The Devil-Tree of El Dorado

The Devil-Tree
of El Dorado
Frank Aubrey

MINT EDITIONS

The Devil-Tree of El Dorado was first published in 1896.

This edition published by Mint Editions 2021.

ISBN 9781513298801 | E-ISBN 9781513224602

Published by Mint Editions®

 MINT
EDITIONS

minteditionbooks.com

Publishing Director: Jennifer Newens
Design & Production: Rachel Lopez Metzger
Project Manager: Micaela Clark
Typesetting: Westchester Publishing Services

Contents

Shall Roraima[1] Be Given up to Venezuela?

S hall Roraima be handed over to Venezuela? Shall the mysterious mountain long known to scientists as foremost among the wonders of our earth—regarded by many as the greatest marvel of the world— become definitely Venezuelan territory?

This is the question that hangs in the balance at the time these words are being written, that is inseparably associated—though many of the public know it not—with the dispute that has arisen about the boundaries of British Guiana.

Ever since Sir Robert Schomburgk first explored the colony at the expense of the Royal Geographical Society some sixty years ago, Roraima has remained an unsolved problem of romantic and fascinating interest, as attractive to the 'ordinary person' as to the man of science. And to those acquainted with the wondrous possibilities that lie behind the solution of the problem, the prospect of its being handed over to a country so little worthy of the trust as is Venezuela, cannot be contemplated without feelings of disappointment and dismay.

This is not the place in which to give a long description of Roraima. It will suffice here to say that its summit is a table-land which, it is believed, has been isolated from all the rest of the world for untold ages; no wilderness of ice and snow, but a fertile country of wood and stream, and, probably, lake. Consequently it holds out to the successful explorer the chance—the probability even—of finding there hitherto unknown animals, plants, fish. In this respect it exceeds in interest all other parts of the earth's surface, not excepting the polar regions; for the latter are but ice-bound wastes, while Roraima's mysterious table-land lies in the tropics but a few degrees north of the equator.

Why, then, it may be asked, have our scientific societies not exhibited more zeal in the solving of the problem presented by this strange mountain? Why is it that unlimited money can, apparently, be raised for expeditions to the poles, while no attempt has been made to explore Roraima? Yet, sixty years ago, the Royal Geographical Society could find the money to send Sir Robert Schomburgk out to explore

---

1. The Indians of British Guiana pronounce this word Roreema.

British Guiana—indeed, it is to that fact that we owe the discovery of Roraima—but nothing has been done since. Had the good work thus begun been followed up, we should today have been able to show better reason for claiming Roraima as a British possession. But, as the writer of the article in the *Spectator* quoted on page 3 says, "we leave the mystery unsolved, the marvel uncared for." This article is commended to the perusal of those interested in the subject, as also are the following books, which give all the information at present available, viz.— Mr. Barrington Brown's 'Canoe and Camp Life in British Guiana,' and Mr. Boddam-Whetham's 'Roraima and British Guiana.' Mr. Im Thurn's 'Among the Indians of British Guiana' should also be mentioned, since it contains references to Roraima, though the author did not actually visit the mountain, as in the case of the first named.

As an illustration of the confusion and uncertainty that prevail as to the international status of this unique mountain, it may be mentioned that in the map of British Guiana which Sir Robert Schomburgk drew out for the British Government, it is placed within the British frontier. But in the map of the next Government explorer, Mr. Barrington Brown—'based,' he says, 'upon Schomburgk's map'— it is placed just inside the Venezuelan boundary; and no explanation is given of the apparent contradiction. Again, another authority, Mr. Im Thurn (above referred to), Curator of the Museum at Georgetown (the capital of the colony), in his book says that Roraima "lies on the extreme edge of the colony, or perhaps on the other side of the *Brazilian* boundary." These references show the obscurity in which the whole matter is at present involved.

Apart, however, from the special interest that surrounds Roraima owing to the inaccessible character of its summit,[2] it is of very great geographical importance, from the fact that it is the highest mountain in all that part of South America, *i.e.*, in all the Guianas, in Venezuela, and in the north-east part of Brazil. Indeed, we must cross Brazil, that vast country of upwards of three million square miles, to find the nearest mountains that exceed in height Roraima. Consequently, it forms the apex of the water-shed of that part of South America; and it is, in fact, the source of several of the chief feeders of the great

---

2. Mr. Barrington Brown says the mountain can only be ascended by means of balloons (see article previously referred to on page 3); and Mr. Boddam-Whetham came to the same conclusion.

rivers Essequibo, Orinoco and Amazon. Schomburgk, in pointing this out, dwelt strongly upon the importance of the mountain to British Guiana, and insisted that its inclusion within the British boundary was a geographical necessity.

Finally, Sir Robert's brother, Richard Schomburgk, a skilled botanist, who had visited almost all parts of Asia and Africa in search of orchids and other rare botanical productions, tells us that the country around Roraima is, from a botanical point of view, one of the most wonderful in the world. "Not only the orchids," he says, "but the shrubs and low trees were unknown to me. Every shrub, herb and tree was new to me, if not as to family, yet as to species. I stood on the border of an unknown plant zone, full of wondrous forms which lay as if by magic before me. . . Every step revealed something new." ('Reissen in Britisch Guiana,' Leipzig, vol. ii, p. 216.)

Are our rulers, in their treatment of the question, bearing these facts sufficiently in mind? Are they as keenly alive as are the Venezuelans to the importance of Roraima? If they are, there is no sign of it; for while, in the Venezuelan statements of their case, there are lengthy, emphatic, and repeated references to the importance of Roraima, on the English side—in the English press even—there is scarcely a word about it.

From these observations it will be seen that there is reason to fear we may be on the point of allowing one of the most scientifically interesting and geographically important spots upon the surface of the globe to slip out of our possession into that of a miserable little state like Venezuela, where civil anarchy is chronic, and neither life nor property is secure.

One of the avowed objects of this book, therefore, is to stimulate public interest, and arouse public attention to the considerations that actually underlie the 'Venezuelan Question,' as well as to while away an idle hour for the lovers of romance.

It has been suggested that, if it is too late to retain the wonderful Roraima as exclusively British—and to effect this it would be well worth our while to barter away someother portion of the disputed territory—then an arrangement might be come to to make it neutral ground. Standing, as it does, in the corner where the three countries—Brazil, Venezuela and British Guiana—meet, it is of importance to all three, and, no doubt, in such an endeavour, we should have the support of Brazil as against Venezuela.

With regard to the oft-discussed question of the situation of the traditional city of Manoa, or El Dorado—as the Spaniards called it—most authorities, including Humboldt and Schomburgk, agree in giving British Guiana as its probable site. We are told that it stood on an island in the midst of a great lake called 'Parima'; but no such lake is now to be found in South America anywhere near the locality indicated. An explanation of the mystery, however, is afforded by the suggestion that such a great lake, or inland sea, almost certainly existed at one time in precisely this part of the continent; in that case what are now mountains in the country would then have been islands.

Indeed, most of British Guiana lies somewhat low, and it is estimated that if the *highlands* were to sink two thousand feet the whole country would be under water—the mountain summits excepted—and there would then be only 'a narrow strait' between the Roraima range and the Andes. In this great supposed ancient lake the group of islands now represented by mountain summits might well have been the home of a powerful and conquering race—as is today Japan with its group of more than three thousand islands—and Roraima, as the highest, and therefore the most easily defensible, may very well have been selected as their fastness, and the site of their capital city.

Schomburgk thus states his speculations upon the point, in his book on British Guiana, page 6:—

"The geological structure of this region leaves but little doubt that it was once the bed of an inland lake which, by one of those catastrophes of which even later times give us examples, broke its barriers, forcing for its waters a path to the Atlantic. May we not connect with the former existence of this inland sea the fable of the lake Parima and the El Dorado? Thousands of years may have elapsed; generations may have been buried and returned to dust; nations who once wandered on its banks may be extinct and exist no more in name; still, tradition of Parima and the El Dorado survived these changes of time; transmitted from father to son, its fame was carried across the Atlantic and kindled the romantic fire of the chivalric Raleigh."

As a natural sequence to the foregoing arises the inquiry, What sort of people were those who inhabited this island city, or who 'wandered on the banks' of the great lake? Here much is to be learned from the recent discoveries of the Government of the United States who, of late years, have devoted liberal sums to pre-historic research.

The money so expended has been the means of unearthing evidence of a startling character—relics of a former civilisation that existed in America ages before the time of its discovery by Christopher Columbus. The Spaniards, as we know, found races that were white, or nearly so; but these later discoveries go to show that long anterior to these—at a time, in fact, probably coeval with what we call the Egyptian civilisation—America was peopled with a white race fully as cultured, as advanced in the sciences, and as powerful on their own ground as the ancient Egyptians; and as handsome in personal appearance—if some of the heads and faces on the specimens of pottery may be accepted as fair examples—as the ancient Greeks.

It has long been known that America possesses extraordinary relics of a former civilisation in what are known as the great 'earthworks,' which are still to be seen scattered about in many parts of the continent, and which, as vast engineering works, challenge comparison with the pyramids themselves. But now discovery has gone much further; bas-reliefs and pottery have been found that set forth with marvellous fidelity many minute details concerning this pre-historic people—their personal appearance, and their ornaments and habiliments; the style of wearing the hair and the beard; and other particulars that can be appreciated only by inspection and study of the reduced facsimiles lately printed and issued by the Government of the United States.

Many of them relate to the custom of human sacrifice which, as most people are probably aware, prevailed largely in America when the Spaniards first landed there; though few, perhaps, know the terrible extent to which it was carried. Prescott tells us that few writers have ventured to estimate the yearly number of victims at less than twenty thousand, while many put it as high as fifty thousand, in Mexico alone! If we consider that the lowest of these estimates represents an average of some four hundred a week, or nearly sixty a day, such figures are appalling! And now we learn, beyond the possibility of a doubt, that the same practices obtained in America in times that must have been ages before the Spanish conquest, and, judging by the frequency of the representations of such things in these old bas-reliefs, as extensively. In these sculptures we can see the very shape of the knives used; the form of the plates or platters on which severed heads of victims were placed, and other such details; and in a certain series we are enabled to note the curious point, that, while the officiating priests always wear full beards, the victims appear to have usually possessed no hirsute adornments, or to have 'shaved clean,' as we term it. It may be added that these ancient white people seem to have been a totally different race from those the Spaniards found on the continent; and that between the two there is believed to have been a gap lasting for many ages, during which the country was overrun by Indian or other barbaric hordes; though how or why this came about is one of those mysteries that will probably never be unravelled.

IN CONCLUSION, I HAVE TO acknowledge my indebtedness to the writers whose books of travel I have named for the information I have made use of; as well as to express a hope that the writer of the review in the *Spectator* will regard with indulgence the liberties I have taken with his admirable article. I am sanguine enough to believe, however, that I shall have the sympathy and good wishes of all these in the endeavour here made to arouse public attention to the real meaning and importance of the 'Venezuelan Question'; and to add to the number of those who feel an interest in the future status and ultimate exploration of the mysterious Roraima. I wish also to express my thanks to Messrs. Leigh Ellis and Fred Hyland, the artists to whom the illustrations were entrusted, for the thought and care they have bestowed upon the work, and the successful manner in which they have carried out my conceptions.

For the rest—if objection be taken to the accounts of the mountain and what is to be found on its summit given by the characters in my story—I desire to claim the licence of the romance-writer to maintain their accuracy—till the contrary be proved. If this shall serve to stimulate to renewed efforts at exploration, so much the better, and another of my objects in writing the book will thereby have been attained.

FRANK AUBREY

I

"Will no one explore Roraima?"[1]

B eneath the verandah of a handsome, comfortable-looking residence
near Georgetown, the principal town of British Guiana, a young
man sat one morning early in the year 1890, attentively studying a
volume that lay open on a small table before him. It was easy to see
that he was reading something that was, for him at least, of more than
ordinary interest, something that seemed to carry his thoughts far away
from the scene around him; for when, presently, he raised his eyes from
the book, they looked out straight before him with a gaze that evidently
saw nothing of that on which they rested.

He was a handsome young fellow of, perhaps, twenty-two years of
age, rather tall, and well-made, with light wavy hair, and blue-grey eyes
that had in them an introspective, somewhat dreamy expression, but
that nevertheless could light up on occasion with an animated glance.

The house stood on a terrace that commanded a view of the sea, and,
in the distance, white sails could be seen making their way across the
blue water in the light breeze and the dazzling sunlight. Nearer at hand
were waving palms, glowing flowers, humming insects and gaudily-
coloured butterflies—all the beauties of a tropical garden. On one side
of him was the open window of a sitting-room that, shaded, as it was,
by the verandah, looked dark and cool compared with the glare of the
scorching sun outside.

From this room came the sounds of a grand piano and of the sweet
voice of a girl singing a simple and pathetic ballad.

At the moment the song ceased a brisk step was heard coming up
the path through the garden, and a good-looking young fellow of tall
figure and manly air made his way to where the other still sat with his
eyes fixed on vacancy, as one who neither sees nor hears aught of what
is going on about him.

"Ha, Leonard!" the new-comer exclaimed, with a light laugh, "caught
you dreaming again, eh? In another of your reveries?"

---

1. The Indians of British Guiana pronounce this word Roreema.

The other roused himself with a start, and looked to see who was his visitor.

"Good-morning, Jack," he then answered with a slight flush. "Well, yes—I suppose I must have been dreaming a little, for I did not hear you coming."

"Bet I guess what you were dreaming about," said the one addressed as Jack. "Roraima, as usual, eh?"

Leonard looked a little conscious.

"Why, yes," he admitted, smiling. "But," he continued seriously, "I have just been reading something that set me thinking. It is about Roraima, and it is old; that is to say, it is in an old number of a paper bound up in this book that a friend has lent me. I should like to read it to you. Shall I?"

"All right; if I may smoke the while. I suppose I may?" And the speaker, anticipating consent, pulled out a pipe, filled and lighted it, and then, having seated himself on a chair, crossed one leg over the other, and added, "Now, then, I am ready. Fire away, old man."

And Leonard Elwood read the following extract from the book he had been studying:—

"Will no one explore Roraima, and bring us back the tidings which it has been waiting these thousands of years to give us? One of the greatest marvels and mysteries of the earth lies on the outskirt of one of our colonies, and we leave the mystery unsolved, the marvel uncared for. The description given of it (with a map and an illustrated sketch) in Mr. Barrington Brown's 'Canoe and Camp Life in British Guiana' (one of the most fascinating books of travel the present writer has read for a long time) is a thing to dream of by the hour. A great table of pink and white and red sandstone, 'interbedded with red shale,' rises from a height of five thousand one hundred feet above the level of the sea, two thousand feet sheer into the sapphire tropical sky. A forest crowns it; the highest waterfall in the world—only one, it would seem, out of several—tumbles from its summit, two thousand feet at one leap, three thousand more on a slope of forty-five degrees to the bottom of the valley, broad enough to be seen thirty miles away. Only two parties of civilised explorers have reached the base of the table—Sir Robert Schomburgk many years ago, and Mr. Brown and a companion in 1869[2]—each at different spots. Even the length of the mass has not been determined—Mr. Brown says from eight to twelve miles. And he cannot help speculating whether the remains of a former creation may not be found at the top. At any rate, there is the forest on its summit; of what trees is it composed? They cannot well be the same as those at its base. At a distance of fifteen hundred feet above sea-level the mango-tree of the West Indies, which produces fruit in abundance below, ceases to bear. The change in vegetation must be far more decided where the difference is between five thousand and seven thousand feet. Thus for millenniums this island of sandstone in the South American continent must have had its own distinct flora. What may be its fauna? Very few birds probably ascend to a height of two thousand feet in the air, the vulture tribe excepted. Nearly the whole of its animated inhabitants are likely to be as distinct as its plants.

"Is it peopled with human beings? Who can tell? Why not? The climate must be temperate, delicious. There is abundance of water, very probably issuing from some lake on the summit. Have we here a group of unknown brothers cut off from all the rest of their kind?

"The summit, Mr. Brown says, is inaccessible except by means of balloons. Well, that is a question to be settled on the spot, between an engineer and a first-rate 'Alpine.' (What is the satisfaction of standing on the ice-ridge of the Matterhorn, or crossing the lava-wastes of the Vatna-Jökull, compared to what would be the sensation of reaching that aerial forest and gazing plumb down over the sea of tropical verdure beneath, within an horizon the limits of which are absolutely beyond guessing?)

"But put it that a balloon is required, surely it would be worth while for one of our learned societies to organise a balloon expedition for the purpose. No one can tell what problems in natural science might not be elucidated by the exploration. We have here an area of limited extent within which the secular variation of species, if any, must have gone on undisturbed, with

---

2. Since then Roraima has been visited by two or three other travellers; but their accounts have added little to our knowledge. They entirely confirm Mr. Brown's statements as to its inaccessibility. (See Preface.)

only a limited number of conceivable exceptions, since at least the very beginning of the present age in the world's life. Can there be a fairer field for the testing of those theories which are occupying men's minds so much in our days? And if there be human beings on Roraima, what new data must not their language, their condition, contribute for the study of philologers, anthropologists, sociologists?

"One more wonder remains to be told. The traveller speaks of two other mountains in the same district which are of the same description as Roraima—tables of sand-stone rising up straight into the blue—one larger than (though not as high as) Roraima itself. It is only because of their existence, and because, for aught that appears, they may be equally inaccessible with Roraima, that one does not venture to call Roraima *the* greatest marvel and mystery of the earth!"

"What is that taken from?" asked Jack Templemore when the reader had put down the book.

"It is from the *Spectator*.[3] I say, Jack, what a chance for an explorer! Fancy people spending their money and risking their lives in exploring an icy, cold, miserable, desolate region, like the Arctic Circle, when there is a wondrous land here in the blue skies—yet no wilderness of ice and snow—waiting to be won; and no one seems to trouble about it! I do wish you would do as I have so often suggested—set out with me upon an expedition and let us see whether we cannot solve the secret of this mysterious mountain. You have the leisure now, and I have the money. Dr. Lorien and his son are now on their way back from near there; if they can undertake the journey, so could we. Besides, it is not as though we were novices at this kind of travel; we have been on short trips to the interior times enough."

Jack Templemore looked dubious. He was, it is true, used to roughing it in the wild parts of South America. He had been trained as an engineer, and, for some years—he was now twenty-eight—had been engaged in surveying or pioneering for new railways in various places on the Continent. His father having lately died and left him and his mother very poorly off, he was now somewhat anxiously looking about for something that would give him permanent occupation, or

---

3. This article appeared in the *Spectator* of April 1877.

the chance of making a little money. He and Leonard Elwood were great friends; though they were, in many respects, of very different characters. Elwood was, essentially, of a romantic, poetic temperament; while Templemore affected always a direct, practical, matter-of-fact way of looking at things, as became an engineer. He was dark, tall and sturdily built, with keen, steady grey eyes, and a straight-forward, good-humoured manner. Both were used to hunting, shooting, and out-door sports, and, as Elwood had just said, they had had many short hunting trips into the interior together. But these had been in previous years, since which, both had been away from Georgetown. Templemore, as above stated, had been engaged in railway enterprises, Elwood had gone to Europe, where, after sometime spent in England, during which his father and mother had both died, he had travelled for a while 'to see the world,' and finally had come out again to Georgetown to look after some property his father had left him. On arrival he had gone at first to an hotel, but some old friends of his parents, who lived on an estate known as 'Meldona,' had insisted upon his staying with them for a while. Here he found that his old friend Jack Templemore was a frequent visitor, and it was an open secret that Maud Kingsford, elder of the two daughters of Leonard's host, was the real attraction that brought him there so constantly.

Now Jack Templemore, as has been said, was more practical-minded than Leonard. He had not shrunk from the hardships and privations of wild forest life when engaged upon railway-engineering work, when there had been something definite in view—money to be made, instruction to be gained, or promotion to be hoped for. But he did not view with enthusiasm the idea of leaving comfortable surroundings for the discomforts of rough travel, merely for travel's sake, or upon what he deemed a sort of wild-goose chase. He had carefully read up all the information that was obtainable concerning the mountain Roraima, and had seen no reason to doubt the conclusions that had been come to by those who ought to know—that it was inaccessible. Of what use then to spend time, trouble, money—perhaps health and strength—upon attempting the impossible?

So Jack Templemore argued, and, be it said, there was the other reason. Why should he go away and separate himself for an indefinite period from his only surviving parent and the girl he loved best in the world, with no better object than a vague idea of scrambling up a mountain that had been pronounced by practical men unclimbable?

Thus, when Leonard appealed to him on this particular morning, merely because he had come across something that had fired his enthusiasm afresh, Jack did not respond to the proposal with the cordiality that the other evidently wished for.

"I don't mind going a short trip with you, old man," Jack said presently, "for a little hunting, if you feel restless and are a-hungering after a spell of wandering—a few days, or a week or two, if you like—but a long expedition with nothing to go upon, as it were, seems to me only next door to midsummer madness."

Leonard turned away with an air of disappointment, and just then Maud Kingsford, who had been playing and singing inside the room, stepped out.

Leonard discreetly went into the house and left the two alone, and Maud greeted Jack with a rosy tell-tale flush that made her pretty face look still more charming. In appearance she was neither fair nor dark, her hair and eyebrows being brown and her eyes hazel. She was an unaffected, good-hearted girl, more thoughtful and serious, perhaps, than girls of her age usually are—she was twenty, while Stella, the younger sister, was between eighteen and nineteen—and had shown her capacity for managing a home by her success in that line in their own home since her mother's death a few years before. The practical-minded Jack, who had duly noted this, saw in it additional cause for admiration; but, indeed, it was only a natural outcome of her innate good sense. She now asked what her lover and Leonard had been talking of.

"The usual thing," was Jack's reply. "He's mad to go upon an exploring expedition; thinks we could succeed where others have failed. It's so unlikely, you know. Now, if he would only look at the thing practically—"

Maud burst into a merry laugh.

"You do amuse me—you two," she exclaimed; at which Jack looked a little disconcerted. "*You* always insisting so upon being strictly non-speculative, and Leonard, with his romantic phantasies, and his dreams and visions, and vague aspirations after castles in the air. You are always hammering away at him, trying to instil practical ideas into him with the same praiseworthy perseverance, though you know that in all these years you have never made the least little bit of impression upon him. Your ideas and his are like oil and water, you know. They will never mix, shake them together as you will."

"But—don't you think I am right? Isn't it common sense?"

"Quite right, of course; and you *are* persevering; I'll say that for you."

"For the matter of that, so's Leonard," said Jack with a good-natured laugh. "He's as persevering with this fad of his as any man I ever met in my life. I do believe he's got a fixed idea that he has only to start upon this enterprise, and he will come back a made man with untold and undreamt-of wealth and—"

"And a princess for a bride—the fair maid of his dreams," Maud put in, still laughing. "We have not heard so much of her, by the bye, lately. He has been rather shy of those things since his return from Europe, and does not like to be spoken to about them. We began to think he had grown out of his youthful fancies."

The fact was, that, from his childhood, Leonard had been accustomed to strange dreams and fancies. These five—Leonard, Templemore, and Mr. Kingsford's son and two daughters—had been children together, and in those days Leonard had talked freely to his childish companions of all his imaginative ideas; and as they grew older, he had not varied much in this respect. Moreover, Leonard had had an Indian nurse, named Carenna, who had encouraged him in his fantastic dreamings, and who had, by her Indian folk-lore tales, early excited his imagination. Her son Matava, too, had been Leonard's constant companion almost so long as he could remember, first in all sorts of boyish games and amusements, and later in his hunting expeditions; and both Matava and Carenna had been always more devoted to Leonard than even to his father and mother.

But when Mr. and Mrs. Elwood left the estate they had been cultivating, to go to England, the two Indians had gone away into the interior to live at an Indian settlement with their own tribe. About twice a year, however—or even oftener, if there were occasion—Matava still came down to the coast upon some little trading expedition with other Indians; and at such times he never failed to come to see the Kingsfords and inquire after Leonard.

The Dr. Lorien, of whom mention had been made by Leonard, was a retired medical practitioner who had turned botanist and orchid-collector. He had been a ship's doctor, and in that capacity had voyaged pretty well all over the world. Since he had given that up he had travelled further still by land—in the tropical regions in the heart of Africa, in Siam, the Malay Peninsular and, latterly, in South America— in search of orchids and other rare floral and botanical specimens. The vicinity of Roraima being one of the most remarkable in the world for such things—though so difficult of access as to be but seldom visited by white men—it is not surprising that he had lately planned a journey thither.

From this journey the doctor and his son were now daily expected back. One of the Indians of their party had, indeed, already arrived, having been despatched in advance, a few days before, to announce their safe return.

Thus it came about that Templemore and Maud, while still talking, were not greatly surprised at the sudden appearance of Matava, who stated that he had come down with the doctor's party, who would follow very quickly on his heels.

Maud, who knew the Indian and his mother well, received him kindly; and, to his great delight, was able to inform him that his 'young master'—as he always called Leonard Elwood—had returned to Georgetown, and was at present with them.

Matava had, indeed, expected this, for he had heard of Leonard's intention at his last visit to the coast some six months before. He was greatly pleased to find he was not to be disappointed in his expectation. Moreover, the Indian declared, he had news for him—"news of the greatest importance"—and begged to be allowed to see him at once. So Maud sent him into the house—where he knew his way about perfectly—to find Leonard; and then, turning to Templemore, she said, laughing,

"I wonder what his 'important' intelligence can be? Some deeper secret than usual that his old nurse has to tell him, I suppose."

"I hope it's nothing likely to rouse a further desire to set off on this mad-cap expedition he has so long had in his mind," Templemore returned; "for," looking at her with a sigh, "if he *should* make up his mind to start, I am, in effect, pledged to go too, whether I wish or not."

"Why should you expect it? and how are you obliged to go?" Maud inquired with evident uneasiness.

"I know that Leonard saw Dr. Lorien in London before he came out last, and had a long talk with him. When he learned of the expedition upon which the doctor was then setting out, he was much annoyed at being unable to join him. He said, however, that he should be in Georgetown himself in a few months, and hoped to see the doctor on his return; and he particularly asked him to try to collect for him all the information and particulars he could concerning the best route by which to make the journey to Roraima. Dr. Lorien told me all this before he left us, adding that he felt certain Leonard's object in coming again to Georgetown was quite as much to arrange for an expedition as his ostensible one of looking after his property. And *I* know, too, from what I have seen since Leonard has been back, that his thoughts are full of the idea. You say he does not now talk much of it to you or to others?"

"No; and as I told you just now, we had begun rather to think he had given up his former romantic yearnings for adventure; and, when you have referred to them before him, I have thought that you were only teasing him a little about old times."

"Oh dear no; by no means. Whatever he may say, or leave unsaid to you and his general acquaintances, he is, in his heart, just as much set upon it as ever."

"It is odd, that," Maud observed thoughtfully, "because he used to be so fond of telling us about his dreams and visions and all the castles in the air and half-mystical imaginings he used to build upon them. But," she went on slowly, "I have noticed that, since his long absence from us, Leonard Elwood is very different from what he was as I remember him. He seems, at times, so reserved and distant, I almost feel inclined to call him 'Mr. Elwood' instead of 'Leonard.' And he is, in a manner, unsociable, too. He is so preoccupied always, so silent, and so wrapped up in himself, that you generally have to wait, if you speak to him, while he collects his thoughts—brings them back from the distant skies or wherever they have gone a-wandering—before he replies to you. Not that he is intentionally cool or distant, I think; and I am sure he is just as good-hearted as ever. Yet there *is* a change of some sort. Stella says the same. And, do you know, he sometimes gives me a sort of feeling as though he were not English at all, but of someother race, and that he feels half out-of-place amongst us, a fish out of water, as it were? I wonder whether he is in love!" And Maud gave a ringing little laugh.

Templemore shook his head.

"If he were, it would be with some young lady on the other side of the Atlantic," he returned. "And he would not be desirous of prolonging his stay on this side. No; *I* know what is the matter with him. He talks freely enough to me. And, now that he is expecting Dr. Lorien back, he is gradually working himself up into a state of excitement and expectation. He has quite made up his mind for some news or information—Heaven only knows why—and that is what makes him by turns restless and preoccupied. If, therefore, what Matava has to tell has anything to do with what I know to be so much in his thoughts, it may be the means of deciding him to go; and then I should have to go too."

"But why? I don't see what it has to do with you, Jack."

"It has this to do with me, dear Maud," said Templemore, taking her hand; "Leonard, sometime ago, made me a very handsome—to me a very tempting—offer if I would make up my mind to start with him on this vague expedition. He offered me £300 clear, he paying all expenses, and giving me, besides, half of whatever came out of it. Unfortunately for myself, I am not now in a position to say 'no' to such an offer. I have been, now, nearly a year waiting for something to 'turn up.' My mother has barely enough to live on, and depends upon me for ordinary comforts, to say nothing of little luxuries; and what I had saved up from former engagements is steadily getting less and less, and will shortly disappear. I do wish with all my heart I could get anything else, almost, rather than this wild-goose affair of Leonard's. Yet nothing has offered itself; so what am I to do? For your sake, for the hope of being able one day to provide a home for you—"

"Nay, Jack," Maud interposed, with a deep flush, "do not say for *my* sake. I would not have you set out on an enterprise of danger and difficulty for my sake. But I see clearly enough you must do it, if it be again offered, for your mother's sake. Yes, for hers, you must." The girl hesitated, and it was easy to see she found it hard to say the words, but she went on bravely, "So, I repeat, if it be again offered, you must accept it, Jack. And be sure I will look after your mother, and comfort her while you are away."

"That is spoken like my own dear girl," Templemore answered with emotion. "Yes, I cannot well refuse; and I know I may look to you to console my mother. You will comfort each other."

Just then they heard Leonard's voice calling out in excited tones for Templemore. A moment or two later he came rushing out of the house.

"Jack, Jack!" he cried. "Such a strange thing! Here is our opportunity! Matava has brought some extraordinary news!"

Leonard was so incoherent in his excitement, that it was sometime before his hearers grasped his meaning.

His news amounted, in effect, to this. A white man had been staying for sometime near the Indian village at which Carenna and her son Matava lived; and he had had many talks with both about a project for ascending the mountain of Roraima. It being an arduous undertaking, he sought the co-operation of one or two other white

FRANK AUBREY

men; and Leonard's old nurse had urged him to communicate with her young master, who would shortly be in Georgetown, assuring him that he would be the very one—from the interest and enthusiasm he would feel—to join him and help him to achieve success if success were possible. Matava, who knew of Dr. Lorien's presence in the district, had suggested to the stranger to go to see him, and a meeting had thus been brought about. The doctor would tell him the result; but the main thing was that the stranger had sent an invitation to Leonard to join him and to bring, if he pleased, one other white man, but no more. The doctor was now at the Settlement, near the mouth of the Essequibo, transferring to the steamer, from the Indian canoes in which they had been brought down the river, his botanical treasures and other trophies of his journey. If Leonard wished to go back with the canoes and the Indians who were with them, he would have to let them know at once, and they would wait. Otherwise they would be on their way back in a day or two; which would involve the organising of a fresh expedition—a matter of great trouble—should Leonard make up his mind to proceed later.

The enthusiastic Leonard needed no time to make up his mind.

"I shall go," said he. "If you will come too, Jack, I shall be only too glad. But, if not, I may be able to find someone else; or I shall go alone. So I shall send word at once to keep the boats and the Indians."

"But," objected Maud Kingsford, "consider! You know nothing of this stranger; he may be a blackleg, an escaped murderer or desperado, or all sorts of things."

"No, no! Carenna knows. She has sent word that I can trust this man, and she knows. She is too fond of me to let me get mixed up with any doubtful character. Dr. Lorien, too, and Harry have seen him, and talked with him, and think well of him; so Matava says. I shall know more when I see them in a day or two. Meantime, I shall keep the canoes and Indians, and risk it."

Then he rushed off to have a further talk with Matava, and, as he said, see about getting the Indian "some grub."

Jack and Maud, left alone, looked at each other in dismay. It had been one thing to talk vaguely of what they would do in case Leonard should take what at the time seemed a very unlikely step. It was quite another to be thus suddenly brought face to face with it.

Maud turned very pale and seemed about to faint. She felt keenly how hard it would be to see her lover depart upon an adventure of this uncertain character, the end or duration of which no one could even guess at. But she recovered her self-possession with an effort and, looking steadily at Templemore, said,

"What you said you would do for our sakes is to be very quickly put to the test, it seems. You—will—go, Jack?"

"Yes," he answered firmly; "since it is your wish."

"You must," she answered. "It is hard to lose you; it will be hard for us both. But go—and go with a good heart. Be sure I will be a daughter to your mother while you are away."

He took her hand in his and pressed it to his lips.

"For your sake, dear Maud, I shall go," he said. "For your sake and for my mother's; in the hope that some success may result; but not— Heaven knows—for the mere sordid hope of gain."

II

MONELLA

Two days later Dr. Lorien and his son arrived in Georgetown and, after taking rooms at the Kaieteur Hotel, went at once to call upon the Kingsfords. This haste was, in reality, prompted by Harry, whose thoughts were bent upon his hopes of once more seeing the pretty Stella; but the ostensible reason that he urged upon his father was somewhat different, and had to do with the message of which they were the bearers from the white stranger they had met in their travels.

At the evening dinner the matter was discussed, Mr. Kingsford and his son Robert and the others being present.

The two travellers had much to tell of their adventures, which had been full of both interest and danger, apart from the matter of the stranger's message.

"And yet, I think," observed the doctor, thoughtfully, "our meeting with this stranger, and his behaviour, impressed me more than almost all else that happened to us."

"How so? What is he like?" asked Mr. Kingsford.

"In figure he is very tall; of a most commanding stature and appearance. _I_ am not short."

"Why, you are over six feet!" put in Harry.

"And yet I almost think, if he had held his arm straight out, I could have walked under it with my hat on, and without stooping."

"I'm sure you could, dad," Harry corroborated.

"As to age—there I confess myself at sea. As a doctor I am accustomed to judge of age; yet he thoroughly puzzled me. If I could believe in the possibility of a man's being a hundred and fifty years old and yet remaining strong and hale and vigorous, I should not be surprised if he had claimed that age. On the other hand, if one could believe in a young, stalwart, muscular man of thirty with the face and white hair of an old-looking, but not _very_ old man, then I could have believed it if I had been told he was no more than thirty. In fact, he was a complete puzzle to me; a mystery. But the most remarkable thing about him was the expression of his eyes; they were the most extraordinary I have ever seen in my life."

"Wild—mad-looking?" Templemore asked.

"Oh no, by no means; quite the reverse. Very steady and piercing; but wonderfully fascinating. Mild and kind-looking to a fault; and yet changing to a look of quiet, almost stern resolution that had in it nothing hard, or cruel, or disagreeable. In fact, I hardly know how to describe that look, or convey an idea of it, except by saying that it was something between the gaze of a lion and that of a Newfoundland dog. It had all the majesty, the magnanimity, the conscious power of the one, with the benevolence and wistful kindness and affection of the other. Never have I seen such an expression. I really did not know the human countenance could express the mingled characteristics one seemed to read so plainly in his—all kindly, all noble, all suggestive of sincerity and integrity."

"You *are* enthusiastic!" said Robert, laughing.

The old doctor coloured up a little; then took out his handkerchief and wiped his face.

"I know it sounds strange to hear an old man of the world like me speak so forcibly about a man's appearance," he returned; "but, if it is true, I do not see why I should not say it. Ask Harry here."

"I couldn't take my eyes off his face," Harry declared. "He fairly fascinated me. I felt I should have to do anything he told me; even to taking my pistol and killing the first person I met. I do believe I should have done it—or any other out-of-the-way thing. And he made you feel, too, as though you liked him so, that you longed to do any mortal thing you could to please him."

"What's his name?" asked Templemore.

"Monella."

"Monella? Is that all? No other name?"

"None that I heard. And as to his nationality, I cannot even so much as guess. I have been in Central Africa, in Siam, in India, in China, in Russia, and have picked up a smattering of the languages of those countries; but this man jabbered away in all; additionally, he spoke French, German, Spanish and Portuguese, besides English. So much I know. How many more he speaks I can't say."

"Injun," said Harry.

"Oh yes, I forgot that. We had some of three different tribes with us, and he spoke to each in his own tongue."

"And what is his object in going in for this Roraima exploration?" asked Mr. Kingsford.

"He has a curious theory. He declares that the ancient island-city of El Dorado—or Manoa—was not at the lower end or part of the Pacaraima mountains, as some have surmised, but at the further and highest point of the range, which is Roraima itself. He holds that the great lake or inland sea of Parima once washed around the bases of all those mountains, making islands of what are now their summits; and that the highest and most inaccessible of all, Roraima, was selected by the Manoans for their fastness, and for the site of their wonderful 'Golden City.'"

"But that theory won't help him to get up there, will it?" Jack asked.

"Ah, but there is something else. He states that he was brought up by some people, the last members of what had once been a nation, but has now died out. They lived in a secluded valley high up on the slopes of the Andes. He has travelled all over the world, and went back to these friends of his, only to find that they were all dead, save one, and that he was fast dying. This survivor gave him an ancient parchment with plans and diagrams, by means of which, it was declared, the top of the mountain can be reached, where will be found whatever traces may be left of the famous city of Manoa or El Dorado. This man, Monella, has other old parchments which he can read, but I could not—he showed me some—and from these he declared his belief that there is almost unlimited wealth to be gained by those who find the site of this wonderful city."

All this time Leonard had been listening with sparkling eyes and flushed cheeks, though in silence. Here he glanced with a satisfied smile at Templemore, and said,

"There's method in all that; at all events he is not undertaking the thing in a haphazard way and without something to go upon, that's certain."

Jack did not look hopeful.

"It is probably just as wild and hopeless an adventure all the same," was his reply. "What 'directions' or 'plans' or 'diagrams' can help a man today after the lapse of hundreds and hundreds of years—even if they were reliable, and the old party who handed them over was not mad— as he probably was?"

"As to Monella," observed the doctor, "I could see no sign of madness in him. He is one of the most intelligent, best-informed men I ever met. I cannot say anything, of course, of his informant."

"Has he any money, do you suppose—this man?" Robert asked.

"I don't know. But he pays the Indians well, and has got together a lot of stores, it seems; which must have been a costly thing to do. They have been brought over the mountains from Brazil. And he specially said you need not trouble to load yourself up with much in the way of stores—only sufficient to get to him. After that you will be all right. And he said nothing about money being wanted. But," and here the doctor hesitated, "he is very particular as to the character and disposition of those he purposes to work with. In fact, he subjected me to a long sort of cross-examination respecting our friend Leonard here. He had already gained a lot of information about him from the old Indian nurse, it seemed, and I was surprised at the details he had picked up and remembered. In fact, Master Leonard," continued the doctor, addressing the young man, "he seemed to know you almost as well as if he had lived with you for years. And your friend Mr. Templemore, too, he seemed to know about him, and to expect that he would join you."

"How could that be?" Jack demanded.

"Oh, from the old nurse and Matava, I suppose."

"To tell you the honest truth," Harry interposed, "I believe there's some hocus-pocus business about those two. She is reputed to be a witch, you know; not a bad witch, but a good sort. And I quite believe Monella to be a wizard; also of a good sort. And when those two laid their heads together, they could know a lot between them, I suspect. I should not at all wonder if he were not magician enough to lead you to the 'golden castle,' or 'city,' or whatever it is, and find its hidden stores of gold. I wish I had a chance to join him. But dad's wanting me somewhere else. So I am out of it."

"Yes," observed his father. "We have to go on to Rio, where I have some law business on. But we shall not be away a great while, and then we are going back to that district."

"Going back?" said Templemore in surprise.

"Yes, there is a lot to be done there. It is a wonderful place for my sort of work, and we really saw but very little of it after all. So we are going again when we return from Rio; but I cannot at all tell when that may be."

The doctor was a fine-looking specimen of a hardy, bronzed traveller. He was, as has been said, over six feet in height; his hair and beard were iron-grey, his complexion was a little florid beneath its tan, and his expression good-humoured and often jovial. His son, Harry, was somewhat slight in build, but wiry, and had been used to knocking about with his father. He was a young fellow with boundless animal spirits and plenty of pluck and courage. His ready kindness to everyone made him a general favourite; and the lively, captivating Stella and he were special friends.

Mr. Kingsford asked the doctor whether anytime had been estimated for the length of the expedition.

"That would be difficult," Dr. Lorien answered. "Apart from the long and tedious journey there, there is the girdle of forest that surrounds Roraima to be cut through. That may take months, I am told."

"Months!" The exclamation came from Maud who, with Stella, had been a silent but appreciative listener.

"Yes. It is a curious thing, but this forest belt is never approached even by any of the Indian tribes. They look upon it with superstitious awe and will not even go near it. Indeed, they all regard Roraima with a sort of horror. They declare there is a lake on the top guarded by demons and large white eagles, and that it will never be gazed on by mortal eyes; that in the forest that surrounds it are monstrous serpents—'camoodis' they call them—larger far than any to be found elsewhere in the land; besides these, there are 'didis', gigantic man-apes, bigger and more ferocious and formidable than the African gorilla. Altogether, this wood has a very bad reputation, and no Indian will venture near it. Indeed, the mountain of Roraima and all its surroundings are looked upon as weird and uncanny. As a former traveller has expressed it, 'its very name has come to be surrounded by a halo of dread and indefinable fear.'"

"How, then, is the necessary road to be made through this promising bit of woodland?" asked Templemore.

"*There* has been Monella's difficulty," returned the doctor. "But for that, doubtless, he would not have troubled about anyone else's joining him. But, though he is very popular amongst the Indians, they cannot get over their fear of the 'demons' wood,' as they call it. They are, in fact, quite devoted to him, for he has done much that has made him both loved and feared—as one must always be to gain the real devotion of these people. He has effected many wonderful cures amongst them, I was told; but, more than that, he has saved the lives of two or three by acts of great personal courage. So that, at last, he even prevailed upon them to enter the 'haunted wood' with him. But they are making very little progress, it appears; he cannot keep them together, and they give way to panic at the slightest thing and make a bolt of it; then he has to go hunting over the country for them, and it takes days to get them together again—and so on. He is in hopes that the presence and example of other white men will inspire them with greater confidence and courage."

"A promising and inviting outlook, I must say," said Jack, eyeing Leonard gravely.

"Never mind," Leonard exclaimed with enthusiasm. "If he can face it, so can we; and if it is good enough for him to brave such difficulties, it is good enough for us. It only shows what sterling stuff he must be made of!"

At this Jack gave a sort of grunt that was clearly far from implying assent to Leonard's view of the matter.

There was further talk, but it added little to the information given above; and, inasmuch as Leonard had already made up his mind, almost in advance, and had to ask no one's permission but his own, he determined at once to set about the necessary preparations; and Jack Templemore—though with evident reluctance—agreed to accompany him.

"I have a list of all the things I took with me," remarked Dr. Lorien, "and notes of a few that I afterwards found would have been useful and that I consequently regretted I had not taken; and also some specially suggested by the stranger Monella. You had better copy them all out carefully, for you will find it will save you a lot of time and trouble."

Thus it came about that in less than a week their preparations were all made, and the two, with Matava as guide, were ready to set out. Matava had with him fourteen or fifteen Indians, who had formed the doctor's party, and these, and the canoes with the stores on board, were soon after waiting at the Settlement, ready to make a start.

Then, one sunny day at the beginning of the dry season, the Kingsfords, with Mrs. Templemore, and the doctor and his son, all took the steamer to the "Penal Settlement" (a place a few miles inside the mouth of the Essequibo river, the starting place of all such parties), to see the young men off and wish them God speed. When it came to this point the struggle was a hard one for Maud and for Templemore's mother; but they bore themselves bravely—outwardly at least. The three canoes put off amidst much fluttering of handkerchiefs, and soon all that could be seen of the adventurers were three small specks, gradually growing less and less, as the boats made their way up the bosom of the great Essequibo river—here some eight miles in width.

Their intended journey had been kept more or less a secret; such had been the wish of him they were going to join. Hence no outside friends had accompanied the party to see them off. Those who knew of their going away thought they were only bent upon a hunting trip of a little longer duration than usual.

For two loving hearts left behind the separation was a trying one. For a few days Mrs. Templemore stayed on at 'Meldona' with Maud, and the presence of Dr. Lorien and the vivacious Harry helped to cheer them somewhat; but, when the doctor and his son started for Rio, the others returned sadly to the routine of their everyday life, with many anxious speculations and forebodings concerning the fortunes of the two explorers.

III

The Journey from the Coast

The greater part of the interior of British Guiana consists of dense forests which are mostly unexplored. No roads traverse them, and but little would be known of the savannas, or open grassy plains, and the mountains that lie beyond—and they would indeed be inaccessible—were it not for the many wide rivers by which the forests are intersected. These form the only means of communication between the coast and the interior at the present day; and so vast is the extent of territory covered with forest growth that it is probable many years will elapse before any road communication is opened up between the sea and the open country lying beyond the woods.

Of these vast forests little—or rather practically nothing—is known save what can be seen of them from the rivers by those voyaging to and fro in canoes. There are a limited number of spots at which the Indians of the savannas come to the banks of the rivers to launch their canoes when journeying to the coast; and to reach these places they have what are known as 'Indian paths' through the intervening woods. These so-called paths are, for the most part, of such a character, however, that only Indians accustomed to them can find their way by them. Any white man who should venture to trust himself alone in them would inevitably get quickly and hopelessly lost. Hence—save for a few miles near the line of coast—there are, as yet, absolutely no roads in the country.

Naturally, under such conditions, the forest scenery is of the wildest imaginable character, and its flora and fauna flourish unchecked in the utmost luxuriance of tropical savage life; for the country lies but a few degrees from the equator, and is far more sparsely populated than even the surrounding tropical regions of Brazil and Venezuela.

Fortunately, however, for those who for any reason have occasion to traverse this wild region, there is no lack of water-ways. Several grand rivers of great breadth lead from the coast in different directions, most of them being navigable (for canoes and small boats) for great distances, leaving only comparatively short stretches of forest land to be crossed by travellers desiring to reach the open plains and hills.

Of these rivers, the Essequibo is one of the finest, and it was by this route that the two friends, Elwood and Templemore, set out, under Matava's guidance, to reach their destination. From this river they branched off into one of its affluents, the Potaro, noted for its wonderful waterfall, the Kaieteur, which they visited *en route*. Here their canoes were left and exchanged for lighter ones, hired from the Ackawoi Indians, who live at a little distance above the fall; their stores and camp equipage being carried round. So far the journey had been uneventful, save for a little excitement in passing the various cataracts and rapids; but the two young men knew their way fairly well thus far, having visited the Kaieteur with Matava some years before.

When, however, the journey was resumed above the Kaieteur, the route was new to them; and, among the first things they noticed, were the alligators with which the river abounded. In the Essequibo they had seen none, and not many below the fall; but from this point, as far as they ascended the river, they saw them continually. Once they had a narrow escape. They were making arrangements for camping on the bank, and were nearing the shore in the last of the canoes, when a tremendous blow and a great splash overturned the boat, and they found themselves struggling in the stream. An alligator had struck the canoe a blow with its tail and upset it. Fortunately, however, it was in shallow water; and the Indians, seeing how matters were, made a great splashing, and thus frightened away the reptile. The contents of the canoe were partly recovered, not without difficulty; but some were damaged by the water.

As they proceeded up the river, the rapids and cataracts became more frequent, and the negotiation of them more difficult, till they reached a spot where further navigation was impossible, and they had to take to the forest, their stores and baggage being henceforward carried by the Indians.

This marked the commencement of the really arduous part of the journey. So long as the stores were carried in the boats, the Indians had been cheerful and docile, and easy to manage. But now their work was harder, and food was scarcer—for game is difficult to shoot in the forest. Then, after two or three days, the gloom of the woods began to have an evident effect upon their spirits; they first became depressed, and then began to grumble. This would not have been of so much consequence, perhaps, but that Matava became apprehensive that they might desert. They were not people of his tribe, it seemed; they had come with Dr. Lorien from a different district; and when they began to understand that the eventual destination was Roraima, they became still more depressed.

All the Indian tribes who have heard of Roraima, in anyway, have the same superstitious dread of it; and those now with the two young men were evidently not exceptional in this respect. Templemore and Elwood began to feel anxious and, to make matters worse, food ran short for the Indians. The latter live chiefly on the native food, a kind of bread called cassava, and, of this, a good deal of what they had brought with them had been lost or spoiled by the upsetting of the canoe.

In consequence, Matava advised that they should interrupt their direct journey to turn aside to an Indian settlement that he knew of, about a day's journey off the route they were pursuing; there they would be able to replenish their stores, he thought; and to this course a reluctant assent was given by the two friends.

It turned out to be more than a day's journey, however; but they reached the place on the second day. It was called Karalang; there were not more than a dozen huts, and the people at first said that they had no food to spare; but eventually promised to procure some if the travellers would wait a few days; and this they were perforce compelled to do.

This village was situated on a hill in a piece of open country in the midst of the great forest; and, during their enforced rest, the two friends were enabled to engage in a little hunting, and to see more of the wild life of the woods than they had seen before.

The first thing they did on arrival was to procure a couple of fowls for cooking, of which there were plenty in the village. But these were of no use as food for the Indians, who never eat them. Throughout the country this is everywhere the case; the Indians keep fowls, yet never eat them; and it is said that, were it not for the vampire bats and tiger-cats, these would increase beyond all reason. Though, however, they object to fowls as a diet, they have no dislike to fish, and they were not long in discovering that there were some in a stream that ran near the village; and a supply was caught by their method of poisoning the fish in such a way that they float on top of the water as if dead, but are nevertheless palatable and wholesome as food. The poison is prepared from a root.

Amongst the miscellaneous stores the two had brought they had a liberal supply of firearms—five Winchester rifles, half-a-dozen revolvers and two guns, each with double barrels, one for shot and the other for ball. The extra weapons were in case of loss or accident, and Templemore had a good stock of tobacco, for he never felt happy for long together without his pipe.

On their way up they had had very little shooting. Jack had indeed killed an alligator, by way of relieving his feelings after the upsetting of the canoe; but there had been very little time to spare for sport. Every morning they had started as soon as the morning meal had been eaten, and had gone into camp at night only in time to cook a meal before it became dark. For in this part of the world night closes in at about half-past six on the shortest days of the year, and a little before seven on the longest. Practically, therefore, the varying seasons bring little difference in the length of the days. One cannot there get up at three or four o'clock and "have a good long day," with an evening keeping light till eight and nine o'clock, as in summer-time in Europe. Hence the days seem short for travel and sport, and the nights very long.

"I think we've stuck to it pretty well," Jack observed in the evening, as he sat smoking by the camp fire, outside their tent—for though the day had been hot the evening was chilly—"and we deserve a rest. So it is just as well. We will have two or three days' shooting, and a look round, before we go on to tackle 'the old man.'"

'The old man' was the one they were on their way to see—the one Dr. Lorien had met and described so enthusiastically. Jack was a little sceptical as to whether the good-natured doctor had not sacrificed strict accuracy to his friendly feeling for the stranger. Leonard, too, felt full of curiosity upon the same point.

"I can scarcely believe, you know," Jack continued, "that our friend will turn out all that the doctor pictured him."

"I shall be glad if he does, at any rate," Leonard made reply. "He would be almost worth coming to see for himself alone."

Jack laughed.

"That's rather stretching a point, I think. However, I am keeping an open mind on the subject. The gentleman shall have 'a fair field and no favour,' so far as my judgment of him goes. I won't let myself be prejudiced in advance, either one way or the other."

During the following days they enriched their stores by the skin of a fine jaguar, shot by Templemore, a great boa-constrictor—or 'camoodi'—twenty-four feet long, shot by Leonard, and many trophies of lesser account. Then, a fresh lot of cassava having been procured for the Indians, the journey was resumed.

In about three weeks from the time of their start, the party emerged from the forest into a more open country, where rolling savannas alternated with patches of woodland. Here the air was fresher and more bracing, so that the depressing effect of the gloomy forest was soon thrown off. They could shoot a little game, too, as they went along; there were splendid views to be had from the tops of the ridges and low hills they crossed. The ground steadily rose and became first hilly and then mountainous, till, having crossed a broad, undulating plateau, they once more entered a forest region, but this time of different character. The trees were farther apart; there were hills, and rocky ravines, and mountain torrents, steep mountains, and deep valleys. The way became toilsome and difficult; game was scarce, or at least not easy to obtain, owing to the nature of the ground; the cassava ran short, and, once more, grumbling arose and trouble threatened.

At last, one evening, Matava, with perplexity in his face, led the two young men aside to hold a consultation.

"These people," he said in his own language, "say they will not go any farther!"

"How far do you reckon we are now from your own village?" asked Jack.

"About four days. If we could but persuade them to keep on for two days more, we could fix a camp, and I could go on alone and bring back some of my own people to take all the things on."

"Ah! a good idea, Matava. Well, let us see what persuasion will effect. Anyway, we had better get them to go as far as we can, and then encamp at the first likely camping-ground."

In the end the Indians were prevailed upon, by promise of extra pay, to go the additional two days' journey. Beyond that they would not budge.

"They think that mountain over there in the distance is Roraima," Matava explained; "and I cannot get them to believe it isn't. And they are frightened, and won't go any nearer to it."

There was, therefore, nothing to be done but to adopt Matava's suggestion. It was agreed that the two friends would stay in camp and keep guard over their belongings, while he started next day for his village, to bring help.

The spot was a convenient one in which to camp for a few days, with a stream of water near. That evening, therefore, the Indians were paid, this being done in silver, which they knew how to make use of. The next morning, when Elwood and Templemore got out of their hammocks, they found they were alone with Matava. All the others had disappeared.

"Ungrateful beggars!" said Jack. "They might, at least, have gone in a respectable manner, and not like thieves slinking away. Let's hope they are not thieves."

But they were not. An examination showed that nothing had been stolen.

"The poor fellows were only frightened," Leonard observed. "They are honest enough."

Matava, meantime, was making ready to set off alone for carriers from his own village. When he was ready, Templemore expressed a desire to walk a little way on the road with him 'to take a peep over that little ridge yonder'; which is a wish common to travellers in a country that is new to them. But when they reached the ridge, there was only to be seen another short expanse of undulating savanna, whereupon Jack decided to return, leaving Matava to continue on his way.

Leonard, left to himself, finished the occupation he had in hand—the cleaning of his double-barrel—and, having loaded it, strolled out of the camp in another direction, to take a look round. He left the camp to itself, not intending to go far, and expecting that his friend would be back in a quarter of an hour or so. Not far away a 'bell-bird' was ringing out its strange cry, that has been compared by travellers to the sound of a convent bell. He had heard these birds often in the forest since leaving the boats, but, in consequence of the density of the woods, had never been able to get near one. Here, where the trees were more open, there seemed to be a better chance, and he followed, as he thought, the sound. But soon he came to the conclusion that he had been in error; or the bird had flown across unseen; for the direction of the sound seemed to have changed. He, therefore, turned off towards where he fancied the bird now was; and this happened several times, till at last he became confused and found he had fairly lost his way. It is a peculiarity of the 'bell-bird,' as it is of many other birds of the forest, that their notes are often misleading; it is one of those cases of what has been termed by naturalists 'Ventriloquism in Nature,' many examples of which the traveller in these wild regions comes across. Leonard had arrived at the head of a small glen, and found himself on a grassy bank beside a little stream, sheltered from the glare of the sun by over-hanging branches. He laid down his gun and went to take a drink of the inviting limpid water, and then sat awhile on the bank looking down the picturesque ravine. It was very quiet and peaceful all around, and he fell into one of his day-dreams. At such times the minutes pass on unheeded; and he sat for a long while oblivious of all that went on about him. But presently, behind him, a silent, cunning enemy crept up unseen and unheard till near enough for a spring; then there was a loud roar, and the next moment Leonard was lying on the ground in the grasp of an enormous jaguar.

For a minute or two the beast stood over him growling, but not touching him after the first blow that had knocked him down; while Leonard lay dazed and helpless, with just enough consciousness to have a vague idea that the best thing he could do, for the moment, was to lie perfectly still. Then, with another roar, the animal seized him by the shoulder and began to drag him down the slope towards some bushes. At that moment Leonard, whose face was turned away from the brute, saw, like one in a dream, the undergrowth through which he himself had come, part asunder and three figures appear. Two of them were Templemore and Matava, who stood rooted to the spot with horror-stricken faces; the third was a tall stranger who towered above the other two, and who also stood still for a second or two eyeing the scene, while the jaguar growled threateningly.

Then the tall stranger advanced, and the animal released its hold and was itself seized and pulled from over Leonard. In another moment he felt himself lifted in two giant arms, and, looking up, saw the stranger bending upon him a gaze in which there seemed a world of tender anxiety and compassion. Everything appeared to swim around him, and he knew that consciousness was leaving him; yet, for a space, the fascination of that look seemed to hold him chained.

"You—must—be—Monella!" he said, softly. Then he fainted.

IV

The first view of Roraima

When Leonard came to himself sufficiently to see and understand what was going on around him, for the moment he thought himself once more in his days of childhood; for the first face he recognised was Carenna's, his Indian nurse, who was bending over him in much the same way and with the same expression as of yore. But, when he looked round, he saw that he was in an Indian hut; and slowly the memory of what had occurred came back to him.

Carenna, when she saw that he was himself again, gave a joyous cry; then, conscious of her indiscretion, put her finger on her lips to imply that he must remain quiet. He felt no inclination to do otherwise, and soon fell into a refreshing sleep, which lasted for sometime.

When next he opened his eyes they rested on another pair, large and steady, and that seemed to have a wondrous depth and meaning in them. Then he saw that they belonged to the stranger who had pulled the jaguar off, and was now sitting alongside the mattress on which he lay.

"Keep thee quiet, my son," said he in a low, musical voice. "All goes well, and in two or three days you will be as strong as ever again."

There was something soothing in the mere glance of the eye, and in the very tones of the man's voice; and Leonard, reassured by them, remained passive for a while, till Carenna again appeared with a drink she had prepared for him.

When, later, Jack Templemore came in, and Leonard was able to talk, he found he had been ill for a week, and that he was then in the hut of Carenna at the village of Daranato.

"I've had an awfully anxious time of it," Jack said; "but Monella seems skilled in doctoring, and Carenna has been most devoted in her nursing and attention and would brook no interference; so I've had to hang around and pass the time as best I could."

When once Leonard had 'turned the corner,' as Jack called it, he recovered rapidly, and was able, in a few days, as Monella had predicted, to get about again. Nor was he any the worse for his mishap; for the beast's teeth had just missed scrunching the bone.

When he wished to offer his thanks to Monella, the latter put him off with a quiet smile.

"We think nothing of little incidents like that, my son, in a land such as this. Your thanks are due to God who sent me to you at the moment; not to me. Being there, I could not well have done otherwise than I did."

It appeared that Monella had come out from the village a day or two before to look out for them, and had fallen in with Matava. The Indian had led him towards the camp, near which they had met Jack, who was wandering about in search of Leonard. On learning that he was missing, Monella had proceeded to the camp and thence—by some method known only to himself—had tracked Leonard's footsteps—a thing that even Matava confessed himself unable to do—and thus had come upon him just in time.

"When I saw how matters stood," said Jack, "my very heart seemed to stand still. Neither I nor Matava dared to risk a shot, for the brute stood up nearly facing us and holding you in his mouth. But that wonder, Monella, quietly laid down his rifle and drew his knife, keeping the beast fixed with his eye all the time; then he walked up to it as coolly as though he were going to stroke a pet cat, put out his hand and caught it with such a grip on the throat that it nearly choked and had to let go of you at once. And presto! Before it could get its breath, whizz went the knife into its heart! And he lifted it up and threw it away from him, clear of you, as easily as one might a small dog. Then he picked you up and carried you to the camp, as though you were but a baby. The whole affair took only a few moments, and passed almost like a dream. It's fortunate he happened to come out to meet us. How could he possibly know we were coming?"

"I have always told you," said Leonard dreamily, "that there seems to be a strange sympathy between my old Indian nurse and myself. She tells me she 'felt' that I was in the neighbourhood, and sent word to Monella, who at once went to her, and then came on to try to intercept us. Only, you know, you never believed in those things. Yet here, you see, Monella must have believed her, or he would not have had such confidence in our coming as to wait about for us as he did."

"It's very strange," Jack admitted. "I confess I do not understand you 'dreamers.' I am out of the running there altogether.

"They say," he continued, "that from the top of yonder low mountain before us you can see Roraima pretty plainly. But I had no heart to go out to look for it while you were so ill, and, since you have been getting better, I have preferred to stay and keep you company. But now, I suppose, it will not be long before we set eyes, at last, upon the wonderful mountain that is to be our 'El Dorado'!"

When Elwood heard this, he became anxious to get a sight of the object of their journey; so, two days after, they started before dawn, with Monella, to walk to the top of the low mountain Jack had pointed out.

They reached the summit of the ridge just when the sun was rising, and there before them, like a veritable fairy-land in the sky, they saw the mysterious Roraima, its pink-white and red cliffs illumined by the morning sun, and floating in a great sea of white mist, above which showed, here and there, the peaks of other lower mountains like the islands they once were, but looking dark and heavy, in their half-shadow, beside the glorious beauty of this queen of them all, that reared herself far above everything around.

It is impossible to give an adequate idea of the impressive grandeur of this mountain, which might be likened to a gigantic sphinx, serene and impassive in its inaccessibility.

Or it might be likened to a colossal fortress, built by Titans to guard the entrance to an enchanted land beyond; for the cliffs at its summit appeared curiously turreted, while at the corners were great rounded masses that might pass for towers and bastions.

In places, with the light-coloured cliffs were to be seen darker rocks, black and dark green and brown, worked in, as it were, with strange figures, as though inlaid by giant hands. And everywhere the sides were perpendicular, smooth, and glassy-looking. Scarce a shrub or creeper found a precarious hold there; but down from the height, at one spot, fell a great mass of water—like a broad band of silver sparkling and glistening in the sunlight—that came with one mad leap from the top and disappeared in a cloud of spray and mist two thousand feet below. Further along could be seen other narrower falls like silver threads.

There was no crest or peak as with most mountains. The top was a table-land, beyond whose edge one could see nothing. This edge was fringed with what looked like herbage, but, seen through a powerful field-glass, proved to be great forest trees.

Then, as the sun rose higher and warmed the air, the mist cleared somewhat around the lower part of the precipitous cliffs, so that far, far down could now be seen the foliage that crowned the great primæval forest—the 'forest of demons'—that girdled the cliffs' base. Gradually the mist descended, and the full forest's height showed up like a Titanic pedestal of green, itself floating in the haze that still remained below.

By degrees the mist rolled down the mountain's side, for below this extensive forest-girdle the actual base and lower slopes began slowly to appear, with waterfalls, and cascades, and rushing torrents and great rivers dashing and foaming in their rocky beds. Then other intervening ridges and patches of forest and open savanna gradually came into view, with the full forms of the surrounding smaller mountains, the whole making up a panorama that was marvellous in its extent and in the variety of its shapes and tints.

But scarcely had the sun revealed this wondrous sight to their astonished eyes, when a cloud descended upon Roraima's height.

Almost imperceptibly it grew darker, then darker still and yet more sombre, till the erst-while fairy fortress seemed to frown in gloomy grandeur. Its salmon-tinted sides, but now so airy-looking in their lightness, turned almost black, and seemed to glower upon the brilliant landscape. The forest also lost its verdant colouring and looked dark and forbidding enough to pass for an enchanted wood peopled by dragons, demons, and hobgoblins to guard the grim castle in its centre.

Then the cloud descended lower still, and castle and haunted forest passed out of sight, as swiftly and completely as though all had been a magical illusion that had vanished at a touch of the magician's wand.

Leonard rubbed his eyes and felt half inclined to think he had been dreaming. All this time not a word had been exchanged. Each had seemed wrapped up in the weird attraction of the scene; and the new-comers, even the practical Jack, had been astounded, almost overwhelmed, at the sight of the stupendous cliffs and tower-like rocks of the mysterious mountain, and its changes from gorgeous colouring and ethereal beauty to black opacity and shapelessness.

Presently Monella turned and led the way back to the camp, the others following, each absorbed in his own thoughts.

Templemore was more impressed by what he had just witnessed than he would have cared, perhaps, to own. Never before had he seen such a mountain, though he had crossed the Andes, and had looked upon the loftiest and grandest on the American Continent. To him there was something about Roraima that was wanting in all other mountains; a suggestiveness of the unseen, of latent possibilities. He could now understand why the Indians regarded it with fear and awe. It was, indeed, impossible to look upon it without believing that some wonderful story was hidden in its inaccessible bosom; some mysterious secret that it kept jealously concealed from the rest of the world. For, perhaps, the first time in his life, he was conscious of a feeling that bordered on the superstitious. What if that which they had witnessed were meant to shadow forth a warning; to be an omen! Did it portend that, should they gain the summit of Roraima, they would find there indeed a sort of earthly Paradise, but that it would turn—as suddenly and completely as the fairy-like first view had changed that morning— to the darksome solitude of a charnel house?

But Leonard, for his part, when he came to talk upon the matter, was only more enthusiastic than before; and Monella smiled with indulgent approbation when, with the ingenuous impulsiveness of youth, he enlarged upon his delight and expectations.

When they returned to the Indian village preparations were begun for a forward move to the place Monella had made his head-quarters; not far from the commencement of the mysterious forest the Indians regarded with such dread.

During the march thither they had many more glimpses of Roraima; finally they emerged upon the last ridge that faced it, from which a full view of its towering sides and of the forest at their base could be obtained.

Between them was a deep ravine, along which flowed a narrow river dotted with great boulders. Having crossed this with some difficulty and ascended the other side, they reached an extensive undulating plateau, an open savanna with here and there small clumps of trees. They were now almost under the shadow of the great cliffs, and before them, three or four miles away, was the beginning of the encircling wood.

Rounding the end of a thicket distant a mile or so from this wood, they came suddenly upon a large and substantially built log hut, and this, Monella told them, was his temporary residence. Near it were several smaller huts roughly but ingeniously formed of boughs and wood poles, which the Indians who worked with him had constructed for themselves.

As they entered the larger dwelling Monella thus addressed them:

"This, my friends, is where we shall have to live until our work in 'Roraima Forest' shall be completed. Make yourselves as much at home as the circumstances will permit; we are likely to occupy it for sometime."

And a fairly comfortable home it was; far more so indeed than the young men had ventured to expect. There was rough furniture, there were lamps for light at night, a number of books, and many other things that took them altogether by surprise.

"It must have taken you a long time," said Jack Templemore, "to get all these things transported here, and this place built and its furniture made."

"It has taken me years!" was the reply.

The Indians who accompanied them, numbering about twenty, were all of Matava's own tribe; altogether a different race from those who had accompanied them nearly to Daranato and had been paid off and gone home. When Monella had left his abode, temporarily, at Carenna's request, to come to meet the two, all the Indians had gone with him, objecting to be left so near to the 'demons' wood' without him. Now, however, they quickly distributed themselves among the huts, one acting as cook and servant in the house, and Matava attending to all other matters as general overlooker.

So far little had been said between the young men and their strange host as to the objects and details of their enterprise. The circumstances of their introduction had been so unusual that the discussion had been tacitly postponed until Leonard should have recovered sufficiently to take part in it. And even then, when Jack had broached the subject, Monella had remarked,

"You had better wait till you have been to my cabin near Roraima, when I can better explain the nature of the undertaking. Then, if you do not care to join me in it, or we seem unlikely to get on well together, we will part friends and you will merely have had an interesting bit of travelling." So all farther explanation had been adjourned.

"I call this more than a 'cabin,'" said Leonard, when they had had time to make a sort of tour of inspection. "I think we ought to give it a better name. Suppose we call it 'Monella Lodge.'" And 'Monella Lodge' it was henceforth called.

V

In the 'Demons' Wood'

The following day, Monella led the two friends to the road he had begun to cut into Roraima Forest; but first he showed them two llamas that were kept in a rough corral near his dwelling.

"I brought them all the way from the other side of the continent," he said. "You know that there they are the only beasts of burden, and in this country there are none. They will be useful to us later."

As to the so-called 'road,' it was really but a pathway; and, in places, almost a kind of tunnel. The great trees of this primæval forest were so high and dense that but little daylight penetrated to the ground beneath; and on all sides the undergrowth was so thick and tangled that almost every foot had to be cut out with the axe. Here and there one could see for a few yards between the giant trunks, and at these spots the path had been made wider. One curious thing Jack noted: the path did not start from that part of the wood opposite to 'Monella Lodge'; nor even from the margin of the wood itself.

Asked why this was, Monella thus made answer: "If in our absence others should come here, they might hunt up and down for the path a long time before they hit upon it—and very likely never find it. On this stony ground the tracks we leave are very slight and difficult to trace."

"But," said Jack, "your Indians know the way."

Monella smiled.

"Not one of them would ever show another man the way," he replied, "let him offer what he might."

"But why all these precautions?"

"Later you will understand."

But, when Jack came to look round, his heart sank within him.

"I should not care to have a few miles of railway to cut through wood like this," he said. "It's the worst I ever saw. I do not wonder you have found it more than you could manage—only yourself and these Indians—and it's a wonder you ever got them to join at all, considering all the circumstances."

"Yes; that's where it is," Monella answered. "Many men would have despaired, I think. We have had trouble, too. Two Indians met with accidents and were badly hurt; though now they are recovering. Then, some of the small streams that issue from the mountain became suddenly swollen once or twice, and washed away the rough bridges we had made across them; and we have met with many unexpected obstacles, such as great masses of rock, or a fallen tree, some giant of the forest that was so big it was easier to go round it than to cut through it."

That evening, Monella explained his project, and showed the young men the plans and diagrams Dr. Lorien had spoken of, and then went on to say,

"If you decide to join me, you ought to know something of the language in which these old documents are written. I both read and write it, and I speak it too. You will find it interesting to decipher them, and an occupation for the evenings."

Jack was not enthusiastic at this suggestion; but Leonard cordially embraced it.

"To learn the language of an unknown nation that has passed away will be curious and *very* interesting," he declared, "and will, as you say, help to pass the time. You may as well learn it too, Jack. You speak the Indian—why not learn this? Then we can talk together in a tongue that no one but ourselves and our friend here can understand."

"And where did these ancient people 'hang out'?" asked Jack irreverently.

"Have you heard of the lake of Titicaca and the ancient ruins of the great city of Tiahuanaco; a city on this continent believed by archæologists to be at least as old as Thebes and the Pyramids?" Monella asked.

"*I* have," Leonard answered, "though I know very little about them. But I believe I was in that country when very young, and had a curious escape from death there."

Monella turned his gaze quickly upon the young man.

"Tell me about it. What do you remember?" he asked.

"Oh, I do not remember anything; I was too young. But I have been *told* how that my father went somewhere in that district on a prospecting expedition, and, not liking to be separated from my mother, took her with him, and my nurse, Carenna, and myself. Whilst there they came across a small settlement of white people, as I understand, and remained with them sometime. There was amongst these people a child of my own age, and so exactly like me, that my nurse grew almost as fond of it as she was of me, and used to like to take the two out together. One day, it seems, we both went to sleep on the grass, and she left us for a few minutes to gather fruit. When she returned a poisonous snake crawled hissing away, and she found the other poor little child had been bitten and was dead."

"That's all I know about it. Who the people were, and where the place was, I cannot say. I have always understood, however, that it was somewhere in the direction of Lake Titicaca. But Carenna could tell you more."

"And what about this ancient people of yours?" Templemore asked of Monella, who still gazed thoughtfully and inquiringly at Leonard. Templemore had heard of Elwood's early adventure many times before.

"High up on the eastern slopes of the great Andes is an extensive plain, as large as the whole of British Guiana," the old man replied. "It is twelve thousand feet above the level of the sea, and there, at that great height, is also the largest lake of South America, Lake Titicaca, over three thousand square miles in extent, on the shores of which was once a mighty city called Tiahuanaco. It is now in ruins; yet, even amongst its ruins, it boasts of some of the oldest and most wonderful monuments in the world. Two thousand feet above this again, are another large plain and another lake, little known to the outside world, being, indeed, almost inaccessible. It was there my people dwelt, and tradition asserts that they retired thither when driven out of Tiahuanaco by some invasion of hordes from other parts of the continent."

"Is it a very old language, do you suppose?" Jack asked.

"Undoubtedly one of the oldest in the world; and yet not difficult to acquire by those who know the language of Matava and his tribe—as you do. It has some affinity to it."

As regards the tongue spoken by the Indians, Leonard had learnt it from Carenna in his childhood; and Templemore had picked up a good deal from the same source, as well as on his hunting expeditions with Leonard and Matava.

When it came to discussing terms, Monella declared that he had none to make, except that on no consideration whatever should any other white man be invited or allowed to join them. As to the rest, he simply suggested that any wealth they might acquire by their enterprise should be shared equally between them.

"Suppose one of us were to die," observed Jack. "How then? Might not the survivors choose someone else to join them? Though," he added thoughtfully, "if it were *you*, we should not be likely to go on."

"*I* shall not die, my friend, until my task be finished," replied Monella with conviction.

"You cannot say," was Jack's rejoinder.

"No, I do not say I *know*, yet I can say I *feel* it. No man dieth till he hath fulfilled the work in life allotted to him by God," Monella finished solemnly.

The others already knew him, by this time, as a man with deep-seated religious convictions; though he made no parade of his beliefs. He seemed to have a simple, steady faith in an overruling Providence, and showed it, unostentatiously, in many ways, both in his actions, and in the advice he gave, on occasion, to the young men.

In the result, the bargain—if it can be so termed—was concluded. Elwood and Templemore formally enrolled themselves under Monella's leadership, and henceforth performed the duties he assigned to them; amongst other things assisting almost daily in the formation of the path that was to take them through the forest. When not so engaged, they would go out with some of the Indians on hunting or fishing excursions in search of food.

Monella had with him, amongst other things, a beautifully finished theodolite of wonderful accuracy and delicacy; with this he settled the direction of the road from day to day. Often, obstacles were encountered that made it impossible to go straight; these had to be worked round and the proper direction picked up again by means of Monella's calculations.

Another circumstance worthy of note and that caused the two young men at first some surprise, was the fact that Monella had with him some mirrors specially prepared and fixed in strong cases for carrying about in rough travel, and intended for heliographic signalling. They frequently took these out and practised with them by sending messages to one another from the ridges of hills far apart. Monella tried also to instruct Matava and some of the Indians in the work, but without success. They were indeed afraid of the glasses, and looked upon it all as some kind of magic.

"Wouldn't it be simpler to go up the bed of this stream that you seem to have been following more or less all the time, even if it be longer?" observed Jack one day.

Monella shook his head.

"No use, my friend. It divides into so many branches; and then again, in case of a rise of its waters, we should have all our road submerged at once."

On Sundays they always rested. This, it appeared, had been Monella's custom all along.

In his conversations in the evenings and during their Sunday strolls, he would instruct and amuse his hearers with his reminiscences and adventures in all parts of the world, or with his intimate knowledge of the wild life around them. From his account, he had undergone, at times, terrible and extraordinary hardships and privations on the plains and in the forests of India and Africa; of Australia; the Steppes of Tartary; the Highlands of Thibet; the interior of China and Japan; the wilds of Siberia; of Canada; the prairies of North America, and the pampas, plains, and rugged mountains of South America—all, as Dr. Lorien had said, seemed to be alike known to him. Nor was he less familiar with the countries and cities of Europe; yet he spoke of his travels and experiences in a simple manner that had in it nothing of boastfulness or ostentation, but as though his sole object were to amuse and entertain his two young friends.

As they penetrated farther into the forest, their work became harder and the progress slower. This latter was unavoidable, since each day they had to walk farther and farther to and fro. Moreover, the Indians, who had displayed greater courage—so Monella had said—now that they had two more white men with them, once more began to show signs of nervous apprehension and fear.

This was doubtless due to the great difference in many ways—some definite enough, others indefinable and vague—between this forest and those generally to be found in the tropical regions of South America. Not only were the trees still more gigantic—making it gloomier—and the undergrowths more dense and tangled, but the birds and animals, judging from their cries, were unfamiliar to them. Many of the sounds usual to forest life in British Guiana were absent; the constant note of the 'bell-bird' was not heard, nor was even the startling roar of the howling monkeys. Instead were heard other sounds and noises of an entirely novel and peculiar kind, unknown even to the Indians who had been used to forest travelling all their lives; sounds that even Monella either could not explain—or hesitated to. One of these was a horrid combination of hiss and snort and whistle, loud and prolonged like the stertorous breathings of some monstrous creature. Some of the Indians declared that this was the sound traditionally said to proceed from the great 'camoodi,' the monstrous serpent that is supposed to guard the way to Roraima mountain; while others inclined to the opinion that it was made by the equally dreaded 'didi,' the gigantic 'wild man of the woods,' that also had, as they averred, its special haunts in this particular forest. At times, a startling, long-drawn cry would echo through the wood, so human in its tones as sometimes to cause them to rush in the direction it seemed to come from, in the belief that it was a cry for help from one of the party who was in danger. This strange, harrowing cry, the Indians called 'The cry of a Lost Soul'[1]; and they were always seized with panic when it was heard.

There were other cries and sounds equally mysterious and perplexing; and, so the Indians began to declare, strange sights too. Of these they could give no clear account, but they maintained that, in the shadows in the darker places, or just before nightfall, while returning from their work, they now and then caught passing glimpses of vague shapes that seemed to peer at them and then disappear within the gloomy forest depths. And even Elwood and Templemore were conscious of the occasional presence of these silent unfamiliar shapes, and sometimes fired at them, though without result. These facts they made no attempt to conceal from one another, though, in their intercourse with the Indians, they put a bold face on matters, and affected to disbelieve the stories told them.

Monella alone was—or appeared to be—entirely undisturbed by all these things. If conscious of them, he gave no sign of it, but went

---

1. This strange cry is often heard in the depths of the forests in this region, and has never been accounted for, the only explanation given by the Indians being the one stated above, viz., that it is 'the cry of a Lost Soul.' It is alluded to by the American poet, Whittier, in the following lines:—

> "In that black forest where, when day is done,

> *　　*　　*　　*　　*

> Darkly from sunset to the rising sun,
> A cry as of the pained heart of the wood,
> The long despairing moan of solitude
> And darkness and the absence of all good,
> Startles the traveller with a sound so drear,
> So full of hopeless agony and fear,
> His heart stands still, and listens with his ear.
> —The guide, as if he heard a death-bell toll,
> Crosses himself, and whispers, 'A Lost Soul!'"

about whatever he had to do as though danger were to him an unknown quantity.

There was, however, one unpleasant fact that could not be ignored, and that was the unusual number of 'bush-masters' of large size in the wood. This is a poisonous snake, very gaudily coloured, whose bite is certain death. It does not—like most serpents—try to get out of the way of human beings, but, instead, rushes to attack them with great swiftness and ferocity. It is the only *aggressive* venomous snake of the American continent. It usually attains a length of five or six feet; but, in this forest, the explorers killed many of eight or nine feet, and two— that came on to the attack together—were nearly eleven feet long, with fangs as large as a parrot's claw. In consequence of the frequency of the attacks of these reptiles, so much dreaded by the Indians, and indeed by all travellers, one or two of a working party, armed with shot guns, had to be told off to keep watch; rifles being of no use for the purpose.

Templemore, as it happened, had had a bad fright when a child from an adventure with a snake; and this—as is frequently the case—had left in his mind, all the rest of his life, a great horror of serpents. He found, therefore, the presence of these 'lords of the woods,' as their Indian name implies, a source of ever-present abhorrence.

Besides the 'bush-masters,' there were the 'labarri'—also a large venomous snake, but not aggressive like the other—and rattlesnakes. There were also, no doubt, boa-constrictors, or 'camoodis,' of the ordinary kind; but, thus far, only one had been seen, and that, though large, was nothing out of the way as regards size for that country.

Nor were serpents their only visible enemies; there were others of a kind new to the two young men. One day, while with the working party at the farthest part of the track, they heard the whole forest suddenly resound with a perfect babel of discordant noises. There were shrill cries and squeals, hoarse roars and growls, then a kind of trumpeting. The Indians retreated, throwing down their axes to pick up their rifles. As they hastily retired, four large animals sprang into their path, one after the other, with loud roars and growls. But Monella, who was behind Elwood, stepped forward and rolled two over with his repeating rifle, and Jack stopped another of the beasts with his. The fourth, apparently not liking the way things were going, leaped into the thicket and disappeared; though, judging from the sounds that came from the direction it had taken, there were many more of its fellows close at hand. Gradually their cries grew fainter, until they died away in the distance.

Meanwhile, further shots had given the *coup de grâce* to the three that had been knocked over, and the victors went up to examine them. They seemed to be a kind of panther or leopard of a light grey colour, approaching white in places, with markings of a deeper colour.

Neither Templemore nor Elwood had ever previously seen any animal, or the skin of one, at all like these. They were, moreover, of different shape from either the jaguar or the tiger-cat; larger than the latter, and more thick-set than the former.

"These must be the 'white jaguars' that the Indians say help to guard Roraima," Jack observed, looking in perplexity at the strange creatures.

"Yes," said Matava, who had now come up, "and they are 'Warracaba tigers.'"[2]

"What on earth are they?" asked Leonard.

"Warracaba tiger," Monella said, "is the name given to a species of small 'tiger' (in America all such animals are called 'tigers') that hunts in packs, and is reputed to be unusually ferocious. They have a peculiar trumpeting cry, not unlike the sound made by the Warracaba bird—the 'trumpet-bird'—hence their name."

"They look to me more like light-coloured pumas," Jack remarked.

"No; pumas are not marked like that, and do not make the sounds we heard. Besides, you need never fear a puma, and should never shoot at one, unless it is attacking your domestic animals."

Both Templemore and Elwood looked up in surprise.

"I always thought," the latter said, "that pumas were such bloodthirsty animals."

"So they are, to other animals—even the jaguar they attack and kill. But men they never touch, if let alone. I do not believe there is a single authenticated instance of a puma's hurting any human being, man, woman or child. In the Andes and Brazil—where I have lived long

---

2. A vivid account of an adventure with these formidable animals will be found in Mr. Barrington Brown's 'Canoe and Camp Life in British Guiana,' page 71. Very little is known about them, but they are believed to have their haunts in the unexplored mountain districts, from which they occasionally descend into other parts. Mr. Brown states that the Indians fear them above everything; and, while comparatively brave as regards jaguars and tiger-cats of all kinds, give way to utter panic at the mere idea that 'Warracaba tigers' are in their neighbourhood. It is said that nothing stops or frightens them except a broad stream of water—not even fire.

FRANK AUBREY

enough to know—the Gauchos call the puma 'Amigo del cristiano'— 'the friend of man'—and they think it an evil thing to kill one."[3]

A few days after, they were attacked again by these furious creatures, and this time did not come off so well, for two of the Indians were badly mauled. But for Monella's cool bravery, indeed, matters would have been much worse; and Templemore had a narrow escape. Then, a day or two later, one of the Indians was stung by a scorpion; and Jack came near being bitten by a rattlesnake—would have been but for Monella, who, just in time, boldly seized the reptile by the tail, and, swinging it two or three times round his head, dashed its brains out against a piece of rock.

Indeed, upon all occasions where there was any kind of danger, Monella's ready, quiet courage was always displayed in a manner that won both the admiration of his white colleagues and the devotion of his Indian followers. Moreover, as Dr. Lorien had stated, and as Leonard had found by actual experience, he was skilled in medicine and surgery. To wounds he applied the leaves of some plant, of which he had a store with him in a dried state, the curative effects of which were reputed among the Indians to be almost marvellous.

But even these incidents were surpassed by a startling experience they had a short time afterwards. On going to their working ground one morning, two or three Indians in advance of the remainder of the party saw, lying across the path, what they took to be the trunk of a tree that had fallen during the night; and they sat upon it, indolently, to wait for the others to come up. Suddenly, one of them sprang up, exclaiming, "It's alive! I felt it move! It is breathing!" They all jumped up, in alarm, when the great snake—for such it proved to be—glided off into the wood. Most likely the others would have ridiculed their story, but that Templemore happened to come up in time to witness what occurred. And through the underwood, on both sides of the path, was plainly to be seen a sort of small tunnel that marked the place where the serpent had been lying asleep.

---

3. A very interesting account of the South American puma will be found in 'The Naturalist in La Plata,' by Mr. W.H. Hudson. He states that the puma has a strange natural liking for, or sympathy with, man; that, though ferocious and bloodthirsty in the extreme as regards other animals, yet it never attacks man, woman, or child, awake or asleep. He quotes many authorities, and gives numerous instances, of a very remarkable character, from the accounts of hunters and others whom he has himself seen and questioned.

Matava and his fellows, of course, insisted that this was the great 'camoodi,' that Indian tradition had long declared existed in this forest—set there specially, by the demons of the mountain, to guard it from intrusion.

These constant dangers and adventures made the task of keeping the Indians from deserting doubly difficult, and rendered the work both harassing and tedious to the others. Only Monella showed no weariness, no sign of the strain it all involved; so far from that, these troubles seemed only to increase his vigilance, his power of endurance, and his determination.

And all the time they were cutting their way through vegetation that would have astonished and delighted the heart of a botanical collector such as Dr. Lorien. Not only within the wood, but in the whole district round, unknown and wondrous flowers and plants abounded. But the explorers had neither time nor inclination to take that interest in them they merited, and would, at any other time, have undoubtedly excited.[4]

4. See extract given in the preface (page viii) from Richard Schomburgk's book 'Reissen in Britisch Guiana.'

VI

The Mysterious Cavern

When the time drew near for the adventurers, if Monella's calculations proved correct, to reach the base of the towering rock towards which they were making their way with so much labour, a suppressed excitement became apparent throughout nearly the whole party. It was clearly visible in the Indians and in Elwood; and Templemore, even, showed signs of anxiety. Monella alone was imperturbable as ever, and, if any unusual feeling arose in his mind, there was no trace of it to be seen in his placid manner. Perhaps a close observer might have seen, at times, a little more fire in the gaze of his keen eyes; but it was scarcely noticeable to those around him.

Elwood did not attempt to hide the state of expectancy into which he had gradually worked himself; but while he, on the one hand, grew more excited, Jack Templemore, on the other, became steadily more pessimistic and moody. Since the adventure of the great 'camoodi' he seemed nervous and depressed, and he no longer troubled himself to conceal the discontent that now possessed him. The continued sojourn in that terrible forest was becoming too much for his peculiar temperament. Its gloom oppressed him more and more each day; and he had become silent and unsociable, often sitting for long intervals stolidly smoking and, if addressed, replying only in monosyllables. They had now been for some weeks in the wood, camping in it every night, and going back to 'Monella Lodge' only for the Sundays. To this rule Monella rigidly adhered; but, since it took the greater part of a day to reach the edge of the forest from the point they had now attained, but little work was done at the path-making on Saturdays, Sundays, or Mondays. Hence their progress had become slower, and Templemore's discontent and impatience increased in proportion.

One morning, after breakfast, Jack was sitting on a log moodily smoking, while Elwood was busying himself clearing up after the meal recently finished. Monella and all the Indians had gone to the path-end, and were out of sight; but the strokes of their axes, and their calls one to another, could be heard distinctly, now and again, echoing through the almost silent wood. Very little else broke the stillness, but once or twice they had heard that weird sound, half hiss, half whistle, that the Indians attributed to the monstrous serpent. Presently, Jack took his pipe from his mouth and addressed Elwood:—

"You heard what Monella said last night, that he hoped today or tomorrow would see the end of this work. Supposing, as I expect, that we find that we merely run against inaccessible cliff, I want to know what you intend to do. To attempt to work either to right or to left, along the foot of the rock, in the hope of finding an opening would be, I feel convinced, a mere wild-goose chase, and would lead us only farther into this hateful forest, and uselessly prolong our stay in it. Now, Leonard, is it agreed that the thing is to end when we get to the cliff? I've asked you again and again as to this, but you always put me off."

"I put it off—till the time comes for deciding about it; that's all, you old grumbler. What is the use of talking before we see how Monella's calculations come out?"

"If I grumble, as you call it, it is because I am anxious for others. I gave a solemn promise before I left my poor old mother that I would not rush into any obvious and unnecessary danger; any danger, that is, beyond the ordinary risks of travel in a country like Guiana. Now—"

"Well, what dangers have we courted that are beyond the 'ordinary risks of travel,' as you call them?" Elwood demanded cheerfully. "We have come safely through forests and plains thus far, and now we are in another forest—"

"Yes, but what a forest! I have been, as you know, pioneering in the furthermost recesses of Brazil and Peru; I know a little—just a *little*— you will allow, of wild life; but never have I seen the like of this wood! No wonder the Indians shun and fear it; indeed, it is a marvel to me how Monella ever induced them to enter upon this work, and it is still more wonderful how he has managed to keep them from deserting him. Heaven knows what we have experienced of the place is enough to try the courage of the best—the most ferocious 'tigers,' the biggest serpents of one sort ever dreamed of, and the more deadly and more fiercely aggressive venomous ones; strange creatures that one can only catch glimpses of and can never see; sounds so weird and unnatural that even the Indians can offer no explanation. That great serpent, alone, fills me with a continual cold horror. We never know where it may be lurking; it may make a rush at one of us at any moment, and what chance would one have with such a beast? What consolation, to think it would probably get a bullet through its head from one of us, if, while that was being done, it crushed another to a jelly?"

"Your old horror and dislike of serpents make you nervous, old boy. I wish you could get over it. In all else, you know, you are as bold as—as—well, as Monella himself; and that is saying a lot, isn't it? You must admit that, if our enterprise has its dangers, we have a leader who knows what he is doing."

"A splendid fellow! but—a dreamer—or—a madman!"

"A madman! He has method in his madness then! I admire him more and more everyday. He is a man to lead an army; to inspire the weakest; to put courage into the most timid. I do not wonder the Indians are so devoted to him. *I* would follow him anywhere, do anything he told me! His very glance seems to thrill you through with a courage that makes you ready to dare everything! He is a born leader of men! He carries out, in every action, in his manner, his air, his principles, his extraordinary cool courage, and his gentle, simple courtesy, all my ideas of a hero of romance of the olden time—the very *beau idéal* of a great king and chivalrous knight. *I* can see all this; his very looks, his slightest motions are full of a strange dignity; never have I seen one who so excited alike my admiration and my affection! Yet, I do admit he is a mystery. One knows nothing—"

"Exactly," Jack burst in, interrupting at last the speech of the enthusiastic Leonard. "It is true, what you say, in a measure. He seems to have in him the making of such a man as you, I can see, have in your mind—a hero, a leader of men. Yet here is he, an unknown wanderer on the face of the earth, giving up the last years of his life to a fatuous chase after El Dorado, with a few Indians and a couple of credulous young idiots joining in his mad quest. I like him; I admire him; I believe in his sincerity. But I say he is mad all the same, a dreamer; and for the matter of that, so are you. You suit each other, you two. Two dreamers together!" And Templemore got up and began pacing up and down, restless in body and disturbed in mind.

Leonard watched him with a half smile; but Templemore looked serious and anxious.

"We are surrounded by hidden enemies—many of them deadly creatures," he went on gloomily. "Already three of us have fallen victims, and we know not who may be the next. Even the most constant and watchful vigilance does not avail in a place like this; and the never-ceasing worry of it is becoming more than I can stand. One wants eyes like a hawk's and ears like an Indian's. One cannot feel safe for a single minute; you want eyes at the back of your head—"

Leonard went up and put his hand on the other's arm.

"All because you are so anxious about *me* and others, dear old boy," he said. "If you really thought of yourself alone you would never trouble; but you make a great affectation of nervous apprehension for yourself, while all the time you are thinking only of me."

Templemore shook his head.

"I don't know how it is," he returned, "but the thought of that great snake *haunts* me. I feel as if some terrible trouble were in store for us through it. A kind of presentiment; a feeling I have never had before—"

Elwood burst out laughing.

"A presentiment! Great Scott! *You* confessing to a presentiment! You who always deride *my* presentiments, and dreams, and omens! Well, this is too good, upon my word! Who is the dreamer *now*, I should like to know?"

Just then they heard a call, and, looking along the path, saw Monella at some distance beckoning to them.

"Bring a lantern," they heard him say, "and come with me, both of you."

"A lantern!" exclaimed Jack. He took one up and examined it to see that there was plenty of oil. "What on earth can he want with a lantern? Is he going to look for the sun in this land of shadow?"

When they came up to Monella they looked at him inquiringly, but no sign was to be had from a study of his impassive face. Yet there seemed, Jack thought, a softer gleam in his eyes when he met his gaze.

"I think our work is at an end," he said to the young men; "and," addressing Jack more particularly, "your anxiety may now, let us hope, be lightened."

Then he turned and walked on with a gesture for the two to follow. And Templemore felt confused; for the words Monella had spoken came like an answer to the thoughts that had been in his mind; so much so that he could not help asking himself, had this strange being divined what he and Elwood had been talking, and he (Jack) had been so seriously thinking, of?

However, these speculations were soon driven away by surprise at the change in the character of the wood. The trees grew less thickly, and the ground became more stony, the undergrowth gradually thinner; more daylight filtered down from above, and soon they found they could see between the trunks of the trees for some distance ahead. And then, in the front of them, it grew lighter and lighter, and shortly the welcome sound of falling water struck upon their ears. Then they came upon a stream—presumably the same that they had been, in a measure, following through the wood—rushing and tumbling in a rocky bed—for they were going up rising ground—and splashing and foaming in its leaps from rock to rock. The trees became still sparser, and the light stronger, till, finally, they emerged into an open space and saw, rising straight up before them, the perpendicular flat rock that formed the base of Roraima's lofty summit.

It was here fairly light; indeed, a single ray of sunlight played upon the splashing water in the little stream, and the spray sparkled in the gleam. But still very little sunlight ever entered the place. The great wall of rock that reared itself in a plumb-line two thousand feet into the sky, overshadowed it completely on the one side; and on the other were the great trees of this primæval forest towering up three hundred feet or more, and extending their branches above across almost to the rock, though below, the nearest trunk was quite fifty yards away. They stood, in fact, upon the edge of a semi-circular clearing that extended for a distance of perhaps a hundred yards, its radius being about fifty yards if taken from the centre of the exposed portion of the cliff. At each end of this space the trees and undergrowth closed in again upon the rock in an impenetrable tangled mass, denser, and darker even, than that through which the explorers had been slowly cutting their way.

Some of the Indians were grouped round the stream, two or three enjoying the luxury of wading in it, or sitting on the bank and dangling their feet in the clear cool water. Matava and the others were busy upon some kind of rough carpentering. Templemore and Elwood saw that the stream issued from a hole in the rock near one end of the clearing; and this was of itself a matter for surprise. They were, however, still more astonished when Monella, with a strange smile, pointed out another aperture in the rock near the centre of the open portion of the cliff. It was about sixteen or eighteen feet from the ground, and was not unlike a window or embrasure in a stone building of considerable thickness. Within—at a distance of eighteen inches or so—it seemed however to be closed by solid rock.

The two gazed in silence at this unexpected sight; Elwood showing in his eager manner the hopes that it aroused, and Templemore pondering in silent wonder as to what it all meant. That Monella's 'calculations' had led them to a most unexpected result thus far—whether by accident or otherwise—he could not but admit. Of the fact there was now no doubt. But a clearing of this character, opposite to what looked like an opening in the rock, or entrance to a cave, was a fact too startling to be the outcome of a mere coincidence, or a lucky chance. He knew that a party of explorers might spend years—centuries, indeed, if they could live long enough—in a search for such a place in that forest and never find it, unless guided by the most exact information. Then the fact that the opening was so nearly in the centre of the clearing had a significance of its own; the question whether it was actually the entrance to a cave or merely a curious accidental hollow in the rock was thus answered, as it were, in advance. Besides, just below the 'embrasure' a small stream trickled out, and, falling down the rock, found its way amongst the stones to the larger water-course beyond. Here there seemed presumptive evidence that the space at the back of the rock was hollow—was, in fact, a cave. But in that case the entrance must have been purposely closed by human hands. If so, by whom? and when? and why?

These thoughts revolved rapidly in Templemore's mind while he stood looking at the rock. He glanced around at the giant trees, and thought of the almost impenetrable character of the forest they had come through, and he felt that, if the ideas that had come into his mind were correct, it was impossible to suppose that such a cave could be the retreat say, of any unknown Indians living at the present time. Therefore, the puzzle seemed the greater. *Who* could have been there before them—and how long ago?

But Matava now approached the cliff bearing a sort of rough ladder that he had constructed under Monella's directions; this he placed against the rock just under the opening, planting the ends firmly in the ground. He had cut down two young saplings and, partly by means of notches, and partly by twisting some strong fibres to hold them, had fastened cross-pieces at short intervals, and so fashioned the whole into a very serviceable ladder.

Monella signed to him to hold it firmly, and proceeded to test its strength. Then, satisfied as to this, he quietly mounted it till he could insert his hand into the aperture. After a moment or two he called to Elwood and Templemore to assist in steadying the ladder; and, when they had come to the assistance of Matava and another Indian who was with him, Monella leaned over into the opening and, exerting all his great strength, pushed away the stone that was closing it, exposing to view a cavern beyond. After a brief look inside, he asked for a lighted lantern and a long stick, and, while these were being handed up, the expectations and curiosity of his companions became excited to a lively degree. The Indians, who had been amusing themselves in the water, came crowding round, half pleased, half afraid at this unexpected development of events.

"You're never going to venture into that place?" Templemore asked. "It may be full of deadly serpents. For Heaven's sake do not be rash enough to risk it. Send one of the Indians—"

Monella replied with a look—a look that Jack remembered for many a day after. His eyes simply flashed; and then he said quickly,

"Did you ever know me bid another go where I would not venture myself?"

Then he took the lighted lantern, swung it into the cavern at the end of the stick, and, having satisfied himself that the air within was not foul, he threw the stick in first and followed, himself, into the semi-darkness.

A minute after, his head and shoulders reappeared, just when Jack was half way up the ladder to follow him.

"Wait a few minutes before you come up," he asked him. "I just want to give a glance round, and there is but one lantern. Or—well—suppose you come up and wait inside. But tell the others to keep to the bottom of the ladder, and be ready to hold it in case we should wish to beat a hasty retreat."

This seemed prudent counsel, and was carried out. When Jack got off the ladder into the opening, he was told to jump down inside; and he found there a level rocky floor about three feet below the aperture, which had thus a resemblance to a veritable window. By the dim light it gave he could see that he was in a cavern of considerable height and extent, and Monella, with his lantern, disappearing through an arched opening at some distance that seemed to lead to another cave within. He had brought with him his double-barrel, one barrel loaded with small shot, the other with ball, and he gave a look at the revolver in his belt while he stood waiting at the entrance and gazing curiously about him. He saw that a small stream of water ran through one side of the cave; there were, in fact, two streams, for one ran in a ledge at some distance from the ground; but when it came to the opening they had come through, it fell to the floor and joined the other stream, the whole finding its way out through a fissure in the rock and running down outside, as has been before described. Now the stone slab that had closed the 'window,' as Jack called the opening, had rested on a continuation of what may be termed the sill, and, on being pushed, had rolled off. It was a thin slab, roughly circular in shape; not unlike what one might suppose a millstone to be in the rough. Jack regarded it with close attention, almost indeed with awe; it spoke so plainly of human beings having inhabited the place, or, at least, of their having fashioned this method of closing the entrance to the cave. How long ago had they been there? And, when they went away, why had they closed the entrance so carefully?

Monella seemed a long time away; so long that Jack at last began to think of starting to look for him—they had already sent for another lantern in case it should be required—when he heard his footsteps in the distance, and shortly afterwards saw the gleam from his lantern. When he came closer, Jack scanned his face keenly, but, as usual, read nothing there.

"You can call Elwood," said Monella, "and I will take you to where I have been. You need have no fear; the place is quite free from reptiles."

When, however, Leonard was called, a difficulty arose; Matava and his fellows objected very strongly to being left alone outside; but it also appeared that they objected still more strongly to coming into the cavern. On no consideration whatever would they enter 'the demons' den,' as they had already named it. But, since they had to make a choice, they elected, in the end, to remain outside and wait.

When Elwood was inside and had had a few moments in which to get accustomed to the obscurity and peer wonderingly about him, Monella pointed out how the opening had been closed.

"I want you to notice," he observed, "that this stone was *cemented*, and this little stream of water that has accidentally found its way round here, has, in the course of time, loosened the cement; else I could not have pushed the stone away. We should have had to blast it."

"Yes," said Jack; "and it also shows that it was closed *from the inside*. Whoever last closed it never went out again—at least not by this entrance. Where then did they go to?"

"That's what we have to see about," returned Monella. "Now, follow me, and I will show you something that will surprise you."

VII

The Canyon within the Mountain

Monella, with the lantern in his hand, led his two companions through an arched opening into a second cavern which seemed to be larger and loftier than the first; and this, in turn, opened into a third, at one end of which they could see that daylight entered. Monella stopped here and, lifting the light high in one hand, pointed with the other to side-openings in the rock.

"They are side-galleries, so to speak," he said, "but do not appear to be of any great extent. I have been to the end of two or three. They all seem to be perfectly empty too; not so much as a trace of anything did I see, save loose pieces of stone here and there, that had, no doubt, fallen from the roof. Now we will go to the entrance on this side." And he turned and walked on towards the place where they could see the glimmering of daylight.

Quite suddenly they turned a corner and saw before them a high archway, leading out into the open air; and, before the two young men had had time to express surprise, they had stepped out of the gloomy cavern into a valley, where they stood and stared in helpless astonishment upon a scene that was as lovely and enchanting as it was utterly unexpected.

They saw before them the bottom of a valley, or canyon, of about half a mile in length, and nearly a quarter of a mile in width; its floor, if one may use the expression, consisted chiefly of fine sand of a warm tawny hue; its sides, of rocks of white or pinkish white fine-grained sandstone, with here and there veins, two or three feet wide, of some metallic-looking material that glistened in the sunlight like masses of gold and silver. In other places were veins of jasper, porphyry, or some analogous rock, that sparkled and flashed as though embedded with diamonds; other parts again were dark-coloured, like black marble, throwing up in strong relief the ferns and flowers that grew in front of them.

At the further end of the valley a waterfall tumbled and foamed in the rays of the sun which, being now almost overhead, threw its beams along the whole length of the canyon. The stream that flowed below the fall widened out into clear pools here and there, fringed by stretches of velvety sward of a vivid green. The water of this stream was of a wonderful turquoise-blue tint, different from anything, Templemore thought, that he had ever seen before; and he and Elwood gazed with admiration at its inviting pellucid pools. But most extraordinary of all were the flowers that nearly everywhere were to be seen. In shape, in brilliancy of colouring, and in many other respects, they differed entirely from even the rare and wonderful orchids and other blossoms they had come across in the vicinity of Roraima. Of trees there were not many, though a few were dotted about here and there by the side of the river; and, in places, graceful palms grew out of the rocky slopes at the sides and leaned over, somewhat after the fashion of gigantic ferns. Though the valley was so shut in, and the heat in the sun very great, yet the amount of green vegetation on all sides, the blue water, and the light-coloured, cool-looking rocks, made up a scene that was gratefully refreshing after the gloom of the forest scenes to which the explorers had been so long accustomed. Moreover, by stepping back into the cool air of the cavern, they could look out upon it all without experiencing the drawback of the intense heat.

Elwood was in ecstasies. The triumphant light in his eyes, when he turned round and looked at his friend, was a thing to see.

"You confounded, wretched old grumbler," he exclaimed, "what have you to say now? Is not *this* worth coming for? Or is it that even *this* will not suit you? Perhaps it is all too bright, the water too blue, the flowers too highly coloured, or"—here a most delicious scent was wafted across from some of the flowers—"they are perfumed too highly to please you! You haven't found fault with anything yet, and we have been here nearly five minutes!"

Jack laughed; and Leonard noticed that it was more like his old, easy, good-natured laugh.

"I think you are too severe upon me, Leonard," he replied. "Don't you think so, Monella?"

Monella, the while, had been standing gazing on the scene like one in a dream. More than once he passed his hand across his eyes in a confused way, as though to make sure he was awake. When thus addressed, however, he seemed to rouse himself, and, without noticing the bantering question that had been addressed to him, and, extending one hand slowly towards the valley that lay before them, said,

"I praise Heaven that I have been led, after many days, to the land that I have seen in my visions. *Now* do I begin to understand why they were sent. And you too, my son," he added, looking at Leonard, "you have had your visions and your dreams. Tell me, does this not remind you of them?"

"Indeed it does," returned Leonard seriously. "Though, till you spoke of it, I had not thought of it. I felt so glad to think we had been successful so far, and that your expectations were being justified. It is all very strange."

"I am out of all that," observed Jack, with a comical mixture of offended dignity and good-natured condescension. "You dreamers of dreams have the best of such beings as I am. *You* are led on by visions of what is in store for you, as it would seem, while *I* have to work in the dark, and follow others blindly, and—"

"And think of nothing but how best you can serve and protect your friends," said Monella, looking at him with a kindly smile. "We are not all alike, my friend. It is not given to all to 'dream dreams,' anymore than it is given to all to have true manly courage combined with almost womanly affection for those they call their friends. We three have little to boast of as between one another, I fancy. Would it were so more often where three friends are found grouped together or associated in any undertaking. But now to consider what is next to be done. It seems to me we could not have a better place for our head-quarters in our future explorations than this cavern. Here we have all we want: shelter from rain, and sun, water—pretty well all we could ask for. We must see about getting our things along here." He paused for a moment and then continued, "On second thoughts I see no reason why you should not remain here. There is no more baggage than the Indians can carry amongst them, and that is all we have to trouble about. I will go back, and you two stay here."

"That seems scarcely fair," Jack protested. "I have been lazy all the morning. I propose I go and leave you here."

Monella shook his head.

"You cannot manage the Indians as I can," he answered. "Indeed, that is one reason why I think you would do better to remain here. When they find you do not return, and that they have to obey me or remain in the forest alone, they are more likely to do what we require. But I will ask you not to go far away, and not to fire off a gun or anything, unless in case of actual danger and necessity."

"You do not believe that the place is inhabited?" Jack exclaimed in surprise.

"Who can tell?" was the only reply, as Monella took up the lantern and turned away.

Left to themselves, Jack pulled out his inevitable pipe, the while that Elwood sought, and brought in, a couple of short logs from a fallen tree to serve as seats; and the two then sat down in the shade of the cavern-entrance.

Jack was very thoughtful; but his thoughtfulness now was of a different kind from his late moody silence. He, indeed, was ruminating deeply upon Monella, who was everyday—every hour almost—becoming a greater mystery to him. He had been particularly struck with his manner and the expression of his face when they had stood together, looking out upon that curious scene. In Monella's *words* there had not been much perhaps, but in other respects he had strangely impressed the usually unimpressionable Templemore. There had been in his features a sort of exaltation, a light and fire as of one actuated by a great and lofty purpose, so entirely opposed to the idea that his end and aim were connected with gold-seeking, that Jack Templemore confessed himself more puzzled with him than he had ever been before. Too often, as he reflected, when a man sets his mind, at the time of life Monella might be supposed to have reached, upon gold-seeking, he is actuated by sheer greed and covetousness. But by no single look or action whatever had Monella ever conveyed a suggestion that the lust of gold was in his breast. Yet, if that were not so, what was his object? Did he seek fame—the fame of being a great discoverer? Scarcely. Again and again he had declared, on the one hand, his contempt for and weariness of the world in general, and, on the other, his fixed intention never to return to civilised life. Jack began to suspect that all his talk about the wealth to be gained from their enterprise had been chiefly designed to secure their aid, and that for himself it had no weight—offered no incentive. What, then, *was* Monella's secret aim or object? What was the hidden expectation or hope, or belief, or whatever it was, that had led him into an undertaking that had appeared almost a chimera; that had so taken possession of his mind as to have become almost a religion with him; that had enabled him to support fatigue and physical exertion, privation, hunger and thirst, as probably could few other men on the face of the earth; and that had become such an article of faith—had made him such a firm believer in his own destiny, that no danger seemed to have any meaning for him? Neither storm nor flood, lightning nor tempest, savage beasts nor deadly serpents—

none of the dangers or risks that the bravest men acknowledged, even if they faced them, seemed to have existence so far as this strange man showed any consciousness of them. Never had they known him to step aside one foot, to pause or hesitate one moment, to avoid any of them. He simply went his way in supreme contempt of them all; and, until quite lately—till within the hour almost—Jack had attributed all this either to madness, or to an inordinate thirst for riches for riches' sake—which, as he reflected, would be, in itself, a sort of madness. Now, however, his opinion was altering. The liking he had all along felt was changing to surprised admiration. He remembered the calm, unwavering confidence with which Monella had led them through all their seemingly interminable difficulties and discouragements to their present success—for success he felt it was, in one sense, if not in another. In the strange flowers and plants before them, alone, there were fame and fortune, and what might there not be yet beyond, now that they had in very truth penetrated into that mysterious mountain that had so long defied and baffled all would-be explorers? Monella, he still felt, might be a bit mad—a dreamer or a mystic—but, evidently, he was a man of great and strange resources. Few engineers, as Jack himself knew, could have led them thus straight to their goal from the data he had had to work upon. Yet he showed now neither elation nor surprise, and in particular, as Jack confessed to himself rather shamefacedly, no disposition to remind him of his many exhibitions of contemptuous unbelief. With these thoughts in his mind, and the remembrance of Monella's unvarying kindness of manner—to say nothing of the way he had exposed himself to danger on his behalf—Templemore began to understand better than he ever had before the affection that the warm-hearted Leonard entertained for their strange friend, and he became conscious that a similar feeling was fast rooting itself in his own heart. In fact Monella was now, at last, exercising over the practical-minded Templemore that mysterious fascination and magic charm that had made the Indians his devoted slaves, and Leonard his unquestioning admirer and disciple.

Presently, Leonard, who had fallen into one of his daydreams, woke up with a slight start and exclaimed,

"What a paradise!"

Jack smiled, and said, "I wonder whether it is a paradise without a serpent, as it is without an Eve? But your dreams, Leonard, if I remember, were mixed up with a comely damsel; and there is none here.

I fear we shall have to regard her as the part that goes by contraries, as they say."

Leonard looked hard at him, and there was evident disappointment in his glance and tone when he asked,

"Do you then think this place is uninhabited?"

"I do," was the reply. "And I will tell you why. That stone that closed the entrance from the forest was placed there by someone, no doubt, and by someone inside. Yes; but how long ago? A very long time! Hundreds of years, I should say. It has taken quite that time for that stream of water to hollow out the little channel in the rocky side of the cave and play upon the cement until it has become loosened. The wood outside tells the same tale. It must be hundreds of years since any human beings made their way to and fro through the wood, to or from this place. *Once* there were many people here; and they were not ordinary people either, I can tell you. Not Indians, I mean, for instance. They were clever workers in stone. That 'window,' as I call it, through which we came in, is artificial."

Elwood gave an exclamation of surprise.

"Yes; I noticed it, though you did not. I have little doubt that Monella noticed it too. The cavern was formerly all open, or, at least, it had a large opening, and I am almost certain its floor was originally level with the ground outside. If so, the present floor is artificial, and there are probably vaults beneath. Outside, the stonework is so artfully done that you see no trace of it; it appears to be all solid rock; but inside I saw distinctly traces of the joints. Then, look at these archways, at the one we are now sitting under! They have been worked upon too—to enlarge them, probably; to give more head-room when the floor was made higher. See! here are marks of the chisel!" And Templemore got up and pointed to many places where the marks left by the tool were clearly to be seen.

"Well," said Elwood, "I suppose we shall solve the problem and set all doubts at rest before many days are over. For my part I am in a curious state of mind about it—half impatient, half the reverse. If it is to turn out as you say, I am in no hurry to terminate the uncertainty. This strange spot, the fact that we are really, at last, inside the wonderful mountain—these things open such a vista of marvellous possibilities that I—it seems to me—I would rather, you know—"

"Oh, yes, I know, you old dreamer," Jack exclaimed, laughing. "You would rather wait and have time to dream on for a while than have your dreams rudely dispelled by hard facts. Now suppose we go and take a look round in the shade over there. We need not go out of sight of this entrance; so that Monella will find us immediately he returns."

The sun had now moved so far over that one side of the valley was lying in shadow, and they strolled out to observe more closely the new flowers and plants they had thus far seen only from a distance.

VIII

Alone on Roraima's Summit

When Monella returned about two hours later, the two young men had much to tell him of the wonderful flowers and plants they had found, of strange fish in the water, and curious *perfumed* butterflies that they had mistaken for flowers.

There were many of these extraordinary insects flying about. In colouring and shape they resembled some of the flowers; when resting upon a spray or twig they looked exactly like blossoms, and upon nearing them, one became conscious of a most exquisite scent. But just when one leaned a little nearer to smell the supposed flower, it would flutter quickly away, and insect and perfume disappeared altogether. Many of the flowers that were scattered about the rocks were shaped like exquisitely moulded wax bells of all sorts and kinds of colours and patterns, white, red, yellow, blue, etc., striped, spotted, speckled. So distinct were they from anything the explorers had before seen, that they had picked some and brought them into the cavern to show Monella; but he could not give them a name.

The stream from the waterfall, they found, disappeared into the ground just before it reached the cavern. No doubt this was the stream they had seen issuing from the rock upon the other side.

At the further end the valley began to rise, following the stream, which came down in a series of small falls or cataracts. About this part they had found someother caves; but had not entered them.

"And most remarkable of all," said Templemore, "we have not seen a single snake, lizard, or reptile of any sort or kind. Yet this is just the sort of place one would have expected to be full of them. Nor have we seen either animals or birds."

Monella told them the Indians still refused to enter the cave. They all three, therefore, went to the 'window,' and assisted to get their camp equipage inside, the Indians bringing the things to the top of the ladder and handing them through the opening. They preferred, themselves, to camp outside, and had already made a fire to cook some monkeys they had killed with bows and arrows.

When all their things were safe inside, Leonard and Jack took some fishing nets and soon caught some fish in the pools of the stream in the canyon. They then made a fire just outside the cavern entrance, and cooked them for their evening meal. The fish seemed to be a kind of trout, but of a species they had never seen before.

Monella expressed his regret that all attempts to persuade the Indians out of their fear of 'the demon-haunted mountain' had failed.

"They will neither come inside nor remain outside by themselves; that is, if we go away from here to explore farther. It seems to me, therefore, that we ought to have all our stores brought here before we start, and then let the Indians go back by themselves. We may be here for months, so had better get them to fetch everything we can possibly require from 'Monella Lodge.'"

Such was Monella's advice.

"It will take two or three days at least—possibly more," he continued, "to transport all our stores here. During that time we must be content to attend to nothing else, and postpone any further exploration of the mountain. Besides, when we once start, none can tell how far we may be led on. Better have our 'base of operations' settled and secure first. How far away are those other caves that you saw?"

"About a quarter of a mile," Jack answered.

"We will have a look at them in the morning," Monella said thoughtfully. "It may be wiser to hide some of our stores and belongings in different places, so that, if any accident should happen to one lot, the others may be all right. Eh, Templemore?"

"Just the very idea I had in my head when I spoke to you of those other caves," Jack responded. "We can take half an hour or so to explore them in the morning."

"Better take longer," observed Monella. "Better take the day, and do it thoroughly. Much may depend upon it hereafter. Suppose, therefore, that you remain here while Elwood and I return to 'Monella Lodge' and see about packing and bringing some of the 'belongings'? Then, if we find another journey necessary, you can go next time, and Elwood and I will remain here on guard. But we cannot get back tomorrow night. Do you mind staying here alone?"

"Not I!" said Jack, laughing.

"Very well then; we will arrange it so. We shall load up our two animals, and perhaps one journey will suffice after all. Anyway, you hunt for the best and most secret hiding-places you can find. See that they are dry, you know. There are the three casks of powder—"

"What! Will you bring them too?"

"Certainly. We may have blasting to do before we have done with what we have in hand. The extra arms, too, we will divide, and secrete in different places."

"I see the idea," Jack assented. "Rely on me to do the best that can be done."

The three went back, after their meal, to where the Indians were camping just outside the 'window.' Matava looked grave, and shook his head dubiously, when Leonard told him of the arrangements come to.

"My heart is heavy, my master," he said in his own language, "at the thought of leaving you to fight the demons of the mountain. It is not good this thing that you are about to undertake. Doubtless the demons have left this place open as a trap to tempt you to enter their country. When you are well inside they will close it and have you securely captured and we shall never see you more. Alas! that my mother should ever have said aught to lead you on to this terrible enterprise. Better had she died first. I feel sure, if you go inside there, we shall never see you again!"

Elwood only smiled, and bid him be of good cheer.

"We shall return," he replied, "and, I trust, not empty-handed. And, if so, you and my old nurse shall share in my good fortune. But, if you think there is danger, why do you not come with us to help? It is not like a brave Indian to be afraid!"

The Indian shook his head and sighed.

"Matava is no coward," he responded. "His master knows that well. Against all earthly dangers Matava will help him to his last breath, but to battle with the demons of Roraima is but madness—and it is useless. No mortal man may brave them and live. *Some* one must take the tale to those left behind. It is not good that they should never know."

"That is a nice way of getting out of it, Matava," said Templemore, who had just come up and heard the last sentence. "But please don't take intelligence of our fate till you have learned it. Above all," he continued seriously, "do not alarm our friends in Georgetown by any wild, preposterous—"

"Oh, don't trouble as to that," Elwood interrupted. "Our friends know Matava and his superstitions about the mountain too well by this time. Besides, we will leave letters with him, to deliver, in case he returns before we get back."

It was now getting dark, and the three white men went back into the cavern to prepare their sleeping arrangements. First, it was determined to make a more thorough examination of the side-galleries, and this was soon done, for they were found to be of very limited extent. In passing the archway that led into the canyon, however, Leonard happened to glance out, and uttered an exclamation which called the others to his side. They also looked out into the valley, and were as much astonished as at their first sight of it that morning. It seemed to be lighted up!

On all sides, high and low, small lights were seen. They were of various colours, and hung, some singly, some in groups or clusters. Many drooped over the water, and were reflected in the pools below. The effect was extraordinary. The place seemed a veritable fairy land; and exclamations of astonishment and admiration burst from each of them while he stood and gazed upon the scene.

Then they went out to the nearest lights, and the marvel was explained. The bell-shaped flowers that had excited their curiosity during the afternoon all glowed with radiance. Inside each was a small projection apparently of a fungoid character, that was phosphorescent. It sent forth a light nearly as brilliant as that of a firefly; and this illumined the bell-shaped blossom, which then appeared of different hues according to its colouring by daylight. Even those that Elwood had picked, and thrown down at the entrance of the cavern, glowed with appreciable glimmer.

"I've heard of some kinds of toadstools and fungi being phosphorescent," Templemore remarked, "but never of such a thing in flowers."

"Yet," observed Monella, "if you come to consider the matter, there is nothing more remarkable in the one case than in the other."

The night passed without incident, and all were astir before dawn, making preparations for the day's work. After a light meal, all except Templemore set out on their way to 'Monella Lodge,' while Jack went out into the canyon to seek for caves and likely hiding-places for their stores, and to look about generally. He took with him his usual two-barrelled gun, a supply of cartridges, and some biscuits and other provisions. Water he knew he could get in plenty. He also took a lantern to enable him to explore the caves. Before leaving the 'window,' as he now always called the entrance by which they had found their way into the first cavern, he drew up the ladder, and then, with some difficulty, rolled the stone that had closed it into its place again. Most likely he could not have given any reason for this action if he had been asked;

but probably a vague hatred of the gloomy forest, and satisfaction in shutting it out of view, were what chiefly prompted him.

"I will take all I want round to the other side," he said to himself. "I like that side best. It's a more cheerful outlook."

He thoroughly explored the caves, and decided that they were fairly suitable for the purpose they had in view. Then, quite accidentally, he came upon another that was so hidden by a tangled mass of creepers that its existence would never have been suspected. He fancied he had seen a small animal disappear behind a bush, and trying with a stick to see whether he could rout it out, he found what at first he thought was a large hole; but, on pushing back the creepers, which hung like a curtain across it, he found a large opening about eight or nine feet high. Inside was a roomy cavern with many recesses here and there, like high shelves in the rock, and many short side-galleries. Just the very place they wanted, he decided. Neither here nor elsewhere did he meet with any signs of his pet aversion—the serpent tribe.

He now began the ascent of the canyon, following always the course of the stream that came down it. In some places the way was easy and direct; indeed, as he could not but remark, there was every appearance that a well-defined, wide pathway, with steps here and there, had at one time existed. But in places it was broken away; the steps cut in the rock had crumbled, or trees growing in the fissures had rent them asunder. In other places masses of rock, fallen from heights above, blocked the road; and, occasionally, the trunk of a fallen tree. Then he came to a wayside cave, and was glad to rest in its shade from the heat of the sun, which began to pour down into the canyon with intolerable fierceness. He had proceeded so far that he imagined he must be half way to the top; and he looked up the canyon still beyond him and at the overhanging cliffs with curiosity, wondering how much farther he would have to go to reach its head, and what he would see when he arrived there.

While he sat quietly pondering this question, and enjoying a smoke following upon a light lunch, the idea grew upon him to complete the ascent that afternoon. He knew that, if he did so, it would be impossible to return that night, and this meant passing it in the open air. But that he did not at all mind; he was accustomed to it; and, since he saw no signs of serpents anywhere, there was an absence of the only thing that troubled him in such case. Monella and the others would not return till the following evening; he had plenty of time to do it in, and nothing else to occupy his time.

But would Monella like it? Why, however, should he object? He could do no harm in going to the top and back. It was not as though the place were inhabited and he might get involved in any adventures with the 'natives.'

The more he thus thought about it, the more strongly did the feeling grow upon him to make the venture. True, he had not much with him in the way of provisions; but he had enough for supper and breakfast if he put himself upon short rations. In the end he resolved to risk it.

Accordingly, so soon as the sun had gone across sufficiently to shade the path, he started off once more, and made his way still upwards. He encountered many obstacles that delayed his journey, but eventually, just when night was falling, he arrived at what he calculated must be the top of the ascent. It was a grassy plateau of a few hundred yards in extent, facing cliffs that rose still higher and shut out the view and were inaccessible. Down these the stream still flowed, though much smaller in volume than was the case below. What, however, caused him dismay, was to find that he was shut in on the other side by a belt of forest that seemed to be almost as dense and impenetrable as the hated wood below. It was too late to think of going back; there he must stay and pass the night. It was cold, too, up there, and he had no rug in which to roll himself. In fact, he began to wish himself back in the cavern, where he could have cooked himself a good supper and then rested comfortably. There was not even a view; he had hoped to have a glorious prospect and, having brought his field-glass, even that he might be able to look across the forest and savanna and make out 'Monella Lodge'; possibly see his friends, who would now be nearing it. Instead of that, he was shut in upon a narrow ledge beside an unknown forest that might be full of wild animals of a dangerous kind.

Altogether Jack felt he had not acted wisely. He went a little way into the wood; but, finding it very dense, and fearful of losing his way in its dark recesses, he soon returned to the clearing. Finally, as it grew dark, being tired and drowsy after his exertions in climbing the canyon, he fell asleep.

IX

Vision or Reality?

The following afternoon, a long train of Indians, with Monella and Elwood at its head, was making its way slowly along the tunnel-like road that had been cut through the heart of Roraima Forest. They all carried loads, and they had with them, besides, Monella's two llamas, which were also loaded with as much as they could carry. All looked more or less wearied from their long march, and cast many anxious glances ahead as they approached the end of their journey. When they reached the part where the path opened and the trees became thinner, Matava fired two shots, the agreed-on signal to Templemore; they were answered at once by one from him, and, shortly afterwards, he was seen making his way towards them. He relieved Elwood of a few things he was carrying, and inquired whether they brought any news.

"None," said Elwood; "and you?"

"First of all," returned Jack, "here's a very curious and awkward thing. I have come across a large *puma* that has taken a great fancy to me, and has become somewhat of a 'white elephant.' At the present moment it is looking out of window, anxiously awaiting my return; and, though it has not yet learned to scramble down the ladder, I'm not at all sure it won't acquire that accomplishment shortly—or it may even risk the leap down. What I am thinking of is the animals you have with you—they might tempt it; otherwise, it seems tame and good-natured enough, and I do not think it will hurt either you or the Indians."

"Does it seem like an animal that has been tamed, then?" asked Monella. "And where did you come across it? Inside, I suppose?"

"Why, yes. But I'll tell you later. Meantime, can't we halt the animals here, and keep them out of sight for awhile? My new friend is as big as a lioness, and of the same sex—and would have one of them down in a moment, if she felt so inclined. You can't tie her up, you know, without a collar and chain, even if one cared to make the attempt. I tried to drive her away, but it was of no use; and I've been sitting there racking my brains as to what on earth I was to do when you came, and hoping against hope that the beast would take herself off." And Jack looked the picture of comical perplexity and bewilderment.

Meantime, the train had come to a halt, and Matava and the other Indians crowded round Templemore and examined him with great curiosity and attention. There were many strange Indians who had been induced, for a consideration, to accompany the party, and these were equally inquisitive. Some came and touched him, as though to make sure he was real flesh and blood. Since Jack seemed inclined to resent this, Leonard laughingly explained.

"They can scarcely believe that any man can have passed a night in the mountain and live to tell the tale," Elwood told Templemore. "Their idea is that you have been eaten up or captured by the 'demons,' who have sent back a ghostly presentment of their victim to lead on the others. So they are anxious to know whether it is really yourself or a spectral imitation. You may be sure, too, your 'lioness' will be a matter of serious speculation to them. She will be looked upon as a familiar spirit, to a certainty."

Monella had said little; but he now proposed to go on to the cave at once with Jack and Elwood, to see how matters really stood, leaving the others to await their return.

On nearing the 'window' they saw, sure enough, the head and paws of an immense tawny-coloured animal that gave a cry—a sort of half-whine, half-roar—of recognition on seeing Jack. The ladder was lying on the ground outside.

"There you are," he observed with a mixture of mock gravity and real anxiety; and he waved his hand towards the animal. "Let me introduce you to the 'Lady of the Mountain.' I only hope to goodness she will behave herself and receive you in a friendly manner; for, if not, *I* have no control over her. I disclaim all responsibility."

Monella and Elwood looked curiously at what they could see of the animal. It seemed, as Jack had said, nearly as large as a lioness.

"It is a puma," said Monella decidedly, "though a very large one. I never saw one anything near the size. However, there is no need to be afraid of it; you have heard me say you need never fear a puma."

"Yes," returned Jack, "and here is an opportunity of testing your faith in your own theory. I confess, if I did not already know she was well-disposed towards myself, I should think twice before I ventured upon going near her."

"Nonsense!" said Monella, taking up the ladder and placing it against the opening. "I will show you the creature is tame and friendly enough. I could see it at the first glance." And he ascended the ladder and entered the cavern, pushing the puma on one side as coolly as if it were a pet dog. Then he turned and called to Elwood to follow.

Jack also went after them, and found the puma already on friendly terms with both, much to his own relief; for he had had misgivings.

"The question now is what about the llamas?" he next said. "Do you think she is to be trusted there—and with the Indians?"

"With the Indians—yes—though *they* probably would object," replied Monella; "but, with the llamas, it is doubtful. So we had best be on the safe side, and keep them, if possible, out of her sight."

"She's wonderfully playful," observed Jack; "just like a great kitten. I've been playing with her with my lasso, and she will run about after it by the hour together, just for all the world like a kitten. If you want to keep her out of the way on the other side, all that need be done is for one of us to stay there and play with her."

"Let Elwood do so then," Monella decided. "He is tired; and you can come and help unload."

The animal had, in fact, already begun to show a liking for Leonard, and, when he went out towards the canyon, it followed him at once. Jack watched this with some surprise, and affected much disgust.

"Just like the generality of females," he remarked, "inconstant and changeable. Here have I been at the trouble of capturing the beast, and being worried with her all day, only to see her transfer her affections and allegiance to someone else at the very first opportunity!"

The unloading was then proceeded with, and before dark everything they had brought was placed within the cavern temporarily, to be moved on to other places, as might subsequently be determined.

When all had been brought in, the Indians set to work to cook their evening meal, while Jack did the same outside the canyon entrance. The hunters had shot an antelope, and with some of this and some fish a satisfying meal was provided; the puma lying down and watching the proceedings with evident curiosity, but with no more attempt at interference or stealing than in the case of a well-trained dog. Needless to say she was rewarded for her patience with a share.

When the meal was over, and Jack and Leonard took out their pipes, Monella, looking at the former, said,—

"You have something of importance to tell us. What have you seen?"

At this Elwood turned and regarded Jack with surprise.

"Why, what is it?" he exclaimed. "You have said nothing about it all this time!"

Jack looked a little sheepish. He was somewhat taken aback, too, by Monella's direct question. It brought to his mind the query that had often arisen before—could this strange being read his thoughts?

"I scarcely know whether I have seen something or only dreamed it," he began hesitatingly; and seeing Leonard, at this, open his eyes, Jack went on desperately: "Well, yes! I may as well out with it and make a clean breast of it! I *have* something to tell you, and for the life of me, I cannot make up my mind whether I actually *saw* it, or dreamed it—whether, in short, it was reality, or only a vision!"

Leonard opened his eyes wider than ever, and gave a long whistle.

"*You* having 'visions'!" he exclaimed in unbounded astonishment. "*You*, the scoffer, the hard-headed, prosaic-minded derider of dreams and visions! Great Scott! Is the world then coming to an end? Or have the demons of the mountain in truth bewitched you as Matava declared they would?"

"Ah! I knew you would laugh at me, of course. And I feel I deserve it. However, if you want to hear what I have to tell, you will have to keep quiet a bit. I cannot explain while you are talking, you know."

"I'll not say another word; I'm 'mum,' but amazed!" Elwood answered. "Now go a-head."

"Well, yesterday, after you left, I pulled up the ladder and carefully closed the 'window' by rolling the stone back into the place, as we first found it. I thought to myself I would shut out the gloomy forest. Then I went up the canyon to explore the caves we spoke of, and soon, by accident, found a new one, so curiously hidden from sight, that it seemed the very thing we wanted; so there was no need to search farther. Then I thought I would stroll up the canyon a bit, and reconnoitre; and I found another cave about half way up, and, finding the sun getting warm, went in and had a rest. When it grew shady again, I thought, instead of coming back, I would go on to the top to see the view."

Monella uttered an exclamation.

"Ah! yes. I know you mean I ought to have kept below. However, no harm has been done, and I could see no objection to going up and taking a peep from the top. I had my glasses with me and thought I might even catch a glimpse of you on your way to 'Monella Lodge.' However, by the time I reached the top it was getting dusk, and, after all, I found myself quite shut in by yet higher rocks on one side that I could not climb, and a thick wood on the other. There was a grassy knoll of a few hundred square yards in extent, and there I had to make up my mind to pass the night. I was tired out; and, soon after it grew dark, I fell asleep."

Templemore paused, and glanced doubtfully at Monella, as if expecting him to say something; but he remained silent, and Jack proceeded:—

"I seemed to wake up after being asleep for an hour or two. I say *seemed* to wake up—I really cannot say—but either that, or I dreamed the whole thing. Well, I seemed to wake up, and fancied I heard distant shouts. I looked sleepily round and was surprised and alarmed to see a very unmistakable glow in the sky through the trees. It struck me at once that the forest must be on fire, and if so, I thought, my position might be an awkward one. If the wood were burning, and the fire travelling in the direction of where I was, to have to retreat down the canyon in the dark would be anything but agreeable. After some consideration I decided to venture a little way into the wood, and climb a tree in the hope of getting a view of what was going on. I could hardly, I reflected, lose my way, for, when I wished to return, I should only have to turn my back on the direction in which the fire lay and march straight back. Accordingly, I made my way into the wood; at first it was very dense, but soon it grew thinner, and, encouraged by this, I went straight on, when I emerged on to a high plateau, where an extraordinary sight presented itself. I seemed to be on the edge of an extensive sort of basin; I could see for miles; and in the centre, as it appeared, there was a broad lake, and beside the lake were lofty buildings lighted up on all sides, the lights being reflected in the water. There seemed to me a large city; there were buildings that looked like grand palaces; there were wide noble-looking embankments and promenades and bridges, all well lighted; and, on the lake, boats, also lighted, were going to and fro, filled with people. I could hear shouts and cries, though of what nature it was impossible to say; and through my glasses I could plainly distinguish numbers of people moving about. It was as though some kind of *fête* were going on. The large buildings towered into the air, and their cupolas and turrets glistened as though built of gold and silver. In effect, it was a wonderful sight, and how long I stood watching it I cannot say; but, after a time, the lights went down and all became silent and dark. I managed to find my way back to my camping ground, and, while thinking it all over in astonished wonder, I fell asleep again, as I suppose. At any rate, when I finally awoke, the sun was shining and this animal was lying on the grass by my side."

"What! the puma?" Leonard asked.

"Yes. I was rather upset at first sight of her, you may be sure. To wake and find oneself in a wild place at the mercy of a great animal like that is a startler for anyone's nerves, I can assure you. No chance to use one's rifle or anything, you know. However, while I lay very still and watched it, not knowing what to do, I saw it must be a puma, though an unusually large one. Then I thought of what you, Monella, had told us—that we need never be afraid of a puma. And then the beast turned round and began licking my hand! It stood up, too, and purred, and put up its tail just like a tame cat; so I made friends with it and found it was quite disposed to be on good terms. After a bit my dream came back to me, and I went into the wood some distance, but could see nothing. The forest seemed awfully thick, and to get denser at every step; so I finally came away, thinking I must either have had a remarkably vivid dream or vision, or that I had really been the sport of some demons of the mountain such as Matava and his Indian friends so thoroughly believe in." And Jack paused, and looked at his two companions with an odd mixture of doubt and bewilderment.

Elwood's face, while he had been listening, had become lighted up with sympathetic enthusiasm. It fell a little at the end of the recital, when Jack made the suggestion about the 'demons.'

"Certainly," he said, "it sounds like witchcraft to hear you, our own matter-of-fact Jack, who never dreams, make such suggestions. But, either one way or the other, it goes to prove that there is something very extraordinary about this mountain."

Elwood looked at Monella.

"What do you think of it all?" he asked.

"I think," he replied, "that our friend ought, in future, to be less ready to deride those who may have to tell of strange things, whether dreams and visions, or out-of-the-way experiences."

"I admit that to be a just rebuke," Jack responded with a good-natured laugh; "but it does not tell us, all the same, what your real opinion may be." But Monella had already risen from where he had been sitting and moved away to speak to the Indians.

"I say, Jack," said Leonard, "can't you *really* say, straight out, whether you *saw* this or only dreamed it?"

"Truly, my dear boy, it seemed so natural that I should say it was real, only for the inherent improbability of the thing. Then, too, I could see nothing this morning to confirm it, you know."

"Surely," Elwood said dreamily, "the Indian tales of demons that can bewitch you cannot have any foundation? There cannot be an unsubstantial city of demons to be seen at night, that vanishes and becomes only plain forest in the daytime? That is taking us back to the Arabian Nights, isn't it?"

Jack shook his head.

"I am more bewildered and puzzled than I can possibly give you any idea of," he returned. "The whole thing is beyond me; the sight I saw, or dreamed; and then, again, the behaviour of this animal here."

"Ah," Elwood said, "this puma! Does it not behave as though it were a tame animal used to the company of human beings?"

"I must say that idea has occurred to me more than once today; but the more I think over it, the more hopelessly puzzling the whole thing becomes." And Templemore, for the time being, gave it up.

X

IN SIGHT OF EL DORADO

The next morning Templemore, after leading Monella and Elwood to the hidden cave he had discovered, set out early with the Indians for 'Monella Lodge' to bring in the remainder of the stores; and, while there, in the evening, he wrote long letters to his friends, to be entrusted to Matava to take to Georgetown. Amongst them, we may be sure, was one to the fair Maud, who, amidst all the excitement of his adventures, was never long absent from his thoughts. His letter to her was grave, almost sad in its tone. He knew he was about to set out upon a critical venture, the end of which none could see, and he warned her not to be surprised if nothing were heard of them for a long time.

When, the following afternoon, he and his party once more made their way back through the forest to where they had left Monella and Elwood, and had halted just out of sight, those two soon came to meet him in response to the usual signal-shots. The first glance at Elwood's face told Jack that he had some important news to impart. While Monella was greeting the Indians and giving directions for the unloading and camping, Leonard whispered to Jack,

"We've been up to the top and have seen all you saw. It was no dream, old man, but simple reality. But don't let the Indians hear anything about it, or they would stampede straight away."

Jack stared in mute surprise, scarce knowing what to think, whether to be most pleased to have it established that he was not 'a dreamer of dreams,' or astonished at the almost incredible fact it conveyed—that the top of the mountain was, in very truth, inhabited.

"And the puma?" he asked.

"Is still with us. You had better go in and have a rest and take charge of her, while we see to the unloading."

This Jack was glad to do, and, on entering the cavern, he was welcomed by the animal with every demonstration of gladness at his return.

"Ah! you have not forgotten me then, old girl," he said, and he patted and stroked the creature. "You're not so very fickle, then, after all. Now come along with me for a while—I'm going to have a wash."

When all the fresh stores had been placed inside, and the Indians were engaged upon their evening meal, and Monella and the two young men were seated at theirs, Jack asked for further details of the wonderful news Leonard had briefly spoken of.

"It is substantially a repetition of what you told us," said Elwood, "save that we managed a little better in the morning than you did. That is to say, we did not go the wrong way into the wood, as I suppose you did; and thus, at sunrise, sure enough, we saw the wonderful city, which Monella avers can be no other than Manoa—or, as the Spaniards called it, El Dorado! We saw its palaces, and towers, and spires, glistening and glittering in the sun—a marvellous sight! So, Jack, old boy, you can be at ease; you are not yet 'a dreamer of dreams.'"

"But your intelligence, all the same, makes me feel quite dazed," answered Jack. "Are you *really* sure about it? Are you certain—do you feel confident that—er—well, that it won't all have melted into thin air by the time we get up there?"

"Scarcely. It is too substantial for that."

"Then it means this—that the mountain *is* inhabited after all," said the puzzled Jack. "If so, what sort of a reception are they likely to give us?"

"Well, that of course remains to be seen. But, meantime, it is certain that all your clever theories about the place 'not having been peopled for hundreds of years' are fallacious."

Jack presently asked Monella what he purposed doing next.

"We must put away our stores," was the reply, "and then arrange our plans for making our presence known to the inhabitants, whoever they may be, of the mountain."

"Yes, and then, if they speak the same language that you have been teaching me," Leonard put in, "Jack will have reason to be sorry he has not stuck to it a little more, I fancy."

Of late, Jack had practically dropped all efforts in this direction, particularly during the last fortnight; while Elwood had neglected no opportunity for using it in his converse with Monella. Elwood had, in consequence, got so far as to be able to speak it fairly well; but Jack was much behind him.

"By Jupiter! But I begin to think there is wisdom in what you say," was Jack's response. "I must do my best to make up for lost time."

The night passed without incident. The Indians stayed on through the following day, and Matava even yielded so far as to enter the dreaded cavern, and take a look into the canyon. Elwood managed to persuade him to do thus much, that he might take back to his friends at Georgetown a description of the scene. Matava was rather afraid of the puma, but the animal was quite friendly. The Indian evidently believed that Elwood and his friends were going to their destruction, and would never again be seen by mortal eyes. However, at Monella's suggestion, he made for them during the day a more substantial ladder, which the nails and tools brought with the stores enabled him easily to do. He also made some poles or struts to form bars to close the stone from within, and, with much perseverance, cut slots in the rock and in the stone to receive them. When completed, and the struts put in their places, the stone was firmly fixed and could not be moved from the outside.

Then Monella made another suggestion. He arranged with Matava a few simple signals that might be made from the mountain-top by flashing small quantities of powder at night, and that Matava could, in turn, answer from the plain beyond the forest, or, indeed, from 'Monella Lodge'. These signals were simply—"All well," "Coming down," "*Not* coming down." It was deemed best not to risk more than these, Matava's intelligence in such directions being limited; and, since he could not read, to write them down would have been useless.

When, on the last morning, the leave-taking came, the scene was an affecting one. The Indians were well pleased with the rewards given them for their services; but they were, one and all, in genuine distress at the thought of leaving the three adventurers to what they thoroughly believed would be a terrible fate. They even besought them to alter their minds and "come away from the accursed place"; needless to say in vain.

Matava, almost in tears, was loaded with messages to those in Georgetown, should he go back before seeing the travellers again; the understanding being that, if he found they did not return within a short time, he was to conclude they would remain for an indefinite period, in which case he would shut up 'Monella Lodge' and return to Georgetown, and only expect to hear of them when he came that way again in the usual course.

At last, the Indians sorrowfully set out and disappeared in the forest, and Monella and his two companions set to work to distribute their stores and spare arms and ammunition. It was decided, after some discussion, to place the larger portion in the secret cave; leaving only a comparatively small part hidden in the cavern they were in, it being obvious that the latter was the one most likely to be searched, if any should be.

In the carrying out of the plan settled by Monella, the whole of the stores were divided roughly into two parts; two-thirds, and all the spare arms, ammunition and powder, being hidden in the secret cave; the other third, including most of their camping equipage, lanterns, store of oil, etc., but no arms, being stowed away in various remote parts of the cavern by which they had entered from the outer forest. This was in accordance with certain anticipations and eventualities that he had carefully thought out. Thus, if the people of the place should prove unfriendly, and they were forced to retreat at once to the entrance cavern, they had there, ready to hand, in addition to the arms, etc., they took with them, all that was really necessary either for a temporary stay or for the journey back to 'Monella Lodge.' On the other hand, if the inhabitants should turn out to be hospitable, and invite the travellers to stay with them, it might be a little while before they returned to the cavern at the entrance; in the meanwhile it might be entered and searched by others, who might carry off what had been left there. But in that case the loss would not be a serious one to the explorers, nor would the thieves find any arms or powder.

Early the next morning Elwood went out a little way into the forest to cut some short poles he was in want of, when the puma—apparently finding the new ladder more to her taste than the old one had been—scrambled down after him and disappeared into the wood.

"We had better leave the ladder and go on with our work," observed Monella, when told she had gone off and not returned. "No doubt she will find her way back presently."

But they saw nothing of her till the afternoon, when she came in, bearing in her mouth a good-sized wild pig, which she laid down quietly at the feet of her astonished friends.

"Why, Puss," exclaimed Jack—he had of late insisted upon giving her that name—"that *is* an accomplishment, and no mistake! You can go out hunting and get your own dinner, can you, and ours too? Well, after this we need not want for fresh meat, apparently, while we stay here."

The meat was not only a welcome addition to their larder, so far as they themselves were concerned, but solved the difficulty that had begun to puzzle them, viz., how to find food for so large an animal. Up to now there had been enough left over from what the Indians had captured and brought in; but, since they had gone away, fresh meat had been growing scarce, and to feed 'Puss' out of their limited stores of tinned meats was, of course, out of the question.

FRANK AUBREY

"You'll have to leave us and go back to your friends, whoever they are, Puss," Jack had said only that very morning. "We appreciate your society and all that sort of thing, and shall be sorry to turn you out of doors; but, unless you can crunch up meat-tins and imagine they are marrow-bones, I really do not see where another meal for you is to come from." Whether 'Puss' understood this speech or not, she had certainly settled the question in her own way, and very quickly.

"You shall go out again, tomorrow, on this sort of expedition, Puss," observed Jack. And she did; and next time brought back a small antelope.

This led to a discussion and a good deal of speculation as to whom 'Puss' might actually belong to.

"I wonder who owns her, and whether they have missed her?" said Jack. "And I wonder too whether there are many more like her on the mountain? If so, why haven't we seen anything of any of the others?" Since, however, no answer could be given to these questions, the speculation remained a barren one.

After the stores had all been disposed of to his satisfaction, Monella decided to stay on another day before making the venture of showing themselves to the inhabitants; this was partly by way of a rest and partly to give them an opportunity of studying the plants and rocks in the canyon. Most of this day he spent in hunting for strange herbs and leaves; while Jack and Elwood were more interested, after the first feeling of surprise and pleasure in examining the flowers had passed off, in searching for signs of gold among the rocks. They found undoubted traces of both gold and silver, but in what quantity they might exist it was not possible at the time to form any opinion.

Every night the canyon was lighted up in the fairy-like manner of the first evening; and, during the day, two harp-birds had visited the valley and enlivened it with their dreamy music. The travellers also caught sight of two or three small animals; but did not obtain a sufficiently good view to make them out, and Monella particularly desired that they should not shoot at anything.

Of fish there was plenty; and bathing in the cool, limpid pools of 'The Blue River,' as Jack had named the stream, was a welcome luxury.

Finally, having completed all their preparations, the three, on the morning of the third day after the departure of the Indians, set out on their enterprise of visiting the mysterious inhabitants of "The Golden City."

They started at daylight, with just sufficient camping things for passing the one night, heavily laden with spare ammunition, and taking their Winchester rifles and revolvers, and one extra gun—a double-barrelled fowling-piece. After a midday rest in the cave that lay about half way up, they reached the summit, as before, at nightfall.

They assured themselves that the strange town was still in the same place—had not vanished into thin air as an illusive creation of the demons of the mountain. Then they settled down to sleep and were undisturbed during the night.

When they woke at dawn on the day that was to prove so eventful, they found that the puma had disappeared.

"Puss has deserted us," said Jack. "She knew she was close at home and preferred the kitchen fireside, I suspect, like a respectable tabby, to passing the night out here; and small blame to her. I shouldn't be surprised, if we happen to come across her when she is in the company of her own friends, to see her pass us by with her nose in the air with a 'don't-know-you' sort of look. You'll see, she won't know us! she would lose caste, I expect, if it were known that she had been away for a week hob-nobbing with a party of houseless vagabonds like ourselves."

XI

Ulama, Princess of Manoa

The morning broke fine, and the sun rose with a splendour that was not often seen even in this land of gorgeous sunrises. As Leonard looked up at the sky above, with its tint of deep sapphire blue flecked with cloudy flakes, and cirri tinted with gold and pink and crimson, he thought he had never witnessed any effect to equal it. But, when they had quietly passed through the narrow belt of wood, and stood just within its cover, gazing down at the wondrous 'golden city' that lay sleeping at their feet, the three friends remained silent and almost spell-bound. The scene was indeed one to which no description can possibly do justice. The sun was just high enough to light up the glistening towers and cupolas; and these, and the spangled sky above, were reflected in the glassy waters of the lake. Beyond and around all was haze of a rose-coloured golden hue, which gave to the centre picture the effect of a vignette. From the upper parts, which showed the clearest against this background of rosy mist, the various buildings grew less substantial as the eye followed their lines downwards, till the bridges and embankments seemed almost ghostly and unreal, yet strangely beautiful in their airy lightness. And the picture was so faithfully repeated in the lake that, but for the reversal of the images, the line that divided the reality from the shadow could scarcely be discerned; while the whole seemed poised, as it were, in the ruddy-golden haze like a *mirage* in mid-air. Just below them a rocky spur jutted out with clear-cut outline against the central scene, the palms and other trees with which it was crowned showing a lace-work pattern of feathery foliage through which naught could be seen but the golden mist. This part alone seemed real; the city, with its towers, its lofty buildings, its bridges, and its lake, seemed too fairy-like a creation to be indeed an earthly reality.

Of the three who were thus looking out upon this glorious sight, it would be hard to say, perhaps, which was most affected by its subtle influence. Templemore, notwithstanding his affectation of putting on ultra-practical glasses through which to regard and analyse everything, had, in reality—as is not infrequent with such characters—a deep undercurrent of appreciation of beauty, whether exhibited in nature or in the works of man. As an engineer, he could appreciate the rare grace and exquisite proportions of the buildings, and of the bridges, viaducts, and other such works, far better than could Elwood's less trained mind; and then, his was a naturally generous and unselfish nature, and—he was in love. Such a temperament cannot look upon anything that charms, that satisfies the senses, without wishing that the loved one were present to participate in the pleasure and gratification experienced. And the absence of that companionship must necessarily strike a chord of sadness and longing. He was one, at heart, deeply sensible of these emotions; so sensible, indeed, that he shrank from displaying them to onlookers; and thus it was that he half unknowingly hid them beneath a veneer of 'matter-of-fact.'

Elwood's younger impulses, on the other hand, bubbled up on all occasions unchecked and uncontrolled. He was of a highly imaginative and poetic turn of mind; he was not in love, and hence, the vague aspirations of his affections had as yet met with nothing upon which to rest, or, as it were, to centre themselves. He was filled with unformed hopes and shapeless expectations. The beautiful was not satisfying in itself; it was but a stepping-stone, an enticing indication of something still more pleasing yet to be met with beyond, in the indefinite future. Thus he was always looking forward to an horizon that lay beyond his ken; while Templemore's hopes and longings, though they also turned upon the future, had found, in the being who had won his love, a settled, definite purpose in life. Not that the latter was altogether uninfluenced by that spirit of adventure which always actuates, more or less, young men of his age and character; though, in this respect, he might be swayed by somewhat more practical considerations than was the enthusiastic Elwood. In the breasts of the two, it could scarcely be but that there was some feeling of exultation and pride in the consciousness that what they had achieved was likely to bring them a high reward either directly or indirectly—in fame, or wealth, or both—even though no sordid, grasping greed mingled with the generous impulses natural to youth.

And Monella? With what feelings was *he* swayed while he silently surveyed the fair city that embodied the fulfilment of what he had been striving after for so many years? He was old, he had no children or other kin (he had declared) to interest himself in. Fame, power, riches, he despised—so he had uniformly given his two companions to understand. None of the motives that prompted the two younger men seemed to apply in his case; yet the fact was patent to them—had been all along, since first they met him—that he had been instigated by some overmastering idea that had become, as Templemore had phrased it, a sort of religion to him, a faith, a belief; that had urged him on unceasingly where success had seemed hopeless and the difficulties of his enterprise insurmountable. Templemore, at Monella's side, could not but reflect upon this now; as he had similarly reflected upon it when first they had found themselves veritably inside—so to speak—of the hitherto inaccessible mountain. But now, mingled with Templemore's admiring appreciation of all these things, there was a new element in his feelings towards Monella, which he could only define to himself as one of reverence. He felt inclined almost to take off his hat, and deferentially salute the indomitable, high spirit that had led them on to success, where success had seemed but a fallacious, impossible, fatuous dream.

But Monella seemed unconscious of all such thoughts. He gazed out on the scene before him with a countenance that expressed only a high and simple joy. His tall, commanding form had never seemed to his two companions so instinct with dignity and latent power as at this moment; and in his eyes, when he turned his glance, with a smile, to meet theirs, there were a kindness, a benevolence, a magnanimity even, that seemed to fill up the measure of the feeling of respect that was growing upon them—that made them wonder they had ever ventured to treat such a man as one of themselves. This strange emotion swayed both of them; they both felt it, though each thought it influenced himself alone. Afterwards they found this out by comparing notes; and yet again, in the time to come, they lived to comprehend that this vague idea had been something more than a fancy; it had been an instinct growing out of a solid, though then unknown, reason. It signified that the parting of their several ways, as between them and him who had been their comrade thus far, had commenced, had been already entered upon.

For a while they continued to gaze with swelling emotions upon the wonderful town. Bathed in the light of the rising sun, it slowly grew more substantial to the view, and its stately buildings gradually assumed increased solidity and reality. Their graceful outlines and proportions, their masterly design and bold execution, the novelty and originality everywhere apparent, impressed Templemore with astonishment, just as they delighted and satisfied the poetic fervour of Elwood. Templemore presently turned to Monella.

"Never have I seen the like of those structures," he exclaimed, "either in the places I have visited or in the pictured representations of the most celebrated cities of the world. Surely this people must be a nation of architects!"

"You speak truly, my friend," Monella returned. "I have travelled the world over and I have not seen the like elsewhere. But, as I have told you before—as I warned you I expected would be the case—we have here the chief town of an ancient people; a race so old that the oldest Egyptian records of which the world has any knowledge relate to peoples, and times, and things that are but as yesterday compared to the remote period to which these people can trace back their history. So is it written in my parchments."

"And is what we see, that glistens everywhere, truly *gold*—upon the very spires and roofs?" asked Elwood.

"I cannot say; but it may well be so, for these parchments of mine assert that gold is the most plentiful metal of any in these mountains. They say that the inhabitants used it for common purposes as other nations use iron; and that, in fact, iron and steel were far less common than gold and silver. But I think it is time we started down the slope to reconnoitre and await our opportunity."

The plan Monella had arranged was that, after concealing in the wood at the top the few camping requisites they had brought with them, they should move down towards the city through the clumps of trees, keeping within their cover, till they came to the point where the trees ended; that they should remain thus concealed for a time to see what sort of people passed to and fro, stepping out and making their presence known only when they saw anyone who might be supposed to be a person of standing or authority.

Following out this plan, the three moved on through groves and plantations of trees bearing luscious, tempting fruits of a kind and nature totally unknown to them. Wonderful flowers, too, they saw on all sides, and many strange and curious birds; amongst them the harp-bird, whose enchanting notes came floating every now and then upon their ears. In due course they reached the farthest and lowermost clump, and here they were therefore compelled to pause. So far they had seen no one; but it was yet early morning.

The thicket within the shelter of which they now stood was upon a knoll that was not a great way from the lake. Looking across its waters of turquoise blue, they now made out that which had so puzzled them before. Moving on its surface were numbers of white swans of gigantic size; and it was these, as they subsequently ascertained, that drew the boats about which had seemed to glide here and there without sails or oars. They had seen these great swans through their glasses, but had believed them to be vessels fashioned in that shape; deeming them too large to be really living creatures.

Suddenly, Elwood gripped Templemore's arm, and pointed to someone—a youthful maiden seemingly—walking along the border of the lake in their direction. She came to within a few hundred yards, and then stood looking dreamily out over the lake at the towering, palatial buildings upon the opposite side.

"Great heavens!" Elwood exclaimed in a whisper. "The face, the form, the very *dress* that I have so often seen in my dreams! Can it be possible? Am I awake, or is this, too, but a vision from which I shall awake by-and-by?"

Monella put his hand upon his shoulder as a sign to him to be silent, and pointed to other forms approaching from the same direction. They all seemed to have come from a great pile of buildings near the water's edge some half-mile away. It was partially screened by groups of waving palms and other trees, which hid from view the entrances.

The new-comers consisted of a tall, handsome man, of a dark-hued skin, and richly dressed, and a following of a score or so of men, apparently a guard or escort. They carried spears that flashed and glittered in the sun, as did their burnished shields and helmets. These seemed to be of gold; they wore short black tunics and sandals. They halted—upon a sign from the one who seemed to be their leader—while he advanced towards the girl. Just then she turned and caught sight of him. At this she uttered a sharp cry expressive of surprise and fear; then walked quickly up the slope towards where the three travellers were concealed.

The man followed and overtook her when she was about a hundred and fifty yards from the edge of the wood. He seized her by the wrist; but she, wresting herself free, turned and confronted him, regarding him with a proud disdain, in which, however, fear was also plainly—too plainly—written.

Now that they were closer, the concealed witnesses could distinguish pretty clearly, through their glasses, the features of the two who stood facing one another, neither for a full minute uttering a word.

As to the maiden, she was in very truth a dream of loveliness. With skin as white and fair as the most delicately reared Englishwoman, glistening golden hair, large grey-blue eyes of entrancing and lustrous beauty, a perfect oval face, and a figure the very embodiment of grace, she appeared indeed more like the creation of a vision than an earthly being of flesh and blood. She was not exactly tall, yet of fair height for a woman. Her dress seemed of silk; it was rich-looking, but quiet in colour, and flowing in design. She wore golden ornaments enriched with glistening gems, and her hair, falling loosely over her shoulders, was confined by a broad gold circlet on the head and was cut short over the forehead. And in her face was an expression of exquisite sweetness—albeit now there were distracting emotions mingled with it. The clear-cut, pouting lip curled in scorn, though, the while, the eyes showed fear, as do those of the hunted hare. Timidly she glanced around, as if for aid; but not a soul was to be seen save those who accompanied the man she feared, and from them, it was clear, she could expect no help.

As to the man himself, he was, as has been said, of fine stature and handsome; but his was not beauty of a prepossessing character. His dark face expressed arrogance and cruelty; in his smile was cold, deadly menace; his haughty features wore a scowl; and his dark eyes fairly blazed with passion. Upon his head he wore a coronet of curious design in lieu of helmet or other covering. His tunic was of black material—silk apparently—with a large star worked in gold upon the breast. A belt as of gold was round his waist, and a short sword and a dagger were by his side. His hair, full beard, and bushy eyebrows were jet black; so far as one might judge he looked about thirty-five years of age. The tunic had short sleeves and was cut low so as to display his neck, round which was a kind of necklace; upon his bare arms were bracelets, and in all these ornaments there flashed, as he moved, sparkling jewels of large size and surprising lustre.

Then ensued, between the two, a hot discussion or dispute, though those within the wood were too far away to understand its purport. The man advanced again and again in a threatening manner towards the girl, who as often retreated a short distance up the slope; then, each time, turned and faced her adversary.

Suddenly, the man seemed to give way to a burst of fury; with a gesture whose murderous import there was no possibility of mistaking, he drew his dagger from its sheath, and tried to seize the girl; but she, eluding him, turned and ran farther up the slope. The man followed, and coming up with her, seized her by the wrist, and raised the hand that held the dagger.

At this moment Monella stepped out from the wood and called loudly to the assailant, at the same time holding up his hand in warning; but Elwood, revolver in hand, rushed forward in advance of him, and levelled the pistol at the moment when the blade was poised in the air and was about to be plunged into the bosom of the girl, who had now fallen upon her knees. He was only just in time; for the weapon had already commenced its fatal downward sweep when the report rang out; the murderer's arm gave a jerk that cast the dagger a distance of some yards, and the man himself fell backwards with a bullet through his heart.

Elwood hastened to the assistance of the girl, who swayed as though about to faint; but the sight of the strangers seemed to rouse her, for she rose to her feet and stood regarding them with wondering and evidently doubtful looks. Then she turned her glance upon the dead man, and shuddered at the thought of the death she had so narrowly escaped. Looking once more at the three who now stood in a group a short distance from her—for Elwood had drawn back on seeing her rise to her feet—she drew herself up with a charming dignity and grace, and, to the surprise of the two young men, asked, in the language Monella had taught them,

"Who are you?"

The words were intelligible enough. The inflection, the accent, or the exact pronunciation, may have been slightly different from Monella's, but the words rang out clear enough.

"Who are you?"

Monella stepped a pace or two towards her. His lofty form seemed to grow in dignity the while he bent his gaze upon her; and, looking up into his face, she could scarcely fail to read the true meaning of the glance she met. She felt its extraordinary fascination, and yielded to its influence, as so many had before. Her confidence went out to him at once; and her look, that for the moment had been proud and distrustful, softened into one of friendly interest. She bowed her head as though in involuntary respect—the respect a dutiful child might show to a parent—and spoke again; this time varying the form of her question:—

"My father, whence come you?"

"We are strangers from far countries, my daughter," Monella made reply. "We came here in peaceful and friendly intent, but fate has so ordered it that our arrival has been marked by the shedding of blood. Still, though of that I am deeply regretful in one way, I cannot pretend to be sorry, if, as I see reason to believe, it has saved your young life."

"Truly it has, and I thank you; and the king, my father, will thank you too; though I know not by what marvel it was accomplished, nor by what other marvel ye have come here, you who wield the lightning and the thunder, who hold men's lives in the hollows of your hands, and yet speak our language."

"Time enough to explain that, anon, my child," was Monella's answer. "For the moment we must know what yonder people are about to do. Their intentions seem scarcely to be friendly."

This referred to the small company of guards or soldiers, who were being harangued by one who appeared to be their officer, and who, when he had ended his speech, formed them into line, as though for a charge upon the strangers.

The girl turned round and looked at them; and, doing so, her face grew pale.

"Alas, yes!" she exclaimed. "I had forgotten them for the moment. They are the special soldiers of Zelus whom ye have slain; and their officer will seek to carry you all before the father of Zelus, the dread High Priest. His vengeance will be cruel and terrible, if you fall into his power; but, if we could but get back to my father's palace, you would be safe; for he would protect you for my sake—for the sake of what ye have done for me today. But alas! How can that be? They are many and ye are but three. Ye have not even swords or spears—unless, indeed, ye can serve them as ye have served this one."

"Fear nothing for us, my daughter. We can truly serve these others in the same way, if the necessity unfortunately should arise. But we seek it not; we have come here, as I have told you, with peaceful intentions, and we have no wish to signalise our arrival by further bloodshed. Will you not, yourself, speak to these foolish people, and warn them not to rush upon destruction? Tell them we are powerful, and that, in your own words, we hold their lives in the hollows of our hands. If they will depart in peace, they may, and bear with them the body of their chief; but, if they dare approach with hostile intent, then shall they fall before us, ere even they have time to come a dozen paces, even as men are struck down by lightning. Tell them this, and urge them to be friendly; for we are not of the nature of those who take delight in slaying. To us, to slay is easy, but abhorrent."

The girl heard this with increasing wonder. She viewed the rifles (which all three were now handling) with a curiosity she did not care to hide. She took them for some sort of magic wands.

FRANK AUBREY

"I will perform your wish," she said, "but I doubt my power to stay them, for they are men used to working their own will, and now they seek your lives in revenge for this man's death. Indeed, they well know they go to their own deaths if they return to Coryon, the High Priest, and bring not with them those who slew his son."

She turned to go towards the soldiers, who were now standing in two ranks, with spears in rest, awaiting the word of command.

"Stay," said Monella. "If they listen to your words, they will want to come here to take up the body of their chief. We are willing they should do so; but it were better we did not meet, for I do not trust them, and they might plot treachery. See!" And he took his lasso from where it hung at his waist and laid it in a straight line on the ground about twenty feet from the dead body. "We will retire towards the wood; and let it be clearly understood that they must not cross that line nor touch that cord. If any man do so, he shall surely die then and there. Let them not think, however, that we retire from fear, because of their number. But now, my daughter, take heed lest they seize you. Be sure you keep near enough to avail yourself of our protection; but stand not between us and them, lest the lightning strike your own form in its course. Once launched, it goes straight to its mark, and blasts all whom it meets upon its path."

"I understand," she answered. "But you need have no fear for me, so far as these people are concerned. Their chief has dared more today than has ever been known before; but none of these would lay hand upon Ulama, the daughter of their king."

"Then," said Monella, "if you feel sure as to that, do not approach them, but go thirty or forty yards to the right, and bid them come near enough for you to address them from there. For the rest we will answer." And, with a sign to his companions, he walked slowly up the slope towards the wood they had left but a few minutes before.

XII

A Preliminary Skirmish

The words that had been spoken on both sides in this conversation the two young men had followed fairly well; though they had listened in silence and made no attempt to join in the discussion. On their way back towards the wood, Elwood was at first very thoughtful; then he turned to Monella and said excitedly,

"How do we know she is safe, out there alone? And what will her father, the king, say to us, if harm come to her? It seems to me we are acting in strange fashion to leave her thus."

"Patience, my son," returned Monella quietly; "we must avoid the shedding of blood, if it be possible. We have come here, as I have already said, with peaceful motives. If violent acts be forced upon us in self-defence, let us keep at least our conscience clear; let us be in a position to show that they *were* forced upon us. Let it not be said of us that we have come into a strange land to introduce dissension, and discord, and internal warfare; and all for no other reason than the gratification of an adventurous spirit."

"But," said Elwood, "*we* have not introduced dissension and trouble. It is clear enough that a terrible murder would have been perpetrated had we not been here to prevent it. Surely, no one can accuse *us* of commencing bloodshed; and, as to the rest, why, what are the lives of two or three scoundrels like these, the infamous myrmidons—if we may believe what we heard—of a bloodthirsty 'high priest'; what are the lives of two or three such wretches, compared with the safety of this gentle, trustful girl, whom we are leaving now almost at their mercy? In my view this is one of those cases in which offence is the best defence. They are showing their intentions pretty clearly; let us anticipate them by shooting one or two. That will frighten the remainder, and stop further hostile action; and, moreover, prevent their coming near this young lady, or princess, as I suppose she really is."

"I am bound to say I rather agree with Leonard," said Templemore. "I see, clearly enough, we are in for a fight, and shall have to kill two or three. Why not as well do it first as last? If, as she says, they are used to do as they please in the land, and if what we have just seen is a specimen of their style, pity is thrown away upon them. And, besides, is it good generalship, Monella? To attack first would be sure to scare them; but, if they make a rush, in absolute ignorance of the power of our rifles, may they not, some of them, charge home? And then we should have a hand-to-hand fight where they would be four or five to one."

Monella passed his hand over his face, and answered almost sadly,

"There is a time to be forward in attack, and a time to be forbearing. If the time come for the former, no man will ever see me flinch from it. But you know what has been said, that the shedding of blood is like unto the letting out of water, and that he who begins it is accursed. If these people begin it, we will not shrink; but at least we shall have clear consciences. Now listen to my plan. We must not enter the wood, or they will think we have fled. If they cross the line I have laid down, let each take the man opposite to him in the line, and bring him down. Then, if they still rush on, fire once more, and step back into the shelter of the wood. If they follow, you know what to do; your revolvers will suffice."

Meantime, Ulama, as she had called herself, had been addressing the soldiers. Their officer had advanced to speak to her, and angry talk had been exchanged, which those standing at the edge of the wood, with rifles at the 'ready', could not hear. But when, finally, she shook her head meaningly, and began to retire towards them, Jack Templemore set his teeth and said,

"I told you so! I knew it meant a fight! We might just as well have begun it, as let them think we are afraid."

"There is yet a chance," replied Monella. "They may hesitate to pass the line I have laid down. In any case, all we can now do is to wait and see." And, as Ulama came towards them, he signed to her to step aside, out of the line of fire.

The officer had returned to his men, and, after a short consultation with one who seemed to be next in command, the two ranks advanced, with the slow, measured tread of a well-disciplined troop, up the slope. On reaching the dead body they were halted while the two officers examined it. They had not understood how their leader had been killed; nor did they understand it now. They had heard the report of the pistol and had seen their chief fall, but the report had not been a loud one; and as Elwood had run forward at the time, for all they could see (Ulama being between them) he might have hurled a spear at Zelus. Yet the sound of the explosion had puzzled them, and stayed them from rushing instantly to the assistance of their leader. Altogether, they were perplexed. The dress of their opponents showed them to be strangers. They appeared to be unarmed, yet had they killed their dreaded master in the face of his guard. This argued conscious power; and it behoved them not to be too precipitate. After this fashion, probably, reasoned the two officers.

If so, the examination of the dead body could but add to their uncertainty; for they found there a wound they were quite unable to account for. It was not a spear thrust; it was not a wound from a sword or dagger. The scrutiny, in effect, yielded them no enlightenment; but the sight of the dead body of their leader and of the blood exasperated both officers and men, and murmurs were heard, and cries for vengeance. They probably began, too, to remember what Ulama had suggested—that if they went back with the dead body of their chief and without the slayer, their own lives would be forfeited. And all this time the strangers stood calmly regarding them, watchful of their movements, but offering neither to retreat nor to attack them.

After some further consultation, the one who seemed to be in command turned towards where the three strangers stood; flinging down his sword, he stepped forward and threw out both his hands, to signify that he desired a parley.

Thereupon Monella also advanced a few paces; then paused for the other to address him.

"Who are you? Whence come you? Why do you enter our land in this fashion by killing one of the greatest in the country?" asked the captain of the guard.

"The answers to your first questions are for your king's ear alone," returned Monella. "As to the last, we came in peace, but interfered to save a maiden from being murdered."

The other's face expressed an evil sneer, and he made answer:

"It is not usual, with us, for men to throw away their lives for women. For what you have done yours may be required. Still," he added diplomatically, "I am not judge nor executioner—unless you resist me. If, therefore, you will surrender like men of peace—as you say you are—and will come with me to tell your tale to my master, I promise you good treatment while in my custody."

Monella shook his head.

"You have had my answer," he said. "We seek your king. We will yield ourselves to no one else. And," he continued, with louder voice, "since you, my friend, dare to deride us for taking a woman's part, know that in the land we come from we are not accustomed to stand still and look on while women are being murdered. What manner of *men* are *ye* who dare openly proclaim so vile a doctrine? Soldiers of a High Priest? Guardians of a 'religion' that teaches things like this? The span that shall be left to such a being as ye serve is growing short. His power is waning, his days are even now numbered." He raised his arm, and extended it towards him he was addressing; then, with gathering force, and even passion, till he seemed like an inspired prophet of old thundering his denunciations against evil-doers—"We came here in goodwill and peace; we may remain to be a withering scourge to you and him you call your master. See to it, and take warning! There must—and there *shall*—be an end of such deeds as we have this day seen attempted by—as ye have no shame in avowing—the favoured son of your High Priest. Hence from my sight, ere scorn and anger overcome me! I have but to move my finger, and you fall dead before me!"

For the first time in their knowledge of him Templemore and Elwood saw their leader, usually so calm and equable, moved by a passion that was almost uncontrollable. They glanced at one another in surprise; and well indeed they might. For whereas, at first, they had felt almost impatient of his equanimity, and had feared he lacked the sternness to deal with those they were opposed to, yet now they thought only how to restrain his sudden and unlooked-for passion, lest it should embroil them further than was actually necessary.

But the fire of Monella's rage expired as suddenly as it had kindled.

"You have heard," he went on, coldly and disdainfully, to the captain of the hostile group. "I have warned you. I spare your life to give you time to do better."

But this contemptuous treatment, so far from having the effect intended, seemed to rouse the other's fury.

"Think not to impose on me by empty threats and vain-glorious boasting," he retorted. "I summon you to yield and come with me. If not, and we have to kill you in striving to enforce obedience, the consequences be upon your own heads."

"And I say that I have warned *you*," returned Monella quietly. He stooped and picked up a stone, then threw it to within three or four feet of the cord that lay between them.

"If," he said, "you but cross that cord so far as that stone, you die."

Instantly the other took up the challenge. He stepped back for his sword, then walked boldly forward, Monella meanwhile falling back in line with his companions; but the instant the other crossed the cord, Monella's rifle rang out, and the fatuous soldier fell prone upon the sward.

Then a tall fellow burst from the ranks and, brandishing his spear, rushed towards the fatal cord; he was followed by an adventurous comrade; but, e'en as they stepped across the line, they both bit the dust. Then all the others turned and fled; all save the second officer, who stood his ground, neither advancing nor retreating. He remained leaning on his sword, and looked, by turns, first at his flying men, then at the dead bodies that lay around him, finally at Monella and his companions.

Monella advanced and thus addressed him,

"How is it you stand thus in hesitation, friend? Are you in two minds, whether to fight or to fly?"

The second officer was a fine-looking young fellow with features that were not unpleasing. With a steady glance he looked Monella in the face and answered,

"I am no coward to run away, and no fool to rush to meet a thunderbolt. Whoever you are, it is plain that we are powerless against you. But indeed," he went on, with something almost like a sigh, "when I heard your words I felt no stomach to fight against you, if so be that they are true."

"I am well pleased to hear you say so, friend," Monella said, laying his hand upon the other's shoulder. "You have seen what it is in our power to do. I call upon you to be a witness in the presence of your king—of all your people—that we did not resort to force until all other means had failed."

"That will I gladly do," returned the officer, bending his head in courteous salutation. "Few would have been so persistent in their merciful intention. For myself, I know my fate if I rejoin my master; therefore, if you will accept my service, I would fain join myself to you. One can but fight and die; better to do so in the service of such a chief as you, than of him I have lately served," and he seemed to shudder while he spoke.

Just then the maiden joined them, and he saluted her respectfully. She looked at him with sorrowful eyes.

"And is it Ergalon," she said, "that could stand by today and see another man raise his hand to slay the daughter of his king, and not move a step to hinder him? Has Ergalon indeed sunk so low as this?"

The words were said in pained surprise rather than in anger; and in the gentle eyes she turned upon him there was no sign of aught but mild reproach. But this seemed to cut him to the heart, when ringing words of accusation would, perhaps, have failed to move him. He fell upon one knee and bent his head.

"Alas! Princess," he cried, "I well deserve your scorn; yet knowest thou not how that against my will I have been forced into this service. Well I know that to ask pardon would be useless—the king will never pardon, should this reach his ears; still less will Coryon. Yet I care not if thou wilt but grant me *thy* forgiveness. If these strangers are thy friends, grant me to serve thee by serving them; and should this service be even to death, it will content me that thou shouldst say of me that Ergalon had done his duty, and redeemed himself in thine eyes."

"Be it so, Ergalon," Ulama answered, her voice and manner charged with a sweet graciousness that quite captivated the three bystanders. Then, turning to Monella, she continued, "My father, I owe you much for what you have done today. I shall try in the future to repay you to some measure. Meantime you will need friends—accept from Ergalon this proffered service. I feel sure, after what has happened, you may trust him—even to the death. I know not who you are, whether immortals, or beings of like nature to myself, thus timely sent by the Great Spirit to my aid. But this I know, that I may trust you; that you have come to be my friends, and my friends from henceforth you shall be."

It would be difficult to convey an idea of the wonderful mixture of simple gentleness and queenly dignity with which these words were spoken. Further, it would be hard to say which of her hearers was most impressed. She had the art of winning hearts without intending or desiring it; and few could long resist the fascination of her presence. Small wonder then if Leonard Elwood had already fallen incontinently, helplessly, irretrievably in love.

"And now," she finished, "I invite you to my home, where my father will bid you welcome."

"And these?" Monella asked, pointing to the dead bodies.

"Ergalon will know what to do," she answered; and moved away in the direction she had indicated.

But by this time a small crowd was on its way to meet them. Those forming it were, as it appeared, chiefly her maidens and attendants and a file of soldiers—her guards. They looked curiously at the strangers, but, at a sign from her, fell in respectfully behind the little party.

"Doubtless you marvel," she observed to Elwood and Monella, between whom she walked, "how it comes about that with all these people to attend and guard me, I was alone this morning. But for that chance the dead Zelus had never found his opportunity of saying that he did to me. He must have been watching for it; perchance had heard that I sometimes like to steal away alone for a little ramble. One gets so tired of always having people around one," she added, with an almost childish wilfulness. "But this will cure me. For the future I shall be more careful."

Templemore, meantime, strolling along behind the others, found himself somehow placed between Ergalon and a dainty little damsel whose name, he afterwards found, was Zonella. She was Ulama's close friend, and was most busy plying Ergalon with questions about what had taken place. At the noise of the firing they had rushed out in alarm; then, missing the princess, had set out to seek her. In reply to her inquiries, Ergalon gloomily referred her to Templemore, and on this slender introduction the two soon found themselves in friendly converse, rather to the increase of their companion's moodiness.

It was well for Templemore that day that his affections were unalterably fixed upon a chosen fair one; else, inevitably, had he lost his heart either to the fair Ulama or to the dark-eyed, captivating Zonella. As it was, he was compelled to own that he had never seen two more fascinating maidens—save—save, of course, Maud Kingsford. In that reservation—and in that alone—lay the salvation of his heart. But this Ergalon knew not; and since he had long ardently—but vainly—sought the favour of Zonella, he was none too pleased to see her so quickly place herself on friendly terms with a total stranger.

But Templemore's acquaintance with the language was so limited, that his part in the conversation consisted more in listening than in talking; and his thoughts were more concerned in observing all that went on around him than in studying Zonella herself.

XIII

A King's Greeting

During the walk—which now more resembled a procession, for they had been joined by numbers of the inhabitants who had heard the rifle shots and had come out in curiosity or alarm to inquire into the cause—Jack Templemore had observed many pumas that, like tame dogs, accompanied the people who crowded round them. They were mostly smaller than the one that had followed him from the mountain top down the canyon, though a few equalled it in size. But he looked in vain for any sign of recognition from any of them; and it really seemed as though his own jesting prophecy were being actually fulfilled.

They now arrived at a colossal edifice that reared its soaring walls and towers high up in the sky. They passed between its open gates, that appeared to be of gold and iron, beneath an archway that, far above their heads, spanned the space between two lofty towers of pink-white stone. In the courtyard within were many other soldiers. These, when the party entered, seemed crowded together in some confusion; but, at sight of Ulama and her attendants, they quickly formed into lines, in obedience to hoarse words of command, shouted by officers in gorgeous blue uniforms, and with white plumes waving in their helmets.

The courtyard was large enough for two or three hundred men to drill and march about in. In the centre was a fountain that threw into the air a jet of water that fell back with a sound of refreshing coolness into a marble basin, from which rose curious-shaped green plants that showed in pleasing contrast to the dainty whiteness of the stonework. Here and there were marble statues, and, between them, large vases filled with flowering plants. Above, a broad gallery ran round the enclosure, and from this a number of richly-dressed people gazed down upon the strangers as they entered with Ulama. The latter, making signs to Monella and his two friends to follow her, proceeded, through lines of soldiers and attendants who fell back respectfully before her, to an apartment at one side, outside which all remained save two or three whom she specially invited to accompany her. Around, were benches or divans and couches covered with richly embroidered stuffs; upon these she bade her guests be seated, begging them to await her while she sought out the king and solicited an audience.

When she had gone, a sudden silence fell on those she left behind; a silence that was the more noticeable, coming, as it did, after the confused hubbub and clank of arms that had filled the courtyard on the arrival of the strangers.

The scene was certainly a curious one. The homely, travel-stained dress of the new-comers contrasted strangely in its nineteenth-century plainness with the elaborate, brilliantly-coloured costumes of Zonella and the half dozen members of the princess's suite who had entered with her; with the luxurious carpets, rugs, and cushions everywhere around; and with the magnificence of the whole surroundings, that spoke more of the sumptuous luxury and elaborate decorations of a Moorish 'Alhambra' than of what one would have expected in this isolated city of the clouds.

Monella stood, lost in thought, with bowed head and folded arms, his rifle, that that day had sent three human beings to their long account, resting against the wall beside him. Elwood, whose eyes had followed Ulama till she had disappeared through the inner door, also stood plunged in reverie, not noticing aught of his surroundings. Of the three, Jack Templemore alone seemed alive to the interest and strangeness of the scene. His keen, steady eyes were making mental notes of every line of the architectural designs, as though with the object of afterwards constructing a like edifice from memory; and, from the building, they travelled to its furniture and decorations, and thence, finally, to the dress and appearance of those of the princess's suite who stood or sat around. Ergalon had remained outside with many more.

Presently, Templemore said quietly to Zonella, somewhat to her astonishment,

"What is the name of this city?"

"What!" she exclaimed, "do you not know then that you are in Manoa? Where did you suppose you were?"

"Manoa! H'm. The same as 'El Dorado,' I suppose, as the Spaniards called it?"

"I know nothing of that, or of who you mean by 'the Spaniards,'" she replied. "Fancy your coming here and not knowing the name of the place! *Where* have you come from? I long to hear all about it. Are all the people there white like you and those with you? We have always been instructed, by our teachers here, that only black demons lived in the world beyond our island—at least we still so call it; though, of course, it is no longer an island; has not been for many, many long ages."

But when Jack attempted explanations, he soon discovered that he knew too little of the language to make things clear to his companion. He became hopelessly involved, his descriptions quite impossible, and, in the end, he had to give it up as hopeless.

"You must wait till I know your language better," he said with a sigh; "or else question my friends, who know far more of it."

"I will wait as patiently as I can until you can tell me yourself," she answered with an arch look. "I shall like better to hear it from you. I feel, too, a little afraid of your friend there—the older of the two. He seems so proud and dignified."

Jack laughed.

"He is anything but that. He is as kind-hearted and good-natured a man as I have ever known. Today he looks more serious than usual, perhaps. You see, we have had a disagreeable adventure, and do not yet know what may be its consequences."

"I think, all the same, he is a man of great pride and dignity," Zonella repeated. "He might be a great chief—a king—so far as one can judge from what one sees. He is not of the same race as you," she went on with decision. "He is more like one of my own people. Your younger friend, too, is not unlike one of our people; though I do not see the resemblance so strongly there, as in the case of the other."

This odd suggestion almost startled Templemore. Curiously enough, the same idea had struck him several times during the past half-hour; since, in fact, the opportunity had offered of comparing Monella's face and form with those inhabitants he had seen. Except that he was taller than any, there were many points in which there was obvious resemblance; and Jack began to ponder upon it as a strange coincidence.

He was also surprised at the confidence with which the young girl had declared Monella to be of different race from himself.

"You must be an unusually quick observer," he said presently, "to distinguish these things so readily. In my land young ladies do not much trouble themselves—"

Suddenly, Zonella laid her hand upon his arm and leaned forward with a look of fervid earnestness.

"*Who* is this man?" she asked. "What is his name, and what brings him here, and just at such a time, too?" This last seemed to be said more to herself than to her companion.

"He is called Monella," Jack told her. "I know of no other name; and, as to why he is here, I can no more tell you that than why you yourself are here. In somethings he keeps his own counsel absolutely, and is altogether inscrutable."

"Ah!" Zonella said this with a long breath. "Then, though he is your friend, and you are here together, you *really* know nothing of him. Is that what you mean?"

"Well," returned Jack slowly, "it's rather an abrupt way of putting it, but—well, I never thought of it in that light before—but—I really think you have about hit it."

"Yes! You and he have met by chance, and have agreed to travel together for a time. And you have let him bring you here, I suppose, without troubling yourself to ask him his objects?" Zonella went on, still with her glance fixed on Monella.

Jack opened his eyes.

"You have a very direct way of putting things, I must say," he laughed. "But again, I am bound to admit you are not far out."

"And your other friend—what do you know of him?"

"Oh, I have known him since he was a child."

"And yet," the girl persisted, "he is very different from you. Are you *sure* he is of the same race as yourself?"

"Quite," Templemore replied, laughing. "We are both of a nation that I suppose you have never heard of, but that makes no small amount of noise in the outer world, I can assure you. We are both English."

Just then a heavy curtain was drawn back, and Ulama entered, and with her an immense puma, larger even than their friend of the canyon, and behind it the latter animal itself!

"Why," exclaimed Zonella, "there is 'Nea,' who has been missing for several days," and she called the animal to her. Great was her surprise to see it, after a brief acknowledgment of her greeting, turn to Jack and his two friends, with every sign of recognition and delight.

"Why, it's Puss, by all that's wonderful!" Jack cried. "At least, that's the name I gave her," he added, by way of explanation to Zonella.

"Do you know her, then? But how can that be?"

"She has been living with us for the last week; but she deserted us last night, and we wondered where she had got to."

"Then that accounts for it. We could not think what had become of her." And she began to chide the animal for its desertion of its home and mate.

"If 'Tuo' had known you were off gallivanting with strange people, 'Nea,' I fancy he would have come after you and marched you back." Then, to Templemore: "But how odd that she should attach herself to you like that; you must have had some strong attraction for her."

"It was not what she got to eat, at any rate," said Jack. "In fact, I fear she was half starved. And at last she got so disgusted at what, I suppose, she thought our stinginess, that she went off hunting on her own account; and what she caught she offered, with a splendid lack of selfishness, to share with us." And he went on to tell how he first met the animal; Elwood, meanwhile, recounting the same story to Ulama; and they learned that the two pumas were named 'Tuo' and 'Nea.'

Presently, the princess gave a sign to her attendants, and they all followed her from the apartment, leaving the three strangers by themselves.

Elwood was the first to speak.

"We are to wait till the king is ready to receive us," he said. "I wonder what he is like, and what sort of a reception he will give us! What say you, Monella?"

The latter turned slowly, and seemed to wake as from a deep reverie.

"I know not what to say, my son; but I am full of pain at all that has happened today. My mind misgives me that civil war will come out of it; yet we can but try to do our best, and leave the rest to a higher power."

It was not long before the curtain was drawn aside again, and one entered who seemed to be a dignitary of the court.

"I have come," said he, "to conduct you to King Dranoa." And, with a ceremonious bow, he motioned to them to follow him.

They passed through many passages, across galleries and large halls, and up broad staircases covered with thick soft carpet that was noiseless to the tread.

On their way they saw many people of various costumes and appearance, who regarded the new-comers curiously, but not rudely. Presently they reached a heavy curtain before a doorway, where stood more soldiers and officers in brilliant uniforms. The curtain being drawn aside, they entered an immense hall, its sides lined with people, but the whole centre part unoccupied. They were ushered up this hall and there left standing, their conductor retiring to one side.

They found themselves confronting a high canopy, beneath which, upon a raised dais, a man, apparently somewhat past middle age, was seated; they had little doubt he was the king. He was a man of a fine presence, and seemed hale and vigorous, though his dark hair and beard were streaked with grey. His features were regular and well formed, his eyes steady and piercing; his expression was not unkindly; but his chin suggested weakness, a wavering and unsettled temperament. He was dressed in a long flowing robe, and large jewels sparkled upon his breast and shoulders, in the belt that girdled his waist and in the hilt of his short sword. On his head he wore a circlet that was simple in design, and scarcely to be called a crown; it was a band of gold with gems set as stars. Ulama was seated by his side; she, also, wore a golden circlet in which gleamed, with softened radiance, one cluster of large pearls. She had changed the simple dress in which she had been clad when they had first seen her, and now appeared in a costume that was fairly dazzling in its richness, yet in exquisite taste, and well chosen for showing to advantage her graceful figure.

At her feet Zonella sat, or rather half reclined, and other members of her suite were grouped around. Upon the other side of the king stood his ministers and officers of state, and his body guard, and, ranged around the hall, were many others of both sexes, looking curiously and silently upon the strangers.

Over the canopy was an immense star wrought in solid gold. Statues on pedestals were to be seen at intervals, and, most curious of all, on the walls were well-executed coloured frescoes depicting battle scenes.

The king rose and addressed them.

"Friends, I know not whence ye come, what brought ye hither, nor how ye succeeded in passing the wood of black demons and forced your way into our land. In ordinary circumstances it would have been my duty to send ye away forthwith, or even to imprison ye—possibly, still worse might have befallen. But my daughter hath told me that ye have saved her life—a life doubly, trebly dear to me in that she is my only child. But that ye came so opportunely on the scene, she who is my heart's pride would e'en now be lying in the cold grasp of death."

Here he paused, overcome with emotion.

"So," he presently went on, "it has been described to me. I understand, also, that, by some strange chance, ye speak our language, and comprehend what I would say. We knew not that there were people outside this land of ours who were white like us, and, above all, could speak our tongue. But these wonders ye shall explain afterwards at your leisure. At this moment not curiosity, but gratitude inspires me, in that ye have restored my child to me. There is not one here"—his eyes travelled round the packed assemblage—"who will not join with me in thanking ye for that which ye have done. What say ye, friends?"—this to his people—"Ye have heard in what dire peril hath my daughter been this day. Shall we not give to those who rescued her a right good welcome?"

At this, the hitherto silent crowd burst out into acclamations. They cheered, they clapped their hands; they waved banners, they raised their spears and swords aloft and flashed them in the air; again and again the shouts went up, till they seemed in very truth to shake the walls.

When, by a motion of his hand, silence had been restored, the king resumed,

"Ye hear! All greet ye, and *I* thank ye. Be assured of my protection an' ye have come in peace. But alas! I grieve to say I am not all-powerful. There are reasons for enjoining upon ye that ye be circumspect in your going to and fro, have always with ye the escort I shall give ye, and visit only places they shall indicate. This is not the time or place for further explanations, nor is it fitting I should now hear the wondrous things I doubt not ye can tell me. I only wish it understood that while I shall give ye my protection, and that of those devoted to me, ye must not hope too much from it; and it may fail ye, if ye observe not the conditions and limitations I have stated; the cause whereof I shall explain hereafter."

"While we return thee our thanks, O King," Monella answered, "on our part, also, let it be understood that we can protect ourselves. The cowardly assailants of the princess thy daughter fell before us like chaff before the fire. We could, an' we had chosen, have destroyed them all, even to the last one; but we spared some that they might noise the tale abroad and warn others of their kind not to raise their hands against us. Yet do I regret that it was necessary to kill any. We came in peace and goodwill, not to maim and slay, or to spread alarm and desolation through thy land. Yet this was forced upon us."

"It hath been so told to me. Perhaps, as ye say, ye can protect yourselves; and it hath been further told to me how ye wield the lightning and the thunder and blast your enemies, hurling them to the ground ere they can reach ye. For all that, if ye would go about in peace, and avoid the need for further exercise of your death-dealing powers, accept the guard I offer. If occasion arise, and they fail ye, and ye can help in your own defence—well, by so much the better will it be."

"Thou hast well said, O King. It shall be as thou hast spoken," Monella returned.

Throughout the interview the king had been eyeing the commanding figure of the man before him, not only with great intentness, but also even anxiously. Indeed, Monella, with his lofty stature and intrepid bearing, his nobly chiselled features, his bold, unflinching glance, would have made no unfitting occupant of the throne. And, possibly, this thought had struck the king, who once more spoke.

"And now I would fain know thy name, and what hath brought thee."

"I am called Monella."

"Monella! It hath a sound as of our own tongue," returned the king. "And thine end in journeying hither?"

"That is for thine ear alone, O King," Monella replied with decision, thereby arousing the surprise of all, the king included. Then, drawing from his breast a sealed roll of parchment he had brought with him, "But here is that which will in part explain." And he handed the document to the king.

The king unrolled the parchment, but, as the first words met his eye, he started; then, growing more intent, he read on. But presently, in evident agitation, he stepped down from the dais, placed his hand on the other's arm, and said in a voice that trembled with emotion,

"I will speak with thee alone. Follow me into my private chamber." And, looking neither to the right nor to the left, he passed down the hall, Monella following, the crowd opening out to give them egress.

No sooner had they gone, than confused murmurs of astonishment and curiosity burst out on all sides. Elwood and Templemore, as much taken by surprise as anyone, looked each in the other's face inquiringly; but Zonella glided to their side and said in a low tone to Templemore,

"Said I not that thy friend was no ordinary man? Monella! Is it not like my name, Zonella? Methought, the moment my eyes rested on him, 'That man is a great man—a wondrous man—and he is one of our people!'"

XIV

Dakla

U lama also left her seat and came forward to the two young men. "Your friend," she said, "has taken my father by surprise; else had he bidden you be seated. Nor did I know that he could not earlier have received you, or I would have sent my maidens to you with refreshment. Come now and sit near us, and I will point out to you my friends that they may be your friends; meantime Zonella will order fruit and wine for your sustainment. Anon you will be invited to our table; but meantime you will need something. We all do," she added, when they made gestures of dissent, "so you will not be conspicuous in partaking here of what we offer you."

Pages then entered bearing luscious fruits and tempting-looking foaming drinks; the former on massive salvers of pure gold, the latter in chalices of gold and silver set with gems. The fruits were all new to them, as also were the drinks; but, on tasting them, they found them to be all they looked.

The fruits were indeed delicious and refreshing; the drinks cooling and exhilarating: to Elwood and Templemore they were as nectar and ambrosia, and they said so, and asked many questions concerning them. But, seeing that the only information they received was a string of names that conveyed to them no meaning, they added little to their stock of knowledge.

They now talked freely with those around them; but found the questions showered upon them from all sides somewhat more than they could answer, so that Templemore said at last in an aside to the other,

"Tell you what it is, Leonard; we shall have to give a public lecture— or perhaps a series—and invite as many at a time as the Town Hall of the place will contain. Pity we didn't bring some magic lanterns and dissolving views to illustrate what we have to tell them. I *would* have done so if I had only known."

They, in their turn, were not less full of curiosity and interest in all they saw around them. The statuary, and, above all, the pictures amazed them.

"It upsets all one's notions of history and all that," said Jack quietly to Leonard, "to find this sort of thing in the so-called 'new' world. We might be back in Ancient Greece."

"Or Babylon, or Nineveh," Elwood answered. "It's like a dream—and, strange to say, I have dreamed much of it before. I keep thinking I shall wake up presently and find that this city, with all that it contains, has vanished."

"I trust not," said Ulama—to whom the last part of the sentence had been addressed—with a smile. "I should not like to think that I, myself, am but a dream. But, since you speak of having dreams of that which you find here, know that I have strange dreams also. All my life it has been thus with me. Of late they have been less frequent than of yore, and the memory of them is confused and indistinct; but I know that in them I have seen—aye, more than once—*your* face, and the face of him you call Monella."

Elwood regarded the maiden in surprise, and she continued,

"Yes, it is true. Tell me, Zonella, have I not often described to thee those I had seen in my dreams; and did not some resemble these? As to face thou canst not know, but as to garb and other details?"

"'Tis true," replied Zonella gravely.

But the matter-of-fact Templemore found it hard to credit this; visions and the like were nothing in his way.

"Are you serious?" he asked.

"Quite," both said.

"And—me—a—I—myself, I mean; was I there too?"

Templemore's manner when he asked this question was so humorously anxious that Ulama laughed—a joyous, ringing laugh, the token of a soul innocent and free from care.

"No, indeed," she answered. "I never dreamed of you."

"And you?" he asked, turning to Zonella.

"No, never"; and she too laughed merrily.

"It really doesn't seem fair," said Jack, with an injured air. "Waking or sleeping, my friend has been a dreamer all his life; when we met with Monella we found he was one of the same sort; so those two were on terms immediately; but I—I am out of it all. Never had a dream in my life worth remembering. Not only that, but—as it now seems—I can't even get into other people's. I put it to you, Princess, am I not a little hardly done by?"

Thus they laughed and chatted, and time passed on, and still Monella and the king were closeted together. It was more than an hour—nearer two—before the king returned; and then alone.

"My friends," he said, "the audience is at an end. Affairs of state demand my earnest thought, and I must now dismiss you. But," beckoning the two young men to him, and taking in his own a hand of each, "once more let me commend these strangers to your care and friendship. They have rendered me today a service that is beyond price, and in rendering it to me, they have rendered it to us all. More I need not say, except to charge you to make their stay with us a pleasant one."

He withdrew, and, with his absence, the crowd began to thin; only those belonging to the court remaining.

And now Ulama spoke.

"I shall hand you over to my good friends here," she said. "Doubtless you will wish to make a change in your apparel and—"

"Unfortunately we brought no change with us," said Jack.

"They will bring you a choice of vestments," she answered, laughing. "You will surely find something to your taste." She bowed courteously, and went out, followed by Zonella and her attendants.

They were now taken in charge by the high chamberlain, whom they already knew by name—Colenna. He, in turn, handed them over to his son Kalaima, a bright-eyed, fair, talkative young fellow with whom they quickly found themselves on pleasant terms. He conducted them to a suite of chambers which would be, he said, reserved to them. They found there various suits which he laid out for their selection, instructing them, with much good humour, in the way in which they should be worn. These were, so he told them, the distinctive dresses of a noble of high degree; and were presents from the king as a mark of his special favour.

Elwood laughed at Jack's expression while he turned over the various articles after Kalaima had left them to themselves, examining in turn the white tunic of finest silk embroidered with strange devices, the cap with jewelled plume, the heavy belt of solid gold, and the short sword and dagger; all ornamented with precious stones of greater value than they could estimate.

"Are you really going to deck yourself out in these things, Leonard?" he asked, with a rueful look. "Am I expected to do so too? Great Scott! What would our friends in Georgetown say if they could see us masquerading in this toggery?"

"When at Rome you must do as Rome does, I suppose," Elwood returned lightly. "After all, I don't suppose it will seem half so strange to the good people here as would our continuing to wear our present dress."

"There's a good deal, no doubt, to be said for that view," Jack said with resignation. "And, since it is intended as a compliment, I suppose we must e'en accept it as such. I only hope I shall be able to keep my countenance when I look at you—that is, before the king and others. At present I feel very much afraid that it may prove beyond my powers."

In their suite of chambers was a bath, with water deep and broad enough to swim in. A refreshing plunge, a reclothing in the unfamiliar raiment, and they emerged from their apartments dressed as nobles of the country. The attempts, honest, but too often futile, made by Templemore to preserve his gravity, caused him at times more personal discomfort than did even the strange garb but, since use accustoms us to pretty nearly everything the efforts required became gradually less and less.

But what sobered him, so to speak, the most, was his meeting with Monella, who was now attired in like fashion to themselves. The change seemed to have made an extraordinary alteration in the man. He looked taller and more imposing than ever, and in his gait and manner there were an added grace and dignity. It could now be seen that his form was supple and muscular as that of a young man's, graceful in the swing of the limbs and in every pose. His eyes retained their unique expression that seemed to magnetise those upon whom they fell; but his face had a greater gravity than ever, and something of a majesty that awed Templemore when he noted it.

"Of a truth," he said to Elwood, "that man seems to alter from day to day even from hour to hour. He is just as kindly, as courteous, and as gentle; just as thoughtful—yet, I feel somehow that there is a gulf deepening between us, and that it is widening, slowly but surely. Yet not because one likes him less—that's just it, you seem to like him and admire him more and more—but you feel you do it from afar—from a gradually increasing distance."

And when, later in the day, they sat down to a banquet at the king's table, and saw Monella seated beside the king, taking the post of honour and accepting it with the easy dignity of one who had been used to it all his life; not only the observant Jack, but the less seriously-minded Leonard, felt, with increasing force, the feeling the former had described.

FRANK AUBREY

During this repast they learned that the Manoans were vegetarians; though their cookery was so skilful that such dishes as the strangers tasted they found both appetising and satisfying. Not only that, but, as they soon discovered, these dishes were fully as invigorating and nourishing as a meat diet. This was due to the presence of some strange vegetable or herb in nearly every dish; but what this was they could not then determine.

At dusk, a new surprise awaited them; for, not only the palace, but the whole city was lighted up by what they quickly recognised as the electric light. They now could understand the brilliant aspect of the city as first seen by them at night from the head of the canyon.

After the meal, Templemore and Elwood went out, with many more, upon a terrace that overlooked the lake; where now boats were going to and fro, some paddled by oars, some drawn by the large white swans. But what at first puzzled the new-comers were the antics of some who threw themselves into the water from considerable heights. Instead of falling almost vertically, as a diver would, they swept down in a graceful curve, striking the water almost horizontally, then bounded up and flew through the air for a short distance, till once more they touched the water and bounded up again. Finally, when the impetus was expended, they swam back to shore or were taken thither in a boat. Of course this style of bathing could not be practised *in puris naturalibus*, or in ordinary bathing dress; so they were furnished with a kind of divided parachute, or twin parachutes, not unlike artificial wings; with these they could descend from towers and great heights and with a long swallow-like sweep, striking the water and rebounding again and again. By practice some had obtained a wonderful dexterity in this amusement, and their evolutions would have deceived a stranger, viewing them from a distance, into a belief that they were actual flying creatures. Some of the children—who chiefly delighted in this pastime—were very expert at it.

While watching the gay scene before them—a repetition of what they had witnessed from afar—Kalaima came to say that the king requested their presence in his council chamber. Following the young man they entered a hall, smaller than that in which they had first been received, and found the king throned under a canopy as before, and Monella seated near him. Around the hall were ten or twelve of his chief ministers and officers, each placed before a small table, Upon which were ink-horns, pens, and sheets of parchment.

Standing in the centre of the chamber was a man of swarthy skin and haughty mien, his expression cruel and deceitful. He wore a black tunic on which was worked a large golden star like that displayed by the ill-fated Zelus. Standing respectfully a short distance behind this man were two others, somewhat similarly attired.

The leader had just finished speaking when Templemore and Elwood entered, and he cast at them a scowl that was almost appalling in its malignity.

The king signed to the young men to seat themselves beside Monella; then, turning to the man who had just spoken, said,

"It avails nothing, Dakla, for thee to come to us with messages of this intent, and with presentments, void of truth, of what befell today. Here are the three strangers who, as thou sayest, opposed themselves to Zelus, the son of Coryon thy master. They slew him, it is true, and some of those who followed him, but it was to save my daughter from his violence."

"It is false, O King! They lie, if they say so! For our lord Zelus had no thought of violence!" This from Dakla.

"If thine errand here is but to charge with falsehood these three men, I'll grant thee audience no longer." The kings voice was stern, and his eyes flashed angrily, so that Dakla trembled, and there was less confidence in his tone when he replied,

"But they are strangers whom the king knows not; wherefore should he accept their word before our trusted servants?"

"Because it is confirmed by mine own daughter, sirrah! And if thou darest again to say it is untrue that Zelus lifted his hand to take her life, thou shalt not return unpunished, be the consequences what they may!"

By the king's impressive manner, and still more by the menace he had thus let fall, Dakla seemed daunted. He had expected to be able to carry things his own way. He hesitated, then said in a milder tone,

"But even so, they should not have taken the life of our lord Zelus, but have brought him before *thee*."

"How could they do that when he had more than a score of men with him, and they were but three? Furthermore, there was no time for parley. An instant's hesitation, my daughter saith, and it would have been too late."

Dakla reflected; then he made a fresh suggestion.

"It will content us if the king remit to us for trial him who, with his own hand, did slay our lord. If, on due inquisition, it shall be found even as the king hath said, then shall he be returned unhurt."

The king's face clouded, and his lips curled with scorn as he replied,

"Out upon thee, with thy tricks and cunning snares! Thinkest thou we do not know thy master by this time? These strangers are my guests—under my protection! Hark ye! I say under my protection! If harm shall befall them, I will seize thyself, an' thou comest again within my reach, or any others of thy master's minions on whom I can lay hands, and their lives shall pay the forfeit."

"Thy words will grieve my master, King Dranoa," said Dakla, with a scarcely hidden sneer. "He careth only for the welfare of the king and of his people. But how shall there be safety for the dwellers in this land if such as these may go abroad and slay at will, and be protected by the king?"

"What safety is there now for any, when even the king's daughter cannot walk near mine own palace without assailment?" the king wrathfully demanded. "Hold thy peace, sirrah! and quit my sight ere worse betide thee!"

At this Monella rose, and, bending towards the king, said something in a low tone to him; the king, assenting with a nod, Monella slowly turned his glance upon the henchman of the priest, and thus addressed him,

"I have the king's permission to send a message of my own to Coryon, since the opportunity now offers. It is well that thou shouldst bear it, and better still if thou takest it to heart. I sent the same message by the murderous crew that followed at the heels of thy late shameful lord—as thou callest him—Zelus. It is this: that such things as he attempted will bring down vengeance and retribution on you all. Bid Coryon take heed and mend his ways; if not, his doom is fixed. We are but three; yet, if we chose, and the king so willed it, we could clear thee and thy master and his brood from off the land—aye, ere another sun has risen and set. And tell Coryon this, by the king's permission we are here, and, as thou hast heard, under his protection. For that protection we are grateful, but we need it not. If thou, or any of thy serpent brood molest us, we will hold you all to such a vengeance as shall repay the wrongs of others and rid the earth of you. I sent this message by Zelus's craven hounds, but my mind misgives me that in their flight they scarce remembered it; or, perchance, they feared to give it. Wilt thou now bear it to thy master?"

"Who art thou that dares to send a message of defiance to the great Coryon?" Dakla asked.

"One who can carry out his words; one who, as the ally of the king, will bring upon your heads that which has been so long deserved. One who, though he spared thy myrmidons today, will spare no more. Beware! Attack us, and we show no mercy!"

With each succeeding sentence he seemed taller, more imposing, and more menacing; until the last words were fairly thundered out, and his eyes flashed fire.

The countenance of Dakla fell before his gaze; he hesitated, panted, turned to go, then turned back, and finally, as one who spoke against his will, he said, with no show of his former mocking insolence,

"Sir, I will bear thy message." Then, with an obeisance to the king, he and his attendants left the place.

"I would give something to know what the king and Monella talked about so long today," said Elwood to Templemore that night, when they found themselves alone together.

"So far as I can gather," Jack replied, "there is a grand old feud on here between these rascally old priests, on the one side, and the king and his followers on the other; and Monella, I suspect, has learnt enough concerning it to lead him to back up the king. Well! So far as I am concerned, I am game to back him up, too, against such a murdering lot as they seem to be. What say you?"

"You need not ask *me*," Elwood answered with some surprise. "But I thought that you—well—that is—"

"Would be rather more slow to get up enthusiasm, eh?" Jack interrupted with a laugh. "Not at all. Fooling about in a dark, gloomy forest, with no apparent end in view, was one thing; taking part in an adventure of this kind to help a lot of people who have received us kindly, is quite another; to say nothing of helping the king, who's a regular brick, and his daughter, who's—"

"An angel!" put in Leonard.

And Jack laughed, but approvingly, and said goodnight.

XV

Marvels of Manoa

During the following days Elwood and Templemore learned much of the strange land in which they found themselves; of its people, of their condition, and other details. But, since to give every separate conversation, incident, or other means by which they gained their information, would be tedious, it will suffice to cite some extracts from Templemore's diary that summarise the knowledge then and subsequently obtained.

"I AM ABLE NOW TO jot down some account of this strange place and its inhabitants, so far, at least, as my limited knowledge of its language and other means of information go.

"The people seem to be amiable, fairly intelligent—considering, of course, that they know nothing of the great world outside—and generally well disposed. Although they maintain a small force of 'soldiers' or 'guards,' and drill and discipline them with as much assiduity as though they might be called upon to engage in warfare, yet, as a matter of course, there are no people with whom they can go to war; nor is there any likelihood of their having to fight, except amongst themselves. And this, unfortunately, has not been unknown; moreover, there are 'signs in the air' that it may not be unknown again.

"An unexpected discovery we have made is, that this mountain is connected with another close to it and called 'Myrlanda.' The connection is underground, and was made originally in the course of mining operations.

"Undoubtedly, *once* these people were a great nation. Their arts and sciences, their buildings, their engineering works, and their knowledge of mechanics, all give evidence of this; but, since a nation, isolated as this has been for ages, must necessarily either progress or retrogress, the Manoans slowly, gradually, but surely, have done the latter. They have numerous museums which are full of wonders of all sorts, pointing to lost arts, lost sciences, lost inventions, lost knowledge of all kinds. The fact that the demand has fallen off with diminishing population has led to the discontinuance of manufactures; though, in the museums, there are evidences that they once existed.

"This is the case as regards chronometric instruments. Their occupations being desultory, they have little need to know the time of day; so the use of clocks and watches has 'gone out of fashion,' and there does not now exist a person in the two 'islands'—as they still call these two inaccessible mountains—who can make a clock or a watch. Yet, in their museums they have many ancient specimens of clocks and watches of various kinds.

"Like remarks apply to many other arts and sciences and manufactures. The cause is likely to be found in the fact of their non-intercommunication with other nations.

"But the most wonderful thing of all, in this land of marvels, is a plant or herb they call the 'Plant of Life.' This, I am assured (though it seems hardly credible), if taken from time to time in certain forms, combined with other plants found here, induces great longevity in the recipients. The king, for instance, who looks between fifty and sixty years of age, I am seriously told is three hundred and forty! Yet that, even, is nothing out of the way here; for—assuming that they speak the truth—there are among the priesthood a few who have lived in the land one thousand, fifteen hundred, and two thousand years and more! I should scarcely take the trouble to write this down, were it not that I find it a matter of such common belief on all sides that it is impossible to avoid regarding it seriously. When first these statements were made to me I sought Monella and reported to him what had been told me, remarking that I thought it somewhat in bad taste on the part of my informants to combine together—as it seemed to me they must have— to palm off such tales upon a stranger. To my utter astonishment, he replied that he had reason to believe that there was truth in what I had been told! He had doubtless heard the same thing—and he is so quick to probe to the very root of whatever excites his interest, and a man so difficult to deceive, that, on receiving his solemn assurance (I asked for it) that he was not jesting, I felt bound to regard the matter attentively. I, therefore, set to work to get at all the facts as well as I could, and to see and examine the wonderful plant for myself. In this way I have arrived at the following data:—

"The plant, which is called 'karina' in the language of the country, is of a curious delicate, clear, blue tint—almost transparent in appearance, and in texture smooth and glassy-looking as to the leaves. It grows to a height of two or three feet, and is succulent in character; exuding freely, when squeezed, a juice which has a very strong bitter-sweet taste. It is prepared in several ways—many having, it is believed, secret recipes which have been handed down from father to son from generation to generation; but they all relate more or less to a tea or infusion of the leaves, with or without the admixture of other herbs or drugs. To have the full effect it must be taken regularly, almost from infancy; indeed, it is so powerful that those not accustomed to it must take but very weak doses at first for a long time, till the system learns to assimilate it; otherwise, it may even act as a poison. Taken, however, regularly from childhood, it produces and maintains perfect health, defying all those usual fevers and diseases that afflict humanity in other parts of the world, and carrying the body unimpaired in all its functions—accidents, of course, excepted—into extreme age, without loss of vitality or strength.

"People do not, however, live forever; there is one disease and only one that the 'karina' cannot cure. This is called the 'falloa'; there is also another name for it signifying the 'don't care sickness.' Those attacked with it gradually sink, and die painlessly and easily. This disease, no doubt, must come to all sooner or later; but it is generally believed that the priests—and they alone—are aware of some way of so preparing the 'karina,' that they can either cure even the 'falloa,' or keep it at bay for very much longer periods than other people succeed in doing.

"It is certainly a remarkable fact that throughout the land disease, in the sense in which we understand it, is unknown. Consequently, physical pain is almost absent, save in case of physical injury. Nor is it necessary to be continually taking the preparation of the 'karina.' When once the system becomes inoculated with it, as it were, it is sufficient, afterwards, to repeat the doses at long intervals; and a traveller, as I gather, might take sufficient of the dried plant with him on his travels to keep him in perfect health for many years in any part of the world.

"And when, at last, the 'falloa' attacks its victim, it causes neither pain nor suffering of any kind; only melancholy, and a distaste for life in general; while its approach is so gradual as often to be unnoticed.

"There is little doubt that the absence of ordinary diseases exerts a corresponding effect upon the physical development; and this alone is sufficient to account for a fact that is very noticeable here, viz., the beauty of the inhabitants. Both the women and the men are remarkable in this respect; and probably not in all the rest of the world put together could so many beautiful women and handsome men be found as one sees in this small, but strange country; and this applies to the old, in a measure, as well as to the young generally. Whether it also applies to the old amongst the priests, one cannot say, for they seem to keep entirely to themselves.

"As regards these 'priests,' there are two sects in the country, called respectively the 'Dark,' or 'Black,' and the 'White.'

"The religion of the 'White' priests, or 'Brotherhood,' resembles, in many respects, that of the Hebrews, save that for 'God' they use the term 'Great Spirit,' or 'Good,' or 'Almighty' Spirit. These have, however, now no influence in the country, and have been exiled to Myrlanda, where they confine themselves to a small 'domain,' have few followers and very little communication with the general inhabitants. The chief of these is named Sanaima.

"The chief of the 'Dark Brotherhood'—as they denominate themselves, and well they deserve their name, from all I hear—is called Coryon; and he and Sanaima are both popularly supposed to be more than two thousand years old! But, since both these millenarian gentlemen keep themselves shut up amongst their own immediate adherents, and seldom show themselves to the people, it would not be very difficult to keep up a tradition of this sort without a word of truth to back it. It may be urged in support of it, however, that we see many going about who, we are assured, are three, four, or five hundred years old; and these assert that they have not the true secret of preparing the 'karina'; this being known only to the priests.

"But whatever be the truth as to their longevity, the 'Dark Brotherhood' seem to be a set of bloodthirsty, licentious tyrants, ruling the people with a rod of iron, for the king, though nominally an autocrat, has but little real power; but his rule, so far as it extends, is mild, and his people appear loyal and well disposed towards him.

"The real ruler of the land is Coryon, the High Priest of the 'Dark Brotherhood'; a man who, though never seen beyond the limits of his own domain, makes his power felt everywhere. What I have heard of him and his chosen band sounds too atrocious to be true; yet I am assured I have heard only a part; the whole truth is of such a nature that men shrink from speaking of it to one another.

"It is said that they have many wives, whom they choose at will from amongst the daughters of the people; but what becomes of them afterwards no one knows, for they are never seen again when once they disappear behind the gates that shut in the domain 'sacred' to the

'Brotherhood.' Further, they lay a 'blood-tax' upon the population for 'religious sacrifices'; at certain intervals these victims are selected, it is *said*, by a sort of ballot, and from that moment vanish like the others, and their fate is never known; or at least no one professes to know. It is, indeed hinted, that it is too terrible to be published. One or two who have escaped back to their homes have, it is averred, died raving mad; their ravings being of so dread a nature that it could not be determined whether they referred to scenes actually witnessed, or were the offspring of their madness. What becomes of the children of these 'priests'—or at least of a large proportion of them—is also a matter for conjecture. They cannot well all live, or they would probably overrun the land. It is darkly whispered that all but a certain definite proportion are sacrificed. At any rate they are seldom heard of. Zelus, the one Elwood killed, was an exception, it would appear. He is described as the 'only remaining' son of Coryon; but what has become of his other children, if any, is not known. Zelus had set his mind upon taking Ulama from her father to make her, against her will, his wife—or one of them. Now it is generally understood that the king and his family, and the members of his household, are safe from molestation by the 'Brotherhood.' Therefore, in seeking to force Ulama, Zelus was offending against the strict law; yet, such was his insolent contempt for all law but his own will, that he not only designed to bear her off, but, in his rage at her resistance and the scathing disdain and scorn she showed in her refusal, he would have killed her. And it is quite certain that, had he succeeded, he would have been protected by his father, so that no punishment would have fallen on him.

"If, however, as appears from this, even the king's only child is not safe from these atrocious wretches, what must be the position of the common people? As a matter of fact, though they are by nature cheerful, contented and unselfish, yet over all there seems to hang the shadow of an ever-present dread, the overpowering, constant fear that tomorrow or the next day—this day, even, they or some of those they love, without the slightest warning, may be seized and borne off to an unknown fate. All the information vouchsafed in such a case is that the victim has been chosen by the so-called ballot; but it is hinted, and no doubt believed, that, if one of the priests, or one of their favourite adherents, happen to cast an approving eye upon a daughter of the people—be she maiden or wife—the 'ballot' is pretty sure to fall upon her before very long.

"This is the awful despotism wielded by these 'priests' in the name of religion. Needless to say, it is not confined to the particulars stated. If the priests themselves are not much seen in public, some of their emissaries and followers are continually about, and they domineer over the people and perpetrate many shameful acts of cruelty and injustice, in almost all of which they are supported and protected by those they serve. For, though these wretches are nominally amenable to the civil law, or to be brought before the king, few, even of the boldest of their victims, care to risk the after vengeance that they know would overtake them as the consequence.

"It was these miscreants that the king had in his mind when he insisted upon giving us an escort during our sojourn here. And, though our firearms are undoubtedly our best protection, still, as has been pointed out to us, we have made enemies who are treacherous and relentless, with fanatical adherents, who mingle with the people and might stab one of us in the back without warning, were they allowed the opportunity of coming near us in the guise of ordinary well-disposed or curious citizens. We have thought it, therefore, only prudent to accept the proffered guard.

"Of the 'White Brotherhood' one hears little. Sanaima, their chief, is reputed to be an upright, well-disposed man, who would, if he had his way, assist the king to put an end to the domination of the other sect and its human sacrifices and other evils and abominations; but they do not seem to have the power, or, if they have, they lack the resolution to take any decided or practical steps to shake off the tyranny of Coryon. Nor could it be done without plunging the country into a civil conflict that might last indefinitely and be productive of almost endless suffering; and the king, as a kind-hearted man, shrinks from precipitating such a calamity. So Sanaima shuts himself up in his own domain and gives himself up, it is understood, to abstruse study.

"Turning to another noteworthy and surprising thing—the fact that these people are acquainted with electricity and the electric light—it seems that they collect and store it underground in some way I do not yet understand. But upon all high rocks are placed metal rods—lightning rods, in fact—and it is asserted that at all times, day and night, but more particularly when there are clouds around the mountain, a constant stream of electricity passes down the rods and is retained and stored in insulated receptacles constructed for the purpose underground. The effect of this arrangement is that thunderstorms are unknown

FRANK AUBREY

here. The armature of lightning rods draws off all the electricity from the surrounding atmosphere; and, though thunderstorms are often witnessed in the distance—playing round other mountains, for instance—yet they never burst over Manoa or Myrlanda.

"On this mountain—Roraima, as we call it—a name, by the way, entirely unknown to the inhabitants—the city of Manoa and its lake stand at one end of the great basin that lies within the summit. All around are terraces of rock rising, one behind the other, till they end in high wooded crags that form, in fact, the edge of the summit as seen from outside. Down these crags or cliffs pour numerous cascades that find their way, eventually, into the lake; whence they issue again as the great waterfalls that tumble from the summit—or near it—to the base of the mountain. For though, from a distance, these falls seem to start from almost the very summit, they, in reality, burst out from the level of the lake, more than a hundred feet lower than the highest rocks upon the top of the mountain.

"The rest of the top—apart from the lake and city—is a country of hill and dale, rocks and woods, very picturesque, and forming, in places, minor basins, or vales, of considerable extent and beauty, quite shut off from one another. I estimate the total extent roughly at a hundred square miles; but I believe Myrlanda covers nearly two hundred.

"None of the land in Manoa is given up to cultivation, save in the form of gardens, or orchards, and groves of fruit-bearing trees. The lower rocky terraces around the lake are beautifully laid out in this way. Here, are cultivated fruits of every kind. The trees are planted in such a way as to form shady walks and resting-places; beneath them are seats and fountains that are always playing, fed by the streams that rush down at intervals towards the lake. And across these streams are numerous bridges; some, where the torrents open out on approaching the lake, are necessarily of considerable width; those on the terraces above are small rustic structures—but all are ornamental, and some of exquisite design. Around the terraces flowers grow in profusion, partly wild and partly cultivated. Wonderful orchids, gloxinias, begonias; orange-groves covered with flowers and fruit; and gardenias with their deliciously scented blossoms; with many others that I have never seen before and have not yet learned the names of.

"The cereal and other crops required are grown in Myrlanda, which is principally devoted to agriculture; there also there are numbers of goats, and a kind of sheep, and large quantities of fowls. Pumas, which are kept as pets in Manoa, are not allowed in Myrlanda, for they would play sad havoc amongst the flocks and poultry; though, probably, they live upon them all the same; for the Manoans, being vegetarians, never eat meat, but give the flesh of their animals to their pets. The latter include cats, of which there are large numbers; some of most curious kinds. These two animals, between them, it is said—the puma and the cat—have cleared the land of all wild animals, including serpents; for there is no more deadly enemy of serpents—even venomous ones—than the cat; and the puma will attack and overcome larger non-venomous snakes.

"No one, to see these latter great animals playing continually with the children of their masters—as may be witnessed here all day long—would think they were naturally of such bloodthirsty instincts. It has been said of pumas that, with the possible exception of some kinds of monkeys, they are the most playful animals in existence. One can certainly see ample evidence of this in Manoa, for the creatures, whether large or small, old or young, seem ever ready to start a game of romps with whomever they can get to indulge them—whether little folk or their grown-up elders.

"The large swans that swim about on the lake, though very tame, can scarcely be regarded as pets, though they are frequently to be seen docilely drawing a small boat about; or a team of them will be harnessed to a vessel of larger size. They get their own living among the fish in the lake, and seem able to hold their own with the pumas. I am told that this comes about from the fact that the young pumas, being often foolish enough to attack them in the water, meet with such treatment that—if they succeed in escaping drowning—they ever afterward leave the birds alone. These swans make their nests and rear their young on some islands that lie out near the centre of the lake. Often, towards night, when the sun has perhaps set for the day on the lake and the country surrounding it, these birds may be seen in small flocks circling and whirling in the air, and presenting a very beautiful sight as they rise out of the shadow, and the rays of the setting sun light up their plumage. These are undoubtedly the 'white eagles' that are asserted by the Indians to be the 'guardians of the lake' on the top of Roraima.

"Myrlanda is honeycombed with mines, but hardly any are at present worked, the demand for their products having practically ceased; and such large stocks have accumulated from former workings that I am told they are not likely to be reopened for many years. So far, I have only partially inspected the museums. They are more surprising than even the people, for they speak plainly of a wonderful past history. Here are many strange inventions and machines, the very meaning and use of which are now but a matter of conjecture. They contain, too, stands of arms—spears, javelins, swords, daggers, shields, bows and arrows, etc., as well as suits of beautifully wrought chain armour—sufficient to fit out a small army. Most of these are mounted in gold, and many are ornamented with jewels. All are kept bright and in admirable order.

"The statues are surprising specimens of art, as are the bas-reliefs with which most of the buildings are embellished. Yet there are now no sculptors here, nor any painters. There are potters, but their work is inferior to specimens preserved in the museums. In many other branches of manufacture, also, the artificers of today are evidently unskilful as compared with those of former times.

"In the museums are also preserved manuscripts of great antiquity, and interesting as throwing light on the past history of the nation. Many of the nobles and chief people can write and read; but, printing being unknown, their opportunities of keeping up such accomplishments are necessarily very limited. The materials used for dress are mostly silk—obtained from silkworms—wool, and linen; the last being obtained from a fibre resembling flax. In the manufacture of these materials into fabrics the Manoans are particularly skilful; especially in working or embroidering upon them all kinds of new and quaint designs. Their boats, too, that float about the lake, are exquisite models; so that one can quite believe that the nation was once, as they declare, a maritime people, with fleets of ships, or, at least, large vessels of some kind. In the museums, by way of confirmation, are pictures—very cleverly executed works—of naval battles; and, in these, large vessels with two and three masts are represented.

"It is worthy of remark that in all these pictures representing battle-pieces—and these are many—none but white people are depicted. That different races intermingled in the fighting is indubitable; but the difference consists in dress and other details; not in the colour of their skins.

"It is a tradition of the Manoans that they formerly ruled over 'the whole world.' This may be taken to imply either the whole continent of America, or a large portion of it; but they knew nothing, formerly, of black or red races; and their archives bear this out—their pictures, perhaps, more forcibly than anything else.

"As regards the buildings, their architectural magnificence is undeniable—almost, indeed, defies description. On many structures gold has been freely employed in the roofing, and for other purposes where we should employ lead or iron. They say the gold came chiefly from Myrlanda, and certain neighbouring 'islands'—*i.e.*, mountains—from which they are now isolated. Gold cornices, and embellishments, of every conceivable shape and form, are commonly used for outside decorations; the very conduits to carry off water being often of gold or an amalgam consisting largely of that metal, and wrought into elaborate designs. Indeed, both iron and tin—and lead also—seem to have been much more sparingly employed than gold and silver. Iron seems to have been used only where extra strength and weight were required, and, in the form of steel, for weapons, or for common utensils, tools, etc.; and of copper there is very little anywhere to be seen. Silver, even, is less common in heavy decorative metal work than is solid gold.

"Thus the tales that Sir Walter Raleigh heard of the splendours of the ancient city of Manoa—or El Dorado—and that for many hundreds of years since have been regarded as fables, appear to have been based, after all, upon actual fact."

XVI

LEONARD AND ULAMA

How I should like to see this wondrous outside world that you come from!" said Ulama dreamily. "The more you tell me of it, the more you whet my curiosity, and the more I long to see its marvels for myself."

"And yet," was Elwood's answer, "nowhere will you find so marvellously beautiful a scene as that which now surrounds us. I have travelled a good deal myself; and my friend Jack much more; and Monella, where has he not been? He seems to have visited every corner of the world! Yet he said to me, but yesterday, that he thought this the fairest spot on earth; and in this Jack agrees, so far as his experience extends.

"Since I first came here I have looked upon it from many points of view; from the water, as the boat drifts from one side to the other; from different places round the shore; from various spots on the rocky terraces above; and these different views I have seen under all the shifting effects of sunlight, moonlight, and in the mountain mist. Yet do I find myself unable to decide which I like the best. Whatever I do, wherever I happen to be, I see constantly some fresh enchantment, some new charm, some effect at once unexpected and delightful; till I strive in vain to make up my mind which I admire the most."

It was about a week after the arrival in the city of the three travellers; and Ulama and Leonard were seated in a favourite boat in which the princess was wont to spend a large portion of her time. It was, really, a small barge, of curious but graceful design and elaborate decoration. Over the after part was a white and light-blue awning; the bow ran up in the shape of a bird with out-stretched wings wrought in gold and silver, and the stern was fashioned like a fish with scales of blue and gold, its tail being movable, and running down below the water-line to form the rudder. Upon the sides provision was made for several oars; but this morning Ulama and Elwood had put off alone, content that the boat should drift wherever the slight air or current might direct.

Truly Leonard had not over-rated the beauty of the scene around them; scarce indeed would it be possible to do so. The water was a dazzling blue, yet so clear and limpid that it seemed more like a film of tinted air than water, so that the eye could pierce to great depths where many strange creatures could be seen. The sun, high in the sky, poured down its rays upon the buildings and the trees, in some parts lighting up only the tops and throwing purple shadows over the rest; in other places, touches of vivid green contrasted with the pink-white tints of the faces of the buildings; the whole quivering in the shimmering haze that conveys an idea of unsubstantiality in what one sees—a suggestion that it may be only a mirage that a passing breeze may dissipate.

Ulama was leaning in contented listlessness over the boat's side, her hand playing idly in the water. On the shapely arm, bare to the elbow, was a plain gold band in which was set a single diamond that even crowned heads might have envied. It flashed and sparkled in the sunlight with dazzling fire and power. A gold fillet, set with another matchless diamond, confined her hair, which fell loosely in wavy tresses round her shoulders. Her dress was of finest work, its texture thin as gossamer; pure white with here and there a silken knot of blue. It was gathered into her waist by a golden zone whose clasp was hidden by another and even larger diamond. No other style of dress could have so well set off the perfect symmetry and beauty of her figure. Thus, bending in unconscious ease over the boat's side, the young girl formed one of the rarest models of maidenly grace and loveliness that could that morning have been found amongst Eve's daughters.

Yet, probably, to most observers, the purity and sweetness that looked out from her soft, wistful eyes would have seemed the chief and most attractive charm of this radiant maiden of the 'city of the clouds.' And her gentle, lustrous eyes were the index of the pure and loving soul within.

No wonder, therefore, that she was, beyond compare, the best loved, the most honoured person in the land.

She was her father's chief, almost his only, joy. Apart from her he found but little that gave him happiness. At the same time he loved his people and honestly desired to do his best for them; and gladly would he have made great sacrifices to bring about their emancipation from the priestly tyranny that oppressed them. But he shrank from the extreme step of precipitating a civil war; yet the alternative of allowing things to take their course and continue in the old groove grieved him deeply; so much so that his distress had begun to take the form of settled melancholy. His courtiers, who were devoted to him, noticing this, themselves became a prey to anxious misgivings, fearing in it the first symptoms of the sole incurable disease they knew—that which they termed the 'falloa.'

Leonard's last words had started a fresh train of thought in the young girl's mind, and presently she spoke again.

"Do you then mean that you would fain pass your life with us; you to whom the great world beyond is known, with all its endless interest? It seems strange that! Methinks that, were I in your place, I should deem life here but colourless and childish. For me, certainly, it has sufficed. I have a father who loves me dearly—dotes on me; my mother I never knew. She died when I was very young. I have kind friends around me whom I love, and who love me, and who seem to think far more of me than I deserve. And, were it not for the sadness in the land, I think I should be very happy; certainly I should be contented. Yet, now that you have told me of a spacious world beyond, full of all sorts of mysteries and unheard-of marvels, I confess I should like to see something of it."

"To do so would bring you no lasting pleasure," Leonard answered. "If we—if I—who have looked upon these things, have been brought up amongst them, if I am weary of them, and never care to see them more, and would spend the remainder of my life here, for you they would have no attractions."

Ulama glanced up shyly at him from under her long lashes.

"But are you—would you?" she asked with a slight blush. "Would you truly like to stay here all your life—never to go back to your own land?"

"Yes! I *do* mean that!" And there was a fervid glow in Leonard's countenance. "All my life I have had a restlessness impelling me to seek—I knew not what—in distant lands. All my life I have had strange dreams and visions; not only in the stillness of the night, but also amidst the busy hum of day, and in all these one form was ever present; it hovered round me so that I could almost see and touch it. But—and now comes the strange part of it—that first day I set eyes on you, the moment you drew near, I saw in you the living image of her who had been the central figure of my waking visions, and held sweet converse with me while I slept. Then—when my eyes met yours—I understood it all! I knew then what had led me hither; what it was I had unconsciously been seeking, and wherefore I had been restless and unsatisfied at home. I knew that in you I had discovered all I craved for—the sweet fulfilment of my soul's desire. And then—then—I saw you in the grasp of one who would have slain you! And my heart stood still, for I knew that, unless my hand were steady and my eye unerring, in striving to save your life I might destroy it. Oh, think, think what must have been my anguish! Think, how—Ah! never will you know a tenth of what I suffered in that brief space; or my relief and thankfulness when I saw him fall, and you stand scatheless!"

The young girl looked shyly at him; then, noting the love-light in his eyes, and the glowing flush upon his cheeks, the while he had poured out all that he had felt for her, an answering blush stole over her own fair cheek; while a coy, dainty little smile seemed to flit airily around her mouth, setting into little dimples first here then there; in like manner as a ray of light, reflected from a mirror, will dance coquettishly to and fro in obedience to the hand that moves the glass.

There was silence for a space, she gazing downwards at the water, but now and then stealing a shy glance at her companion.

Then another line of thought passed over her mind and shadowed her face for a moment.

"I wonder," she said with touching innocence, "what people see in me to like so much? I fear it is not always well that this should be. It was that which led—Zelus"—she shivered at the name—"to thrust himself upon, and at last threaten me, and has placed you in danger for having slain him. It is very strange! To like, to love, should mean naught but happiness and loving-kindness and innocent delight; yet here it has led a man to attempt an awful crime, and has placed others in great peril."

"It was not *love* on that man's part," said Leonard, savagely, between his teeth. "At least, not the sort of love that urged *me* on, that has guided me—even as the unwinding of a clue leads the traveller through the maze—to the side of her I loved and worshipped in my visions. Mine is not the love that could ever do its object hurt; that could ever—"

He paused abruptly, seeing her glance up at him with a look of wonder on her face.

"You love me?" she exclaimed. "But that is past believing! 'Tis but a few days since you first saw me. You cannot know what I am really like! How then can you *love* me? I love my father because he has cared for me and loved me all my life; I love Zonella—and—and—other friends, because I have known them for so long, and they have been kind and good to me. How can you yet tell that you will love me? Perchance when you know me better you may even come to hate me."

"Oh! Ulama! What is that you say?" he said impetuously. "You cannot mean it! You are playing with me! But it is cruel play! The love

I mean is not such as the slow growth of a child's affection for a parent or a girl-friend. It is a swift, resistless passion, that centres on one being above all others in the world, and says, 'This one only do I love; this one possesses all my heart and soul! From this one I can never swerve—my love will end only when my heart no longer beats; I cannot live without it.' Such a love bursts forth spontaneously from the heart, as does a tiny spring from the earth's bosom and that, when once it has found vent, forever bubbles up fresh and clear and pure, and, commencing in a little rill, increases to a torrent whose force no power can stem. *That* is the love I mean; and 'tis such a love I bear for you, Ulama. Can you not understand something of all this?"

"I know not," replied the maiden in a low voice, and glancing timidly at him. "You frighten me a little—or you would, but that I like you too well to feel afraid of you—but—I have no knowledge of such love as you describe."

"But, you have *heard* of a love that far exceeds mere friendship—far stronger than affection?"

"Y-es. I have *heard* of it; and—ridiculed it as fiction. Yet—if you affirm its truth, and in your own person have experienced it—I must fain believe you, for I know you would not say what is not true. But"— here she sagely shook her head—"though my ears receive your words, the time has not yet come when they have reached my heart."

Leonard seized her hand.

"But, meanwhile, I have not offended you, Ulama?" he asked entreatingly. "You will let me love you? Indeed, I am powerless to help it. And you will try to—to—like me—ah, you have said you *do* like me already. Will you not try to love me a little?"

"Nay," she frankly answered, "you would not surely have me *try*? What sort of love would that be that we had to *try* to bring into being— to force upon an unresponsive heart? You have said that it should burst forth spontaneously. I scarcely understand when you speak thus."

Leonard sighed.

"You are right, Ulama, as you ever are; and I am wrong; but my love makes me impatient. I will not expect too much of you. I will wait with such content as is in me to command until your gentle heart shall beat in unison with mine; and something in me tells me that one day it will."

Just then they heard the voice of someone calling to them, and, looking round, they saw Jack Templemore and Zonella, with several others, coming towards them in another boat.

When they were within speaking distance, Jack said that Monella had sent him to tell Leonard he wished to speak to him; Leonard accordingly took up the oars and rowed the barge slowly to shore. There he left Ulama with the party, and proceeded in search of Monella who, he had been told, was awaiting him upon a terrace that overlooked the lake.

Here Leonard found him seated with a field-glass in his hand. Monella turned and looked searchingly at the young man, who felt himself colouring under the other's glance.

"I love not to seem to spy upon your acts, my son," Monella began gravely, "but when I caught sight of you in yonder boat holding the hand of the princess, the daughter of the king, who is our kind and gracious host, I could not well do otherwise than seek a talk with you. I fear you have not well considered what you do."

At this rebuke Leonard coloured up still more, albeit the words were spoken with evident kindness. For that very reason, probably, they sank the deeper. It was the first time anything savouring of reproof to him had fallen from Monella's lips; and, up to that moment, its possibility had seemed remote; and now the young man deeply felt the fact that the other should have thought it necessary.

"I think I know what you would say," he answered in a low voice. "I feel I have been wrong—guilty of thoughtlessness, presumption, and seemingly of breach of confidence. I understand what is in your mind. Yet let me say at once that so far little—practically nothing—has been said, and nothing more shall be—unless—you can tell me I dare hope. But oh, my good friend, you who have treated me always as a son, and shown such sympathy and kindness towards me—who have known of my half-formed aspirations, and the ideas that led me on and ended in my coming here, and encouraged me in those ideas—who have learned that in the king's daughter I have found the living embodiment of the central figure of all my dreamings—*you* surely will not now turn upon me and tell me I must stifle all my feelings, and—give—up—the hopes—that had arisen—in my heart?" And Leonard sank wearily into a seat.

Then, for the first time realising his actual position, how next to impossible it was that the king would regard with favour his pretensions, he placed his hands before his face and groaned aloud.

Monella rose, and, going to him, laid his hand kindly upon his shoulder.

"I might bring all the arguments and platitudes of the 'worldly-wise' to bear on you," he said, "but I forbear; and I know they will not weigh with you. Moreover, it is undeniable that the circumstances are unusual and unlooked-for. But they do not justify you in forgetting what you owe to a kingly host and—I may add—to others; to us, your friends, for instance. You know, also, that our position here is critical; there is trouble brewing in the land. If the king should have reason to believe that one of us has abused his confidence in one matter, he may lose his trust in all, as touching other, and far more weighty matters—matters that may affect even his own personal security; to say nothing of our own lives, and those of many of his subjects. Therefore—"

Leonard sprang up and looked at him imploringly.

"For pity's sake say no more," he said, "or I shall begin to hate myself. I understand—only too well. Trust me—if you will; if you feel you can; if you have not lost confidence. You shall not have further reason for complaint."

Monella took Leonard's hand in his and pressed it affectionately.

"'Tis well, my son," he said. "I have full confidence, and will trust you. And you, on your side, must trust me. I may have opportunity to sound the king, and, if it so happen, you may count on me to say and do all that my friendship for you may dictate—and that will not be a little."

Leonard wrung the other's hand and tried to thank him, but a burst of emotion overcame him, and he turned away. When he again looked round he was alone.

XVII

The Fight on the Hillside

It had become the custom of the two young men to go every morning, when the atmosphere was clear, to a height at one end of the valley, from which a view could be obtained over the whole country surrounding that end of Roraima. The spot was a level table of rock under a picturesque group of fir-trees—for on the upper cliffs fir-trees were numerous—and from it, looking in the direction farthest from the mountain, the view was grand in the extreme; while, on the other side of them was the great valley or basin in which lay the lake and the city of Manoa.

It would be but labour lost to attempt to give an adequate idea of the prospect over which the eye could travel on a clear day, when one stood upon this giddy height. It extended to an almost illimitable distance; for, when one looked beyond the surrounding mountains of the Roraima range, there were no more hills to break the view till it reached the far distant Andes, had these been visible. Indeed, it was said that they *were* visible on a few days in the year; but, if that were so, it would perhaps be rather as an effect in the nature of a mirage than what is usually understood by an actual view of the far-away mountains. But nearer at hand, in other directions were mountain ridges and summits in seemingly endless succession, piled up in extraordinary confusion. From Roraima, as the highest of all, one could look down, to some extent, upon the others. Myrlanda was upon the other side, but Marima, and others of the strange group, lay before the eye, and one could see the woods and lakes upon their summits; but enough could not be seen to enable the spectator to decide whether they might be inhabited or not.

The beauty of the expanse of tropical vegetation immediately below was indeed marvellous. Here the explorers gazed down upon the tops of the trees of the gloomy forest that girdled the mountain (though not that part through which they had made their way with so much wearying, but dogged perseverance), and lo! it was a veritable garden of flowers of brilliant hue! For the trees beneath which they had crept, like ants among the stems of a field of clover, were gorgeous above in their display of blossoms, while shutting out the light from those who walked below.

Here and there, amid the green, the great cascades and torrents from the mountain side dashed impetuously from rock to rock; the streams that were in fact some of the feeders of the greatest of all rivers, the mighty Amazon; that river of wondrous mysteries, that pursues its course of four thousand miles through the plains of Brazil, and finds its way round at last into the Atlantic, there to hurl the volume of its waters with such force into the sea, that even the ocean waters are pushed aside to make a path for them hundreds of miles from land!

Here, upon the table of rock, in full view of one of the grandest and most eloquent natural panoramas it is possible for the mind of man to conceive, Leonard and Templemore stood the morning following the former's interview with Monella, looking out upon the scene. A high wind, of bracing and exhilarating freshness, blew in their faces, rushed with a roar through the branches above them, swaying the great trees to and fro, and then, seeming to tear off across the valley at one leap, continued its wild course amongst the trees on the heights that lined the further side. Leonard, on turning to look across the lake, saw Ergalon advancing up the slope and making signs to him. He drew Jack's attention to the signals, and they both descended the terraces of rock below to meet him. Here all was quiet; they were sheltered from the gusts of wind; the roar of the gale no longer met their ears.

All the time they had been in the city they had had a guard. It consisted of a file of soldiers with an officer, and they followed the two young men in all their walks, movements, journeys, never thrusting themselves on their attention, yet always ready to assist and defend them, if occasion should arise. Monella, also, had an escort whenever he went out. He had particularly enjoined on the other two never to stir abroad without their rifles, and this injunction, though they did not always see its necessity, they implicitly observed.

They had not seen much of Ergalon of late; he had attached himself more particularly to Monella, and had, in fact, become his particular attendant. Monella had trusted him so far as to explain to him something of the secrets of the firearms, and had instructed him in the loading of them in case circumstances should arise in which his assistance might be needed. Accordingly, when Leonard saw him coming up the hillside and signifying that he wished to speak to them, he at once called Templemore and left the ledge where they had been standing.

Soon they saw their guard approaching with Ergalon in advance of them, and, following them, Monella, who came on leisurely from ledge to ledge, occasionally giving a glance behind him.

The hillside was marked out in terraces, or tables of rock, most of them covered with greensward and fringed at the sides with belts of trees. Ergalon, who had taken his stand below, made signs to the two to come down to him, and, when they had descended within hearing, he addressed them.

"The lord Monella has sent me to warn you to await him here and to be ready for a contest. There is trouble afoot."

"But why wait here?" asked Jack. "We will go down to him at once."

Ergalon shook his head.

"No," he said. "He particularly desired that you would await him here."

"So be it; if you are sure you rightly understood him. But tell us, friend Ergalon, what all this means."

Ergalon explained that Coryon had unexpectedly dispatched a large force of his soldiers to capture the three strangers. They had hoped to surprise them without giving time for others of the king's soldiers to lend their aid. But he (Ergalon) had, through a former comrade who was still one of Coryon's people, attained intimation of the intended movement, and had been able thus to warn Monella.

"So the lord Monella," he explained, "sent on your guard in advance, and then himself walked up the hill towards you that they might see him. Thus he hoped to draw Coryon's people away from the palace and the houses to this place, where, he says, it will be better to make a stand and fight them, since thus no other persons will be injured in the encounter."

It was strange, but all who spoke of Monella, or to him, gave him some title of honour or respect. Ergalon called him 'lord.' Even Dakla, at the meeting in the king's council chamber—spite of his insolent swagger towards the king—had been awed by this man's look into addressing him by the equivalent in their language of 'sir.'

"How many are there of them?" asked Jack.

"Oh, a hundred—or perhaps more. But the lord Monella has said their number matters not; and he sent me to the king to beg that none of his soldiers should interfere. 'They would only be in the way,' he said.

He sent these extra things for you. See." And he showed a parcel of cartridges he had brought with him.

"Good," said Jack. "He is quite right. That's all we wanted; we can answer for the rest. More soldiers would only be in the way; and some of them would be pretty sure to get hurt, if not killed outright—and all for nothing. I think I see Monella's idea. It is"—turning to Elwood— "to take up our position here and shoot them down as they come across this wide terrace just below us. Not a man of them will ever cross that stretch alive."

"Here are your guards," observed Ergalon. "The lord Monella desired that you should place them somewhere where they would be out of the way, but within call."

"Let them get on to this next ledge, then, just behind us. There they will have a fine view of everything. Did these people think to surprise us, do you think, friend Ergalon?"

"No doubt. Your habit of coming here of a morning has been noted, I suspect, and they had intended, I imagine, to creep round and get up through the woods unseen. But the lord Monella, being warned by me, went up on a high rock, where he could see them in the distance; when they saw they were observed by him, they gave up that plan and came straight on."

"I see. Well, we owe you something for having warned us, friend."

"It is nothing," Ergalon answered simply. "My life was forfeited that day, and you spared me; and through the lord Monella and the princess, I gained the king's pardon. I owe you all my service."

By this time the guards and their officer had arrived, and were placed by Ergalon on a terrace above and behind that on which the two were standing.

"We like it not, this mode of yours—putting us in the background, out of danger, while you stand up in front," observed the officer; "we consent only because the lord Monella so desires it. They are many, but we should not shrink; and others from the king's palace would soon come to our assistance."

"Yes, yes, good Abla. We have no misgivings of your courage. But you could do no good with so few men—they are more than ten to one, I hear—and your men would but impede us. Besides, it will give them a lesson for the future, if we deal with them ourselves, unaided."

Abla bowed and walked away unwillingly, as one who is bound to obey orders, but does so against his will.

Monella now came in view, and was soon standing by their side. After a few words of explanation, he said gravely,

"They thought to have surprised us all three up here; but, when they saw they had failed in that, they took a bold course and came straight on. Now that means, in effect, an open challenge to the king. It means," he continued with increased earnestness, "civil war. Civil war, you understand, has therefore broken out in the land—unless we nip it in the bud, *here, now*, as we can, if we show no untimely hesitation. These men are scoundrels of the serpent's brood; cruel, bloodthirsty tools of the human fiends behind them. They deserve no mercy, no consideration. Let none be shown to them! My plan is simply to shoot them down the instant they appear on that ledge below us. They *must* climb up in front; there is no way round it, nor any means of getting to the height above us. Therefore, they must cross that piece of open ground. One word more. The chief, Dakla, leads them. Do not fire at him. I wish to take him alive, if possible; he will make our best ambassador hereafter."

Under such conditions the battle could not be a long one. Monella had chosen his ground skilfully, so as to make the utmost of the advantage firearms gave him. The black-coated myrmidons of Coryon scaled the fatal terrace only to be shot down the moment that they came in sight. There were only four or five places where they could climb up and, at these, not more than two men could pass together. Those who reached the top and escaped a bullet, turned back when they heard the explosions of the firearms, saw the flashes and the smoke, saw also their comrades fall. Others of those below who could see nothing of what was going on, swarmed up in their places, only to fall or turn back at once in like manner; till, in a short time, every man had been up and witnessed the ghastly sight of the dead and wounded lying around, and had satisfied himself that not one could cross that level piece of rock to come near their foes. Finally, the survivors were all seized with panic when one of the last to show his head above the ridge came back crying out that "the white demons were coming down after them." At this, all those who were unhurt turned and fled. But many had fallen, dead or wounded, and lay at the foot of the rock they had climbed up only to be instantly shot down. Above, on the terrace itself, but at one side, stood Dakla and one of his subordinates. These had been amongst the first to appear above the ledge, and had moved aside to let the men form into line up on the rock; but now they were left alone, and, when Monella quietly descended from the rock above, they had the mortification of seeing all their men who were capable of running disappear in frantic terror down the hillside.

Then he who stood by Dakla made a rush at Monella with uplifted sword, thinking, since he seemed to be unarmed, that he would fall an easy prey; but the man fell with a pistol ball in his breast ere he had gone half way to meet Monella.

"Now yield, Dakla," Monella called to the other. "It is useless either to fight or run."

"We will see to that," Dakla exclaimed savagely. "If thou be man, and not demon, this sword shall find thine heart." And he too made a sudden rush. But, before he had gone three yards, the sword flew from his hand and his arm dropped useless by his side. Monella had shot him in the arm.

"Thou see'st," he said coldly, as he now approached the crestfallen chief, "how ill-advised thou hast been not to give heed to all my warnings. I could have slain thee earlier in the fight; I could have killed thee now, as I did thy friend there; but I have spared thy life. It is not for thine own sake, but that thou mayest bear a message to thy master, and witness to him of that which thou hast seen and warn him once more of the futility of warring against us, the allies of the king. Dost thou understand?"

The other cast a murderous scowl upon Monella, but made no answer for a moment. Then, after reflection, he said in a dogged, surly tone,

"So be it. But thou must give thy message quickly and let me go; for thou hast hurt me sore and the blood flows fast—"

"We will see to thy wound," Monella replied composedly. "Let me bind it up till we get to the king's palace; there it shall be seen to farther."

And Dakla, reluctantly, and with an ill grace, submitted to have his wound bound up by his enemy, who, before commencing, took away the other's dagger.

"I cannot trust thee with these playthings," he observed. "Thou art of the wolf tribe, Dakla."

Meanwhile, the officer and men of their guard had come down to the lower terrace, with Templemore and Elwood, and were looking in awe and horror upon the outcome of the fight—if so one-sided an encounter could be so called. On Monella and the two young men they gazed in wonder; and, gradually, they drew away from them in fear, from that moment treating them with even greater deference than before.

Monella despatched Abla to summon more soldiers from the king's palace to bring down the dead and wounded; and himself set about attending to the latter, first handing Dakla over to Templemore.

"Look you!" said Jack to his prisoner, "if you attempt to escape, I shall not kill you, but hurt your other arm; and, if that does not stop you, I shall hurt your leg, and I know that that *will*. Do you follow me?"

Dakla nodded a sour assent; then stood looking with evident surprise at the trouble Monella was now taking with some of his late enemies. Such singular behaviour he did not understand, and he shrugged his shoulders in contempt.

When, after a time, more soldiers, with some officers, arrived upon the scene, these were at once set to work to bear the dead and wounded down the hill. Monella followed with his friends and Dakla. The noise of the firing had brought out great crowds of people, who were now massed about the palace waiting to receive them. They had watched the precipitate flight of the survivors of the soldiers of Coryon, and rejoiced greatly at their defeat. But, when they saw the dead and wounded, and that Dakla was himself a prisoner, and heard that not one had been hurt upon the other side, their astonishment was complete.

The king himself, with some of his ministers and officials, came out to meet the victors; and his gratitude and emotion, when he noted all these things and greeted Monella and his friends, were profuse and heartfelt.

"Ye have indeed rendered us a service," he exclaimed, "and taught Coryon a lesson he will do well to take to heart. I feared me greatly that harm would come to ye, and that war would follow in the land."

"Nay, we have laid the dogs of war, I trust, at any rate, for the present," Monella returned, with a grave smile. "They will not attack us further, I opine, nor brave thee in the future in this rebellious fashion."

Then they entered the palace, and Ulama came forward to welcome them, with Zonella and many more.

"We have been in such trouble about you," she said, the tears standing in her tender eyes, "ever since they told us that over a hundred of Coryon's people had gone up the rocks to take you. And we heard the noise of the thunder-wands, and were in great fear, till they told us that your enemies were fleeing. Then we looked out and saw them rushing madly down the hill, throwing away their spears, and their helmets, and even fighting one another in their haste to scramble down the rocks. Then Abla came and told us you were all safe, and then—"

"Then," said Zonella, "you sat down and wept." And at that Ulama laughed.

"I fear it is true," she said.

XVIII

THE LEGEND OF MELLENDA

Monella's anticipations of what would follow the severe lesson they had given Coryon's followers turned out to be well founded. For when Dakla, with his arm in a sling, revisited his master, bearing a message from the king, the conditions offered were accepted.

Dakla had been straightly charged that these terms would have to be submitted to; if not that his master and all his followers would be starved into submission. They would be confined to their own colony, supplies of food refused, and any of their number leaving their retreat would be killed at sight.

The conditions imposed were that not merely the three strangers, but all the 'lay' inhabitants were to be free from molestation by Coryon's people; and that no more 'blood-tax' was to be levied.

After many journeys to and fro, and much delay, Dakla at last announced that Coryon agreed to the conditions for a time—for four months. After that, their great festival would be coming on, and—well, time would show.

"It is only a truce," said Monella, with a sigh, to his two young friends. "I would it had been permanent; but it will give us time, and the opportunity of shaping out our course. The people will have a respite from the terrible fear that now is ever with them; and, short of engaging in a protracted civil conflict, for which the people are not yet prepared, I see not what better could have been arranged."

They were thus now able to move about more freely, and without a guard; their rifles, too, could be left behind when they went abroad; though Monella had counselled that they should always carry their revolvers; for he feared they were not altogether safe from treachery, or from some fanatical outbreak on the part of certain of the priests' adherents.

Thus Templemore and Elwood were now able to mingle more freely with the populace and to see more of their social life. And, wherever they went, they were well received, and treated with both confidence and respect. They visited the houses of people of all classes, from the palaces of the nobles to the dwellings of the peasantry, if so the lower classes might be called. There were, however, no poor in the country, in the ordinary sense of the word. The crops grown were supplied to all alike; everyone had plenty to eat, and plenty of clothes to wear, and well-built houses to live in. And, beyond these requisites, there was little in the land to pine for. There were forests, and from these all were free to cut wood for fuel; the electric light was laid on to all alike. The water they required they supplied themselves with from the lake, or from one or other of the streams that everywhere gushed forth from the rocks above. Of shops there were none; but there was a market-place, and a sort of market or exchange was held there once a week. Even this, however, was falling into disuse. There was a currency; and there were many kinds of coins; but they were seldom used. They were of ancient make and were preserved rather as curiosities, seemingly, than for use. There was so little that the people wanted, either to buy or sell, that a simple system of barter sufficed for practically all their needs.

Elwood and Templemore, as they came to know all these things, and gained experience of the simple good-nature of the people, felt increased indignation and resentment against the priests. They saw that the horrible tyranny of these men had turned a land that might have been a realm of perfect peace and goodwill, into one where constant dread and hopeless misery and suffering had become so common, that all seemed helplessly resigned to it.

One day, when the two were in a boat with Ulama and Zonella, Kalaima, and others, Templemore, who had been talking of these matters, asked whether the state of things they had seen had been of long duration.

The reply came from Zonella.

"Ever since the time of the great Mellenda. So we are told. It is the punishment sent by the Great Spirit upon the people for their ingratitude to him."

"And who was Mellenda?" asked Elwood.

"What! You ask who was Mellenda? But I forgot; of course, you have not been here very long, and cannot know our history and legends."

"I have been prying about more in your museums than has my friend," Jack observed, "and I have learned something of Mellenda. But I know nothing of any legend. Pray let us hear it."

"Yes, tell us about it," Leonard urged. "I like fine old legends and tales of wonder."

"Ask the princess to tell you."

"No, no, Zonella," Ulama interposed. "You began it; you finish it. Besides, you are more learned in such things than I am."

"Very well," Zonella said resignedly. "I can only give it as I know it. If you want further details, you must go to the museum, or ask Colenna, the High Chamberlain, who is a very learned man. Only I do not wish you to ridicule it"—this to the two young men—"for, though I call it a legend, yet it is history; and all our people implicitly believe it. You could not offend them more than by treating it lightly or affecting to disbelieve it. I give *you* that as a caution, more particularly," she added, looking mischievously at Jack, "for I know that you are very much inclined to scepticism in such things."

"I will promise to be very good, and to make no frivolous remarks," was Jack's laughing answer.

"Then you must know," Zonella began, "that we deem Mellenda the greatest of our kings; that is, of our later kings. Our ancient line of kings before him had made Manoa the greatest, the most powerful, and the richest country of the world. These mountains that you have seen around us were all islands in a great lake—the lake of Parima. Its waters extended to the great mountains that we can sometimes see from the highest points about Manoa—far, far away. But over those, and over lands in every direction, our nation held sway. These islands were our chief fastnesses, and this one, Manoa, being the highest and the most naturally favoured of them all, was the seat of government, and its city was the capital to which were brought all the wealth and the most valued productions of the other countries that formed part of its empire.

"But, after many mighty kings had lived and died, a weakness seemed to fall upon the people. They were defeated in battle; provinces revolted, and many distant parts of the empire were lost, passing under other kings. At that time, it is said, our kings and nobles and chiefs among the nation were too much given to feasting and enjoyment; and, it is declared, they began cruelly to oppress the weaker of the people. And a change came over the religion. Up to then all had worshipped only one Great Spirit, who was said to be a good Spirit—the great ruler of all spirits, in fact, and his priests were called 'Children of the Light.' Their rule—what they taught—was gentle; it is recorded that they were men of peace and of great—very, very great—wisdom. But another religion had been introduced, coming, it is believed, from some of the lands that had been conquered; and this was the exact opposite of the old one. Its votaries and high priests called themselves 'Children of the Night';

they worshipped, not one God, but many strange and terrible gods; their priests, also, were thought to possess great wisdom, but of an evil kind. They taught that there was but one way to escape the power of the Spirits of Darkness, and that was by propitiating them by constant sacrifices; and they killed many people at their festivals to give them to their gods.

"Then Mellenda came to the throne. He was the only son of the last of the ancient line of kings. While young he had travelled far and gained much knowledge in strange countries; and he had already, as general of some of his father's armies, defeated the enemies of the country, and regained some of the lost provinces. His father was killed in battle, and Mellenda immediately set about plans for reviving the old power and recovering the former empire of the nation. He taught, too, that the White religion was the true religion, and he made endeavours to put down the other. But he was absent for long periods at a time, upon distant expeditions, from which, it is true, he always returned victorious; but, while he was away, establishing peace and order in some distant province, the Dark Priests were craftily at work undermining his authority at home. However, for a long time, nothing came of their plottings, and Mellenda reigned for several hundred years—"

"That's a long time," Jack interrupted, regardless of his promise.

"For several hundred years," repeated Zonella with a reproving look at the interrupter, "which was not very long, considering that his father had reigned for fifteen hundred years, and was then cut off, in the flower of his age, by an accident in battle. He (Mellenda) had restored peace at last throughout the whole empire; reformed the style of living, himself setting an example of great simplicity; and his wisdom and justice and kindness of heart had made him revered and loved wherever the name of Manoa was known. Then, finally, he married a princess he was passionately fond of, named Elmonta, and had four children, upon whom, they say, he lavished the most tender love. But some occasion arose for him to leave Manoa once more, to visit a distant part of his great empire. There was a treaty of alliance to be made with another monarch, or some such matter of importance. He sailed away and returned after a long absence, to find that Coryon—"

"Coryon!" exclaimed Jack, once more forgetful of his promises.

"Yes, Coryon, the same Coryon, as is believed, that we have here in the land today. He had seized upon the government and gained over a vast number of the most dissolute and discontented spirits to his side.

He was then, as now, the chief of the Dark Brotherhood, or Children of the Night. All the crowd of idle, self-indulgent nobles and men of wealth, but of loose life, among the people, whom Mellenda had rebuked and curbed, broke out and joined Coryon's revolt; and they actually seized upon Elmonta, Mellenda's queen, and his children, and offered them as sacrifices to their gods. Coryon set up a king of his own choosing; and, when Mellenda returned, he found his wife and children dead, and the government in the hands of a puppet king controlled by Coryon, who threatened him with death if he landed and fell into his hands. Such was the message sent out to Mellenda when he arrived in sight of our island on his return, successful in the mission that had called him away, and impatient to get back to his wife and children. He had with him a great fleet of vessels; and, though the revolt had spread to the other islands, he could, perhaps, have found followers enough in other parts of the empire to have regained his throne, had he been so minded. But he was broken-hearted, and said that, since his wife and children were no longer living, he had nothing left to fight for, and cared not to take part in a civil war with his own people. Instead, he decreed that their punishment should be that he (Mellenda) would go away and leave them for many ages to suffer under the lash of the foul religion they had supported; till all who had sinned against him saw their wicked error, when he would return to punish finally the Dark Priests and those who still wilfully supported them. Then, and forever afterwards, there should be peace and happiness and justice throughout the land for all his people.

"So Mellenda sailed away, and was never seen or heard of more. Not long after his departure came the great sinking of the waters, and the lake of Parima disappeared. This the better-disposed inhabitants left here regarded as a special punishment for their allowing Coryon to usurp the government and drive away the great, good, and wise Mellenda. And they rose up against Coryon and the king he had set up. But the crafty priest had obtained too strong a position for the movement to succeed. Moreover, he managed to pacify a part of his opponents in a strange way. He declared he had not put to death all Mellenda's children, and produced a boy, who, it is said, was recognised by those who ought to know as one of Mellenda's children. This child he promised to place upon the throne; and afterwards he did so.

"The nation, shut off from all the world, has much decreased in numbers, and is now unknown where it was once all-powerful. For centuries, it is said, the surrounding country was but a chaos of swamp and mud. By degrees there grew up vegetation, and finally trees that, in time, became thick, tangled forests that could not be penetrated. Thus, for long ages, we have been cut off from all the other peoples of the world. Some parties were sent out, hundreds of years ago, to explore the surrounding country; but some never returned, and those who did brought back such terrible accounts of awful woods haunted by fearful creatures, and of deserts beyond, inhabited only by black demons, that it was considered better to keep the country here entirely to ourselves. So I believe the only known way that led out into the woods was sealed up for good; and thus ended the last attempt to communicate with the outside world.

"Many of the White Priests fled to Mellenda's vessels, and were taken away with him when he departed; but the others, including their chief, Sanaima, retired to Myrlanda, where they have ever since maintained themselves.

"That is the story of Mellenda, and of how he left us, and of what befell the proud city of Manoa after his departure. When he will come back we know not; but some old prophecies obtain amongst the people according to which the time of his return is very near, if it is not indeed overpast."

"His return!" said Jack. "You surely would not have us understand that you expect this venerable old fossil to return, in the flesh, to trouble himself about the present state of the descendants of his ungrateful people?"

Zonella stared.

"Why, *of course* we do!" she answered. "There is not a man or a woman—scarcely a child of a few years old—that has not been taught to believe in it."

"I should think so," Ulama exclaimed, almost indignantly. "We all *know* it will be so; we believe it absolutely."

"But," said Jack, "how long ago do you reckon all this took place?"

"About two thousand years," Zonella replied, after a brief, but apparently careful, calculation, counting up on her fingers.

"Two thousand years! And you—you two sensible young people—tell us you expect to see this badly-treated, but respectable, old gentleman turn up again, just much as usual, I suppose, after two thousand years!"

"Why not?" Ulama asked. "We have Coryon and Sanaima, both said to be older than that."

"Yes—but"—looking at Leonard—"I fancy that is like the Pharoahs of old, you know, where there was always a Pharoah on the throne, though kings were born and died. It would be easy to keep up a farce of that sort where, as here, the 'High Priest,' black or white, is so seldom visible—always in the background."

"But if the king is three hundred and forty, may it not be possible to live to two thousand, or more? I can point out many men of more than five hundred in the king's palace," observed Zonella.

The gentle Ulama, even, looked somewhat offended.

"We do not question the wonderful things you tell us about the world outside," she said. "Why should you question what we know to be true?"

"It seems to me," said Leonard, "that it all depends upon the virtues of the 'Plant of Life.' Now, if that herb, or plant, or whatever it is, really has the qualities attributed to it, why, the rest is easy enough."

"I admit that," Jack said, laughing. "When once that is conceded, a man may just as easily live to five thousand years. Only, even in that case, I see a difficulty. How would Mellenda get the necessary 'Plant of Life' away from here?"

"The White Priests who went away with him would not be likely to leave their secret behind," explained Zonella. "Besides, it is specially stated in our historical manuscripts—so Colenna has told me—that those who went out from the island for long periods—governors of distant provinces and the like—not only took a large supply of the dried plant with them, but seeds that they might grow it; and in some places they found the plant do well; though they kept its virtues a secret from the peoples they went amongst. These things would be known to Mellenda and to the White Priests who went away with him; and, probably, they settled in a place where they knew the plant was being grown."

"Were that so, it would explain something of the former far-reaching fame and power of a small nation of islanders like these," said Leonard. "The secret of such a plant—the rapid increase of population when there were so few deaths in proportion—would of course give them a long pull over other nations."

"As to the question whether we seriously expect Mellenda to return to us," resumed Zonella, "in the large museum you will see one of his suits of armour, his banner, and a celebrated sword of his, all kept bright and ready for use and well preserved. They are kept there waiting for him."

"I saw them," Jack remarked. "He must have been a big fine man, if that suit fitted him. But, to go back to the son of this great king, said to have been saved after all, and then put on the throne; did he have any descendants?"

Zonella nodded.

"There have been five kings in the direct line since."

"I see. So that the present king is—"

"A great-great-great-grandson of the great Mellenda," put in Ulama.

"I think it was rather fortunate you managed as you did when you came here," Zonella said after a pause; "for, if Coryon had been the first to know of you strangers being in the country, he would have striven in every way to have killed or captured you. They say he is a firm believer in the early coming of Mellenda, and is in mortal terror about it."

Jack was silent awhile, and then he observed drily,

"Well, all I can say is that I should very much like to see the good gentleman, if he is still about; and I only hope and wish he will arrive while we are here. If he has been travelling around all these years, by this time he must know a thing or two! I wonder whether he will come in a balloon!"

XIX

Hopes and Fears

Amongst other advantages of the peace or truce that had been arranged with the mysterious Coryon, one was that Elwood and Templemore were free to visit the canyon and the caves where their reserve stores lay, and assure themselves that they were all safe. To do this they had to arrange to be away one night, since it was a day's journey each way. That night they passed in the cavern—which they had named 'Monella Cave' in honour of their friend; the canyon itself they called 'Fairy Valley'—and their camp equipage being all found intact where they had hidden it away, they had everything at hand for making themselves comfortable. They found, on examination, that the stone that closed the entrance was in the same position as when they had left it. Having removed the wooden bars, they rolled it to one side, and looked out into the gloomy depths of Roraima Forest.

From this outlook Templemore turned back with a shudder of disgust.

"How I hate that forest!" he exclaimed. "How miserable it seems out there! Verily it is wonderful, if you come to think of it, that we ever had the patience and perseverance to cut our way through to this place."

"We never should have done so, but for Monella's influence," observed Leonard. "How strange it all seems, doesn't it? Now that we are back here, we could almost think all we have been through a dream. One thing is certain; no other party of explorers would ever work their way through this wood as we did; they would get disheartened before the end of the first week. Nor could they possibly do any good by persevering, unless they had that to guide them which Monella had. What is that piece of white over there?"

And Leonard indicated a white patch upon a tree-trunk at the edge of the clearing.

Templemore took out his glasses and looked through them.

"It's a piece of paper," he cried excitedly. "Someone's been here! We must go out and inquire into this!" The ladder was quickly got out, and they hurried down it and across the clearing to the tree that bore the unexpected *affiche*. But, though the paper must have been purposely nailed in its place it was blank; on opening it, however, they found a few straight lines that formed a somewhat vague resemblance to the letter M.

"Matava has been here!" Leonard cried out. "All he can do in the writing line is to make some marks that mean M—his own initial, you know. Poor fellow! Fancy his venturing here to seek for us!"

The paper had been folded many times, the 'M' being in the inside; and it had been nailed just under an overhanging piece of bark, as a protection from the weather.

"He must have executed this elaborate piece of penmanship at 'Monella Lodge'," said Jack, "and brought it with him in case his journey here should be in vain. He's a good fellow! Knowing, as we do, how he and all his tribe abhor this wood and the mountain, we can appreciate the devotion that led him to screw up his courage so far. And then to have come for nothing! It's too bad, poor chap! What a pity we could not have got down here and seen him! Plainly he had some hope we might return, or he would not have left this simple yet ingeniously contrived message for us!"

"His hope would be but a faint one at best," Leonard replied gravely. "Having been here and found the entrance fast closed, and after our failing to make any signals, as arranged, I fear he will carry back an alarming tale to Georgetown."

"I fear so too, Leonard," Jack assented very seriously. "They will be terribly alarmed about us; worse than if he had gone straight back without coming here."

That evening, after they had cooked their evening meal, they sat by the smouldering fire, both silent and both thoughtful. Jack smoked away moodily at his pipe; Leonard was absolutely idle, except that he turned his eyes, now on the glow of failing daylight overhead, then down at the scene around him.

Each knew what was in the other's mind; yet neither liked to be the first to speak of it. But at last Jack spoke.

"It's no use blinking the fact, Leonard," he began, "that this visit of Matava here and the account he is sure to carry back is a serious matter. Our friends will be more than alarmed; they will, perhaps, give us up for dead. This raises the whole question again, What are we going to do here, how long are we going to stay, and what about getting back? We can't stay here forever—at least, *I* certainly don't mean to. I don't like the idea of going away and leaving you here. Where are we drifting to?"

Leonard was gloomy. He had been so more or less ever since that conversation with Monella about Ulama. For a few minutes he made no reply; then said, with a tinge of bitterness in his tone,

"You must wait awhile, Jack. I am not prepared to say yet, but—it may be I shall be ready to clear out soon with you."

Jack raised his eyebrows and gave a brief, but keen, glance at his friend. Then he smoked on stolidly for a while and ruminated.

"There's one who will never go back with us," presently he went on, "and that's Monella. He spoke truly when he said he should never return to 'civilisation.' He seems to have resolved to make his home here for the future. He is now the king's right hand—his 'guide, counsellor, and friend,' with him constantly, except when he's away in the place they call Myrlanda, on some mysterious business. And, perhaps, the oddest thing of all is that he is the most popular man at the court—even with those he has, in a sense, displaced. You would think there would be all kinds of envy, and hatred, and jealousy, and counter-plotting, and general 'ructions,' when a stranger, suddenly come from goodness knows where, stepped upon the scene and became straight away the favourite and confidant and counsellor of the king! Yet, the more he takes that character upon himself, the more they all seem to like him!"

"Who can help liking him?" Leonard sighed. "Who can help loving him? Even where he reproves, he does it so tenderly you only love him the more for it. How can anyone feel jealous, or angry, or envious with a man who behaves to all as he does? For myself I do not wonder; he was born to be a leader of men, as I said long ago; he has that magnetic attraction that makes a great commander—a commander who inspires such devotion that thousands and hundreds of thousands are ready to give their lives for but a glance of approval or a word of praise. There can't be many such men at this moment in the world; there cannot have been many since the world was made. But, when such a man appears, he quickly spreads his influence around him."

Jack gave a little laugh; but not an ill-natured one.

"You are as full as ever of enthusiasm for your hero," he remarked, "though he *has* been a sort of cold shower-bath to you lately, eh?"

Leonard coloured, and shifted uneasily on his seat.

"How did you know that?" he asked.

"I guessed it, old man. In fact, I saw the 'cold shower-bath' in his eye that day—you know."

"Yes—perhaps you are not far out, Jack. However, I promised to leave things in his hands, and there they must remain at present. Of his regard for me I have no doubt whatever—or for us both. If he cannot do the almost impossible, I shall accept my fate, and try to bear it as well as may be. Let us say no more about it now."

Jack, who for all his usual habit of appearing somewhat unobservant, could see most things, thought he could have told his friend of someone else who was displaying signs of unhappiness under Monella's 'cold shower-bath' treatment—Ulama, to wit. She had become very quiet and grave of late; and, indeed, the fresh, childish gaiety she had shown during the first few days after their arrival had disappeared. But Jack discreetly decided to keep these thoughts to himself, and let events take their course. He knew that they were in the keeping of a head wiser and more far-seeing than his own—Monella's. Of late they had seen comparatively little of him; he was most of his time either closeted with the king, or had gone, it was said, to Myrlanda, to visit Sanaima, the chief of the 'White Priests.' On these occasions he would be away for two or three days together. Yet, whenever either of the young men chanced to run against him—or, if they met at the king's table—they found no alteration in his manner. Indeed, he showed, if anything, increased kindliness in both his words and actions, often going out of his way to do some little thing, in a manner all his own, to show, before whoever might be present, his cordial feelings towards them. For the rest, he had the air of one whose mind is charged with anxious and weighty thoughts, and both Templemore and Elwood *felt* rather than knew that he was occupied with fears of trouble in the future.

One morning, a few days after the visit to the canyon, Monella invited Leonard to walk out with him, and they went together to the place they had named 'Monella's Height.'

The day was clear and bright, and a slight breeze came sighing through the tree-tops. The scene around was full of soft repose, soothing and curiously satisfying to the mind. But Leonard noticed it not today; his heart beat fast, and his colour came and went, for something in Monella's manner told him that he was about to hear a statement of moment on the subject that was always uppermost in his thoughts. He tried to brace himself to bear the worst, if it must come; but his effort was not too successful.

"My son," Monella presently began, "I promised to speak with you, when I could, upon the matter we talked about one day. Is your mind still the same concerning it?"

Was it? Did he need to ask? Leonard impulsively replied. And he launched into a rhapsody that need not here be given at length. Monella listened in silence till the young man had finished, and then went on,

"Have you considered whether your wish is a wise—a final one? That, were it granted, you must remain here for good? Never to return to your own people?"

"Why, never?" Leonard asked. "In the future—one day, perhaps—"

Monella shook his head.

"You must clearly understand," he said, "that that cannot be. I have told you all along that I never expected to return from my journey here; and now I know that I shall never leave this place. And you and your friend—you will have ere long to decide either to stay here for good, or leave for good. If you elect to go, the king will send you away rich—so rich that you will no more need to strive for wealth; if to stay, he will give you posts of honour where you can profitably employ yourselves in helping me in the great task I have set myself—the teaching of the true religion of the one great God to these my people; for"—he continued, when Leonard looked up at him in surprise—"it is true that I am one of this nation by descent, and that I have, therefore, 'after many days,' only wandered back to mine own people. But I have seen too much of the world outside to love it; my people desire to keep to themselves, and I can only, from what I have seen and experienced, confirm them in that wish. I cannot find it in my conscience to do otherwise. Therefore, we are resolved that there shall be no intercourse between us and the great world beyond. It is useless to say more upon the subject; it is settled beyond all reach of argument or discussion. Hence, it will be necessary for both you and your friend to decide whether to remain and cast in your lot with us for your whole future lives, or to say farewell and return—but not empty-handed—to your own people. It is a serious and weighty matter for you to decide; therefore should not be settled hastily. Nor is there any need for haste; take as long as you please to think it over. Wait awhile, till you have seen more of the place, and have come to know the people better. Or wait until"—here the speaker's voice became impressive well-nigh to sternness—"until I shall have stamped out this serpent brood that hath too long held this fair land in its loathsome coils. Then shall ye see a new era here—an era of peace, and cheerfulness, and godliness—and ye shall see that it is good to dwell in such a country."

"I do not believe that any amount of reflection can alter my wishes in this matter," Leonard answered earnestly. "Painful as the thought of never seeing my friends again would be, yet it would be still harder to leave here and never look again on her my heart has chosen for its queen—aye, for years before I saw her. No! Now that fate has led me to her, nothing in this world shall part us—if the decision rests with me."

Monella regarded the young man fixedly, and there were both affection and admiration in his glance. Very handsome Leonard looked, with the light in his open honest eyes, and the flush upon his cheek. Then Monella's look waxed overcast as from a passing shadow, and he made answer, with a sigh,

"Youth, with its hopes and aspirations, when they come from honest promptings, is always fair to look upon; more's the pity that these aspirations all lead to but one end—sorrow, and disappointment, and weariness. Verily, all is vanity, vanity! We travel by different roads, but we all arrive at the same goal." He looked dreamily away across the landscape to the far distant horizon; then continued, as though talking to himself: "Yet youth pleases, because it desires to live in love—and love is God and Heaven in one. It is the principal of the only two things—it and memory—we carry with us in our passage from this life to the next. Love and memory are two great indestructible attributes of the human soul. True, we take with us our 'character,' as it may be called, but that counts little, unless it be founded upon love. And memory is the ever-living witness showing forth whether our life here has been influenced mainly by selfishness, or ambition, or hate, or cruelty, or—love. For only the love shall live and flourish again; all the rest shall wither and die. Ye hear of 'undying hate,' but there is no such thing. All hates, even, die out at last; love only lives forever and can never die."

He paused, and remained for a space gazing into the distance. Finally, he turned again to Leonard.

"Come with me, and find your friend; I have that to show you that I wish you seriously to consider."

They walked together down the hill. Meanwhile he continued,

"You say your mind is made up, if the decision rests with you. Well, nominally, it rests with the king, of course; but, in reality, I suspect, in this case with the maiden herself. The king is too fond of her—too anxious for her happiness—to desire to thwart her wishes. And he has remarked of late that she is not as she used to be; that she has fits of sadness and melancholy. Her state alarms him. I think, perhaps, he fears it may be the first sign of what is called here the 'falloa.' But," looking at Leonard with a half-smile, "I suspect there is a remedy for her disease, whereas there is none known for the 'falloa.'"

When Leonard heard these words his heart and pulses bounded, and he felt indeed as though walking upon air. Nor did he forget what he owed in the matter to his friend. His breast swelled with gratitude, and he poured out his thanks with a rush of words that stopped only when he caught sight of Templemore coming towards them.

Leonard ran to meet him, and somewhat incoherently explained what Monella had been saying, while Monella led the way to his own apartments in the palace.

When they were seated there he went over again most of what he had impressed on Leonard—for Jack had understood but little of Elwood's impetuous talk—and added,

"Now I want you to advise your friend and consult with him, lest he should decide too hastily; and that must not be. I also must speak further with the king. You see," he continued gravely, "this is a serious thing. The king's son-in-law will look forward to be king one day; therefore he must not be lightly chosen. Again, to choose one of an alien race is no small thing. For myself, I am free from any worldly prejudices about birth, and 'family,' and 'royal blood,' and all that vain, foolish cant. And the king is of the same mind, and wants only to choose for his child the one who pleases her, provided he is worthy. For that I have passed my word to him. I have lived long upon the earth and have consorted with many men; thus I have learned to judge of character and disposition. And I have met none to whom I would sooner trust a daughter of mine own, than to our friend here. On that point, therefore, I have been able to satisfy the king; and fate seems to have settled the rest beforehand. For, incredible as the sceptic may regard it, these two had met in visions long before they encountered one another in the flesh. Thus, in the present, as in the past, fate points the way, and so it will be in the future. For no one can escape his destiny. For good or ill, each has a destiny prepared for him, and that destiny he must perforce fulfil."

XX

THE MESSAGE OF APALANO

The furniture in use in the city of Manoa, in material and style, was not unlike that found in Japan. That in the palace was of exquisite design and finish, much of it inlaid with gold and silver. It was such a cabinet that Monella now unlocked: he took from it a parchment roll.

"This," said he, "is the document I gave the king the first day he received us. Now, of course, it belongs to him; but I have borrowed it, temporarily, to show you. It was written by Apalano, the last descendant of those 'White Priests' who fled this country ages ago with the king Mellenda. In some of the old parchments in my possession it is described how those who thus went away found the empire going everywhere to pieces, and falling a prey to barbaric hordes of black or red or cruel white races; and how they eventually took refuge in the secluded valley high up amongst the peaks of the Andes, of which I have already spoken to you, and dwelt there through many centuries. They had brought with them, and succeeded in cultivating, the 'Plant of Life,' or 'karina'; but, notwithstanding—and albeit it made them all long-lived—the fatal disease, the 'falloa,' claimed them one after another, till Apalano and I alone were left. Then the 'falloa' laid its withering hand upon Apalano also; he lost his last child, and that affected him very deeply; for, before he died, he wrote this strange letter which tells all about myself that I know with certainty; yet hints, as you will see, at still more to be learned in the future. I will read it to you:—

To Sanaima, the Chief White Priest of Manoa. Or,
If Dead, His Descendant or Successor. Or to the
Reigning King of Manoa, Greeting

"'I, Apalano, the last of the descendants of the White Priests who fled with the great King Mellenda, do commend to your care the bearer of this letter, he whom ye will know by the name of Monella. He is, after myself, the sole survivor of our race outside thy land of Manoa. Treat him with all courtesy, respect and confidence, for he is of royal descent, and the unsullied blood of thine ancient line of kings flows in his veins. Mark well his counsels, give heed to his warnings, and observe his rulings; for he comes to restore the true religion of the Great Spirit, and to bring peace and happiness to our land. Long years ago he did receive a grievous injury to the head in combat with a savage foe. This cast a shadow upon his memory of the past, so that he knoweth naught of what went before, and his former life is blank, save for some vague passing glimpses that, at rare times, come back to him in the guise of dreams and visions. We could have told him much of all that went before, but we have refrained;—first for that he might not have rightly comprehended what we had to tell, and next, in mercy; for he hath suffered much. It was deemed best that the recollections of his sufferings should sleep until the time for his awakening should arrive, when the work for which the Great Spirit hath appointed him shall lie before him and shall form his sorrow's antidote and comfort.

"'The memory that hath untimely been suspended—for we know that it may not be destroyed—perchance may be restored to its full power by such an accident as wrecked it; but, failing that, there is but one sure treatment—namely, to drink of the infusion of the herb called 'trenima' that groweth in Myrlanda and nowhere else. Let the stranger Monella, that bringeth this to thee, drink of 'trenima' in accordance with the rules I have laid down for him upon another scroll; let him, for some weeks, take of it sparingly even as I have written; then more frequently, and lo! all his past life, now hidden, shall be revealed to him, the sun shall light up the recesses of his memory, and he shall know himself and what lies before him.

"'And my dying eyes, though unable yet to pierce the future, still can see that his coming amongst you shall be in itself a sign of the truth of these my words. When he shall appear to you I know not; only that it will be at the time the Great Spirit hath appointed—not an hour sooner nor an hour behind that time—ay, not one minute. And herein ye shall read a message from the Almighty Spirit, and ye shall know that Monella's coming at that special time was marked out by the hand of Destiny. And ye shall find upon his body marks whose meaning will be known unto Sanaima, or to him on whom hath fallen his mantle.

"'With my greeting, I bid ye now farewell—ye unto whom this scroll shall be delivered—my first and last message to the land of my forefathers, and to those that now rule there. Through many centuries we, a faithful few, have kept your memory and our love for you green in our hearts; and I and those who have been with me had hoped, as the appointed time drew near, that the Great Spirit would have deigned to grant to us to see our ancient city and our native land. But it was not to be; all have gone save me and him who brings you this; but in him I send the blessing that we have preserved and nursed for you through long years of persecution and despair.

"'If ye would return our love and care for you, I pray you show them unto him we send. I know that he is worthy of them; and, further, that in his own breast he bears for you the sum of all the love we in our own persons would have shown, had we been spared to greet ye—I and those who have preceded me to the land of the Great Spirit.

Farewell!

Apalano

When Monella had finished reading this strange letter, he leaned his chin upon his hand and fell into a reverie, Leonard and Templemore meanwhile looking on in silence. Presently Monella roused himself, and, with a deep-drawn sigh, passed his hand across his forehead with a look of pain. His action was as though he had half-caught some flitting thought or memory, that had, after all, eluded him; and that the effort to retain it had cost him mental pain. After a short interval he said, with one of his rare smiles and in the musical voice that captivated everyone, so full were they of kindliness,

"Now you know as much about me as I know myself. I did not show you this before, because I had been charged to hand it only to those to whom it was addressed; and this is the first opportunity I have since had, for the king sent it to Sanaima, who returned it only a day or two ago. But, since you must now consider seriously the question of your going or remaining, it is right that you should know all I can tell you of myself. It is very little; yet sufficient to explain my present feelings.

You can understand, now that you have read that letter, that I am now, with all my heart and soul, one with these people. I look at everything from their point of view; I consider only their interest, their welfare, their safety, their advantage. If you shall elect to remain with us—to become one of us—you shall find me ever a staunch friend who will do all he can to make you feel at home amongst us, and will place you in positions of great honour. If, on the other hand, you prefer to leave us, you shall not go without such marks of the king's favour as are beyond, perhaps, your dreams. These are the alternatives that lie before you. Take time to ponder them; there is, as I have already told you, no need for an immediate decision."

When, after leaving Monella, the two were once more alone together, Leonard burst out with the thought that filled his mind,

"I scarcely know how to express my feelings. I am full of sadness and yet of joy, and I know not which predominates."

"I know what it will be," said Jack gloomily. "You will stay, and I shall have to return alone. What excuse I shall give to people for leaving you here—dead to them and to the world forever—or whether I shall ever be forgiven for appearing to have deserted you, God only knows. I wish you would think a little upon all this. For the rest, I congratulate you with all my heart. To be the future king of so ancient and remarkable a nation, is a piece of 'luck' that does not fall to everybody. By Jove!" he exclaimed with increasing earnestness, "upon my word I don't wonder at your going in for it—indeed, if—that is—well, if I had not already set my mind upon something else, I would chuck up the world in general and throw in my lot with you and be your—your Prime Minister—or State Engineer—or someother high functionary." And he laughed good-naturedly at the ideas the suggestion called up in his mind.

"Don't let us meet trouble half way," said Leonard hopefully. "The time of parting is not yet; who knows what may turn up? Monella may make us some concession that will meet the case. And now look here. I have been thinking of a plan for sending a message home."

Jack stared.

"How on earth?" he asked.

"It won't be much of a message, and perhaps it will never reach home; but we can try. Let us find a place where we can get a view in the direction of 'Monella Lodge' and watch at night for camp fires out on the far savanna. We must find a spot screened from observation on this side. Then we will bring some powder up from our stores, and flash some signals as Monella had arranged."

"But what good will that do? Even if they are seen it will only be by Indians who will not understand them."

"Never mind. If any Indians see them they are sure to spread the news about; and probably the first place to hear of it will be Daranato, the Indian village where my old nurse Carenna lives. Matava may have told her about the signals, or even other Indians. At any rate, she will be pretty sure to hear of them and let Matava know when he returns; or perhaps even send a message down by someone going to the coast, to say that signals had been seen that showed we were alive on the summit of Roraima."

Jack reflected.

"Yes!" he presently said slowly. "Yes. There is something in the idea. We will try it; it can do no harm. But, to be of any good, we shall have to signal frequently; once or twice would not be of much use."

"Precisely. Before long, Matava will be back from the coast, and will hear of them, and will come out on to the savanna at night to see them for himself. And he would watch night after night with an Indian's patience till he saw them."

"Yes; I suppose Monella won't object? We ought not to do it without his consent. But for that awful forest, we might even go farther; we might make an expedition for a week or two, and get to 'Monella Lodge' and leave a letter there; or even to Daranato, and leave letters to be taken to the coast by the first Indians going that way."

"No, we can't manage that, nor would Monella like us to be away so long. You never know what trouble might turn up here with these priests and their vile crew. And that reminds me of that letter Monella read today. What did you think of it?"

"An extraordinary letter! Really, I feel almost inclined to go back to my former idea that Monella and his friends were all mad together!"

Leonard stared aghast.

"What! You speak of that again?" he exclaimed, real indignation in his tones. "After the way everything has come out—after all Monella's kindness—"

Jack stopped him with a smile and a touch of his hand on the other's arm.

"Put the brake on, old man," he said. "I don't mean anything disrespectful. But if Monella, who already seems to have been about the world and to have seen as much as three ordinary men of three score years and ten—if the point to which his memory reaches is only a portion of his life—why, you see, he must be Methuselah, or the Wandering Jew himself, or someother mythical being. Already, he has puzzled me, times enough, with his extraordinary tales; at the same time you cannot doubt his absolute sincerity. So that if his 'complete' memory is to go back farther still, why—Heaven help us!—we sha'n't know whether we are on our heads or our heels."

After a short silence Leonard spoke.

"But, if they had this 'Plant of Life' with them—those he was with—would that not in part account for it?"

"It might; but it is making large demands on one's credulity. But what I really mean is this. I am inclined, at times, to think Monella a bit mad. He has a religious mania; he has persuaded himself—and evidently, from that letter, has been encouraged by others to believe it—that he has a religious mission to these people. Well, no harm in *that*, you say. No; and that he is honourable, upright, sincere, I feel very certain. Still, he may be self-deceived. He seems to me to be one of those fervidly religious mystics who can persuade themselves into almost anything."

"Yet he is no fanatic. See how mild and gentle he can be; how slow to anger, how just in his discrimination between right and wrong!"

"I admit all that. Still, I repeat, he might easily deceive himself."

That afternoon Leonard sought out Ulama and asked to be allowed to row her on the lake; and to this she smiled a glad assent. When he had rowed the boat out a long distance from the shore, he laid down the oars, and let her drift. A gentle breeze was blowing, and this served to temper the ardour of the waning sun.

"Do you remember the last time we were thus alone, Ulama?" presently he asked her.

"Indeed I do," she answered, her cheek, that had of late been very pale, now glowing with a rosy flush. "But I began to think *you* had forgotten, and were never going to take me out again."

"Ah! It was not my fault, Ulama."

"Whose else could it be?" she asked.

"Well—I cannot tell you now. But, if you remember the occasion, do you remember also what we spoke of?"

The colour deepened in the maiden's face. She bent her head and fixed her eyes dreamily upon the water; and one hand dropped over the boat's side, as on that day of which he had reminded her.

"I then said," he went on, "that I loved you dearly, and asked you whether you could love me in return. And you said you did not understand such love as I described to you. Do you remember?"

"Yes; I remember," she said softly. "But then I said I could scarce credit such sudden love for me; and that you might change. And it seems you have, for, since then, you have never told me that you loved me."

He seized her hand.

"No, Ulama," he cried passionately, "it was not so. I have not altered. But I feared—that—well, that your father might be angered. 'Twas for that reason that I spoke no more to you of love."

"In that you did my father wrong," she answered frankly. "My father loves me far too well to cause me pain and—"

"Ah! Then—would it pain you were I to go away from here and never see you more?"

She started, and a look of mingled fear and grief came into her eyes.

"You are—not—going away?" she faltered anxiously.

"Not if you bid me stay, Ulama. If you but whisper in my ear that you may come to love me—if only a little—then I will stay—stay on always—forget my country, my own people, my friends; give up everything, and live for you—for you alone, my sweet, my gentle Ulama; my beloved Ulama!"

Gradually her head sank until it rested on her hand; her colour deepened, she made no reply, but still gazed pensively into the water.

"Tell me, Ulama—am I to stay or go? Oh, say that you will try to love me!"

He still retained her hand, and now he passed his own gently over it, she making no effort to withdraw it. Thus answered, he pressed his lips upon it, and at this, also, she showed no resentment.

"I would have you stay," she presently murmured softly; "but indeed I fear it is too late for me to try to love you, for my heart tells me you have my love already."

And the boat drifted aimlessly in the evening light. The sun had set, and the moon, the witness of so many lovers' vows—both true and false—had shown her silvery light above the surrounding cliffs; and still the two sat on and scarcely spoke, yet, in speechless eloquence, recounting to each other the old, old tale.

And, when the sweet Ulama left the boat, her heart could scarce contain the joy that filled it; and in her eye there was a light that it had lacked before, so that the king, her father, drew her affectionately to him and asked her what had wrought this wondrous change.

She shyly bent her head and answered him,

"Tomorrow thou shalt know, my father." Then she hid her blushing face upon his shoulder. "I have a favour to ask of thee; but—I would fain not speak of it this evening."

Then, as though fearing that he would wrest from her the secret of her joy, she stole swiftly to her room, and from her window looked across the lake, now shimmering in the silver moonbeams.

For long she sat there motionless, dreaming youth's fond dreams; dwelling, in loving tenderness, on every word and look she could recall of Leonard while the boat had drifted here and there, and the lap, lap, lap, of the ripples against the sides had kept up a soft musical accompaniment to the rhythm of love's heart-beats.

XXI

The Great Devil-Tree

In pursuance of their design of making signals from the summit of Roraima, the two friends made further explorations of the northern side. And this led them into an adventure, one day, that had well-nigh proved fatal to them both.

On mentioning their intention to Monella, he had at first objected; but, upon Leonard's reminding him of the anxiety and distress Templemore's mother and *fiancée* might be, too probably were, in, he had given a reluctant consent.

"Your friends, Dr. Lorien and his son, talked of coming back again," he remarked. "Do you think they are likely to make the journey with Matava, and to be coming to seek for you?"

"Certainly they are coming into this neighbourhood, after orchids," Leonard replied; "and, now you speak of it—though I had not thought about it lately—the news Matava will probably take back may cause such anxiety that they may hurry to get here sooner than they would otherwise have been likely to, in order to make inquiry about us on the spot."

"Matava might lead them to the cavern, if they came to Daranato," said Monella thoughtfully.

"Yes; of course that is possible."

"And a very little ingenuity or a small charge of powder would force an opening; and their way would then be easy to get up here?"

"Certainly."

Monella's face clouded.

"That must not be; you must clearly understand that you must tell me in time if there seems any such probability. I wish not to seem unfriendly towards your friends—and personally I liked them—but to allow them to come in here would be as the beginning of a flood, as the letting out of water. It cannot, must not be."

"Well, after all, it is only a supposition," observed Jack. "Time enough to deal with it, if the occasion actually arise. They were going on to Rio on some law business which was likely to occupy them sometime; they might be detained there indefinitely, they said."

"Quite so," Monella answered decisively. "Only, remember, I rely upon you to inform me in time. And be very cautious and vigilant upon that side of the country, for, as you know, it is in that direction that Coryon and his people have their habitation."

In their walks they were often accompanied by one or both of Ulama's pumas, and on the day referred to the male one, 'Tuo,' as it was called, came after them when they had gone a little way, and trotted quietly beside them; and this, as it turned out, saved their lives.

They came upon a place they had not seen before. Two great iron gates of highly finished workmanship, and picked out with gold, shut in a narrow opening in a high rock. They were such as might form the entrance to a public garden. A broad road wound round from the inside of the gates; but outside, where Templemore and Elwood were, the rocks rose up fifty or sixty feet, or even more, on either side; and though they followed them a considerable distance on both sides of the gates, the rocks still towered up precipitously for as far as they could see.

"This can scarcely be the entrance to Coryon's 'domain,'" said Jack, "or there would be some people about on guard. It must be some kind of public place."

"A cemetery, perhaps," suggested Leonard.

"I believe you've hit it. Well, there's a gate open, so I suppose there's no harm in our having a peep inside."

"Suppose someone were on the watch, and were to pop round and close and lock the gates when we were inside and out of sight," said Leonard suspiciously. "Monella warned us to be wary and to suspect traps."

"We have our revolvers; and, if the worse came to the worst, we could climb over these rocks."

In the result they went inside; then made their way to a wide terrace that ran round an extensive area of horseshoe shape, half natural, half artificial, as they judged. This terrace extended several hundreds of yards in both directions from the point at which they stood; but it narrowed off considerably on one side of the horseshoe. Above and behind it, cut out of the rock, were other terraces, like steps or rows of seats, but broad below and narrowing as they got higher. These went all round, almost to the top of the rocks. It was, in fact, a vast amphitheatre where many thousands of people could stand or sit. At the farther end it was open; and in the centre was a large arena sunk some fifteen feet below the main terrace on which they stood.

This arena opened out into a deep defile beyond, from the rocky heights of which there issued a rushing stream of water that flowed into a large, dark-looking pool below.

But what at once riveted their attention, almost to the point of fascination, was an extraordinary-looking tree that stood in the arena. This tree had no leaves, but branches only. In colour it was of a sombre violet-blue, tinged in places with a ruddy hue. The trunk was about thirty feet in height, and eight or nine feet in diameter. The branches, which were many—a hundred or more probably—drooped over from where the trunk ended and trailed about the ground. But what was most astonishing, these branches were all in motion. Though there was no wind, they waved to and fro, ran restlessly along the ground like lithe snakes, and intertwined one with another, at the same time making a harsh, rustling sound.

Straight in front of where they stood was a long pier of masonry that ran out towards the tree, which was not in the centre of the arena but was nearer to that part of the terrace where it grew narrow. In order the better to observe the object that had so roused their curiosity, the two young men walked across the terrace and some distance along the pier; and, when they had proceeded a little more than half its length, one of the long trailing branches—some of them appeared to be two hundred or three hundred feet in length—came up over the end of the pier, and, with a rustle, made its way swiftly towards them. It was within two or three feet of where they stood looking at it, when the puma, with a loud growl, sprang forward and bit at it. Immediately the branch curled itself round the animal's body and began dragging it along the pier towards the tree. Then two or three other branches advanced and went to the assistance of the first one, coiling round the poor puma and dragging it farther along, despite its teeth and claws and its desperate struggles. In succession, other branches crept up over the end of the stonework, and, just in time, Jack seized Leonard and dragged him back.

"For Heaven's sake come away, man!" he exclaimed in horror. "That tree is *alive*, and will drag us off, if once one of those branches touch us!"

They had stepped back only barely in time, for a moment after a trailing branch swept over the very spot on which they had halted. When assured that they were really out of reach, they stood fascinated, but filled with horror, while they witnessed the unavailing fight made by the poor animal that had saved their lives. More branches came to the aid of the others; they coiled round its mouth and closed it;

round its legs and bound them; and soon, helpless, a mere bundle in the coiling, curling branches, as it were, it was drawn off the pier to the ground below. Then it was rolled on and on till it had almost reached the tree-trunk, where were shorter but thicker and stronger branches waiting for it. These, in their turn, soon coiled round it; then, slowly, they bent upwards, carrying the poor animal in their relentless grasp, and lowered it into a hollow in the centre of the top of the trunk, where it almost disappeared from sight. Then all the thicker branches coiled round it and shut it completely out from view, forming a sort of huge knot round the top of the tree and remaining motionless; while the longer and more slender branches continued to play restlessly about, seeking for further prey. Then, without a word, the two turned away; nor did they speak till they found themselves safely outside the great gates. Then they looked, horror-struck, at each other.

Jack was the first to break the silence.

"Great heavens!" he exclaimed. "What an escape! What an awful monster! What a frightful death! And that poor animal—that saved us both! What shall we say to the princess? Talk of 'traps'! If this gate was left open as a 'trap'—and it looks to me so—we have reason indeed to be thankful!"

"What *is* it?" Leonard asked at last.

"A 'devil-tree.' It is a carnivorous tree. I've seen a small one before; in a forest in Brazil that we were working through. One of the dogs got caught in it and was nearly killed before we cut it free with our axes. And then it was badly hurt, and so was I; a branch caught hold of my hand and tore some of the flesh off it. And where we cut this branch it *bled*! A dark crimson-blue liquid oozed out that stank! Oh, there, I can't tell you what the stench was like! I've smelt *some* bad smells in my time, but that beat anything I ever came across! But that was only a small bush. I had no idea they could grow into great flesh-eating monsters like this! Why, that thing must have been there a thousand—ah—two thousand years, I should say. Fully that."

"But," said Leonard, "why is it kept here? who feeds it—and—what—is—it—fed—on?"

He asked this last question slowly, and looked at the other in blank, horrified amazement.

"It can't live without food," he continued. "And it must want a lot too. Whoever can take the trouble to get it food of the only kind—as I suppose—that it would care for? And why is it there in the middle of that strange place? One would almost think it was kept there as a kind of show or curiosity; and yet—we have never heard about it all the time we have been here! And it is there, with the gate open, no fence to guard people, or notice to warn them. Well! It's a mystery to me!"

But if they had been astounded and horror-stricken at what they had seen, they were still more mystified and upset by Ulama's behaviour when they told her of their adventure; for she fainted right off and, when she recovered, seemed so overcome with terror as to be unable to say a word. No explanation would she give; save that now and then she murmured, almost in a moan, to herself,

"Then it *is* true! And I never knew! It is horrible—too horrible!"

When Leonard expressed his sorrow about the puma, she hardly seemed to notice it.

"Ah yes!" she said once. "Poor Tuo! I shall miss him—and such a death, too! But oh, he saved you and your friend! And then, he was but an animal—but the others!"

At her express desire they promised not to speak to anyone else about it.

"I will tell you why—or you will know why—later," she added. "But you can speak privately to Monella about it; to no one else just now!"

When they found an opportunity of speaking to him about it, he looked very grave.

"You have had a narrow escape," he said. "Heaven be thanked you did escape. I cannot explain more to you now, but may be able to do so shortly. Meantime, please do as the princess says, and keep this matter to yourselves."

All this time Leonard's relations with Ulama had remained unchanged; they had not been placed on any settled footing. Monella had asked him to take time to make up his mind, and had intimated that nothing would be said or done meanwhile. Leonard had, however, been too impatient to put his fate to the test to be able to wait after the encouragement Monella had given to him. But, whether Ulama had spoken on the subject with her father, he knew not; for it so happened that he had not seen her alone since their love-scene in the boat.

And now she was evidently much discomposed about their adventure with the 'devil-tree'; though she did not refer to it again.

Naturally too, the recollection of it was very much in the minds of the two young men. Leonard asked Templemore, one day, what the branches of the one he had seen were like.

"They were covered with small excrescences," he replied, "that are suckers and piercers in one. They pierce the flesh and then suck the blood. The whole affair is a sort of gigantic vegetable 'octopus,' or devil-fish, only that it has a hundred or more 'arms' or branches instead of eight, as the octopus has. I have heard of devil-fish having been caught as large as eighty feet in length, on the coast of Newfoundland. But I never knew that its vegetable prototype grew to anything like the size."

"Of course I have seen devil-fish," said Leonard thoughtfully; "but they have a mouth—a great beak—to which their arms carry the food. Do you think it is the same here? You saw that the branches carried the poor puma up into a hollow in the top of the trunk. Do you suppose the thing has a kind of mouth there?"

"Goodness only knows! It must be an awful sort of affair, if it is so. The whole thing is monstrous and uncanny. Don't let us talk about it!"

But, as a result of this experience, they sought in another direction for a likely place from which to make their intended signals; and finally they found one convenient for their purpose. Then they made two or three trips to the canyon to bring up the requisite powder. They also brought back from the secret cave a number of things Monella wanted. From the first, at his suggestion, they had told no one except the king, Ulama, and Zonella, of the means by which they had gained access to the mountain; and these had promised to keep the knowledge to themselves.

"The place has evidently been so long unvisited," Monella had remarked, "that probably most of those who once knew of it have forgotten all about it. No need to remind them just now. Many years ago, as I have been informed, a project was started for filling it up."

"Filling it up!"

"Yes, and if you go to the other end of the canyon—that by which we entered—you will find, even now, in the thick wood that everywhere surrounds the top of the canyon, vast numbers of great boulders that were quarried from the surrounding cliffs and hauled to the edge in readiness to be thrown down. They lie, in fact, just over the cavern we came in by. There they have remained for a very long time, it seems. Had that intention been carried out, all our work in cutting through the forest and finding the entrance to the cavern, as you can see, would have been thrown away."

"And what stopped it?"

"It is said that the people threatened a rebellion. The belief in the eventual return of Mellenda—of whom you have heard—is deep-seated; and, though the people here are anxious enough to keep to themselves, they would not assent to closing irrevocably the only means by which their hero could gain admittance, should he ever come."

"Do they expect him to come with a host of followers—a conquering army—or do they expect the great lake to come back, and that he will arrive with a grand fleet of ships?" Templemore asked, with somewhat of a sarcastic smile.

Monella passed his hand across his brow in the half-dreamy manner that was his at times, as though striving to collect his thoughts, or to arrest and force into shape some half-formed conception that had flitted across his mind and escaped his grasp. For a minute he stared vacantly away into the distance and was silent. Then, with a look as though of pain at failing to catch the fleeting image, he turned away, saying simply, "I cannot tell you."

During the days that followed, Templemore passed much of his time in the museums; time that Elwood spent in a lover's dream of happiness with Ulama. In the relics of the former history of this strange people, Templemore took a deep interest; and in the archives and ancient manuscripts he found many evidences of the former existence of scientific and engineering knowledge that astonished and perplexed him. On the true meaning and import of some of these he sought the help of Monella, who would frequently accompany him in these visits, and, from his better knowledge of the language, was able to assist him to unravel their curious contents.

"These people must once have been great engineers and architects!" he exclaimed in surprised admiration on one of these occasions.

Monella smiled and made reply,

"There is nothing so surprising in that, if you comprehend the true significance of the gigantic earthworks still extant in many places on this continent. Have you seen any of them?"

"No; but I have both heard and read of them."

"I have seen them; and I tell you your mind can form no idea of their extent, of the scientific knowledge and the prodigious amount of time and labour that must have been expended on them, unless you actually see them. They are of various forms, mostly geometrical figures upon a vast scale—miles in extent. The wonderful thing is that a certain figure is repeated exactly in different places hundreds of miles apart. Yet you shall take your cleverest engineers of the present day, give them the advantages—or supposed advantages—of all your modern discoveries and machinery, and scientific instruments, and, say, unlimited workpeople to do their building, and *then* it would tax all their skill to construct a work *exactly* similar to one of those great figures. Yet now, upon some of them, trees are growing that must be over a thousand years old!"

"And what were they for—what was their object?" Templemore asked.

Then there came over the other's face again that curious look as of one seeking for a lost recollection; but it seemed to evade him, and he answered somewhat as before,

"I think I ought to be able to tell you," he replied, "but I cannot now seem to remember."

It was while thus together one day that Templemore asked him for some further information concerning the 'Plant of Life.'

"You have told me," he said, "that your people, with whom you lived in that secluded valley high up in the Andes, had with them the 'karina' and cultivated it. Therefore I suppose you yourself have been in the habit of taking it?"

"Always. And in my travelling to and fro in the world I always had with me a good supply of the dried herb. I was accustomed to leave stores of it in certain towns, so that if I lost what I had with me by any accident, there was more within easy reach."

"I see. But what I am puzzled about is this: why, if the virtues of the plant are so great, do people ever die at all? And why do some live longer than others?"

"As to the first question," Monella answered, "man was never intended to live on this earth forever. The human frame *must* wear out sooner or later. As to the second query, some constitutions are naturally stronger than others, and these endure longer, just as is the case in the world outside where the plant is not known. The effect of the plant is simply to keep the blood pure, if originally pure. If, however, there is an inherited taint, that taint will make itself felt sooner or later and undermine the vitality of the system. In this case the plant will only result in ensuring a somewhat longer life than would otherwise have been the case. Sooner or later the vitality will fall off and gradual decay set in, although (the blood being kept still pure) ordinary diseases are kept at bay. Lastly, there is the question of the will."

"The *will*?"

"Yes; that has a most powerful influence. If a man who has inherited a constitution that is absolutely sound, from ancestors who have possessed the same through many generations, and if he has, in addition, a strong *will*, powerful beyond the average, he may live longer—if he is so minded."

"I—do not understand you," said Templemore, somewhat puzzled.

Monella gazed at him with a smile that was full of sadness.

"You would," he answered, "if you were old yourself; if you had outlived all that made life worth having—your wife, and others you love, your ambitions, your hopes. *Then* does the soul grow weary, and restless as well; it is like unto a bird that is caged whose time for migration has come. It will either fret or pine itself to death, or beat itself to death against the bars of its cage. Only two things can then keep the soul from taking its flight; the *will* to live to complete some unfinished work, or a delight in a worldly, wicked life. A nature superlatively evil, like Coryon's, may enable its possessor to live on and on for an indefinite time; where better men take the 'falloa' and die. Or a man, not himself enamoured of life upon this earth, may exert his *will* to carry out to its end some great work to benefit his fellow-creatures, and he too may keep the 'falloa' at arm's length for an unusually long period. In other words, the 'falloa' is a form of melancholia, of weariness with the world, of an inward sense that life's work is completed. It is the result of that feeling that we are told took possession at last even of him who has been called the Wise Man of the World—King Solomon—whose wisdom and riches and power only brought him to the same point I have indicated—that at which the soul declares that all earthly things are but vanity."

On another occasion, Templemore was accompanied by Zonella and Colenna; and the latter took him into a gallery he had not before seen, the door being usually kept locked.

In it, to his surprise, were ranged hundreds of stands of arms and military uniforms, helmets, spears, shields, swords, daggers, and red tunics, all kept in splendid condition, as though for instant use. All the helmets had little silver wings at their sides, and the shields were engraved in the centre with a strange hieroglyphic, the same that he had noticed chiselled upon the fronts of many of the principal buildings.

"There," said Colenna, "are the arms and uniforms of Mellenda's soldiers. Over in Myrlanda, in the great temple of the White Priests, are hundreds more; all kept ready for use, as you see these here. You see the silver wings upon the helmets, similar to those on that of Mellenda's suit that stands in the other gallery. And that figure upon the shields is the sacred sign that was engraved upon his signet-ring. It signifies his seal or sign-manual. Wherever you see that mark, it refers to him; on a building it implies that he designed or built it. His royal colour was red, as the king's today is blue; and these red tunics are for his soldiers."

"When they come," said Jack, discreetly repressing the incredulous smile that almost forced itself upon his lips.

"When *he* comes," said Colenna, lifting his hat reverently. "Yes, when *he* returns to us."

"You don't believe in that, I know," interposed Zonella; "yet we all do; and it is a good thing we do, I think, for I fear many in the land would go mad under their dread of Coryon, if they did not believe in a happier future for the country. But there," she added sadly, "it does not matter to *you*. You have no interest in what may go on here in the future. You intend to go back to your own country, and care little for the sorrows or the fate of those you leave behind."

Colenna had walked away some little distance, to examine a shield that he thought was not quite so bright as it should be.

"Not care!" Jack exclaimed, impulsively. "Why, how can you say that? It is that thought that grieves me all the time I am here; that makes me doubt how I shall ever be able to make up my mind to leave. To leave behind one's dearest—"

Zonella turned to him quickly, with a heightened colour and a bright look. This was so unexpected that he stopped and hesitated.

"Well?" she said. "You said your dearest—"

"My dearest friend, Leonard—of course," he answered, looking at her in some surprise.

But Zonella's face paled, and she turned away.

"Let us go," she said with a shiver, as though a cold wind had blown upon her. "This old gallery is kept locked up so much it gets to smell musty, and makes one feel quite faint."

XXII

SMILES AND TEARS

One morning, Monella sought Leonard and reverted to their former conversation about Ulama.

"You have well considered all the words I spoke to you, my son?" he said. "Are you still of the same mind?"

"I had hoped that you knew me too well to think it necessary to ask the question," Leonard said earnestly. "Since I first looked upon Ulama, my love for her has been given past all recall. I have never wavered in my resolution to remain here for her dear sake, if I may hope to gain the king's consent."

"Then," returned Monella, "the king would talk with you concerning it. Let us go to him."

And, without further preface, he led the young man into the private chamber of King Dranoa, where he left him.

The king, Leonard thought, looked ill and careworn; but he received him with great kindness, and in a manner that quickly reassured the anxious lover.

"It has been no secret to me for sometime," said Dranoa, "that thou hast looked with affection upon my child. She, too, hath spoken to me; I see that she hath set her heart upon this thing, and I love her too dearly to desire to thwart her wishes, unless for some weighty reason. Here I see no such reason; for, though thou art a stranger, yet thou art worthily recommended by one upon whose judgment I have learned to place reliance. He that led thee hither is not a man to act lightly or without full consideration in a matter of such paramount importance; if thou hast gained his confidence and esteem, I doubt not that there are good reasons for it. He hath the unerring eye that pierces to the very heart, and that no hypocrisy, no cunning, can deceive. Were it the case that my dominions were today the great empire over which my forefathers held sway, I would seek such a man's advice in the appointment of my generals, my ministers, my governors for distant districts. Therefore do I feel that I can rely upon his judgment, even in a matter so momentous as the choice of one to espouse my child and to succeed me on my throne. And knowing, as I do full well, that the 'falloa' hath laid its hand upon me and that my days in this my land are numbered, it is grateful to mine heart to feel that my child will be comforted, when I am gone, by one whose affection for her is pure and wholly hers, and who will have at his side a friend and counsellor who will guide his youthful steps in the path that I would have him follow. This conviction hath lifted from mine heart a grievous trouble, and hath enabled me to bear without sorrow or regret the knowledge that the fatal sickness hath taken hold upon me. For the fact that I shall now soon quit this earthly life I care nothing in itself; it hath been the fear of what would then befall that hath filled me with forebodings and with fear. But, if I see—as I hope to see—the power of the Black Coryon broken and destroyed forever; my child wedded to one worthy of her love and honour; my successor aided and advised by one so competent to guide as is thy friend, then indeed I shall feel I can lay down the burden of life with thanksgiving, and take my way to the great unknown of the hereafter without fear, without regret, without a sigh; but, instead, with the great content of one who feels he hath nothing more to wish or hope for upon earth. For know, my son," continued Dranoa with grave emphasis, "no man wisheth to prolong his life for that which it hath yielded, but rather for that which he is hopeful it may yield. The proof of this is easy; no man desireth to live his life over again; therefore he is, at heart, and from actual experience, dissatisfied and wearied with life; not charmed with it. Yet do many cling to it, fatuously believing, in the face of all their own actual experience, that it shall yet, in the future, afford them joys and gratifications they have never found in the past. These, my son, are the words of one who hath lived long enough to gain the wisdom that teacheth how to sift the wheat from the chaff."

Dranoa paused, and remained silent awhile. Then he resumed, with a change of tone,

"But I wish not to weigh down thy young imaginings with the sober knowledge that belongeth not to thine years but to mine. It will be sufficient to give thee counsel that is more suited to the circumstances. Therefore I say this to thee: thou hast a good heart and good instincts—trust them, follow them honestly; and leave the rest to the Great Spirit that ruleth over all. And now I have but one more thing to say; it were better for the present that this that is between us were not known openly. Personally, that will not concern thee. When the time hath come, I will myself announce it to my people. Meanwhile, thy mind will be at rest with the knowledge of my approval of thy suit."

Leonard gratefully poured out his thanks to the kind-hearted king; then went to seek Ulama.

He found her sitting alone in an apartment that overlooked the lake, so deep in thought that she did not hear his coming. She was leaning on the window-sill gazing pensively upon the beauties of the scene that lay outspread before her.

But Leonard thought, as he caught sight of her and stayed his steps upon the threshold, that she herself was the fairest creation of all, posed as she was with that unconscious grace and charm that seemed with her to be innate. For a full minute he stood in silence; then, still without moving towards her, he softly called her name, as though fearing to approach her till he had permission.

She turned her head towards him with no surprise, but with a look of sweetest pleasure in her gentle eyes.

"I did not hear you," she said dreamily, "and yet—I know not why—I was looking for your coming."

"And what were you thinking of so profoundly, sweet Ulama?"

"I was thinking," she replied, "how much more beautiful our lake and its surroundings have seemed to me of late. I scarce noticed them before; I suppose because I have known them all my life. Yet, now that you have pointed out some of their beauties, I not only feel and appreciate them, but I note many others on all sides that I never saw before. It is very strange! I wonder why it is?"

"It is *love*, Ulama," Leonard said, coming quietly to her side and laying his hand lightly on her shoulder. "Love can make the plainest works of nature beautiful; small wonder then if it makes those that are really so display new and unsuspected charms. It is because love has taken up his dwelling in your heart that you now see new beauties in these familiar scenes."

But Ulama shook her head sagely, and smilingly made answer,

"You know you told me that the first time you saw our lake you deemed it the fairest spot on all the earth. And you did not know me then, so could not love me. How then can what you say explain it?"

Leonard laughed and took her hand in his.

"You forget that I had seen you in my dreams and had loved you long before," he said. "Perhaps some instinct told me that here I should find the abode of her who already had my heart. Or, if that explanation does not please you, here is another. Love and sympathy are inseparable; you admire, now, things that you thought little of before, because you see that *I* admire them."

"Yes; that may be," Ulama admitted, with a thoughtful look. "But then, it does not explain why *you* should see beauties where *I* did not. I think you must have a quicker appreciation of the beautiful in nature than is given to me."

"It may be so; and that in turn explains how it came about that I was so quick to realise the beauty of the fairest daughter of Manoa!" And Leonard's look was so tender, so full of loving admiration, that it brought a rosy glow to Ulama's cheek. "And it also reminds me that I sought you here to tell you something of importance, something that has brought joy and gladness to my heart. I have just been talking about you with the king."

The colour in the girl's cheek grew deeper; and now she turned her glance again upon the landscape that lay sleeping in the morning sunlight.

"Dear love," continued Leonard, "think what it means to me— to both of us, I hope—when I tell you that the king has given me permission to ask you to give yourself to me! Ah! Not only has he done that, but he has done it in a manner—accompanied it with kind words of trust and confidence that have filled my whole heart with gratitude. He speaks as though I had already *proved* that which I can only hope to show in the future—my true desire to make myself worthy of your love. His kindness and many marks of friendship towards one who is but a stranger here have overwhelmed me. I feel the whole devotion of my life to you and him can scarce repay such generous, ungrudging proofs of his confidence and favour."

"You have a good friend in Monella," Ulama said quietly. "He never fails to speak well of you when occasion offers. And he is one of our own race, and has had great experience of the world outside, of which we know nothing; and my father knows he can rely on his opinion."

"Yes, I know that is true, dear love, and my heart burns with gratitude to him too. And now, beloved"—and he put his arms round her and drew her to him—"may I not think of you as all my own? Let me hear you say with those dear lips that you know now what love is, that it has sprung up unforced in your pure heart; let me hear you say, 'Leonard, I love you!'"

And, as he drew her closer to him and her head nestled upon his shoulder, a whisper, that seemed but a faint sigh, breathed softly the words so sweet to hear for the first time from a loved-one's lips—"I love you!"

Later in the day Leonard told Templemore of his interview with the king; and, as he did so, a look came over his face that, as his friend expressed it to himself, "did one's heart good to see, even if but once in a lifetime!"

"In your happiness I too feel happy, dear old boy," he said. "And I should have little concern, for the time being, if only those at home knew we were alive and well. As it is, the thought of their anxiety troubles me unceasingly."

"Let us hope our signal flares were seen and will be reported," Leonard answered. "I think they must have been seen; and, if so, Carenna is sure to hear of it, and will find some way of sending word."

This referred to what they had done to carry out Leonard's suggestion. After some perseverance in watching from the spot they had selected, they saw, one evening, camp fires far out on the savanna. At once they made their signals with small heaps of powder, and these they repeated several times. No response whatever came; nor did they expect any. There was nothing for it but to wait patiently in the hope that their signals had been seen.

Then ensued a time, lasting many weeks, which was almost uneventful. To Leonard and Ulama it was one uninterrupted dream of blissful happiness. To Templemore it was pleasant and interesting, for he found plenty to engage his mind. He studied the designs of the chief buildings; of the bridges that spanned the streams that fed the lake. In the arches and general construction of these he formed engineering ideas that were new to him. He visited often the great waterfall that formed the outlet of the lake, and declared that the sight of the vast body of water shooting out in its leap of two thousand feet, its deep, thundering roar, and the play of colour when the sun shone into the mist and spray, made up a combination that threw Niagara itself—which he had seen—into the shade.

One day, when Ulama and Zonella were alone together, the former thus addressed her friend,

"Sometimes of late I have fancied there has been some unpleasant passage between you and Leonard's friend. I myself am so fortunate, so happy, that I like not to see those about me otherwise. I would have all my friends as happy as myself." And she took Zonella's hand and rubbed her face affectionately against it. "Tell me, Zonella, have you two quarrelled?"

For a moment Zonella's face, usually so pleasant to behold, looked hard and almost fierce. Then it softened, and, with a loud cry, she threw her arms around Ulama; she hid her face in the gentle bosom, and burst into a torrent of impassioned tears.

It was sometime before Ulama, greatly surprised as well as pained and puzzled, could understand the meaning of this outburst; but presently Zonella, growing somewhat calmer, sobbed out,

"Ah! *You*—you little know, little think what I have suffered. He cares no more for me than he does for you—perhaps less. His heart is elsewhere; he is set upon going away from our land, and only his regard for his friend delays him."

Ulama's beautiful face bent over Zonella's, and her tears fell upon the other's cheek as she pressed her lovingly to her bosom.

"Alas! Alas! My poor Zonella! And is it possible that love, which has been so sweet to me, should bring to you but pain and suffering? I almost fear for my own happiness; that my selfishness in yielding to it has blinded me to what was going on with the others. But it never occurred to me that love that is to me so wonderful in the joy and pleasure it confers, could also be the cause of misery and sorrow. And yet," she added thoughtfully, "you are not without one to love you. Poor Ergalon has long been faithful to his love for you. Oh, how strange and contrary it all seems! Poor fellow! Perhaps you have made him suffer even as you yourself have suffered. Can his love not console you? I know so little myself that what I say may be only foolishness, yet—"

Zonella smiled faintly, and shook her head. Then she kissed the other tenderly.

"Let us say no more, my dear," she said. "I am sorry I gave way as I did; but you took me by surprise. Perhaps, too, your implied advice is wise. It might be better to try to love the one you *know* does truly love you, than to fret your heart out after one who loves you not, and who is beyond your reach. At least, as you say, there *is* one in the world who loves me."

Thus the time sped on. Monella was much away; sometimes for a week together; so the young men saw comparatively little of him. Templemore, on one occasion, expressed a wish to visit Myrlanda with him, but Monella said there were difficulties in the way.

"It is better you two should remain here for the present," he declared. "At a future time, let us hope it may be different."

But one day Monella came to him with a look of gravity that at once aroused his interest.

"It is time," he said, "that I should show you something of the truth, that you may understand what lies before us. Can you brace up your courage and your nerve to stand a severe trial?"

Templemore opened his eyes in astonishment.

"Need you ask?" he answered. "Have you ever known me wanting in courage?"

"Ah, no. But this that I refer to requires courage of a different sort. Yet it must be faced. But I warn you it will be a shock. Make up your mind to a test that will tax all the nerve you can summon to your aid."

"And Leonard too?" Jack inquired, wondering.

"No. Say nothing to him. Let his dream be happy while it may. Be ready to come out with me tonight, when Ergalon shall come to seek you. And bring your rifle."

XXIII

The Devil-Tree by Moonlight

It was about ten o'clock when Templemore, with Ergalon as guide, came out from the king's palace by a side-entrance that was little used, and the door of which the latter now opened with a key. Outside, at a short distance, they found Monella pacing up and down.

Before leaving, Templemore had told Leonard just so much as would explain his absence; then had managed to slip away unobserved by their friends of the king's court.

The night was fine but chilly, and all three were muffled up. In the sky overhead the moon shone calm and clear, lighting up the valley with great distinctness; but across its face wild-looking clouds were scurrying, showing that a strong wind was blowing up above, though little of it was felt below. Only now and then an eddying gust would sweep down the hillside and stir the trees around them, then die away with a rustling sigh or a low moan.

Ergalon led the way; skirting the town he took a roundabout road that Templemore soon saw led to the neighbourhood of the scene of their adventure with the devil-tree, though they were approaching it from a different direction. Finally, they entered a thick wood that covered a steep hill; and now Templemore's companions made signs to him to observe strict silence and to proceed as quietly as possible. When they had reached the summit of the slope, and stood on the ridge within the shadow of the trees, which here ceased abruptly, Templemore uttered a half-smothered exclamation. Instantly, he felt Monella's heavy hand upon his shoulder grasping him with a grip of iron; and it brought to him the recollection of the caution he had received.

"Whatever you see or hear," Monella had rejoined, "you must remain absolutely quiet and utter no sound; do nothing that might betray our presence."

What had excited Templemore's surprise was the fact that he found himself looking down into the great amphitheatre in which stood the well-remembered tree. Its long trailing branches were still moving about swiftly in their strange, restless fashion; but most of the shorter and thicker branches were curled up at the top of the trunk in the same kind of *knot* as they had formed after carrying thither the body of the puma. Viewed in the bright moonlight, the tree was a hideous monstrosity that had yet a certain terrible fascination which attracted and retained the sight while it revolted and repelled the mind. The coiled branches upon the top reminded one irresistibly of the snakes entwined round the head of the Medusa; they formed a kind of crown, of a character suitable to the frightful monster whose formless head, if one may so term it, they encircled. The appearance of the whole thing was repulsive, ghastly, ghoulish. There was that in the mere form and outline of this gruesome wonder of the vegetable world that instinctively aroused aversion. Its naked branches—that in ordinary circumstances could belong only to a dead tree—its colour—half funereal, half of a deep blood-tint almost unknown amongst botanical productions—its never ceasing movement, so suggestive of an everlasting hunting after prey, of an insatiable craving for its hateful diet of flesh and blood, of sleepless hunger, of tireless rapacity and relentless cruelty—all these made up an unnatural creation that appalled the instincts and chilled the very blood of those who looked upon it. This had been the feeling, or combination of feelings, that had made itself felt in Templemore's mind when he had first seen the spectacle by daylight; it impressed itself much more strongly now that he saw the tree in the cold moonlight—now standing out clear and well-defined, now plunged into semi-obscurity, as the hurrying clouds chased each other across the sky above and threw their fleeting shadows beneath.

From the spot where the three men stood a clear view was presented of the opposite side of the enclosure—*i.e.*, of the side nearest to the tree, which was there sufficiently close to the main terrace for its branches to sweep over it; but the terrace was here protected by a covered-way or verandah formed of metal gratings, the interstices in which were small enough to keep the dreadful writhing snake-like branches from pushing through them. When Templemore had seen the place before, this part of the terrace had been open; for the metal screens, or gratings, were, in reality, sliding shutters that could be withdrawn into grooves in the rock beyond. Here, at the end of the covered-way, was a gateway that formed the entrance to the labyrinth of caverns and galleries in the cliff in which Coryon and his adherents lived.

These sliding screens were movable at the will of those within the gateway. They could be either moved along in their grooves and thus protect those traversing the covered-way, or withdrawn, so that the branches of the fatal tree, in that case, guarded the entrance most effectually; for no man might then venture to approach the gateway and live.

Underneath, there were cells in the terrace, also within reach of the tree; and screened off, in like manner, by sliding grated doors. Through these gratings came faint beams of light.

Templemore noted all these things; yet, while his gaze wandered to them, each time the tree itself attracted it again and seemed to hold it spell-bound; and he waited—waited, hardly daring to breathe; waited for he knew not what; waited as one expectant and oppressed by a dim unshapen foreshadowing of some new and nameless horror.

Nor was it without reason; for, slowly, the coiled 'crown' unfolded, and *something* came little by little into view. Gradually the *something* rose out of the hollow in the trunk, was carried up clear of it, then lowered over the side towards the ground. In shape it was cylindrical, and of a colour that could not be discovered in the fitful moonlight. Soon it was deposited upon the ground, and the branches that had lowered it released their hold, and it remained for a brief space untouched. Then other branches crept up to it with tortuous twistings and, coiling round it, raised and swung it to and fro, then quickly dropped it. Anon, yet other branches would do the same; only, in their turn, to drop it or to hand it on to others. Thus was it passed about; now lifted high in the air by one end, then by the other, anon dangled horizontally in mid-air. In time it made the circuit of the tree; but each branch, or set of branches that laid hold of it, rejected it eventually, as though, by some fell but unfailing instinct, they knew there was nothing left in it to minister to their hateful appetite. And all the while the shadows came and went, and the moon looked down between them and lighted up the hideous scene.

Meantime, from out the dark and filthy water and thick slime of the large pool a few hundred yards away, crawled uncouth monsters the like of which Templemore had never looked upon, save, perhaps, in some fanciful representations of creatures said to have existed in pre-historic times. These mis-shapen reptiles were from ten to twelve feet in length. They had heads and tails like crocodiles, and in many other respects resembled them; but in place of the usual scales they were covered with large horny plates several inches in diameter; and in the centre of each plate was a strong spine or spike, thick at the base but sharp at the point, and four or five inches long.

These creatures crawled up to the fateful tree; and it was quickly evident that they came to claim their share in the foul repast—the dry husk and bones from which the tree had sucked the rest. Their armour made them safe against the tree; for the branches no sooner touched their bodies than they recoiled, baffled by the sharp points they everywhere encountered. Two or three of these horrid reptiles began to drag the dead body towards their haunt, and finally carried it away, but not without several tussles with the twisting, curling branches which seemed loth to relinquish their prey; or, perhaps, wished to play with it a little longer, as a cat might with a mouse.

Monella had handed his field-glass to Templemore, still keeping a hand upon his shoulder. The young man placed it to his eyes, and in an instant gasped out,

"Great heavens! *It is a human body!*"

Yes!—if that may be so called which was but the mutilated husk of what had once been a living, breathing, human being! But now there was little left beyond a shapeless form!

Templemore felt sick, and almost reeled; but Monella's grasp up-held him, and was a silent reminder that he was expected to master his emotions, however strong and painful they might be.

"It is no time to give way," Monella whispered in his ear. "Wait and watch!"

It was, however, almost more than Templemore could do. He felt like Dante led by his guide to witness the tortures of the damned. But here, as it seemed to him, was a scene that rivalled in horror, if not in agony, even the scenes in the 'Inferno.' He set his teeth and clenched his hands; his breath was laboured, and his heart almost stood still. But for Monella's hold upon his shoulder he must have fallen.

But now there came out of the covered-way two figures; they stood on the terrace and bent their gaze upon the scene, silent and motionless. They were dressed in flowing robes of black, or some dark colour, that were emblazoned on the breast with a golden star.

Grim, weird figures were they; their dark forms showing sharply against the light-coloured rocks behind them, the while they gazed with cruel composure upon the ghastly contention between the loathsome reptiles and the tree.

When it was ended, and the beasts had disappeared with their prey into the dark waters of the pool, one of the figures on the terrace put a whistle to his mouth, and a low piping sound reached the ears of the concealed watchers.

Immediately a rumbling noise was heard; and one of the sliding gratings beneath the terrace rolled back, thereby disclosing a cavernous cell, in which was a lighted lamp on a rough table. Then a figure seated by it, his face buried in his hands, sprang up with a loud cry, and retreated into the thick gloom beyond. But the terrible trailing branches swept in after him, twined round his legs and threw him down, then quickly drew him out feet foremost. Vainly he shrieked, and clutched at this and that; at the table, at the edge of the sliding door; relentlessly, inexorably, he was dragged from one futile hold to another, upsetting the lamp in his struggles, till he was outside. Other branches swooped down upon him, coiling round him in all directions, and stifling his cries as, slowly, with an awful deliberation and absence of hurry, or even of the appearance of effort, he was hauled high into the air and disappeared into the hollow of the fatal tree. The great branches silently arranged themselves into their knot-like circle; at another sound of the low whistle the sliding door returned to its place with a sullen rumble, and the two dark-robed spectators turned and left the place.

Then Monella and Ergalon also came away; and it is no disparagement of Templemore's courage or 'nerve' to state that they had almost to carry him between them. When they had got to a safe distance, Monella placed him on a boulder, and held to his lips a flask containing a strong cordial. Templemore, who had been on the point of fainting, felt revived by it at once; the liquid seemed to course quickly through his veins, and the feeling of deadly sickness, after a time, passed away.

Monella, meanwhile, contemplated him with compassion and concern, but said no word. Presently Templemore gasped out,

"What horrors! What frightful, cold-blooded atrocity! What a race of foul fiends! Great heavens! To think such things go on in this fair land—a land that seems so peaceful, so contented, so free from ordinary pain and suffering!"

"Ah, my son," replied Monella, and there was an indescribable sadness in his tones, "*now* you can understand the great horror in the land; that which has oppressed it for many long ages; that casts a gloom upon people's lives; that turns to gall and bitterness what, but for it, would be a life of innocent enjoyment."

"But why—?" Templemore exclaimed almost fiercely; but the other checked him.

"I think I know what you would say," Monella went on. "You would know two or three things, I think. To the first question (as I read it) I reply that the reason you have not heard of this thing from other people is that they have learned, from long habit, never to refer to it, even to one another. Almost incredible, you think? Not more so than are many things that happen in your own life, in your own country. I could name many known to all, yet alluded to by none—often wrongly, as I hold. Still, there is the fact. It is the same here. This horror in the land broods over, enthrals the people; yet, because they hold it in such dread, they make an affectation of pretending not to know of its existence; perhaps, in mercy to their children.

"Next, it surprises you that *I* have not told you sooner. The answer is simple. You are not like myself; I am one of this people; you are but a sojourner in the land—a visitor. I had the desire to make your sojourn here as pleasant as it could be; that your interest in the many curious things you see about you should not be lessened, nor your stay here rendered unhappy by the knowledge of that which you have seen tonight—the earlier knowledge of which could have done no good to anyone.

"Lastly, you naturally desire to know why, in that case, I have now chosen to enlighten you. For this reason: the time is approaching when certain plans of mine and of the king's will be completed, and when I devoutly hope we may be able, with God's help, to end this thing forever. In that I shall ask you to help us—I hope you will aid us all you can."

"I will," said Templemore impetuously. "Against such a hellish crew as that I am with you heart and soul. I think I begin to understand—"

"Yes, I never doubted your readiness to take part with us. But it was necessary to give you absolute proof of what goes on, that you might understand those with whom we have to deal. You have now seen for yourself—"

"Ay, I have seen!" Jack shuddered.

"And will now understand that, when the time comes to extirpate this serpent brood, there must be no hesitation, no paltering, no half-and-half measures, no mercy. It will be of no use to kill the old snakes and leave the brood to grow up again, or eggs to hatch. Do you take in my meaning?"

"Yes, and think you will be right and well justified."

"Good. If you wonder why, knowing all this, I have done nothing heretofore, it is that the king's plans could not sooner be matured. Meantime we have stayed the horror for a while."

Jack uttered an impatient exclamation.

"Oh, yes," Monella declared, "we *have*, and you have helped to do it. These wretched creatures you have seen sacrificed to this horrible 'fetish-tree' of theirs, are their own soldiers—those who escaped from us by running away. They deserve no pity. They themselves have given many an innocent victim—even women and children—to that tree—"

"I know that to be true," Ergalon interposed.

"The truce we forced on Coryon," resumed Monella "has had this effect at least—it has saved the lives of numbers of poor creatures who would have been seized and sacrificed during the time that we have been here. Instead of that, however, the arch-fiend Coryon has had to content himself with making victims of his own wretched myrmidons by way of punishment for their running away from us. They are as bad as he—very nearly. At any rate they are not worth your pity."

"Well, I am glad to hear that, at least," said Templemore. "It takes away a little of the load of horror that turned me sick. Truly, of all the diabolical atrocities that the mind of man in its depths of cruelty and wickedness ever conceived—"

Ergalon shuddered now in his turn.

"I can look on at the sacrifice of victims such as these," he said gravely, "because I know that everyone of them has deserved his fate by acts of cruelty; but when it is a case, as it has been in the past, of women, young girls, and poor little children—"

"For Heaven's sake say no more," Jack entreated; "I begin to feel sick again at such suggestions! I will fight to the death against such wretches. As it is, for the rest of my life I shall see before me in my dreams what I saw tonight. Surely no wilder phantasy, no more outrageous, blood-curdling nightmare ever entered the most disordered brain. And now it will haunt me to my life's end!"

XXIV

Trapped!

One day the king announced his intention to fix a day for Leonard's formal betrothal to Ulama according to the usage of the country. Immediately the people began preparations to do honour to the event; and congratulations and marks of friendship and goodwill were showered upon the young couple by all those who were well affected towards the king.

In the opposite camp, however, as might be expected, the announcement was differently received; and, indeed, the crafty Coryon took advantage of it to sow dissension among some of the people, and to suggest opposition to the proposal. His adherents had certain supporters in the land; people who bought their own security by aiding Coryon secretly against their neighbours. This was why the king had shrunk from pushing matters to the extreme against the priest. He knew that these half-hearted or doubtful ones were quite as likely to side with Coryon, at the last moment, as with himself, and that thus a civil war would be inaugurated.

Monella, since he had come into the country and espoused the king's side, had thrown more energy and method into the cause than had been previously bestowed upon it. Through the Fraternity of the White Priests, and their covert friends and sympathisers, and through Ergalon, who had secretly gained over some of Coryon's people, an active work had been carried on amongst all classes, and with satisfactory results. But Coryon, on his side, had been busy too; though hitherto with less success. Now, however, he found a useful aid in the objection many felt to seeing the king's only daughter wedded to one who—as it was cunningly suggested to them—was a stranger, an adventurer, come from no one knew where, and unable to show such evidence of descent and other qualifications as should entitle him to seek alliance with the daughter of their king.

But Coryon's emissaries worked silently and unseen; and there was nothing outwardly to show that two undercurrents were gradually gaining strength and approaching that point whence the slightest accident might bring them into active opposition.

Indeed, in announcing the proposed betrothal, the king had, for once, acted directly against Monella's advice. The latter had counselled that the matter should be kept secret until the contest with Coryon—now in abeyance—had been finally decided; for he foresaw the use to which Coryon would put it.

Leonard and Ulama were too much taken up with each other and with their own happiness to trouble themselves about the 'pros and cons' that had weighed in the minds of Monella and those who thought with him. That the effect of the proclamation would be to hasten his marriage was, of course, sufficient to commend it to Leonard; and he left all the rest to others.

Templemore knew not sufficient of what was going on around him to have any opinion upon the subject. Since the night when the real use to which the great devil-tree was put had been revealed to him, he had been very unhappy. He felt as might one who had been slumbering peacefully in sight of a terrible peril, to whose existence he had suddenly been awakened. Not that he had any fear for his own safety; yet he was filled with a nameless dread, a vague sense of horror and distrust, of unreality, in the life about him. He could not but realise that there would be no real peace, no security for life or property, until an absolute end had been put to Coryon and his atrocious crew, and their abominable fetish-tree destroyed. But when would that be? he wondered. His sense of disquiet was increased by having to keep from Leonard the knowledge he had gained, and being thus debarred from discussing matters with him. Not, however (as he acknowledged to himself), that that would have been of much advantage; for Leonard was too much absorbed in 'love's young dream' to be likely to discuss such things coolly and critically.

Three days before that fixed for the ceremony of betrothal, which was to be marked by a still grander entertainment, the king gave a preliminary *fête*. There was much feasting for all and sundry; boats, gaily decorated with flowers and banners and coloured streamers, glided to and fro upon the lake; the young people skilled in diving from great heights into the water with their parachute aids, contended for prizes, and there were many other forms of gaiety and festivity.

Leonard and Ulama, seated upon a terrace, looked upon the scene, and waved their hands in frequent recognition of friendly faces and signals here and there amongst the crowd. Ulama's lovely face was radiant, and the soft light in her gentle eyes, her pleased acknowledgment of the tokens of affection and the good wishes she received on every side, and her grateful smiles for all, were charming to behold. Her wondrous grace and beauty seemed, if possible, enhanced by her half-shy, half-proud glances, and the flush that mounted to her cheeks when she turned her eyes with love on Leonard. Never before, even in that country where the charms of the daughters of the land exceed the average, had such a vision of lovely maidenhood and such rare beauty been beheld. And yet all those who knew her, loved her as much for the innocence and sweetness that beamed ever in her face and guided all her thoughts and words and actions, as for the physical perfection that compelled their admiration.

She stole her little hand into her lover's and sighed quietly.

"I am so happy, and yet my eyes are full of tears. And I feel half frightened too; frightened lest my happiness should be too great to last. Is it wrong, then, to be happy, think you? It almost seems so, when I know so many others are unhappy."

Leonard fondly pressed her hand, and gazed deep down into her eyes.

"If you feel happy in your love, dear heart," he answered, "it is because you love so much; and surely to love cannot be wrong, or to take pleasure in it. Besides, in that you think so much of others you but show your sweet unselfishness. Therefore, trouble not yourself about the regrets for others that accompany your love. For, if today they sorrow, they have had their times of happiness in the past, or may have them in the future."

"It may be so," replied Ulama. "I doubt whether in all the world there is another maiden who loves as I do, and therefore who could know the dread that weighs me down. But as for me—ah, I tremble at my own great joy, and fear it is too great to last. And everyone is so kind to me and seems so rejoiced to see me happy—that—that I can hardly keep from crying."

And for a brief minute the gentle-hearted girl placed her hands before her face to hide her tears—tears that were born of the great gladness of her love and her tender sympathy for others.

And so for these two the day passed, like many that had gone before it, in a blissful dream; but it was a dream from which they were soon to be roughly awakened to the dark knowledge of what wickedness can achieve.

For, amid the feasting and among the revellers, were evil beings who had plotted in their black hearts to kill the joy of the gentlest-hearted maiden that ever with her sweetness brightened this sorrow-laden earth; wretches that even then were spinning around her the treacherous web designed by the fell Coryon to end her dream of happiness forever.

When Templemore woke up the next morning he gazed about him in surprise. He was not in his usual sleeping apartment; but, instead, in some room that was strange to him. It was small, dingy and ill-lighted, and the couch upon which he found himself was not that on which he had lately slept. He sprang up and, in vague alarm, looked round for his clothes and his arms; the clothes were there, but there was no revolver, and his rifle was nowhere to be seen. Even his sword and dagger, that formed part of his usual dress, had been removed. Dressing himself hastily, he rushed to the door, but it was fastened.

"Great heavens!" he exclaimed, "I am a prisoner; my rifle and pistol have been taken away in my sleep. Oh, what, what has happened to Leonard? What can it all mean?"

He hammered at the door, but no answer came. Then he tried to look out of the window, but it was too high for him to be able to see anything through it but the sky. There was nothing to be done but wait; so he sat down upon the bed, a picture of misery and bewilderment, and forthwith began to formulate all sorts of theories and ideas to account for what had happened to him.

When, after a long interval, the door was opened, a man entered whose dress showed him to be one of Coryon's black-tunicked soldiers. He brought in some food, and a pitcher and a mug, which he deposited upon a small table, and was turning to go, when Templemore sprang up and addressed him. He felt so incensed at the sight of this emissary of Coryon's that he could indeed scarcely refrain from hurling himself upon him, despite the fact that the man was armed. But just outside the door, as he could see, were other soldiers; he could hear, too, the clank of their arms, so he knew that to attack the one before him would be worse than useless.

"What is the meaning of this?" he demanded.

The man, who was just on the point of going out, turned back for a step or two, and then said in a low tone,

"You are the prisoner of the High Priest Coryon."

"But how, and why, and where?"

The man shook his head quietly. He was not an ill-favoured fellow, and regarded his prisoner in a half-friendly manner, Templemore thought.

"You are still in the king's palace," he continued, "but your friend and the princess have been taken away to Coryon's abode."

"Taken away to his place? Great God help them and help us all, then!" Jack moaned, as the picture of what he had seen there that well-remembered night rose up before his mind. "And how has all this come about? and where is Monella, and where is the king?"

"I may not talk to you," the soldier answered. "I have disobeyed orders in telling you thus much. But Ergalon was a friend of mine and I know that he is a friend of yours." And he went out, closing and fastening the door behind him.

Here was terrible news! Leonard and Ulama prisoners of Coryon; perhaps immured in one of those awful dungeons within reach of the terrible tree, where the very sight of what went on beyond those barred and grated doors was enough to drive the bravest mad; and where, at any moment, that whistle—a door run back—and then—!

"It's too dreadful—too horrible to think of!" Templemore exclaimed. He sprang up and began pacing restlessly up and down. "I shall go mad myself, if I dwell upon such thoughts."

The hours dragged slowly by till evening, when, just when it was growing dark, the door was once more opened and the same man came in and, looking at Templemore, made a sign to be silent. Then he returned to the door and led in a muffled figure, and, without a word, retired. The figure threw back a hood that covered the head, and Templemore, with glad surprise, saw that it was Zonella.

He ran forward and took her hand in his.

"Zonella!" he exclaimed. "This is surprising, and gladdening too. It does one good to see your face after all that I have been imagining. Tell me—what does it all mean?"

She laid her finger on her lips and said in a hushed voice,

"It means that the cunning, treacherous Coryon has played a trick upon us all, and made you prisoners. Your friend and our beloved princess have been carried off, the king himself is kept a prisoner in his room, and so are many of his ministers."

"And Monella and Ergalon?"

"Monella was away in Myrlanda, as you know, and so has escaped; and Ergalon—who is free too, but in hiding—has sent a trusty messenger to warn him."

"And you?"

"I am virtually a prisoner too. That is, I am forbidden to leave the palace. But I am free to go about within it. The whole place is full of Coryon's soldiers."

"Can you tell me how it was managed?"

"The 'loving cup' was drugged. All who partook of it fell into an unnaturally heavy sleep. You remember almost everyone throughout the palace drank some, in honour of your friend and our poor princess. Alas! alas! My dear, my loved Ulama!"

She sobbed bitterly, while Jack marched excitedly up and down the place.

"Is there no hope—nothing to be done?" he exclaimed despairingly.

"There is only one thing," was answered in a low, hesitating tone.

"What is that?" he asked eagerly.

"I have come to try to aid you. If you wrap up in this cloak and go out quietly now, while it is half dark, you may get clear out of the palace unobserved. One of my maids is waiting for me without, and will show you the way. I warned her of my plan, and she is to be trusted."

"What! And leave you here in my place to suffer Coryon's vengeance? Why, Zonella—dear, kind friend—what must you think of me?"

"I can think of nothing else," she answered simply. "And for me—I care not. Whatever may befall me, *you* will be able to get away; perhaps even to serve your friend."

Jack took her hand in his, not noticing that she seemed to shiver under the touch.

"Such an offer is too kind, too much, my dear, good friend," he said. "It cannot be; we must try—"

"For *my* sake, then," she exclaimed impulsively. "I would rather die myself than see you carried off to yonder dens. Or"—she paused confusedly, and then went on—"for your friend's sake. Think! Consider! Do you refuse merely from any thought about me? Think what you might be able to do for others—for your friend, for Ulama!"

Templemore passed his hand over his face; the tears were coming into his eyes. When he tried to speak again, he felt half choking.

"You are a noble girl, Zonella," he answered with emotion; "and when you appeal to me on *their* behalf you cannot know how hard it is to me to stay on here, knowing that I have the chance—just the chance—of saving them. But it cannot be, dear friend, it cannot be;

but—I thank you. My whole heart thanks you." He pressed her hand, and turned sorrowfully away.

Presently, she spoke again, this time in a different tone; indeed, her voice sounded hard and strained.

"Then Ergalon shall risk his life for you," she said. "I know that which will induce him to attempt what today he said could not be done. I will seek him at once. For now, goodbye; do not go to bed, but be ready, if you hear someone at the window. You can reach it, if you stand up on the table." And, without further explanation, she left him.

Templemore sat for long pondering upon this strange interview, and wondering too what she had planned; and the time seemed to drag wearily while he waited for some signal at the window.

It was about midnight, as he judged, when there came a tap, tap from the outside. He sprang on to the table; then by the dim light that came through the window he could discern the upper part of a man's body swinging on a rope.

"Is that Ergalon?" he whispered.

"Yes," came back the answer. "If I send you in a short rope and you wait till I have gone down, you can then pull in the rope I am on, get on to it, and come down yourself. Do you dare try it?"

"Yes."

"Then here it is. Now wait till you find you can pull this one in."

Templemore felt about and caught hold of a small cord that was hanging inside the window—which was open to the air—and he pulled lightly at it till he felt the strain upon the rope to which it was attached, relaxed. Then he pulled harder, and a portion of a thicker rope came inside. By its means he was able to climb up on to the sill. With some trouble and manoeuvring he got outside and was soon sliding down the rope, which Ergalon steadied from below. It was very dark, and he descended amidst some trees where it was darker still. When he touched the ground, at first, he could see nothing; but Ergalon turned on the light of a bull's-eye lantern. It was one of those Monella had brought with him, and lent by him to Ergalon.

A voice, that he knew to be Zonella's, whispered,

"That has been well done. Now what do you propose to do?"

"I must get down to the canyon by which we came into the mountain. There we have left spare weapons. But I can't get down in the dark; not even, I fear, with the lantern."

"There will be a moon later; perhaps that will help. Let us go in that direction."

"What! you, too?" Jack asked in surprise.

"Yes, why not? I shall be as safe with you as in the midst of Coryon's hateful minions, and I may be of service."

"You couldn't climb down that place and up again," Jack reminded her.

"Then I can wait near the top, and Ergalon can go with you to help you carry what you want."

"But we shall be a long time, all day tomorrow."

"No matter, I will manage."

Then the three made their way with much difficulty, owing to the darkness, to the top of the canyon. Here they sat and talked in guarded voices till the moon had risen high enough to light the hazardous descent.

Templemore learned how Coryon's plans had been carried out; how Ergalon's escape had been due to his absence from the palace, awaiting the return of a messenger from Monella. At a late hour, on his way back to the palace, he had been warned by a friend amongst Coryon's people. On this he had sent on the messenger to Monella to inform him of all that had occurred. The man had been only just in time to get through the subterranean road before Coryon's soldiers took possession of it and closed it.

Templemore's escape had been planned by Zonella. She had smuggled Ergalon into the palace and up to the roof disguised as one of her own maids; and in this she had been aided by one of his friends amongst the soldiers of the priest. Ergalon had at first objected strongly, conceiving that the attempt was foolhardy and could not succeed; that he would only lose his own liberty and, perhaps, his life, and that Monella might be displeased. In short, he had considered himself bound to do nothing that was in anyway risky until Monella had communicated with him. But Zonella had contrived, by some means, to persuade him; and had herself stolen out and steadied the rope for Ergalon in his perilous descent.

From his friend in the opposite camp Ergalon had learned one very important thing—that nothing was likely to be done to Leonard or Ulama till the day that had been named for their betrothal. That day Coryon had fixed upon, with cruel irony, for the holding of a sort of trial, the result of which would be a foregone conclusion.

"Therefore," said Ergalon, "if you can get back by the morning of tomorrow" (it being then already morning) "you will be in time; though I fear you will find it difficult to effect much good alone, and I cannot yet tell when the lord Monella may be able to get through the subterranean passage to come to your assistance."

"We will try, anyhow," said Jack, setting his teeth with grim determination. "And, if I fail, we will die together. One can but die once. I think it is possible to get back with a couple of rifles and pistols and the necessary ammunition by the morning. If human effort can do it, it shall be done; and I can then put a pistol into your hands, too, my good friend."

XXV

'In the Devil-Tree's Larder!'

Leonard awoke from a deep sleep, on the morning after the *fête*, to find himself, like Templemore, in a place that was strange to him.

So profound had been the slumber induced by the drug that had been mixed with the drink, that he had been carried all the way to Coryon's retreat in absolute unconsciousness. When he at last woke up, he was in one of the cells under the terrace within the reach of the great flesh-eating tree.

No words can describe the horror and anguish that filled his breast when, by degrees, he realised the dreadful truth. Not only did he shudder at the thought of his own too probable fate, but the fear that his sweet Ulama might share the same awful doom drove him almost to the verge of madness. He cursed the false sense of security that had led up to this terrible result. A few simple precautions would have frustrated this treachery! But it was too late!

Through the grated door he could see the great devil-tree, hear the swishing of its long, trailing branches, watch them come up to the grating and search about over its face for some opening large enough to penetrate, even trying to wriggle in through its small slits and perforations. In the centre of the cell was a block of wood fixed in the ground to serve as a table. A small stream of water ran down from a pipe above and fell into a channel in the floor, and a pitcher stood beside it. For chair there was a smaller log of wood; the 'bed' on which he had found himself was simply a bag of straw whereon were laid two or three rugs. An iron door shut off the back from an interior gallery, and the cell was partitioned off from others, on each side, by grated screens, like that in the front. The occupants of adjacent cells could, therefore, see each other.

As Leonard looked round in astonishment and alarm, and exclaimed, involuntarily, "Where am I?" a discordant peal of mocking laughter rang out from the cell upon his right.

"Where is he! He doesn't even know where he is!" a harsh voice cried out. "He—one of the gods that wielded the lightning and thunder! After all, caught by Coryon, and brought here like the rest of us! Ha! ha! ha!"

Leonard, shocked and amazed, went to the side whence the sounds proceeded, and there saw, peering through the bars, a horrible face that grinned at him with hideous sneers and wild-looking eyes. The hair and beard were matted and dishevelled; the face and figure, so far as he could make them out, looked gaunt and thin. He was dressed in the black tunic with gold star that denoted one of Coryon's soldiers.

"Ha! ha! ha!" laughed the mocking voice. "You don't know where you are, eh? I'll tell you, my lord, son of the gods, that can kill us soldiers with a magic lightning wand, but can't keep yourself out of Coryon's clutches—you are in the 'devil-tree's larder'!"

"The devil-tree's larder!"

"Yes, my lord; the devil-tree's larder. That means that they have put you here to keep you cool and in good condition, before they hand you over to be food for their pet out there." And he pointed to the tree.

Leonard shuddered, and the awful truth of the man's statement forced itself upon his mind, in spite of his wish to believe it too atrocious to be possible. He went up to the door in the front and examined it. He saw that it ran in grooves at the top and bottom.

"Ah," said the mocking voice behind him, "that's right. You see how it's done now. They run that back from inside, sudden-like, sometime when you don't expect it; and in come the twisting branches that lay hold of you, and out you go to make him a nice meal. Ha! ha! ha!"

Leonard turned and stared in helpless horror. Was it possible that there was such cold-blooded, fiendish cruelty in the world? Yet—he remembered the fate of the poor puma. He trembled, and turned sick and faint; while the one in the next cell continued to jeer and mock at him.

"Where is your lightning-wand, my lord? Why have you not brought it to try it on the tree? You managed to get *me* brought here; and now you've managed to get here yourself!"

"I got *you* brought here? How? What then are you doing here?" Leonard asked, his surprise overcoming his disgust.

"What am I doing here? Why, the same as you—waiting in 'the devil-tree's larder' till I'm given to him for a meal—as you will be. And it's all through you; because you killed some of us and we others ran away; this is what they do with us."

Leonard shuddered again, while the man went to the stream of water that, as in Leonard's cell, was pouring down from a pipe above, and, filling the pitcher, took a long drink.

"Makes you thirsty, this sort of thing," he said, with another jeering laugh. "You'll find that water there mighty handy if they let you stay here long enough. Ha! ha! ha!"

The man was evidently in a state of high fever. The place was full of foetid odours given off by the foul tree; and, apart from that, the want of sleep would superinduce fever, if, indeed, it did not drive mad the wretched occupants of the cells; for who could sleep for more than a minute or two at a time in one of those dens, where, at any moment, the door might be run back and the miserable prisoner delivered over to the fatal branches? It was this constant, ever-present dread that banished sleep, and must inevitably end in madness for the victims, provided they were kept there long enough.

Then the thought flashed upon him that Ulama also might be an occupant of one of these awful cells; and at that such a burst of grief and agony came over him that he hid his face within his hands and groaned aloud.

"Yah! don't give way like that, my lord. Being here's not so bad when once you're used to it! Look at me! You don't see me worry and cry like a great girl. I take it quietly; I've been too used to seeing others here. Many's the time I've had the pulling back of these doors and have seen a man or a woman hauled out squealing and kicking like an animal going to be killed; and I've laughed at them. I thought it such fun! And now those who used to help me and laugh with me, they're waiting to see how I like it; and they will laugh at me, too, just the same. But I don't care. What does it matter? It's nothing, I tell you, when you're as used to it as I am."

The wretched creature thus trying to delude himself with boastful talk and jeering at his fellow-captive, was himself, it was easy to see, worked up into the highest state of nervous dread and fear. The least sound made him start and look with straining eyeballs in the direction from which it came. He kept going to the pitcher for draughts of water, and never remained still for a single instant. If he sat down for a short space, the twitching of a foot, or leg, or hand, spoke of agitation within that would not be controlled.

Leonard turned from the sight with mingled feelings of disgust and loathing and, going to the other side, looked through the grating of the adjoining cell, to see whether it was occupied. And, looking, his heart seemed to come up into his throat when he saw a silent female form seated with its back to him. The exclamation that escaped him caused the form to turn, when he saw that the woman was a stranger. Her face was pleasing in its features, and good-looking, but had in its expression such a burden of unspeakable horror and despair that he shivered as he met her glance. At sight of it, for the moment, he almost forgot his own misery, and he asked gently,

"And who then are you?"

For a few seconds there was no reply; then, in a voice that had in it the suggestion of much sweetness, albeit now forced, and unnatural,

"I scarcely know. Once I was a happy young girl; then a well-beloved and loving wife and mother; now I am only something with which to feed yonder monster."

"Yes," continued the woman dreamily, "I was once good-looking, they said. Certainly, my husband thought so; and that was enough for me. But it was my curse, alas! for Skelda, the chief of the priests next to Coryon, thought so too. He stole me away from my home and my children and forced me to become one of his so-called wives. And now, because my sorrowing and pining have seared and furrowed my good looks, even as they had eaten into my heart, he has tired of me, and has sent me to the fate that, sooner or later, we all come to here—all of my sex, at least, as well as many of the other among those who are not priests. Yet," she added, "it is but five years since they brought me here. What I look like now you can see for yourself!"

Leonard looked at her with pity; and there came into his mind the remembrance of Ulama's words of the day before—"It seems almost wrong to be happy when I know so many others are unhappy"—and his own light rejoinder. And he reproached himself in that he had been content to bask in love and self-enjoyment while, close at hand, there were such abuses, such direful sufferings. True, he had not actually known their whole nature and extent; but he *had* known of the so-called 'blood-tax'; and had heard enough to make it certain, had he given the matter due consideration, that there were evils in the land that cried aloud for remedy.

Then his thoughts reverted to Ulama, and he asked,

"Do you know aught concerning the Princess Ulama?"

"I know that she was to be brought to this place, and that she was to be put into the cell I occupied before they brought me here yesterday. It is underground; a long way from this part."

At least, then, the poor child, Leonard thankfully reflected, was not in one of the cells in sight of the dreaded tree.

Presently he asked the woman whether she had known Zelus, the son of Coryon.

"Ah yes! Who did not in this land?" was the reply. "The monster! A great spasm as of relief and joy came upon us all—all the women, I mean—when we heard of his death. He was the worst of them all, though one of the youngest. No one was safe from him. Even the princess he sought to bring here to treat as he had treated so many others!"

"I know. I killed him when he was in the very act of raising his cowardly hand against the king's daughter," said Leonard quietly.

The woman turned and looked at him with more of interest in her manner than she had yet shown. She scanned him closely.

"Then," she said, "you must be one of the strangers of whom we heard. But you are young, and not, as I have been told, of our race. We heard of one older, one who, it was said, belonged to our people. And when we heard that, we all rejoiced; for surely, we said, he brings us tidings of what all have been expecting. Therefore, we who were held here in a bondage that is a daily, hourly torture, a never-ceasing degradation, we welcomed your coming as a sign that the Great Spirit had at last brought our long punishment to an end. I, even I, dared to hope I should escape the fate that has befallen all others, and should live to see again my husband and children before I die. But, alas! it was but a dream—a delusive, passing hope, a thing too good to come in my time. Four months have passed and nothing has occurred, though ye smote the hated Zelus quickly; and even Coryon was filled with fear and dread. Why have ye failed to do more, and, instead, fallen victim to Coryon?"

Ah! why? It was a question that now sank deep into Leonard's soul and tortured him with vain regrets and self-reproach. For he had a heart that swelled with kindness towards his fellows, and a tender conscience; and the more he thought things over, the more difficult he found it to feel that he was without blame. He had been too selfishly wrapped up in his own personal feelings, he now acknowledged; too little interested in those very matters that, as the king's future son-in-law, should have taken, if not the first, at least a prominent position in his mind. And then, to be ignobly trapped, at a time when there was nothing but feasting and amusement in their minds! Their arms taken from them—they who could have kept at bay all Coryon's soldiers and dispersed them, had they but been vigilant and wakeful! It was a cruelly humiliating thought—it was worse; for the child-hearted, innocent

Ulama, who had a right to rely on his protection, had been sacrificed also to his self-abandonment and want of watchfulness.

Thus did Leonard reason, now that his opportunities had vanished. He knew not what was the true explanation of the position in which he found himself; but a vague, half-formed idea crept into his mind that Coryon would hardly have ventured upon such a daring stroke unless he had felt he could rely upon the support, or, at least, the indifferent neutrality, of a certain proportion of the people. And if he, Leonard, had shown more interest in the affairs of the people over whom he was one day to be king, he might have gained so firm a hold on their confidence and affections as would have rendered Coryon's schemes hopeless from the very start.

But such thoughts, whether well or ill-founded, came now all too late. Here he was, caged, and at Coryon's mercy. His relentless enemy had but to give the signal and he would be consigned to an awful death.

He had some further talk with the woman, who told him terrible tales of indescribable barbarities and iniquities perpetrated by the priestly tyrants under the covering of their 'religion'; tales that made the blood within him boil, and filled his soul with savage, though helpless, indignation. Then he asked the woman's name, and was told it was Fernina.

At last, he asked the question that, though often upon his tongue, yet he had shrunk from giving voice to.

"And what do you suppose will happen—here?"

She sighed and shook her head, hopelessly, despairingly.

"Only what always happens," she answered, in a dull, listless tone. "None that are once placed here ever escape the fatal tree; except that sometimes they are carried up above and laid on what they call 'the devil-tree's ladle.'"

"'The devil-tree's ladle?'"

"Yes; it is a contrivance on wheels; a kind of long plank shaped at one end like a great spoon. Those who are to be given to the tree are laid upon it, bound so that they cannot move, and then pushed out along the stone-work till they are within reach of the branches; those who push the plank at the other end being far enough away for their own safety. It is part of the system of terrorism and torture here," Fernina added, "to place some of us, at times, in rooms that are in the rock above, and that overlook this place, and to keep us locked in there for days and nights, that we may be cowed and frightened at the scenes that are enacted here. Often, a hateful fascination compels you to become an unwilling witness; in any case, you cannot avoid hearing the shrieks and moans; imagination supplies the rest."

Leonard turned away, not caring to hear more, and sat down to brood, eating his heart out with keen regrets, all now unavailing. The jeering of the half-mad wretch in the other cell had ceased; he, too, had fallen into a sort of brooding lethargy, and so was quiet; but a constant tap, tap, tap, of one foot on the stone floor told he was not asleep. Thus the hours dragged by in silence, save for the intermittent, stealthy rustle of the branches outside, as they came prowling over the face of the gratings in their sleepless seeking after the prey they seemed to scent within.

Once, a small grating at the bottom of the door of each cell was opened, and a platter with coarse food upon it was pushed in; then the space closed up again. The sounds made them all, for the moment, start; then they relapsed again into the stupor of despair. None touched the food or even noticed it. But the man in the further cell had now seated himself near the little stream of water and, every now and then, he roused himself to take long draughts.

When it grew dark, a lighted lantern was pushed under the door into each cell, as the food had been. Leonard felt drowsy and longed for rest; yet was afraid to lie down or to close his eyes. Now and again they even closed against his will in a short doze; but it was never of long duration, and each time he woke it was with a renewed sense of the horror of his situation.

He had just roused from one of these brief snatches of sleep, and had had time to remember once more where he was, when a low rumble made him spring up and look around. Then the man in the next cell gave an awful cry—a cry that rang in Leonard's ears for many a day—and at the same moment the grated door of his prison slowly began to move. In his demented terror he banged himself against the partition between the two cells, tried to get his fingers into the slits that he might cling to it; then climbed up on to the wooden block in the middle of the cell. But the rustling branches neared him, sought for him on every side, and soon mounted the log and caught him in their deadly embrace. Slowly, but irresistibly, while he never ceased his cries or his vain struggles and clutchings, the coils around him tightened and dragged him out into the darkness, where his cries gradually became weaker, and were finally heard no more; and when they ceased, and he heard the door rolling back, with dull rumbling, to its place, Leonard tottered to the pile of rugs in the corner of his cell, and fell upon them in a swoon.

When he returned to consciousness a bright light was shining through the grated door. He got up and, like one who is but a helpless on-looker in a fevered dream, he went to the bars and gazed out. It was bright moonlight outside, and there he saw the same ghastly scene repeated that Templemore had witnessed a short time before. He saw the dead body of the latest victim of the tree's insatiable thirst for blood dangling amongst the branches; caught up, now by the neck, and now by the feet, and passed on from one branch to another in what seemed a new dance or sport of death; and finally carried off by the great crawling reptiles that had come up to claim their share in the repast.

While the scene lasted, Leonard seemed incapable of volition; his limbs refused to obey the will of his reeling brain and to bear him away from the sight. But, when the creatures had disappeared, he turned and made his way once more to the low bed, where he remained in a state of torpor till the day was far advanced.

After what seemed a long interval, he sat up and rubbed his eyes, after the manner of one just awakened from the horror of a nightmare. Then he saw the woman who occupied the next cell standing with her eyes fixed on him; and, when she found he was once more awake and conscious, she addressed him.

"I am sorry for you," she said. "Even in my own misery I am not so blinded but that I can see that your burden of sorrow is a heavy one—more than you can bear. Yet methinks, were I a man, I would not thus give way to it. I am but a woman, but my greatest wish—since nothing else is left me—is that I may see Coryon once more—stand face to face with him—and show him that all his calculated cruelty and subtle ingenuity of torture have not subdued my spirit, nor the scorn that a heart conscious of having done no wrong can feel for such as he. I would give him back look for look, hate for hate, as I have before today; and make his wicked eyes quail before mine with the consciousness that the spirit of one he has unjustly oppressed can show itself greater than his own. But with *you*—he will but laugh at you—for I feel, somehow, you will be taken from here to meet him. I suspect he has sent you here first to crush your spirit with the sight of the horrors that are perpetrated here. He—have you ever seen him?"

"No," Leonard answered, staring at her in amazement.

"Ah! then you know not what he is like. I tell you," the strange woman went on, her eyes lighting up with unexpected fire, "he is a man whose mere glance strikes terror into the souls of ordinary men. There is that about him that makes you shrink as from some unearthly incarnation of all the powers of evil; and in that he delights, yea, more, even, than in torturing his victims."

Here she broke off abruptly; then resumed, in a different manner.

"I have been wondering whether you are he who was to have wedded the princess?"

"Alas! yes. You have divined aright," Leonard answered sadly.

"Then," said the woman, with increasing warmth, that gained as she went on an energy that was almost fierceness, "then, the greater the reason you should throw off this weakness and gird up your strength to meet the haughty tyrant and show him that your spirit is equal to his own. In all his ill-spent time upon this earth—and they say it has been a very long one—it is his boast and his pride that scarce any can meet his glance without quailing under it. Think! Think how he will triumph over you—how he will point the finger of scorn—turn the look of cold contempt upon the one who aspired to be the future king of this country—and *that* means to stand on an equality with himself—and yet, as he will declare, is but a weak, puling, or ordinary mortal. Ah! would I were in your place! You can but die. But I would make him feel that I had a heart, a spirit, more dauntless, more unconquerable than his own. Ay! I would die knowing that for many and many and many a year to come, the remembrance that he had met *one* spirit he could not intimidate or master would be to him an instrument of defeat and shame, eating into his proud heart, even as the suffering he has caused to me has gnawed into my own."

The woman spoke at the last with a force that almost electrified her hearer. Leonard felt roused as, perhaps he had never been roused before.

"You are right, my friend!" he exclaimed, "and I thank you. As you truly say, he who aspires to high things should show himself worthy to achieve them, and not even the shadow of a dreadful death and cruel sufferings should have the strength to cow his spirit in the presence of this most cold-blooded and revolting tyrant. If I have shown weakness, it was not from personal fear, but from thought of the suffering of one dearly loved, and my self-reproach for having been the unintentional cause of it. It is well that I met you; for you have taught me how I should meet this Coryon!"

"And," said the woman, "if you want one unerring shaft to launch at him—one that I know will pierce the armour of his pride and drive him to the verge of madness—tell him you know one woman whose spirit more than matches his; tell him that she is called Fernina."

XXVI

CORYON

At sunrise on the morning of the day that was to have witnessed Leonard's public betrothal he was sitting staring gloomily, through the grating of his cell, at the never-resting branches without, when the sounds of drums, on which a long tattoo was being beaten, broke on his ear. The sounds came from both near and far, some half-muffled in the galleries and caverns of the cliff, others echoing from one side to the other of the rocky enclosure till they died away in the far distance.

Since the previous morning nothing further had occurred; the woman was still in the cell on one side of him; no new victim had been brought to occupy the other.

The roll of the drums caused Leonard to start up and look about him. He was haggard and worn from want of sleep, but his step was firm, and his face was stamped with a look of quiet resolution that showed he had taken to heart his fellow-prisoner's advice. When he rose up she spoke.

"It is as I thought," she said; "they are to have one of their gatherings today, when the tree will be given its meal in sight of all who are summoned to be present. That is why one of us was not given to it last night, no doubt." And she gave a short, hard laugh, that was far from pleasant to hear.

"No doubt it is your turn," she went on in a softer tone. "You must summon all your fortitude. Be brave! If one must die, one needs not show such craven fear as that half-mad wretch exhibited the other night."

"You speak well, my good friend, and what you have said to me has braced me up. Would that, before we part, I could say or do something to serve or comfort you."

"That cannot be; only remember what I told you—if you want a taunt to hurl at the tyrant's head, a taunt that will stab him through his self-admiration, you know now what to say. Soon they will be here for you. Ah!" here she broke off, as though a new thought had come to her. "On these days they are all assembled outside—all the men. Only the women and children are left within their dens. Oh, if I could but get free for half an hour! I know some of their secrets, and could play a trick upon them that would go far to square accounts between us. But, of course," she added mournfully, "it is foolishness to think of it."

Overhead could now be heard the scuffling of many footsteps, and, anon, more drum-beating, with much blowing of horns and trumpets. Next, there were shouting and cheering, followed by what appeared to be a speech from someone; but the words were not intelligible to the two anxious listeners.

At one time the noise had brought a faint hope into Leonard's mind that it might portend the approach of friends; but the words Fernina had just spoken quickly dissipated any such idea.

Presently, steps were heard in the gallery outside, a key was inserted in the lock, and two of Coryon's black-coated soldiers entered. They were both armed with drawn swords; and one of them, addressing Leonard in gruff accents, said,

"You are to come with us." Then, turning to his comrade, he asked, "Have you the cord?"

"No," was the reply, "I thought you had it."

"And I thought you were bringing it. Go, get it."

The man went out.

Then he who had remained, raising a warning hand to Leonard, addressed him in low, guarded tones.

"The lord Monella," he said, "is hastening to thine aid with many armed followers; but he has been detained in the underground pass. Whether he will arrive in time, I know not; if not and thou be harmed, thou wilt be avenged."

"Who art thou, then?" asked Leonard.

"A friend of the lord Monella's."

"And my other friend—what of him?"

"He was a prisoner, but escaped, and has gone—I know not whither."

"Heaven be praised for that! Ah, I can guess where he has gone!" Just then a sudden thought came into Leonard's head.

"See, friend," he said earnestly, "canst thou not turn the key in the lock of the next cell and give the poor creature there one little chance for liberty?"

"I do not know, but I will see. If the key fits, I might."

"Quick, then, ere thy fellow returns."

The man hastily took out the key and tried it in the lock of the woman's cell; it fitted, and he unlocked the door; then withdrawing the key, he replaced it in the door of Leonard's cell.

"Roll that log to the door to keep it close till you think it safe to venture out," Leonard advised the woman. She had but just done so when they heard the steps of the other soldier in the gallery.

"What is thy name, friend?" Leonard asked him in a whisper.

"Melta," the man answered; and then, when the other made his appearance with some cord, he began to rate him for having been so long.

Leonard was bound in a loose fashion, just sufficient to prevent his free use of either arms or legs, and led away. On his way out he said a kindly word to Fernina.

"The Great Spirit help you," was the reply. "I have no fear for you now; you will die with courage, if it be so fated. A heart that can feel and think for a stranger in the midst of such distress as is yours today is the heart of a brave man. But we may yet meet again."

Leonard shook his head sadly.

"I have no false hopes," he answered. "I do not expect that help can now come in time. I may be avenged; that is the most I can hope for."

"Yes!" said the woman in a meaning tone; "you will be avenged; and so shall I."

The man who had been sent for the cord laughed jeeringly at the woman when she said this, but took no further notice of her; and the three proceeded along the gallery till they came to some steps at the end. Ascending these they entered a broader gallery or corridor above; then, turning back, they passed out through the gateway and along the covered-way, finally emerging on the main terrace of the great amphitheatre.

Round the sides of the enclosure a large number of people were gathered. Among these were black-coated soldiers to the number of, perhaps, two hundred; the others, of whom there were from four to five hundred, also carried arms of some sort, spears or swords. When Leonard cast his eyes around and noted them, the heart within him sank, for he saw how difficult would be a rescue, even with the armed followers that the man Melta had said accompanied Monella.

In the centre of the great terrace, upon a high chair carved and emblazoned, and with a great banner waving above his head, sat the dreaded Coryon. Round him were grouped, first his nine priests in black robes, and Dakla and others of his chief officers; then, ranks of soldiers and, among them, some of the king's ministers and chief functionaries, all bound as Leonard was. But the king himself was not there; nor was Ulama; and Leonard, when he had assured himself of this, turned his gaze on Coryon.

It was well that he had been warned that he would need all his courage to enable him to look upon this man unflinchingly. Even thus prepared he found it barely possible to keep down the emotion the sight excited in his breast.

He saw before him a man of great height and powerful frame, clad in a black robe with a star on the breast worked in virgin gold and set with jewels. His grey hair and beard were unkempt and long, his skin of a dark swarthy hue, his forehead, albeit broad, was receding, and furrowed, and wrinkled into a sinister scowl, and his lips were parted or drawn up in a set snarl that disclosed teeth more like a wild beast's fangs than a human being's teeth. When Leonard first caught sight of him, he was standing with one arm extended as though he had just finished some harangue; but, when Leonard was brought up, Coryon sat down. Then he slowly turned his glance upon the prisoner.

And beneath that glance a feeling of cold horror stole into Leonard's breast; he felt as though an icy hand were about to seize his very heart and wring it in a grip of iron. It was the nameless dread that a man may feel in the presence of something that his instincts tell him is a deadly enemy, yet of which he cannot discover the form, or size, or nature; whether earthly or supernatural. Here, certainly, the outward shape was that of a man, but in the eyes there was something suggesting that their owner was not a man at all, but a living incarnation of depravity—a demon with eyes, for the moment quiescent as with the cold glitter and deadly malignancy of the serpent, but instinct with suppressed power, and ready to flame up with terrible, relentless, overwhelming energy. Mingled with the snake-like glitter of malevolence there were lurid flashes that darted forth perpetually, causing the beholder to recoil as though from actual darts. At sight of him one thought of some nameless monster coiled up and meditating a spring upon its prey; a monster that was the implacable foe of the whole human race, that embodied, in human form, all the power, the attributes, the cruelty, of an arch-demon from another world.

From such a being the soul shrinks with a horror that is less earthly fear than the natural loathing of evil things that is implanted within the breasts of all endowed with pure and holy instincts; and this was Leonard's feeling while he stood, half sick and faint, enduring and returning Coryon's fixed look.

But just when it came upon him that he must either shift his glance or drop helpless to the ground, the thought of all the child-like, innocent Ulama must have suffered through the shameless treachery of this fiend in human shape came into his mind; and, with the thought, forth from his heart rushed out the blood, bursting through the icy grip that had all but closed upon it, and coursing through his veins in a leaping torrent, like one of those great waves of fiery indignation that sometimes, for a while, gives to one man the strength of ten. With a sudden impulse that forgot everything but his righteous anger, he put forth such an effort that he broke the cords that bound him; then, rushing impetuously upon Coryon, before anyone could interfere, he actually had him by the throat in a clutch that, spite of the other's own gigantic strength, would have ended his vile life if, for a few seconds longer, his assailant had been left alone. But a dozen hands laid hold of him and pulled him back, bruised and panting, to the custody of the men he had escaped from. But, though baffled and injured in the struggle, there was in his eyes a light almost of triumph when he turned round and faced his enemy once more.

"Aha!" he shouted. "Coward! Hateful murderer of women and children and unarmed men! Thou darest not come down and meet me man to man! Though thou art near twice my size, I had choked the foul life out of thee, had we been left alone!"

At first, Coryon made no answer, except to glare at his late assailant with his evil eyes; but they fell away under the other's dauntless look, and he put his hands to his throat as if in pain.

"This will cost thee dear," at last he said, in a harsh, croaking voice; but Leonard replied with a cold smile,

"Thou canst but kill me; and I would not beg mercy from such as thou. Why dost turn thine eyes away, coward Coryon? Dost feel at last that so foul a thing may not endure the glance of an honest man?"

Coryon sprang up and stood for a moment with his hands extended towards his prisoner, his fingers closing and opening convulsively as though he half intended to accept the challenge in the other's words and looks. Then he managed to control his passion and sat down again, first addressing a few words in a low tone to a priest who stood beside him.

XXVII

On the 'Devil-Tree's Ladle!'

When Coryon sat down, a kind of buzzing or hum or talk in low tones broke out on all sides. Exclamations and expressions of astonishment were heard, for never had such audacity been known in a prisoner standing thus on the very brink of death and almost within reach of the clutch of the fatal tree.

Leonard was now bound again, and Dakla sent two or three of his subordinate officers to stand beside him. But, even while they bound him, the guards, as he could hardly fail to see, treated him with a measure of involuntary respect; and well they might, for there was not one amongst them that durst look the evil Coryon in the face.

Then was brought out the contrivance called the 'devil-tree's ladle'; it was simply a long plank widened out at one end, and mounted, in the centre, on wheels. An irrepressible shudder passed through Leonard when he saw this grim apparatus. But there was little outward sign of his emotion, and his eyes were soon again fixed on Coryon, who rose and thus addressed those present,

"Friends, ye all see here a confirmation of that which I have already explained unto you this morning. Yonder stands one of the strangers whom the king hath admitted to his friendship; the man he was about to honour by alliance with his royal house. Ye can see for yourselves the untutored passions by which this youth, who was, forsooth, to have been your future king, is swayed, and his lack of seemly behaviour in the presence of one like myself, who hath for so many years held a high position in the land, and hath conferred so many benefits upon it. Not the least of these, my friends, is that which I have just achieved—only just in time. I have, with the joint help of those powerful gods whom we all here serve, been able to defeat and overcome even the magic with which these men were armed. Ye all know, or have heard, how they came provided, by some enemies of our race outside the country, with magic wands that brought down lightning and thunder and death upon those opposed to them; and to their seeming power the king weakly yielded, and allowed these strangers to assume high stations in the land. Zelus, my well-beloved son, early fell a victim to their lawless intrusion into our domains, as did many of my people whom I sent to capture them. But in the end I have prevailed against them; I have taken from them their magic wands, and now they are, as ye all can see, but ordinary men. But a punishment hath fallen upon the king, for he is sick to death, and that is why he is not here today. He hath not long to live, and soon the country will be without a king. Now it seemeth to me certain that the people are averse from accepting this young stranger as the successor to their dying ruler, and that they desire one of their own race. This hath caused me much anxious thought, but I have at last, I think, discovered a solution of the difficulty. I will espouse the Princess Ulama, and become the king's son-in-law; thus will your minds be set at rest; for ye will know that whenever the king dieth he will be succeeded by a ruler who is not only of your own race, but hath served his country long enough to satisfy all objectors as to his experience, or his ability, or his solicitude for the welfare of his native land."

While uttering these words, Coryon looked with a hardly-veiled smile of malice at Leonard, who, listening to the infamous proposal wrapped up in such unblushing hypocrisy, started as though he would have rushed again upon the speaker; but he was held too firmly by those who now surrounded him. He could scarce keep from groaning aloud at what he had just heard.

Coryon marked with evident satisfaction this effect of his announcement, and proceeded, in an unctuous voice, and with an affectation of great resignation,

"In doing this, good friends, I have, I assure you, no thought, no feeling save the welfare of my country. I had not thought ever to take to me another wife; though I had looked with favour upon the desire of my son Zelus to ally himself with our king's daughter. But, since this young stranger hath rendered that impossible by slaying treacherously mine only son, I will accept the necessities of the situation, and sacrifice my own feelings for the general good. Perhaps, after all, it is as well; for in me ye will have, as ye all know well, one who thinks always only of his people's weal. For long ages I have guarded the land from outward foes by making friends of the powers of darkness. This, and this alone hath protected us from invasion by the hordes of wild men that we know exist beyond our borders. The powers, whose High Priest I am, have guarded us through many centuries, and have planted around the limits of our island a forest impenetrable and filled with terrible creatures for our protection. True, they let these strangers through, but only as a warning of that which might befall if we forgot, even for a moment, our religion, or rebelled against the sacrifices it requires and that our gods look for from us and will insist upon. True, we have to sacrifice some of those we love to our sacred tree, but what is that compared with the benefits and advantages that the rest receive? We have peace, prosperity, contentment, freedom from invasion, from wars, from enemies and dangers of all kinds; and, compared with these, the price that hath to be paid is, after all, but small. Henceforth, too, there will be a stronger guarantee for peace throughout the land, in that your king and the head of your religion will be one. And you, my faithful followers, who have served me well," continued the arch-hypocrite, casting his eyes around, "will no more be called upon to reside in the rocky fastness that has been so long our home; for I shall take up my abode in the palace of the king and there shall ye all follow me." At this a loud cheer went up from all. "And now to more immediate duties. I have condemned this murderer of my son to death; he shall end his life befittingly as a sacrifice to the gods whose power he hath defied in coming here—defied only to his own doom. So shall perish all who brave me; and so shall perish this man's friends, his murderous abettors who, too, are in my power. And now, sirrah, if thou hast aught to say, thou hast just a minute. If thou hast aught to ask me, now is thy final opportunity."

When he ceased speaking, Coryon sat down, first casting at Leonard a hideous glance of triumph. Leonard saw the sneer and knew that his enemy's desire was to excite him to a farther display of useless anger; but the knowledge only served to calm him, and, when he spoke, it was in a voice that had in it neither bitterness nor passion, but only a great sadness. He did not wish to gratify Coryon by exhibiting anger; and thus he spoke,

"It is true I have something I would say, but it is not to thee, O Coryon, but to those who are not Coryon's degraded servants, but free agents, who have been misled into supporting him here today. To you, good people, I address myself." And Leonard cast his eyes around upon those who were not wearers of Coryon's uniform. "I have much to say and much to ask. Know that the power of this boastful tyrant who declares with mock humility his wicked purpose to force the youthful daughter of his king into an alliance that revolts her—know, good people, that his power is almost at an end, and that he will never enter into that palace, in which he has promised to find place for his credulous followers. He may kill me if he will, but my death will naught avail;

a few hours hence he will be either a prisoner in the hands of those who came with me, or hiding in his underground haunts like a hunted animal that dares not show its face above the ground. But the end will be the same. He will quickly be hurled out, and a terrible punishment will be meted out to him and to all those who abet him—everyone, that is, who shall support him. Therefore I say this to you, when my friends come—as come they will—do not help Coryon's myrmidons against them. They will come armed with a fearful power that you can scarce conceive; you shall see the very rocks fall away before them in crashing thunders as they hunt these rats out of their holes. If you fight on Coryon's side, they will mow you down like grass before the scythe. On the other hand, if you side not with these doomed ones, but, instead, ask for mercy, you shall find it; for we came not to this land to teach cruelty and murder, but to deliver it from the tyranny that has so long oppressed it. That is my advice to you; what I would ask is that you tell your fellow-citizens that I am sore distressed in that I have done far less than I might to win their affections and their confidence. That I have made a terrible mistake, that it has led me to this situation, I now see. But my error I shall expiate with my life; when I am dead, and you see the benefits my friends will shower on the land, then tell all that I was of the same mind, and was full of naught but kindly feelings. But—my great—love for one so fair—as your young—princess—took up my thoughts, perhaps, more than should have been the case." Leonard's voice almost failed him here; but by a strong effort he recovered himself and went on. "That is all that I would ask; let them remember me and think kindly of me. You will see in those days who has spoken truly—whether I, or Coryon. You will know how false has been every word he has said to you today. Even what he says about my friends is false; they are *not* in his power, nor has he deprived them of their magic power, as you will all quickly see. To say that by his atrocious so-called religious rites he has guarded and advanced this country is a lie—"

"Silence!" exclaimed Coryon, who had all this time been moving restlessly in his seat.

"I come from a land—the greatest on the earth—that has an empire upon which the sun ne'er sets; we have no such wicked murders called sacrifices; yet we are safe against our enemies, and—"

"Silence, I tell thee! What think'st thou we care about thy country or thyself?" Coryon burst out.

"I say," Leonard went on, disregarding him, "that every word this man utters is a lie. He cannot say one single sentence without uttering a lie—"

"If thou sayest more, I will have thee scourged as well as killed," Coryon cried, in growing rage. "It speaketh well to these good people for my patience that I have let thee have thy say thus far. Never, for many a year, has mortal dared to flout me to my face as thou hast done."

"O Coryon!" Leonard exclaimed, turning and facing him, "truly did I say that thou could'st not speak one single sentence without uttering some lie, and now thou art convicted. For I know of one, at least, that has flouted and dared thee to thy face; one whose spirit thou could'st not quell; and she but a woman—her name Fernina!"

At this a perfect howl of rage escaped from Coryon's lips. He sprang up and clutched at the air, and gasped; and, for a moment, Leonard half thought he would have a fit. But he recovered himself, and shouted, in a screaming voice,

"Seize him! Gag him! Lay him on the feeding-ladle of our sacred tree! We will see how he fancies its embrace!" Then, turning round and addressing someone near him, he cried out,

"Bring forward the princess, that she may witness this my act of justice towards the murderer she would have taken to her bosom. Let my future wife look on. Ha! ha! ha! My future wife! How dost thou like the title, murderer of my son, and would-be king?"

His rage was something fearful to behold; many even of his own myrmidons trembled, and they made speed to do his bidding.

Leonard was seized and bound to the wheeled plank, and, after trying in vain to turn his head to take one last look at Ulama, he closed his eyes and resigned himself to prayer. At the same time Ulama, looking but the mere ghost of her former self, was led to the side of Coryon's chair between two women, and forced to look upon the dreadful scene. At the sight of Leonard bound to the fatal plank, and the grim tree with its restless branches ever twisting in avid hunger for their prey, a look of stony horror came over her face; she gave one gasping, sobbing cry, and fell back unconscious.

For some moments Coryon paused; he was inclined to wait till Ulama should be restored to consciousness, for he wanted to prolong the torture of the lovers somewhat before finally consigning Leonard to his fate; but his fury mastered him, and he gave the signal to the two men holding one end of the plank to push it out along the stone pier.

They had just begun to move it when a shot was heard, and one of them fell to the ground; and Leonard, turning his head, saw Templemore, high on the rocks above, kneeling with his rifle at his shoulder.

Coryon saw it too, and, with a shout, and many threats, urged the other man to push out the plank; but, instead, he started back in terror, and only just in time to escape a second bullet that came singing past his ears and wounded a soldier standing near.

Coryon, mad with rage and disappointed malice, snatched a spear from a soldier beside him, and ordered others in front of him to seize the plank and push it out, prodding at them with the spear to force obedience; but one, who stepped forward at his bidding, fell before he could reach the plank. Meantime, Templemore, followed by Ergalon and the brave Zonella, had come leaping down from ledge to ledge, threatening all who barred his way, and shooting down one or two who tried to stop him. He now stood, a revolver in each hand, at the end of the plank, and there he kept a circle around him, while Ergalon cut the cords by which Leonard was bound, released the cloth that had been tied round his mouth to gag him, and helped him to his feet. Immediately he rushed to Templemore.

"Give me a rifle, Jack! Let me shoot down that son of Satan and rid the earth of him forever."

Ergalon was carrying three rifles, the one Templemore had been using and two spare ones; one of these he handed now to Leonard.

But, in the interval, Coryon's chief officer, Dakla, had taken in the situation; and having already had experience of the weapons with which he saw Templemore was armed, had advised Coryon to retreat into the covered-way.

"It is useless to stay here, my lord," he said. "Thou wilt surely be killed! Haste to the shelter while there is yet time! There I think thou wilt be safe. If not, thou canst retreat within the gates."

"Dost think the danger is so great, good Dakla?" Coryon asked, incredulously.

"I am sure of it, my lord. Haste thee—and take some soldiers with thee and keep them between thee and thine enemies, or thou wilt never reach the shelter alive. I will leave some men here and take others up on to the rocks above, whence we can hurl down great stones upon them. Haply, if no more come, we may yet prevail against these."

Coryon and his priests and immediate followers hastened away, accordingly, leaving the still unconscious Ulama, in charge of the two women, behind his chair. He was only just in time, for a soldier he forced to walk beside him fell by a shot from Leonard's rifle a moment before they gained the shelter of the covered-way.

Leonard saw the women beside Coryon's chair, and, though he knew not that Ulama was lying there unconscious, he guessed she was near the spot; therefore he feared to fire more shots in that direction; while he knew it would be useless to fire at the iron-work of the covered-way. For a space, therefore, there was a pause; but soon Dakla's men appeared on the rocks above them and began to roll down stones and boulders.

The position of the little band was now becoming critical. To retreat, leaving Ulama in the hands of Coryon, was not to be conceived. Yet they could not advance, for a compact body of men stood ready to receive them; and at these they durst not fire lest they might hit Ulama or one of her attendants. Yet every minute they stayed where they were increased their danger. Great masses of rock, started by persons above who showed only an arm or hand above the ridge, came crashing down and shooting past them. And, when a head was raised above it here and there to take a hurried aim, it was seen only for a second, and gave little opportunity for a shot.

They had had two or three narrow escapes, and had avoided injury only by leaping out of the path of the rocks that came crashing and bounding down. Jack urged Zonella to go back, but she stoutly refused; and he was at his wits' end what course to take, when loud shouting was heard in the direction of the entrance of the enclosure. Soon, a rush of armed men in red tunics came along the roadway at the rear of the black-coated soldiers standing around Coryon's chair. Instantly Coryon's men gave way, and rushed across the terrace towards the covered-way; while the red-coated men poured in and spread themselves out on either side.

And now could be seen men carrying flags and banners, and amongst them two of mighty stature; one of them, the taller, dressed in the coat of mail and the helmet with silver wings that had been preserved so long in the museum and that was said to have belonged to the legendary Mellenda. He wore, too, the great sword that belonged to the suit, and it seemed, upon his towering form, to be of no more than usual and proportionate size.

As this majestic figure came more closely into view, accompanied by Colenna and someothers of the king's officers, Leonard and Templemore's astonishment were great at recognising no other than their friend Monella!

XXVIII

Rallying to the Call

To make clearer the events described in the previous chapters, it should be stated that, when Templemore and Ergalon had returned from their journey down the canyon in quest of arms and ammunition, they found with Zonella, who was anxiously awaiting them, a messenger from Monella.

It was not yet daylight, and the two who had made the descent and ascent of the difficult path under conditions of considerable hardship, were very much exhausted. They were therefore glad, though surprised, to find that, in their absence, Zonella had provided both food and wine for them.

"How pleased I am to see you I need scarcely say," she exclaimed. "But first, eat and drink, while I talk. I have much to tell, and there is yet time to spare. Therefore, rest and refresh yourselves, while I relate what has been made known to me.

"Your friend, Monella, has done wondrous things. It seems—as Ergalon here no doubt has been aware—that he has long been quietly making preparations for some such crisis as the present. Coryon, it is true, by his treachery, has stolen a march upon him, but he is being gradually and surely enmeshed in the net that the lord Monella has drawn around him. For a long time Sanaima has been secretly drilling numbers of his followers in Myrlanda, where he has a large store of arms, and he and Monella have gained over many of Coryon's men; in particular, some of those sent to close the subterranean pass. When, therefore, the two, with many armed men, presented themselves at the entrance to the pass and found the gates closed against them, instead of making a desperate fight of it in which many must have been killed on both sides and the news of it have been carried to Coryon's ears, they waited for their friends inside to act. Soon, those of them amongst the soldiers who guarded the approach, seizing their opportunity, fell upon their fellows in their sleep, bound them, and opened the gates. The same thing has occurred in the palace; all Coryon's soldiers really devoted to him have been quietly made prisoners, and the palace is now in the hands of Monella and Sanaima and their friends; and Coryon knows it not.

"Now, when Monella found that you had escaped, he divined whither you had gone, and sent messengers here to await your return; and I sent them back at once to tell him I expected you here ere long. And now another has arrived with instructions, in case you should return in time to put them into execution, as—the Great Spirit be praised!—you have. Monella has sent two or three of Coryon's own people to him with various messages to allay his suspicions; and Coryon quite believes that you are still a prisoner, and that Monella is still in Myrlanda, unable to get through the pass. Others of Monella's men, dressed in black tunics taken from the prisoners, are now placed at intervals on guard at all the approaches to Coryon's retreat; where already, by this time, nearly all his followers and his adherents amongst the people are assembling. There will be some hundreds altogether; all hostile to you and your friends. But, when they are all assembled, Monella will gather together also many hundreds from the people outside, and march them to the amphitheatre and so surprise Coryon and all with him."

"But how," asked Templemore, "if Coryon gets to hear of it?"

"He will not. No move will be made till all are gathered in the amphitheatre; after that, any stragglers going thither from the town, and any messengers sent thence by Coryon, will fall into the hands of Monella's disguised soldiers, and will be quietly seized and bound."

"I see. And now what is to be done to make sure of the safety of our friends?"

"The directions are these. You are to go quietly, through the forest, to the wood at the edge of the amphitheatre where—"

"I understand," broke in Ergalon. "It is the place,"—turning to Templemore—"where we stood and looked down upon the great devil-tree that night. I can take you by a route that leads through the woods all the way, and thus we shall not be seen."

"Yes, that is right," resumed Zonella. "When you get there, you are to remain concealed, and watch all that goes on, and, unless compelled, do nothing till the arrival of Monella and his friends. But, if it should be absolutely necessary to interfere before that to save our friends, why, then, of course, you must do the best you can."

"I only hope we may be in time to save them," said Templemore, with a sigh. "I am terribly anxious. Let us be going; it is already getting light."

The three then started—for Zonella insisted on accompanying them—and the messenger was sent back to inform Monella. When they approached the amphitheatre, four black-coated soldiers suddenly sprang up before them from among the bushes, where they had been lying concealed. Templemore drew a pistol, but Zonella stepped in front of him, and said something in a low tone to the soldiers, who at once gave way and let them pass.

"What did you say to them?" asked Templemore.

"I gave them the password," she answered quietly.

"And what is that, if I may inquire?"

"It is a word you do not regard with the same feelings as ourselves," she answered gravely. "But in Manoa it has always been a word to conjure with, and, so it is today—it is 'Mellenda.'" And, while she spoke, she looked at Templemore half defiantly.

But he made no reply, and they walked on in silence, and now with all caution, to their destination.

Meanwhile, so soon as the sun had risen, messengers were hurrying hither and thither amongst the populace, knocking at doors, and summoning all friendly to the king and the princess, to assemble in the great square where stood the large museum. And, in reply to excited questionings, they often only gave the magic word, 'Mellenda,' or said, 'Mellenda calls you.'

Most of the population were early astir that morning, restless with anxiety and fear for the princess and her betrothed, who had, they were told, been carried off by Coryon. As stated, by the great mass of people their princess was much beloved by the people; and Leonard, if he had not gained their affection, had the sympathy, for her sake, of all loyal subjects, and they were many. Indeed, all they wanted was a leader; they were too cowed to take action for themselves.

No wonder, then, that when such a leader came, announcing himself as the long-expected, legendary Mellenda, the whole population, outside those who were gathered around Coryon in the amphitheatre, rallied to his standard, and clamoured to be armed and led against their oppressor. That there were plenty of arms in the museum all well knew; and, when the messengers ran to and fro, spreading the news of the return of their hero-king, all the men who heard the tidings left at once whatever they might have in hand, and hurried to the museum. There they found Sanaima with a number of followers already equipped in the well-known red tunics and winged helmets; and Colenna and others engaged in giving out arms and uniforms to many more.

And when, shortly after, Monella appeared at the top of the wide flight of steps, clad in Mellenda's coat of mail, with the well-known banner floating above him, and wearing at his side the mighty sword, every man and woman and child amongst the crowd below gave a great shout and knelt before him. Then Monella drew the mighty sword, that an ordinary man could hardly wield, and, flourishing it in the air as easily as though it were but the lightest cane, addressed the kneeling people in sonorous tones that were heard by all, and were delivered with an air of exceeding majesty and dignity,

"Yes, my children! I have returned to you! After many days the Great Spirit hath led my weary steps back to my beloved country, there to finish my life's work, and end a long and troublous journey. My pilgrimage through the ages hath been a punishment to me, even as the same dreary time hath been a punishment to you; a punishment to myself for having placed too high a value, in the times that are long past, on power and conquest and dominion; to you, for that your forefathers forsook their faith—the worship of the one Great Spirit— and embraced the religion of the powers of darkness, and supported the atrocious Coryon in a rebellion against their lawful king, and in the murder of those near and dear to him. For that, the punishment hath been that they should be oppressed and cruelly ill-treated by him they thus supported, through many generations. But, at last, the anger of the Great Spirit is appeased. He hath led me hither to deliver this fair land from the horror that broods over it. I come to you, not with great fleets of ships, with armies and generals, as of yore; but as a simple wanderer returning to his home. Yet in my coming the Great Spirit sent you all a sign; for I arrived but just in time to save her who is the child of Manoa's ancient race of kings and—my own descendant. This was the sign—this and the death of Zelus at the same time; which was a warning to Coryon that he heeded not. But time presses, and I may not say more now. The princess and our friends are in great peril, and I go to save them. I go to break Black Coryon's power forever, and to punish him as he deserves. Then will I bring again to this fair land peace, and happiness, and security for all."

Then, amid acclamations, and shouts and cries of delight, Monella— or Mellenda, as he now called himself—moved off towards the place where Coryon, in fancied security, was boastfully proclaiming his intention to espouse the princess, and to live henceforth at the palace as supreme ruler of the country.

Those of Sanaima's followers from Myrlanda, who had been instructed in their duties, took charge, as officers, of ranks and companies of the newly-recruited men. They were assisted by many officers of the king's guard who had been held prisoners in the palace, but had been released, and had now changed their blue uniforms for the red tunics and winged helmets in the museum.

Some, however, remained behind, to equip and despatch reinforcements as men continued to arrive asking to be enrolled. Thus, if trouble should arise with Coryon, Monella would have at his back, eventually, an overwhelming force. And as the men kept marching off in companies, the crowd of women and children and old men collected in the square in which was the museum stood about in anxious groups, awaiting news; hardly daring to hope for what all so fervently desired— the final downfall of their ruthless tyrant.

XXIX

'Thou Art my Lord Mellenda!'

To return to the scene in the amphitheatre. Monella, and those with him, advanced with measured tread; but suddenly his eyes fell on Ulama. For a few moments he bent over her, then he came slowly to the front and looked around him, and in that rapid survey he seemed to take in everything.

Beckoning to Leonard and Zonella he said, when they had joined him,

"The princess lies there in a dead faint. This is no place for the poor child. Bear her tenderly outside. My people will protect you." Then he turned again to look around.

In their surprise at the unexpected inrush, those on the heights had ceased hurling down the rocks, and now they gazed in wonderment at Monella and those with him. Beside him stood a tall man in a white robe upon which was worked a figure of the sun in diamonds that flashed and sparkled as he moved. His long hair and beard were snowy white, his forehead, high and massive, was clear, and curiously free from lines and wrinkles. It had the impassive look of one who suffers few earthly cares to trouble him. His features were pleasant and benevolent in expression, and the clear grey eyes were open and candid in their glance. Like Monella, he was far above the usual height; and, like him, was of imposing presence and stately mien. Altogether, one would say of him that he was a *good* man, a man to be trusted and respected; he had at the same time the air of one deeply engrossed in intellectual pursuits, or leading an ascetic life. He lacked just that touch of tender human sympathy that made Monella's mere look so fascinating to those with whom he came in contact, and that bound so thoroughly to him those who yielded to its subtle influence.

Ergalon had already whispered to the others that the stranger was Sanaima, the ancient chief of the White Priesthood; and Templemore regarded him with interest and curiosity.

Above their heads waved great red banners with strange devices and elaborately carved standard poles. At a sign from Monella, Coryon's banner, that floated above his chair, was pulled down and trampled in the dust; then the largest of the red ones was hoisted in its place.

Next, Monella quietly seated himself in Coryon's chair and gazed around the enclosure, his features set and stern, and his steady, piercing eyes seeming to read the very heart of everyone upon whom he turned his gaze. The king's ministers and other prisoners had been unbound, while Templemore had been hastily explaining, to the best of his ability, all that had taken place.

Presently Monella rose, and, waving his hand towards the people not clad in Coryon's uniforms, he thus addressed them,

"How comes it, that in this place of evil deeds and heinous crimes, I find many of the king's peaceful subjects—or they who should be peaceful—ranged round and calmly looking on at acts of cold-blooded cruelty against the king's own child and those he calls his friends? What have ye to say in excuse or extenuation? Choose the highest among ye for a spokesman, and let him come forward and explain this shameful thing, if so he can. Else I may include ye all in the punishment I am here to mete out to these evil-doers."

At this there was a great hubbub and commotion. Some of Coryon's companions in the covered-way turned in a panic to make their escape into the interior gallery; but found, to their dismay, that the gates were fast closed and barred against them from within. And when they glanced out at the rocks above, they saw red-coated soldiers, who now lined the heights and kept still arriving in ever-increasing numbers. Dakla and his principal officers had withdrawn at their advance, and now stood, with the priests, crowded together just inside the covered-way. Outside the iron screens the long, trailing branches swept up from time to time, as though seeking to get at those within.

After a hurried conference among the people, one of their number stepped down on to the main terrace and placed himself before Monella.

Templemore stood on one side of Monella's chair, rifle in hand, with Ergalon close by holding the spare rifles, all ready loaded. He watched with growing wonder the continual arrival of red-coated soldiers on all sides of the rocky ridges. They all carried spears, or swords and shields, and wore the curious helmets ornamented with little silver wings that he had seen in the museum. And now, amongst them, were to be seen many citizens in ordinary dress. But all kept a space between themselves and those who had been there on their arrival; their manner towards these was evidently unfriendly and threatening; and, since the newcomers outnumbered the others, including all Coryon's people, the position of the latter was growing anything but comfortable. And still the red-coated men kept coming, pushing those in advance of them into positions lower down and farther round the terraces of the enclosure.

There was a general hush when the one who had been chosen spokesman came forward and stood in front of Monella, who asked curtly,

"Thy name?"

"Galaima," was the reply, given in a clear, unhesitating voice. "I have been chosen by those whom thou didst but now address, to speak in their name. Seeing that punishment hath been spoken of, we desire first to ask what authority thou hast to speak in the king's name; by what right thou dost threaten us; and who thou art?"

"You have the right to ask those questions," returned Monella coldly. "Know then that I am King of Manoa—thy king, and the king of Coryon, and of all in this country."

"King of Manoa!" echoed Galaima in surprise, while similar exclamations broke forth around. "But, my lord—I speak with all respect—how can that be?"

"The King Dranoa is sick even unto death. His illness hath been hastened in its course by acts of base treachery perpetrated by Coryon—with whom I shall deal anon. Finding himself dying and unable to lead his soldiers to the rescue of his child, he hath abdicated in my favour, for me to hold the post so long as I think fit in the interests of the nation. Here (taking out from his bosom a roll of parchment) is his sign-manual duly sealed and executed in the presence of the High Priest Sanaima and others who are with me; and here is his sceptre of office, and this is his signet-ring—these being given to me by him in token of my authority, and also in the presence of Sanaima and many others you see around me. Is it not so, friends?" Monella demanded, turning to Sanaima and the others near.

A loud shout went up in confirmation; then, at a wave of Monella's hand, there was again a deep, expectant silence.

Coryon had come out from the covered-way on hearing the unlooked-for and unwelcome news, and now stood, a little in advance of his own people, an attentive listener and observer of what was going on.

"Thou hast heard," resumed Monella, in the same cold, stern tone. "I come duly armed with authority to punish, and I have the power. Do thou and thy fellows yonder desire to take part with the traitor Coryon, and fight against us; or do ye disavow him and throw yourselves upon my mercy?"

"My lord, with all respect, I ask for the reply to my last question. We came hither—of a certainty I and my immediate friends so came—to protest against the king's choice of a son-in-law. We were unwilling to have thrust upon us, as our future king, one who is of a different race—who is a stranger in the land—and who, so far as it appeareth, hath no claim to royal dignity. Now—with all respect, I say again—for all we know, those same objections apply to thine own case. If, however, I am wrong in this, and thou canst convince us that thou hast reasonable claim to the dignity the king hath conferred upon thee, then we are ready to submit ourselves as loyal subjects."

"Thy logic is good," observed Monella with bitter emphasis, "for thy present purpose; but it faileth to explain how it came about that, instead of making known your sentiment in a petition and awaiting the king's friendly explanation, as befitted faithful subjects, ye supported Coryon in his treasonable acts—in kidnapping the king's daughter and his friends. Further, ye were all proceeding, at Coryon's mere suggestion, to put to death this stranger, without giving him either time or opportunity to afford the information ye now profess yourself so anxious to obtain. However, thou shalt have thy question answered—and, that done, let me warn thee that I am in no mood to suffer further trifling. King Dranoa's good-natured weakness, and my own misplaced leniency, have already wrought too much misunderstanding. Ask thy question of the lord Colenna, the king's High Chamberlain."

Then Colenna stepped forward, and, in a loud, sonorous voice, that resounded throughout the vast amphitheatre, cried out,

"Know ye all, by the command of King Dranoa and the unanimous assent of his ministers, that the great lord Mellenda, who hath been hitherto known amongst us as Monella—which in ancient times had the same signification as the word Mellenda—hath made himself known to his people, and hath assumed the office of ruler of the countries of Manoa and Myrlanda."

At this extraordinary announcement Coryon moved back into the covered-way with unsteady and almost tottering steps; while Monella rose and, with another wave of the hand, signalled for silence. Turning to Sanaima, he asked, with quiet dignity, but in a ringing voice that all could hear,

"And thou, august head of our religion, faithful through so many years of persecution and despair, who dost *thou* say I am?"

Then Sanaima raised his hands to heaven as though to invoke a blessing, and said, solemnly,

"In the name of the Great Spirit whom I serve, I recognise and welcome thee, my lord Mellenda!"

But still Monella waved his hand for silence; and, raising his voice, he cried,

"Come forth, Black Coryon! I command thee! Come forth!"

And Coryon came forward, and stood before him; but he durst not meet his eyes.

Monella slowly raised his arm and straightened it, pointing his finger at his enemy.

"And who, foul Coryon, who dost *thou* say I am?"

For the space of a few seconds Coryon looked his questioner in the face. There was a brief struggle to hold his own and to repel with proud defiance the glance Monella turned on him; then, bowing his head, he murmured humbly,

"Thou art my lord Mellenda!"

Then a great shout went up. Again, and again, and yet again it was repeated. "Mellenda! Mellenda! Mellenda!" It rang out from far and near. It was taken up by a crowd of women and children without the gates, and thence it travelled back and echoed from one side of the rocky amphitheatre to the other.

When, once more, there was silence, Galaima dropped upon one knee and begged for clemency for himself and friends.

"Lay down your arms, each one of you, and go!" the answer came. "Let me not look upon your faces again yet awhile."

Then Monella, turning to Coryon's soldiers, commanded them also to lay down their arms and surrender themselves prisoners.

Here Coryon showed the first signs of resistance he had yet exhibited, and his officers, who had stood watching for a sign from him, withdrew in a body into the entrance to the covered-way, seeing in it the best opportunities for a last desperate fight.

"My lord forgetteth," said Coryon, "that he hath given no assurance that the lives of my people and servants will be spared."

"I can make no terms with thee or with thy minions. I came here to punish the evil-doers, as well as to save my friends," returned Monella with grave meaning. "Thou hast been warned again and again since I came into the land; I sent thee word that, if I came to thee, I would bring retribution in my hand."

"But surely," urged Coryon, in the smooth, oily manner he could put on at will, "if we submit, my lord will require no more? Thy friends are safe; no harm hath been done to them. May it not be that I remain here with mine own people, within mine own domain—the domain that hath been mine for centuries—in friendly alliance—"

"What!" exclaimed Monella, turning wrathfully upon the crafty hypocrite with a blaze of anger in his eyes, as might a lion turn upon a snapping cur. "Thou darest to speak to me of *alliance*! Alliance with *thee*! With a thing so foul, so loathsome, so detestable as thou! Shall the eagle ally himself with the carrion crow? Enough!" He broke off, in indignation at the insult, and, turning to the officers of his own party who stood near, cried,

"Seize them and bind them! Everyone! Let not one escape! But take them alive, if possible."

A large number of the red-coated soldiers, led by their officers, now advanced upon the crowd of Coryon's people gathered at the entrance to the covered-way. Many of the latter came forward at once and threw down their arms; while others stood irresolute. Coryon, himself, made no effort to escape, and was seized by a couple of men, who quickly bound his hands behind him. But Dakla and all Coryon's priests and some half-dozen of his lieutenants and a few soldiers—perhaps those who felt themselves most guilty—stood defiantly some little distance within the gallery, determined to resist capture to the last.

XXX

A Terrible Vengeance!

O f all the spectators of what had occurred in the amphitheatre, no
one, probably, was so utterly astonished and helplessly bewildered
as was Templemore. At Monella's assumption of the royal office he
felt no great surprise. It seemed almost a natural thing, taking all the
circumstances into account, that the king, finding his daughter stolen
away and himself too ill to pursue and punish her captors, should
delegate his authority to the man in whom he had of late reposed
such confidence. But at Colenna's announcement that in Monella he
recognised the long-expected, legendary Mellenda, Templemore was, as
may be supposed, considerably startled; and his perplexity was increased
when Sanaima, in his turn, subscribed to Colenna's declaration; but
when Coryon himself affirmed his belief in the marvellous assertion,
Templemore's ideas became so hopelessly confused, that he knew not
what to think or what to make of it. In other circumstances he would,
no doubt, have quietly settled matters in his own mind by deciding that
all present had become victims to a passing fit of madness or transient
delusion; but the grim realities of the strange drama that was being
played before him made it impossible to explain things by any such
hypothesis.

It was in the midst of the conflict thus proceeding in his mind, that
Dakla and his fellows took up their attitude of defiance; so Templemore
promptly decided to postpone further thought upon the matter. It was
sufficient, for the moment, that there was the prospect of a fight in
which his friends would need his help; and he began handling his rifle
significantly, glancing while he did so at Monella.

The latter had laid his hand upon his shoulder as though to stay
him until he should have had more time to study the situation, when
a rumbling noise was heard, and an iron door shot out from the inside
wall a little distance from the end of the covered-way, completely
closing it and shutting out from view the men within. So suddenly had
this been done that Dakla was almost caught by it, and would have
been jammed against the iron pillar into which it fitted, but that he had
managed to withdraw himself inside just in time to escape it.

The impression upon the minds of those outside was that this unlooked-for obstacle that intervened between those within the protected gallery and their enemies, had been purposely made use of to gain time to force open the interior gates and thus assist their escape into the labyrinth of passages beyond. The first effect was to dishearten those of Coryon's adherents who were still outside in a state of indecision. Seeing themselves thus, as they thought, incontinently abandoned by their leaders, they threw down their arms without further ado, submitted to their captors, and, in few minutes, were pinioned and marched out of the way.

It now became a question what steps were to be taken to follow up those who had so cleverly escaped, temporarily, at all events, from their pursuers. These were, after Coryon himself, the most guilty of the whole atrocious confederacy; and Templemore turned to Monella with a look of inquiry.

"What say you," said he, "shall we try whether that door is bullet-proof?"

But Monella again laid his hand upon the other's arm, and gazed, as though in expectation, first at Coryon—who was standing out in the centre of the terrace, guarded by two soldiers—and then, from him, to that part of the covered-way nearest to the rocks that ended it. His quick eye had noticed that Coryon seemed as much taken by surprise as all the rest, and that there was, in his face, no trace of that triumphant satisfaction that might have been expected if this manoeuvre of his chief friends had been looked for. Instead, there was a fixed look that was momentarily changing from surprise to terror.

Templemore, following Monella's gaze, noted all this—and so did others. A hush fell upon all present; everyone looked at Coryon, and, from him, to the length of grated iron screens, over the face of which the branches of the fatal tree were playing with busy sweep, evidently aware, by some unfailing instinct, that there was plenty of prey for them within. And it was now noticed that the larger number of the longer branches had gathered themselves upon that side.

Gradually, the look on Coryon's face changed into one of absolute horror, the while he stood staring at the outside of the covered-gallery.

To make what follows clear, it is necessary to describe this covered-way a little more in detail. It has already been explained that it formed the approach to an opening in the rock—closed by gates—which was the principal entrance to Coryon's retreat. When unprotected by the sliding gratings at the side, it was so near to the great devil-tree that the longer branches could sweep its whole width for some distance in front of the gates. At the side was some masonry, above which the rock rose steep and almost over-hanging. At the end, above the entrance, the rock rose also abruptly, and then followed the line of the arena, shutting in the latter at this part by a rocky wall that rose perpendicularly some fifty or sixty feet. But the part within reach of the tree was roofed over by iron gratings, forming a sort of verandah, which, in turn, could be rendered safe from the terrible branches by sliding grated doors or shutters that could, by machinery within, be moved forward in telescopic fashion along the whole length accessible to the tree, and a short distance beyond. Thus, when the side 'shutters' were withdrawn, the entrance-gates were very effectually guarded by the tree itself. When they were extended, they, in conjunction with the roof, constituted an efficient protection to the covered-way. But herein lay also a cunningly-devised and deadly trap; for, just within the entrance of this covered-gallery, was another iron door that could be moved across the passage so as to imprison anyone caught between it and the gates at the other end. This door came out of a scarcely noticeable slot in the masonry at the side; and it was situated far enough along to place those thus caught within reach of the tree, if the side shutters were withdrawn.

Doubtless, many had fallen into this frightful trap. Thinking the gallery well protected they would walk unsuspiciously along it towards the closed gates, when those watching from within could close the gallery behind them and open the sides; and their fate would then be sealed.

This was the only part of the main terrace within reach of the tree. Round the remainder of the amphitheatre it was far removed from it, and was of ample width. Only at this part, and upon the stone pier that jutted out towards the tree from the centre, or down in the arena itself, was there danger to anyone moving about within the vast enclosure.

At a point in the cliff, high above the covered-way, was a small grated door in the rock. This was another entrance to Coryon's fastness; but it was sufficiently protected by the nature of the steep and narrow path by which alone it could be reached.

While those gathered around the enclosure, following Coryon's fixed gaze, were watching the outside faces of the sliding doors or shutters, these doors began to move; and, amidst a hush of awe-struck expectation, they disclosed a gap which gradually widened, and through which the fatal branches quickly darted. Then, from within, arose a fearful and appalling cry, as the miserable prisoners caught in this trap of their own contriving began to realise their situation. The gap grew wider, and, anon, another opened farther on, and into this the searching branches likewise entered, hungry for the prey within. And, as the gaps grew wider, they disclosed to view an awful scene. Some dozens of terror-stricken wretches could be seen fighting and struggling with the writhing branches and with each other, amidst a deafening din of screams, and shrieks, and yells; the officers and soldiers using their swords, and the priests and others their daggers, in a hopeless contest with the twisting branches that kept coiling around them. In their mad struggles and desperate efforts the combatants fought with one another, the stronger striving to push the weaker in front of them; the latter, in turn, stabbing backwards at those who thus tried to make use of them. Three or four, in headlong terror, leaped from the terrace on to the ground beneath, where they fell with dull thuds, and probably broken limbs; but, ere they could rise, their legs were entangled in the ubiquitous branches and escape became impossible. Dakla was seen, with a sword in one hand and a dagger in the other, at one moment slashing furiously at the branches that assailed him, at another striving to hold in front of him Skelda, the next in rank to Coryon. Two of the priests were seen engaged in a hand-to-hand struggle, apparently unmindful of the coils that gradually encircled them and presently dragged both out, locked together, and still frantically fighting with each other. They were carried up to the top of the tree, and disappeared, still fighting, within the cavity. But, though the rapacious tree had now as much as it could, for the time, dispose of in this way, it had no intention of giving up its hold upon the others. These it grappled in its toils, dragging them about hither and thither, dangling them now this way and now that, but never giving one a chance of escape—evidently bent on saving all up for future meals—perhaps days hence. It was a gruesome scene that shocked and sickened the spectators, for all they were so incensed, and justly so, against the victims.

Meanwhile, the iron door in the rock above had opened, and a woman was seen hurrying down the dangerous path. Her hair was streaming loosely about her shoulders, her eyes were wild and fierce, and she laughed and gesticulated in a fashion that made those who watched her think her crazy. She made her way to where Coryon still stood, a silent witness of what was going on before him; and she then paused and surveyed the awful scene with a smile that was almost devilish.

Just then Skelda leaped out of the covered-way on to the ground beneath; then, rising to his feet, looked round despairingly, and, glancing up, he met the fierce gaze and cruel smile of the woman he had so shamefully betrayed. She pointed her finger at him.

"Ha! ha!" she cried triumphantly, "this is *my* work, Skelda! *I* closed the gates and shut you all in with the outer door. My love to you, my— *husband*!" This last word was hissed out at him between clenched teeth. "My love to you, dear friend." And she mockingly threw him a kiss on the tips of her fingers. Then, when the wretched Skelda's feet were dragged from under him by a branch that had coiled round his legs, she addressed herself to Coryon, who had now fixed his eyes upon her, his evil face twitching convulsively with the fury he could not suppress.

"See, great Coryon! Mighty Coryon! All-powerful Coryon! See my handiwork! Yes, *mine*! See what a woman's wit hath done for thy precious friends. What a day to live to see! I saw thee in the clutch of thy prisoner; heard thee called 'coward' to thy face. It was sweet that; and sweet to see thy prey escape thee! And this is sweet too! Look at thy great friend Skelda; see how he kicks and shrieks! Think of it—all my doing! See how Dakla glares! Now he and Palana are fighting one another! Oh, but it is a brave sight to look upon! Fit even for the gods ye have served so well! I think I am almost avenged; but the sweetest of all is yet to come—when I see *thee* given to the tree, as I *shall*!"

Coryon struggled, but vainly, to get at her. She shrugged her shoulders and turned her back upon him, then slowly approached Monella; the look of triumph died away, and an expression that was partly of sorrow, and partly of hard determination, took its place. Arrived in front of him, she threw herself humbly on her knees.

"My lord," she cried, with clasped hands, "I crave justice at thy hands, I *demand* it! In the names of the countless women and fair children whom yonder monster hath given over to the same awful death that hath now overtaken his own creatures; in the name of my own bitter wrongs and sufferings, I demand that this loathsome being shall not escape his just reward. I ask that he be given up to that tree to which he has consigned so many; and that first he be confined in the same cell from which I have escaped. I will lead thy officers to it. Let him be kept there till the wicked tree, with recovered appetite, shall be ready to devour him! Let him there endure the tortures he hath inflicted upon me and countless others!"

"Who art thou, daughter?" asked Monella gently.

She shook her head mournfully and replied, much as she had to Leonard,

"I am called Fernina, lord. Once, I was a joyous-hearted wife and mother; but Coryon stole me away from my home to give me to his friend Skelda. What I am now I scarcely know; misery and suffering, and shame and infamies unutterable have made me—alas, I know not what!"

"From my heart I pity thee, my daughter. Thy wrongs cry out for punishment, and thy prayer is just. Show my officers the place. Coryon *shall* be the last meal of the accursed fetish he has fed with the blood of so many victims."

"I will go back by the way by which I came," Fernina answered, "and will make safe again the covered-way; then will I open the gates, that thine officers may take him in that way."

By this time the covered-way was empty; every occupant had been dragged or had leaped out and was held in the toils below. There was, therefore, nothing to prevent its being used again. Fernina went up the path and disappeared from view; then soon the sliding shutters were seen to move back in their places; and, shortly after, she appeared at one end of the covered-way and beckoned to those in charge of Coryon to follow her. He was led down and placed in the same cell she had occupied, and there shut in and left to himself, and to look out, if he chose, at his friends in the tree's tenacious arms outside. Some of them were so close he could have spoken with them.

After Coryon had been removed, Sanaima turned to Monella; then raised his hands and eyes towards heaven.

"Let us thank the Great Spirit," said he solemnly, "that hath, at last, delivered our enemies into our hands, and that without the loss of a life, or so much as a wound upon our side!"

And Monella added a heartfelt "Amen."

"Of a truth," he added reverently, "the wicked have been caught today in their own snare. At last, we may truly rejoice that the curse hath been removed, forever, from the fair land of Manoa. But this is a fearful sight; let us hasten from it. But ere we do, Sanaima, send kindly and trustworthy people to care for the poor woman Fernina and the other women and children who are somewhere within. I cannot now stay longer; I must look after the princess and return to the palace."

"I will remain and look to them myself," answered Sanaima. "Now that the Great Spirit hath at last given them into my charge, it is a trust that belongeth to me, and to me alone."

During the foregoing events, several messengers had passed to and fro delivering messages, in low tones, to Monella or some of his officers, and speeding away again with their replies, or upon other errands. In this way Monella had learned that the princess had recovered from her long swoon and expressed a strong desire to return to the palace to her father, and he had sent back word to Leonard to accompany her.

When, therefore, Templemore, with Monella and many more, reached the great gates on leaving the amphitheatre, they found Ulama and all those with her gone, and they now hastened to the palace after them.

XXXI

'THE SON OF APALANO!'

On leaving the amphitheatre, Monella and his followers formed a long and imposing procession. Only a few had been left behind to guard the prisoners. These last were immured in cells pointed out by Fernina, who was well acquainted with the interior arrangements of Coryon's retreat. For within the rocks was an almost endless series of passages and galleries opening, at the further end, on to an extensive hanging terrace on the very face of the great precipice that formed one end of Roraima's perpendicular sides. Even those of Coryon's followers who had gone over secretly to Monella, were only partially acquainted with the interior of this fastness; hence Fernina's assistance was found of great use by Sanaima and those who remained with him.

It can scarcely be said that the procession, as it left the great gates of the amphitheatre, exhibited, at first, many signs of having just been engaged in a victorious and successful expedition. Those who formed it were, for the most part, silent and preoccupied; for the scenes they had witnessed—and that, as they knew, were still in progress—were of too horrible a character to be readily dismissed from the mind. But, as they proceeded on their way, they met and were joined by fresh bands of red-coated sympathisers; and these, not having the same reasons for repressing their elation at the result of the day's proceedings, broke out into cheering as they passed the groups of people who were now coming out to meet them. For messengers had gone on in advance to tell the news, and the crowds who had been waiting so anxiously in the city, soon learned that Coryon's downfall was an accomplished fact. They had already heard the good tidings of the rescue of the princess and her lover and friends, and were only waiting for this last crowning announcement; when it came, they became almost delirious with joy, and soon poured out to meet the victors and give them an enthusiastic welcome.

Thus the procession that started so quietly—almost in sadness, as it seemed—from the dismal amphitheatre, became at last, as it entered the city, a veritable triumphal pageant, meeting on all sides, and returning, cheers and shouts of joy and exultation. And when Monella, with Templemore, Colenna, and others came into view in the centre of the long array, every head was uncovered and every knee bent. Then, when he had passed, the excited crowds rose and shouted again louder than ever. And well might they do so; for they—and only they—knew the full meaning of the horrors from which they had that day been delivered.

By the time they had neared the king's palace, the crowd had grown so dense that it was with some difficulty that space was cleared for the passage of the principal persons into the building. At the entrance, under the great archway, Leonard, looking pale and anxious, awaited them. Running forward to meet Monella, he said,

"I have heard the news and congratulate you all. But I am in sore distress about the princess. We had much ado to bring her here, and I fear she is very ill. Let me entreat you to go and see her at once, and then let me know what you think about her."

"Certainly will I, my son," replied Monella kindly, and hurried away; while Leonard turned and greeted Templemore and the others with him. Then they all entered the palace and went up one of the great staircases and on to a terrace overlooking the open space where the crowd was assembled, and there awaited Monella's return.

Presently he came to them.

"The princess is weak and much depressed," he said, "and will require care for awhile; but I see no cause for anxiety. Naturally, the poor child is terribly upset. She grieves, too, about the condition of the king her father, and wishes to help nurse him, but this she has not strength for at present. Patience, my son. Be patient and of good heart." He looked with pity and concern at Leonard's haggard face with its hollow, dark-ringed eyes and its worn-out look. "You have suffered—cruelly—I can see," he added, placing his hand gently on the young man's shoulder. "You have been sorely tried."

"Ah!" returned Leonard with a heavy sigh. "You cannot imagine what I have been through! My thoughts still dwell upon the horror of it; my eyes still see the sights I gazed upon! I feel as though I shall never be my old self again. And Ulama! Though I do not yet know how much she saw or knew, I sadly believe she shares my feelings."

"You are both worn out—exhausted, my son. Wait but a space—while I speak to the crowd and dismiss them—and then I will give you a cordial and refreshment; after that you must lie down and have a long sleep."

"I fear even to sleep," said Leonard, shaking his head sadly. "I dread the thought of sleep, for I know but too well what my dreams will be."

"Nay, my son, have no fear. I will promise you dreamless, restful sleep," Monella answered, and moved away to the front of the terrace.

At the sight of his commanding form and upraised hand the shouts and noise and all the subdued roar that till now had been continuous were hushed. Then, as with one accord, all uncovered and fell upon their knees. He spoke a few brief words and then dismissed them, pointing out that his friends were in need of rest and quiet.

The crowd, in respectful obedience, quietly dispersed, and Monella, motioning Elwood and Templemore to follow him, led them into his private apartments and there mixed and administered to both certain drinks that had an immediate and wonderfully revivifying effect. These potions had also the advantage of stimulating their appetites, so that they were the better enabled to take the nourishment he pressed upon them. Then he accompanied them to their sleeping chambers and bade them lie down and take the repose they so sorely needed. None of the three had had any sleep or rest—for Leonard's swoon in his cell and subsequent state of torpor could scarcely be so called—for the past two nights. The two young men were not only worn out, but in that excited state in which the brain seems to insist upon going over and over and over again the events of the previous troubled time, in that ceaseless, monotonous whirl that makes all efforts at sleep so useless. But Monella—who alone showed no sign of the strain all had undergone—sat down by the side of each in succession for a short time, and talked to him in his low, musical tones. What he talked of, or what he did, neither could afterwards remember; but the effect was magical. As Leonard afterwards expressed it, a soothing, delicious sense of drowsy rest crept over his senses; a rest that was not sleep, for he could still hear the usual sounds around, but gradually growing hushed and muffled. Then came a sensation as of being lifted and wafted away by a gentle wind; and in the sighing of the breeze there seemed a delightful strain of music, a dreamy lullaby that carried with it a restful peace sinking imperceptibly into untroubled repose.

The strangest thing, perhaps, is that even the unimpressionable Templemore was affected in the same way, as he afterwards admitted. Nor was that all; for, on awaking, he was conscious of having had the most delicious dreams, though he could not quite recall their subject. For sometime he lay in a state of blissful ease, striving to recollect the dream that had left sensations so delicious, and afraid to rouse himself for fear the remembrance should vanish altogether. He could hear the usual sounds going on in the palace, the tramp of armed men, and clashing and jingling of arms; but he was only half-conscious of them. Then he heard his name called in tones that seemed to come from the far distance, and, opening his eyes, he saw Monella standing beside his couch and regarding him with a grave smile.

"Wake up, my friend," he said. "It is time you roused yourself. I wish to have some talk with you and Leonard. You have slept for eight-and-forty hours!"

Templemore sat up and rubbed his eyes.

"I feel as if I had slept for months," he answered in a half-dazed way. "And I've had such curious dreams, or visions; I feel quite sorry to be awake again. It's a strange thing for *me* to talk like that, I know," he added with hesitation.

"What did you dream of?" asked Leonard, who had entered in time to hear the other's concluding words.

"That's the strange part of it," returned Templemore, looking perplexed and somewhat sheepish. "I've had a most extraordinary dream of some kind, or a vision or something—*that* I know, yet I cannot remember what it was. All I can now tell you is that it was something so extremely pleasant that it has left the most agreeable sensations behind it. My very blood seems in a warm, delicious glow from it. What can it be?" he added, looking in a bewildered way from one to the other.

But Monella made no comment, and went away.

"It's been just the same with me," said Leonard, in a low voice, that had an expression almost of awe in it. "Monella woke me about half an hour ago and I felt much like what you have described."

"It's very odd," Templemore returned thoughtfully. "It must be the drink he gave us. Do you remember what Harry Lorien said of him? That he believed Monella was a magician? I begin to think him a wizard myself. But, dear boy, how much better you look!"

"So do you, Jack; and he tells me Ulama is the same—and it's all his doing, you know. He *is* a wizard; and that's all there is to be said about it."

"The question is," Jack went on, "what was it he gave us? Here it has made us sleep nearly forty-eight hours; and it seems, has done us, in that time, as much good as one would have thought would have taken a week or two to accomplish, and yet it has left no dull, drowsy, listless feeling, such as opiates generally do. I can't make it out." And, shaking his head gravely, Templemore went to take his morning plunge.

When they sought Monella, he bade Leonard give him the particulars of all that had occurred to him. Leonard recounted them.

"It seemed very terrible to me," he said when he had finished, "at the time; and truly I thought I should never get over it. Yet—now—it seems such a long while ago—so far off."

"That is well, my son," returned Monella. "For it has been a sore trial. I have heard about *you*," he continued, turning to Templemore, "from the lady Zonella and from Ergalon."

"I owe a great debt to her—to him—to both," Templemore replied. "Without their aid I fear things would have gone badly with Leonard, and myself too."

"Yes, Coryon had ably laid his treacherous schemes, and we all have reason to be thankful for their failure," said Monella solemnly. "Things came to a crisis just then. I had just matured certain plans that Sanaima and I had laid out; and only the day before my long-lost memory returned to me, and I remembered, all in a flash, as it were, the whole of my former life."

"That you were—that is—are—" Templemore began; but stopped and looked confused.

"Yes, that I am indeed Mellenda," was the reply, given with an air of grave conviction. "I know the statement sounds incredible to you; you are of that nature, have been brought up in that kind of school, that makes such a thing sound impossible. But if *I* myself feel and know that it is true, and if my people around me know it and not only admit it but rejoice in it, then, for me, that is sufficient."

"Certainly," Templemore assented, feeling very uncomfortable under the other's gaze.

"Still—to you—let me be, while you remain here, simply what I have been before—your friend Monella. I am the same being today that you have known and, I hope, liked—that you have joined with in facing danger and adventure—I am the same! The mere fact that I remember things now that I had forgotten before makes no difference to me or to our friendship."

This was said with a look of such kind regard that Templemore felt his own heart swell with responsive feeling. It was true he had a strong inclination to regard the other as a sincere, but self-deceiving mystic; but, apart from that—apart from this strange delusion, as he deemed it, about Monella's being the legendary Mellenda—Templemore looked upon him with feelings of the greatest admiration, affection, and respect. And he had never been so conscious of those feelings as at this moment. He took the hand that the other extended to him, and bent his head respectfully.

"Sir," said he in a low tone, "no son could respect and reverence a beloved and honoured father more than I do you. No one could feel prouder of the love and esteem you have been kind enough to show me; no people, I feel satisfied, could have a worthier, a more disinterested, or exalted ruler. If I find it difficult to realise the marvel that you have related, if I have the idea that, perhaps, you are mistaking your own dreams for actual realities, it is not from any doubt of your sincerity or veracity—only that in that way alone can I bring myself to explain the wonder."

"And I, on my side, respect the honesty that will not allow you to pretend what you cannot feel," was the reply. "To you let me be simply Monella, and let us continue on our old terms of mutual friendship and esteem. And now I am going to rouse your wonder and surprise with yet one other unexpected statement. Your friend Leonard here is not the son of the parents he has all his life supposed himself to be."

Leonard sprang up with an exclamation.

"I will explain how. You have already told us"—this to Leonard— "how that your supposed father and mother, with yourself, and your Indian nurse, once stayed sometime with a strange people in a secluded valley among the peaks of the Andes. I was not there at the time, but they were my people."

"Your people!" Leonard repeated with astonishment.

"Yes, my son, my people! Apalano, and two or three others of whom you have heard me speak—all, alas, now dead! I was informed of your visit when I next came back to them, for a while, from my wanderings. I heard of it and what had happened; how Apalano's little child—his only one—had been killed by a venomous serpent."

"The child of Apalano!" Leonard repeated in amaze.

"The two children," Monella continued—"Mr. Elwood's child and Apalano's—were wonderfully alike, and your nurse, the Indian woman Carenna, was very fond of both, and was in the habit of taking them out together. She was out with them thus one day, and left them both sleeping in the shade of a clump of trees while she went a few yards away to gather some fruit. She returned (so she says) in a few minutes; then, thinking one of the children had a strange look she picked it up in alarm; at the same moment a serpent glided out from under its clothes and went away, hissing, into the wood. But the child was dead; and it was the child of the Englishman. Then Carenna, frantic with grief, and afraid to tell the truth to her master and mistress, exchanged the clothes and ornaments of the children. The trick succeeded; for the dead infant was swollen and discoloured; and Apalano mourned the death of his only child, when it went away, in reality, with the strangers and their Indian nurse."

"Then," said Leonard excitedly, "I am—"

"Ranelda, son of my well-beloved friend! Ah," said Monella, sadly, "it was a cruel thing to do. It preyed upon the mind of my friend, and, I truly believe, brought on the fatal sickness. But for that he might have lived, haply, to see at last the land of his fathers—might have been one of us here today."

Leonard felt the tears come into his eyes at the picture called up by this suggestion; and he said in a low tone,

"Alas! My poor father! It was cruel—very cruel!"

"It seems so," Monella returned with a sigh. "But God so willed it. And He has also willed that you should be led back to your own nation—that, after many days, you should join with me in the work that I had set myself."

"It's very wonderful. Yet it seems to me to explain those strange dreams and visions that were ever urging me on to attempt the exploration of the mysterious Roraima! I suppose, when Carenna found out who you were, she confessed?"

"Well," answered Monella, with a half-smile, "I made her do so. People find it difficult to hide anything from me. I saw she had some secret, and compelled her to divulge it. But, since she was so afraid to confess to others, and especially averse to *your* knowing it, I made her this promise, that, if you desired to return from our adventure, you should do so in ignorance of the actual facts. I was only to tell you in case you freely elected to stay here permanently. That is why I have kept it back thus far. I had intended to announce it to you and to the people at the time of your public betrothal. Then they would have received you, with one accord, as one having a right to rule over them. And now you can understand why I have regarded you with such affection from the first; and how glad I was to find, in Apalano's son, one so worthy of my love and confidence. Your father was allied with my line, and you are, therefore, akin to me. Worthy son of a worthy father! Let me join with you in thankfulness that you have, after all, come into the heritage that is yours by right! The young eagle was bound to find its way to the eyrie for which it was best fitted." And Monella stood up and laid his hand affectionately upon the young man's shoulder. Leonard reverently bowed his head, and the other pressed his lips upon his forehead.

There was silence for some seconds. Then Templemore took Leonard's hand.

"And let me too congratulate you, Leonard," he said fervently. "It is good news for you—this; for, since you have elected to pass here the remainder of your life, it will be a great comfort and advantage to you that you have such good claims and qualifications for the position."

"I am thinking about my poor father who died of heartache and disappointment," rejoined Leonard; and in his tone there was a note of genuine sorrow. "And I can scarcely forgive Carenna—fond of me as I know her to have always been—for her cruelty to him."

Presently Templemore turned again to Monella, saying,

"Did Carenna then believe this mountain was inhabited, that you would find here the people you came to seek? Did you yourself think that?"

"As to myself, I can scarcely tell you," was the answer. "'Reason' said that the hope of finding here the people of whom Apalano had so often talked to me—for that was all I then knew—was chimerical; yet Apalano's dying wishes, and some strange sentiment or instinct within me, urged me on. Then, when I met with Carenna, I found she quite thought it might turn out true."

"Carenna thought it?"

"Why, yes; but that is not very surprising, for, according to the Indian ideas, it would not be the only instance in this country. There is a belief amongst the Indians in several parts that some of the unexplored mountains are inhabited by strange and unknown races. This applies to those—and there are many; Roraima is not the only one—that are surrounded by the curious belts of almost impenetrable forest. The Indians believe that, if these forests could be passed, strange peoples would be met with living on the mountains thus encircled; and they say that on clear nights the lights from their fires may often be seen.[1]

---

1. Mr. Im Thurn, referring to this belief amongst the Indians, states that he has himself seen, from a distance, strange lights on the Canakoo Mountains for which he was quite unable to account. See 'Among the Indians of British Guiana,' p. 384.

Therefore Carenna was quite prepared to believe we might find Roraima inhabited."

"I see. Then she, at least, will not have been so very much surprised at our not returning, and may not have given us up for dead?"

"Yes; that is probable enough."

"And if she has heard of the signal flares we made when some Indians— as I suppose they were—were camping in sight of the mountain, she would look upon that as a sign of our being up here alive?"

"I think that is very likely."

"There is the suggestion of a little comfort in that," said Templemore; "for, otherwise, those I left behind, and who are dear to me, must have given up all hope and be now mourning me as dead. With Leonard it is different. He stood alone in the world and has no one to grieve for him more than as an ordinary friend."

XXXII

The Tree's Last Meal

A nd now," said Monella, "I have someother news to give you; for you have slept for nearly two days, and in that time much has been done. While you slept we have been busy."

"Do you *never* sleep—yourself?" Templemore asked.

"Yes; but not for long at a time. However, the long rest you have taken is no reproach to you, for it was my doing. I saw that it was needful to restore your strength and good spirits. You are the better for it; the princess, the lady Zonella, and others have also had long rests and are the better for it, as I have already told Leonard. The king Dranoa, too, is better—in a sense; for he has now no mental trouble, and with his sickness there is no physical pain nor suffering nor distress of any kind. But he is very wishful now that the marriage of his daughter should take place as soon as possible; for only then, he feels, will he be able to die happily. In deference to his earnest wish I have settled for it to be solemnised at the end of a fortnight; and, in view of the fact that the state of his health cannot but be a source of sadness to his people, I have deemed it better to order that it shall be a quiet ceremonial, and not a great *fête*, as had been planned. This will not offend your feelings, my son?"

Leonard looked up with a bright smile.

"After what you have told me," he said, "I feel, with gladness and gratitude that it is not without reason that you have so often thus addressed me—as your son. *Now*, I may indeed claim you as a father."

"You may indeed," Monella assented; "I take the place of my lost friend."

"Then you have no need to ask whether what you think best pleases *me*. If you will be my father, choose for me and instruct me; for I feel I have need of your help to enable me to take up, and bear worthily, the position I owe to you. I felt this," continued Leonard, with great earnestness—"I felt this very strongly when I lay in that foul den that the poor demented wretch called 'the devil-tree's larder.' I made then a vow that, if it should please God to deliver me from the peril that threatened me, I would thenceforth devote my life to the good of the people I had come amongst. I repented sorely that I had given my thoughts too much to selfish—albeit innocent—enjoyment; and I vowed I would not be guilty of that selfishness in the future, if the chance and the choice were offered to me. And now that they *are*, help me—instruct me, my father, I pray you, in all that may enable me to fulfil that vow."

Monella gazed long and fixedly at the young man; and in his eyes there was a glistening as of a tear. Then he rose and went to the window that looked out over the lake, and stood awhile, with a far-off vacant look that told his thoughts were wandering to distant scenes or persons. It was sometime before he looked round.

And, when he again turned to speak to the young men, they were both conscious that some indefinable change had taken place in his manner. His face expressed unmistakably a great and exalted joy; and the eyes, that at all times had had so strange a charm in them, had taken on a new expression. For a little while Templemore strove in vain to ascertain in what the change consisted; but presently it seemed to him that they had lost that half-sad, half-wistful expression he had so constantly remarked; and that they now conveyed, instead, a sense of contentment and repose.

"That which you have now told to me," said Monella, walking slowly up to Leonard, "is as sweet to me as water to the thirsty in the desert." With grave deliberation he placed both hands upon the young man's shoulders and looked into his eyes with fatherly affection.

"Know, my son Leonard—or rather Ranelda, as you rightly should be called—know that in these words you bring to my soul the message it has been awaiting—sometimes in hope, too often, alas! in doubt and in despair—through the long ages. Yours is the hand—the hand of the son of Apalano—that bears to me the key of my fetters; and yours are the lips that announce my coming freedom! My work, then, nears its end, and soon—ay, *soon*—I—shall—be—*free!*"

While uttering these last words Monella raised his hand, and with upturned face looked rapturously above him, as if his sight, piercing the marble ceiling overhead, perceived some far-off scene that, while invisible to his companions, filled him with the most intense delight. Presently, he turned away with a regretful sigh, as though the vision he had been gazing at had vanished, and added, with an absent manner,

"Now, when I leave you, I shall feel—"

He stopped; in his eyes there was a far-off look; and Leonard, who had been looking on with wide-open, wondering eyes that comprehended little, if anything, of his discourse, exclaimed in anxious tones,

"Leave me—leave us! What mean you, my father? You surely do not think of leaving the people you so love, to become again a wanderer?"

Monella shook his head; and, appearing to rouse himself, he replied in quite a different voice,

"You misunderstand, my son; I speak of when I shall be called away—called from this earthly life."

"But that will not be for a long, a very long time yet," urged Leonard, looking with confidence at the stalwart frame, and remembering the many feats of strength the other had performed.

Monella turned his eyes on Templemore.

"Do you remember," he asked, smiling, "a conversation we had one day in the museum; when I explained to you that no 'Plant of Life' or other specific—no power, indeed, of earth—can keep in its earthly cage the soul that feels its work is done, and that, therefore, frets itself against its prison bars?"

"I remember," answered Templemore in a subdued tone, and avoiding Leonard's questioning eyes.

"Ah! then *you* understand me. And now"—this with a gesture that enforced obedience—"now let us go back to that which we were speaking of. I was saying that King Dranoa desires that you and Ulama should be wedded without delay. To spare the feelings of the maiden, and give her time, so that the matter may not come upon her too suddenly, I have named a day two weeks hence. There will be no pageant, no public *fête*; only the necessary ceremony, quiet and solemn."

"I should prefer it so," murmured Leonard.

"Then that is arranged; and it will take place in the great Temple of the White Priests that has been closed for so many years. Workmen are engaged upon it, and it is now being cleansed and renovated. It will be ready in time.

"The next thing I have to tell you is that Coryon has suffered his punishment, and is dead."

"Coryon dead?" the other two exclaimed in a breath.

"He is dead," Monella repeated solemnly. "It seems that during the night after we left, there were dreadful scenes in the amphitheatre. Those large reptiles—they are called 'myrgolams' here—came out of their pool and attacked the half-dead wretches entangled in the tree. But the branches tried hard to retain their victims, and so—well, you can almost imagine what took place. The creatures carried off the miserable beings in scraps; tore them piece by piece from the clutches of the branches till nothing was left!"

He paused for a moment, and his listeners shuddered.

"Thus it came about that the greedy tree was, after all, baulked of most of its intended victims; all, indeed, save three or four; though the deaths the others met with were not less horrible. Yesterday, finding the monster had no victims in its grasp, I ordered the separating door to be withdrawn. In a moment, Coryon was seized and carried up into its awful gorge. With that, the tale of this terrible tree must end. I have no heart to devote more criminals to it; though there are some among the prisoners who are scarcely less guilty than was Coryon. But these Sanaima will deal with; he will punish them as seems best to him; and I have set men to work to dig a mine from one of the cells so as to get underneath the tree. Then it can be blown up with gunpowder. And I designed to ask you to superintend the work for me," turning to Templemore.

"That I will gladly do. And—the—reptiles?" Templemore was doubtful of the name.

"Kill them off, if you can, with bullets. And now, to turn to your own affairs. Think not I have forgotten them; I know you are anxious and will be getting restless and unhappy. As I said to you before, when you go away, you will not go empty-handed. On the contrary, you will carry with you such riches as will place you beyond the need of toil for the remainder of your life. I need not say, 'Do not therefore be an idle man,' for I know that you will never be. Whenever it pleases you to go, some of my people shall escort you through the wood to 'Monella Lodge,' as we called it, and there await you while you go on to Daranato and bring back such Indians as you require. Then, do you, in turn, with your Indians, re-escort my people to the cavern; for, you must remember, they are not used to forest life; nor can they, if left alone, protect themselves against wild animals. Will that please you?"

"Yes, truly it is all I can ask or wish for," Templemore responded.

"I shall wish to know—that is, all here will wish to know," said Monella, "that you get back in safety to 'Monella Lodge.' With the heliograph mirror which you will find packed away at 'Monella Lodge' you can send us back a message to that effect; then, with the one we brought here with us, we can reply, and send you a 'God speed you' to start you on your way. Shall it be so arranged?"

"Gladly," responded Templemore with emotion. "But must I then resign myself to the thought that I shall never see Leonard or any of you anymore?"

"You must," Monella answered quietly, but firmly. "Leonard—or Ranelda, as I prefer to call him—has asked me to guide him and instruct him; and my first and last advice to him is, and will be, to keep his people to themselves. Now let us consider this question from what you yourself would term a practical point of view. The term 'El Dorado' has come to be a synonym in the outside world for a sort of earthly paradise, has it not? Originally handed down from actual facts and history relating to this, the celebrated island capital of Manoa—the Queen City of my once powerful and extensive empire—with the tales of its wonderful wealth and the virtues of the Plant of Life; its memory lingered through the ages long after the waters had receded and left it isolated and unknown. And the Spaniards called it 'El Dorado,' which has ever since been but another expression—as I have said—for 'Earthly Paradise,' or 'summit of every man's ambition.' Is it not so? And seeing that the great curse that so long lay upon the land has been removed, can you say that *now* it does not deserve the term? Have we not here a veritable 'Earthly Paradise'—an actual realisation of what you in the outside world understand when you use the expression 'El Dorado?'"

"Truly I believe it."

"Ah yes! It is so now—or will be henceforth, when those who have had such sorrows here shall have outlived them," said Monella with impressive emphasis. "But what I would put to you, is this; you have, perhaps, seen something of frontier settlements, or miners' camps, and gold diggings—at least, *I* have—and you have heard of them. Now, you know well enough that the only people who would care to brave the hardships of the journey hither would be those led on by the lust and greed of gold. Supposing things were reversed, and you were in Leonard's place, and had here your wife—as he will have—your friends, your own people—all that was dearest in the world, with ample wealth, would you care to allow him, or anyone else, to lead people hither, to turn this 'El Dorado' into a 'Gold diggings,' a 'Miners' camp,' with all their hideous associations, their gambling and drunkenness; their rowdyism and their debauchery, their shootings and murders?"

"No!" said Templemore thoughtfully, "you are right there. Still—surely, between that, and forbidding intercourse altogether—forbidding me even to come to visit my friend—"

Monella smiled and gravely shook his head.

"You think that, between the two extremes, there should be some middle course possible," he rejoined. "Unfortunately—or fortunately—there is none. *You* will have no need to come here seeking for wealth. You would not be likely to undertake the expedition alone. Those who accompanied you would do so from self-seeking motives. Then, again, you will have other ties; you will have your wife, children. You do not contemplate dragging them hither through trackless wastes to greet friends *they* have never known as you have? They would not like it, again, if you, a man of wealth, able to do as you pleased, were to leave them for a long space while you made the journey hither alone! And, finally, the thing is not practical or feasible for another reason. You will have much ado to find your way out from here. You know that in these regions vegetation spreads rapidly unless—as in the canyon we came up, or in the clearing immediately outside around the cavern by which we entered, or out on the savanna—there are special causes that check its spread. Should you come back in a year's time, you would not only find the road we cut out impassable—you could not even trace it. The spread of the undergrowth, the fall of great trees or branches, the hurling down of rocks from the heights above, floods from the streams and watercourses—all these, and other forces of nature in this wild region, will, within a few months, have combined to block up or obliterate completely the path we cut with so much difficulty. Is it not so?"

"I fear you are right, though it had not occurred to me," Templemore admitted with reluctance.

"Then, again, with the wealth you will take back with you, you will not care to remain in Georgetown. You will wish to travel with your wife; in any case, it would be years before you would be likely to think of undertaking another journey."

"If ever you *do*, though, dear old Jack," Leonard burst in impulsively, "if ever circumstances should arise to make you wish to communicate with me, you can always do so by the heliograph, you know, or perhaps by balloon, if I'm still alive."

But, though Leonard put on a cheerful tone, it was easy to see that both he and his friend felt deeply the severance that too clearly lay before them. Yet, after Monella's argument, they saw no alternative.

"I am as sorry as you can be," Monella wound up kindly; "but your duties call you away from us, even as Leonard's call upon him to stay.

And now I must leave you, for many are waiting to see me. First, however"—this to Leonard—"I will lead you to the princess."

Leonard followed him from the apartment into another, where Monella left him; and presently Ulama entered, looking radiant, lovely, beautiful—so Leonard thought—beyond belief.

At the sight of Leonard, she threw herself upon him with a joyous cry; with her face upon his shoulder, she sobbed and laughed by turns.

"Oh, my darling! my darling!" she murmured in gentle accents, "if you only knew how *glad* I am to see you! I've had such dreams—dreams about you—dreams that frightened me so! They *were* only dreams, were they not?"

She looked up anxiously, and fixed her glorious eyes upon his face, and closely scanned it. Then she gave a sigh, the token of relief, and once more she nestled her face upon his shoulder.

"Yes!" she said softly, "after all 'twas but a dream! For you look well, and your eyes are bright and happy-looking; and in my dream you were looking *dreadful*! Your poor face looked so thin, and so *different*, and your eyes so sunken, and they had dark rings around them, and oh! their terrible, despairing look! But it was only a dream, or you could not look well again so soon, as now you do. Yes, 'twas but a dream, my darling! But oh! an *awful* dream. I thought there was a great tree—like that you said you saw one day; and it was a tree that fed on human beings, and you were lying bound and they were going to give you to that dreadful tree! Oh, Leonard, my love, think what a dream that was for me! Think, for a moment, what I felt! And there were other dreadful, awful things!" She shivered and cried softly for a space.

"Yes, my darling," Leonard answered soothingly. "But, as you say, 'twas but a dream!"

"Ah, yes! And now it seems far off; for, after it, came other dreams, that were happy and delightful, so that the bad one receded ever farther. Just when I seemed even at the very point of death from horror, a cool hand pressed tenderly on my brow, and brought me peace. It seemed to cool the fever that had made me think my very brain would burst; and a voice said—oh *so* kindly—'Be at rest, my daughter, I bring thee peace, and surcease of thy sorrow.' Then I opened my eyes and saw a strange form leaning over me. It was dressed in a warrior dress, just like that which stands in our museum and which is called Mellenda's. Helmet, sword, everything the same. Then I felt secure and happy, for I thought the great Mellenda had come to deliver me in my trouble.

But—and this seems so strange—when I looked up at his face, who do you think he was? Ah! you would never guess! But the countenance was Monella's—your friend Monella's! Was not my dream a strange one?"

"Strange, indeed, my dear one," said Leonard tenderly.

"From that moment," went on Ulama, "everything was changed, everything was *lovely*. It seemed to me that *you* then came to me, and led me from that scene of horror. Where we went I know not; but, hand in hand, we wandered on, till you led me home. Then once more things became confused—I can scarcely remember—but I'm nearly sure Mellenda seemed to come to me again. And—yes—I remember, he repeated, 'Rest, my child; I bring thee rest and peace.' Then he left me, and we wandered on—you and I, my Leonard—through the loveliest, the most entrancing scenes; among places, people, strange to me, yet all delightful; and, oh, it all seemed *so* sweet, so restful, so grateful, after the horror of that first awful dream! At last I wakened, and they tell me I have slept through two whole nights and nearly two whole days! Did you not wonder that you saw me not the while? Tell me how you have passed your time without me?"

And thus the gentle, loving girl talked on with childlike innocence, Leonard at first evading her inquiries, averse to mar her happiness by telling her the truth.

Indeed, it was not for some days, and then only by degrees and carefully guarded words, that he revealed the truth about her 'dreams.'

XXXIII

The Last of the Great Devil-Tree

Templemore did not find the occupation of directing the operations for destroying the great devil-tree a very agreeable or engrossing one. His memories of the amphitheatre filled him with disgust and loathing both of the place and of the vegetable monster it contained, and he never went near them without reluctance; for all that, he stuck conscientiously to the task now that he had undertaken it. But there was neither excitement nor interest in it to keep his thoughts engaged, and to prevent their brooding upon his desire to get back to those dear to him. Now that everything was settling down peacefully in the land, and there was nothing specially to keep him, he felt he was not justified in prolonging further unduly his friends' suspense. He saw comparatively little, too, of Leonard, who was continually engaged with Monella and others in councils and consultations that naturally had little interest for Templemore; though, no doubt, they would have been glad enough of his company and assistance in their deliberations, had he chosen to offer them.

As a consequence, he wandered about a good deal alone; and took to haunting the spot from which he and Leonard had made their signal flares, and whence he could, with his glasses, just distinguish 'Monella Lodge' and the adjacent open country. Here he would sit by the hour together, wistfully gazing out over the vast panorama spread beneath him, and moodily watching for the slightest sign of life in the far distance. Sometimes 'Nea,' the puma, offered herself as a companion in his walks; at such times, when he went to the amphitheatre, he was always in some concern to keep her out of the reach of the fatal tree, lest she should meet the fate that had befallen her unfortunate mate.

It had been arranged that he would wait till Leonard's marriage, since it was so near. But he had determined not to delay his going more than two days beyond it; and he now awaited the event with something akin to impatience. At the same time, he knew that the journey back to Georgetown would be anything but easy or agreeable. It had been arduous, difficult, wearisome, and dangerous enough on the way up, when he had the company of Leonard with his exhaustless boyish enthusiasm. What would it be like, he asked himself, going all that weary road again alone, for he would be alone in the sense of being the only white man amongst a number of Indians. Then again, he must return with very little to show for all the time, and trouble, and danger he had incurred. Monella, it was true, promised him 'wealth'—and no doubt would keep his promise in the form of a selection of precious stones. *They* were numerous and comparatively cheap in the country; so Templemore had no scruples about accepting such a present. And, when he reached Georgetown, they would mean wealth. That was all satisfactory enough; but there was much, very much more he would have liked to carry away with him; things of much less intrinsic value, but of greater scientific interest. Of these there were more than could be catalogued in a few lines; vessels of gold and silver; wonderful antique jewellery, specimens of their armour, swords, etc., were some; dress-fabrics also; an endless number of curious botanical and zoological specimens, for others—these form only the beginning of a long list of things he had in his mind, and would have liked to carry with him. But well he knew the impossibility; the difficulties of transport were insurmountable. In a country where it was difficult to get carriers even for the bare food required, it was obviously useless to dream of carrying back with him a 'collection' such as he would have wished to take.

There was natural disappointment in all this. It is hard for an explorer to face danger, hardship, discomfort; to separate himself from civilisation and from those he loves, and to risk illness, fever, wounds and death, and then, having achieved success, to have to resign himself to returning without those trophies he would have delighted in exhibiting to an astonished and wondering world. But just, perhaps, when he had convinced himself, by dwelling morbidly upon such thoughts, that he had good cause for dissatisfaction, his good nature would assert itself and remind him of the other side to the picture. Was it a little matter to take back with him wealth enough to make his mother's future secure and comfortable; to marry the girl of his heart, and to be henceforth a man of means and affluence? And if his part in the expedition ended in such result, had he any just cause for complaint? Did he not rather owe a debt of gratitude to those who had urged him on, in spite of his own scepticism, to share in their enterprise? At this thought a rush of gratitude would come into Templemore's mind; then he would torment himself in turn, with misgivings as to whether he was not guilty of ingratitude in now feeling impatient to get away from—to leave forever—the friends who had thrown such good fortune in his way.

And thus Jack Templemore felt anything but happy in the days that preceded Leonard's marriage. And, of course, he was in love, and felt home-sick; so, perhaps, it is not much to be wondered at that he was restless and changeable and ill at ease.

Yet, had he been in a different mood, his stay in the place might now have been very enjoyable, and of surpassing interest. He was free to go where he liked and do as he pleased. The people were not only friendly and willing and anxious to please, but showed pride and pleasure, if he but spoke to them. The story of the rescue of Leonard and the princess had been noised abroad and told and re-told over and over again, and the part that Templemore had taken in it was well known. Then, again, it had also now become known who Leonard really was; and the people felt that what Templemore had done for his friend had been done for them, inasmuch as it had saved for them the life of one who was of their own nation and whom they now valued highly. Thus Templemore was regarded as a hero, second only to Monella (or Mellenda). The people were quite ready to credit him with qualities he did not possess; for was he not the close and trusted friend of their own great hero? If Mellenda had chosen this one from all the people of the outside world—for they knew by this time that there *was* a great world, outside their mountains, peopled with white races—must it not have been for some very good reason? Must he not be a great man, a hero, a wonder, for the great Mellenda to have chosen him as his friend and companion on his return to Manoa?

Thus reasoned the simple-hearted people; and, since it was also known that he was going away from them forever—going back to the outer world that was his home—it created a sort of mystery about him. Must he not be some very great man in that world that could not spare him even to stay and enjoy the friendship and favour of their own great hero-king?

So they regarded him with an interest and curiosity almost amounting to awe. Mothers would bring out their children to look at him as he passed, bidding them remember, for the remainder of their lives, that they had once seen the wonderful stranger, the great friend of their own great hero.

Meanwhile, Ulama had given herself up zealously to joining with Leonard in the work he had set himself among the people. She had been gently and tactfully told the story of all that had occurred; she knew now that her 'bad dream' had been only too true. The knowledge cast for a while its shadow upon her fair face, and she seemed to lose some of her childish gaiety and to become more staid under its influence. But it also called into play all the womanly tenderness and sympathy of her nature. When she heard of unhappy women and children needing care and comforting, she eagerly desired to assist in the work in company with Leonard and Sanaima; and thenceforth she devoted to it all the time she could spare from attendance upon her ailing father.

Amongst those in constant attendance on the princess might now be seen Fernina. She had been brought to the palace by Sanaima, who had discovered that her husband was no longer living. The meeting between her and Leonard was affecting; he presented her to Ulama and commended the poor woman to her kindness. Ulama knew now the particulars of the terrible time the two had passed together in the dread cells within reach of the great tree, and received her with a heart filled with compassion. Fernina's gratitude and pride at the kindliness of her reception were such that they went far to assuage her sorrows. Her two children also were well cared for, and, by degrees, the old look of dull misery in her face gave place to a softer expression that promised to bring back, in a measure, her former beauty. It was understood that Fernina would in the future take Zonella's place; for it had been announced that the latter would shortly be married to Ergalon.

One day Templemore informed Monella that the mine had been completed, that he had placed the cask of gunpowder in position, and laid a fuse.

"And the reptiles?" asked Monella.

"I have left them alone—and for a reason. It seems to me they are inclined to attack the tree; have done so, in fact. They are getting hungry and have nothing else to attack, and, being well penned in, they are beginning to feed on the only thing within their reach. After all, the 'flesh'—if one may so term it—of a 'flesh-eating' tree may quite possibly form an acceptable food for these ugly reptiles when they are starving. If, when we have blown it up—or down—they are disposed to devour it and so clear it out of the way, it may save some trouble."

Then a day was fixed for firing the mine, and a large crowd of the citizens assembled to witness the destruction of their enemy; but many, whose memories of the place were sad, remained away.

When the explosion took place, a long tongue of flame shot up into the air with a thunderous roar, the great tree seemed lifted bodily up, swayed, and then fell with a mighty crash full length on the ground, disclosing a rent in the trunk from which a thick, noisome stream of dark-coloured fluid slowly flowed. This gave off an odour so offensive and over-powering that none could stay in the enclosure; so the crowd quickly dispersed, with loud expressions of wonderment and admiration at all that they had seen. But Templemore remained long enough to see, from a distance, that the foul reptiles had approached the tree, and were greedily drinking up the liquid that flowed from the wound in the trunk. And, visiting the place next day, he found that they had torn the rent still further open, and were busily tearing the trunk to pieces, the branches now showing but feeble signs of life. In the end they fulfilled his expectations and devoured every scrap of the monster. Thus ended the existence of the terrible, horror-laden devil-tree!

It was shortly after he had completed the destruction of the hated tree that Templemore made a discovery that filled him with grave uneasiness. He was wandering about among the heights that lay at one end of the canyon—that immediately over the entrance-cavern—when he found himself amongst huge blocks which had been quarried out (as Monella had one day mentioned) with the idea of precipitating them into the canyon to block it up impenetrably. On examining the quarry from which they had been taken, he observed with alarm that some masses of overhanging rock seemed almost on the point of giving way. A sort of partial landslip had already taken place, and there were fresh-looking cracks and fissures that threatened shortly to loosen the overhanging masses and set them free to fall into the canyon below. He spoke to Monella about this, and he at once accompanied him to the spot, and his opinion confirmed his own. This made Templemore busy himself in earnest with his preparations for departure; for he feared that, if these rocks actually fell, the entrance to the cavern might be so blocked up as to take long and arduous labour to clear it.

It being now within a day or two of Leonard's marriage this was all he could do in the matter. But Monella sent men down the canyon in charge of Ergalon—since the latter now knew the road—to carry in advance and deposit in the cavern some of the things Templemore desired to take with him. They returned on the eve of the wedding,

Ergalon stating that all they had taken down had been duly stored as desired, ready for Templemore when he went down.

That evening King Dranoa was much better and insisted on presiding at the evening meal. He even hoped, he said, to be able to be present at the wedding. Ulama's joy at this, and the sweet delight that lighted up her face, were alone enough to infuse happiness into those around her. She looked at Templemore, too, and smiled and nodded her head in a mysterious way that roused his curiosity; and, later, an explanation came.

At the very end of the repast a mysterious-looking dish or tray, whose contents were hidden by a golden cover, was brought in with a good deal of ceremony and was placed before the king. Then Ulama glanced shyly at Templemore and clapped her hands. At this the king lifted the cover, and displayed to view—not some new eatables, as Templemore had anticipated, but—a beautifully fashioned belt, and several exquisitely-worked purses that all sparkled and flashed with the little diamonds and other stones that were worked in patterns into the silken netting. And, when Templemore looked inquiringly at Leonard, that young man only smiled and nodded mysteriously like the others.

Then King Dranoa thus addressed him:

"My friend, thou hast already heard, I believe, that we do not purpose to allow thee to depart hence without begging thine acceptance of some little testimony of our appreciation of what thou hast done for us. I say we, for all here—all in the land indeed—are deeply in thy debt. Without thy courageous help and unselfish devotion my dear daughter would not now be here happy and joyous as she is tonight, and my kinsman and son-in-law that is to be would, I fear, only too probably have met a dreadful fate. Therefore, we have all joined in subscribing to these presents, of which we beg thy acceptance. The princess hath worked this belt, and inside it are some of her own chosen jewels that thou hast often seen her wear. The lady Zonella, and others of her maidens, have worked these purses—they are for thy friends—and we have all contributed to their contents. I know naught about thy world outside, but understand that what is in these satchels will be of far greater value to thee, and those dear to thee, than to us here. I truly hope it may be so; else I should hesitate to offer them, as being but a poor return for what thou hast done for us. If, however, they can purchase for thee, in the future, any surcease of toil, of trouble, of anxiety, then, and only from that point of view, may they be worth the offering. Take them, my friend; and may the blessing of the Great Spirit go with them, and accompany thy footsteps throughout thy life."

Then Ulama took the belt and poured out its contents upon the tray—a magnificent, glittering heap of superb precious stones. Then she emptied each purse in turn, making other sparkling but smaller heaps. And each purse had a little label with a name to it; and Templemore looked on in wonder as the contents of each were revealed and the names read out by Leonard. There were three large purses, one for his mother, one for Maud, and one for Stella. Smaller ones for Mr. and Robert Kingsford, Dr. Lorien and his son; and two, still smaller, for Carenna and Matava. No one had been forgotten.

Templemore looked from the one to the other, his heart filled with emotion. Even more than the overwhelming value of the jewels, he felt the loving-kindness that had thus taken thought and trouble for those dear to him.

"But—Dr. Lorien and Harry—and—the others—" he said, hesitating. "I don't see—"

"The good doctor," Monella explained, "will be sorely disappointed that he cannot come to see us and take back to the world some of the botanical rarities we have here, and which, to him, would be great treasures. These are to console him. As to the others of your friends—this is the least we can do to show our regret for the sorrow and anxiety they will have borne on your behalf, through us. That is all."

For some minutes Templemore was silent.

"It is too much—a great deal too much!" he got out presently. "I don't know what to say—"

"Then say nothing, dear friend," Ulama interposed, with a merry laugh. "Now let me put them back and show you how they all fit nicely into the belt. You see, while you were working for us at that horrid old tree, we had not forgotten you. Keep the belt always for my sake, and think of us all lovingly in the future, as we always shall of you. Now I want you to take me out on the terrace."

XXXIV

A Marriage and a Parting

In the ancient Temple of the White Priests Leonard and Ulama were solemnly made man and wife according to the custom of the country. King Dranoa was able to be present at the ceremony, and nearly the whole population may be said to have assisted, for they thronged in crowds to the great building where in ages past their kings had all been married; though comparatively few of the populace could find room inside the Temple. The remainder filled all the surrounding open spaces, and waited patiently to greet the bride and bridegroom on their way back to the palace.

Templemore had a place of honour in the assemblage, and watched the function with curious interest. Sanaima, with an array of white-robed priests; Monella, with his commanding form, conspicuous by his noble bearing; the beautiful Ulama, all suffused with blushes; and her handsome bridegroom; the kindly, dignified Dranoa, looking weak and pale, yet well-pleased and content; and the brilliant crowd of spectators, officers in gleaming armour, and courtiers in gorgeous dresses—all combined to form a noble pageant. The building, whose interior Templemore now for the first time saw, was a magnificent structure, and helped to add grandeur to the imposing spectacle.

At the conclusion of the ceremony, the procession, on its way back to the palace, was greeted with excited and enthusiastic cheers and cries that seemed almost loud enough to shake the towering buildings past which it slowly filed.

In the evening there were general feastings and rejoicings. These were continued till the night was far advanced; and it was morning ere the city again subsided unto rest.

The following day, Templemore was busy completing his preparations, and going round to bid farewell to those he knew. But, towards the afternoon, he was surprised to see a large crowd outside the palace; and still more astonished on learning that the people were gathered in his honour. The good-hearted citizens, it appeared, liked not the notion of his going away without some public mark of the esteem in which they held him; so, somewhat against his will, he was called out on to the terrace that overlooked the place in which the people had assembled. Monella, Ulama, Leonard, and all the members of the court and of the king's household, stepped out with him; and the first two each took him by the hand, and led him to a spot where all could see him. Then a great shout went up, and he was cheered again and yet again, till the strange feelings called up by the unexpected warmth of the welcome he received made him go red and white by turns.

"They have come for a sight of you, and a word of farewell ere you leave us," explained Monella. "Will you not give them a few words?"

Templemore was unused to oratory, and he would fain have excused himself; but he saw that to do so would disappoint his friends. So he made them a short speech, assuring them of his appreciation of their friendly feelings.

"The unexpected warmth and kindness you have shown in thus coming here today," he said, "I shall always gratefully remember. If, in company with the friends who led me hither, I have done aught that seems to you to call for commendation, I will only ask you, in return, to keep for me a tender corner in your memories when I have left you. If, when I have gone, you will but think as kindly of me as I shall of you, then indeed I shall be well repaid."

Then Monella addressed them in his sonorous tones.

"My children, I am well pleased that ye should have thus gathered here today, and of your own accord, to show to my friend that you are not unmindful of his part in the events of the past few months. I am glad and proud that he should receive, before he leaves us, this proof that my people are not ungrateful to one who hath done so much for them. A great work hath been accomplished in the land since we three, as strangers to you all, arrived some months ago. At the last, its prompt completion was due in no small measure to your quick response to my urgent call, at a time when hours were precious—and even moments. When I left you in the times long past, I sailed away with fleets and armies; when returning I was a simple wanderer. Yet ye gathered gladly at my summons, and no voice was raised to question my authority. This was well, and helped me to achieve success; yet might we have been too late to save the well-beloved of your princess had not our friend here kept all Coryon's vile following at bay till we could come to aid him. If the dread devil-tree exists, today, no more, and all the wickedness and cruelty that went with it have been trampled out forever, if now your minds are all at peace, and your daughters and your other dear ones are secure—ye owe much of this to our friend's ready courage and devotion; and I am rejoiced to see that ye have not forgotten it!

"Now will my friend know that he bears away with him the love and the good wishes of us all. We wish him all happiness in his future life; our sole regret is that he cannot stay and spend that life with us."

At this there were shouts and roars of applause, and other tokens of assent.

"And now, my children," went on the speaker, "I have somewhat else to say to you. The ancient Temple of the Great Spirit is once more open; see that ye neglect not to there offer up your thanks for the blessing that hath been vouchsafed you. Give heed to the teachings of the worthy Sanaima. See that ye take to your hearts the precepts that he will expound to you. So shall the good work that I have begun be continued and consummated after I shall have left you."

Loud murmurs of surprise and objection were here heard.

"Nay, let not that which I have said arouse your grief, my children. Remember my long life and weary wanderings to and fro upon the earth; these have been a punishment to me, even as events, during this same time, have been to you. Ye would not wish to keep me here when I tell you that my task is done, and my tired soul is seeking rest—rest not to be found on earth, but only in the great domain beyond the skies. I may not linger here now that the work that I was sent to do is finished. I have freed you from the curse that did oppress you; have brought you one to govern you who combines within himself the blood both of your ancient White Priests and of our kings; and in Sanaima ye have a wise counsellor and guide. Seek not then to stay me; when the Great Spirit calleth, weep not and repine not, for then is the hour of my deliverance. Then shall I be united, at the last, to my well-beloved queen, my Elmonta, and my children that have gone before!"

When Monella ended, he raised his hands and face towards heaven, and stood gazing upwards like one inspired. His face seemed transfigured and was lighted up as by a thrilling joy; and, as on the occasion of his talk in the palace with Templemore and Leonard a few days before, he appeared to see something invisible to those around him, but the sight of which filled him with supreme content. Then he dropped his arms, looked around him as though he had just awaked from sleep, and, with bent head and tardy steps, walked silently away.

Ulama caught Templemore by the arm.

"Oh, do you think it can be true—what he says?" she exclaimed in anxious tones, almost a sob. "It cannot be that we are about to lose him? Do you think so?"

"Nay, I see no cause to apprehend it," was Templemore's reply. "Our friend seems as robust and as strong as a man can wish."

"Yes! So think I, and yet—he has spoken in this strange fashion several times of late. His words fill me with foreboding."

She looked at Templemore with such sorrow in her gentle eyes that he scarcely knew what to say to comfort her. And just then he was obliged to leave her to return the salutes of the people, who were now separating and returning to their homes or their various callings.

The next morning, shortly after sunrise, Templemore stood at the top of the hillside, not far from the entrance of the canyon—the spot from which he had first seen the 'Golden City'—looking his last upon the fair scene outspread beneath, and saying the last words of farewell to his friends. Once more the people had assembled to do him honour, and they now crowded the slopes on every side.

Already some of the little party who were to accompany him to 'Monella Lodge' had started and were on their way down the canyon, and Ergalon, under whose charge they were, stood waiting for Jack Templemore. The latter was surrounded by a little group, of whom the chief were Leonard, Ulama, and Zonella, who seemed as if they could not make up their minds to let him go. Monella, his arms folded, stood apart, gravely looking, first at the group, and then out over the landscape with dreamy eyes, his noble figure, outlined against the dark foliage, the centre of a half-circle of officers and courtiers who stood respectfully a short distance from him. Templemore was dressed in the same clothes he had worn on his arrival; beneath them he had buckled on the precious belt with the jewels it contained; his rifle was slung across his shoulder.

Amongst those around were to be seen Colenna and his son, Abla, and others who had been amongst Templemore's first friends; and all showed by their demeanour genuine sorrow at the parting. As a last and special gift—one more token of his remembrance of his boyhood's friend—Leonard had that morning handed to Templemore a deed of gift making over all his property in the 'outer world' to Maud Kingsford.

"It is nothing to give, since it is no longer of any use to me," he observed, with a quiet smile. "But, since I *must* convey it to someone, let it be a dowry for Maud in addition to the purse the others send."

It would be difficult to say how many 'last hand-shakes' were given, or how many times Ulama, with tear-dimmed eyes, pleaded for 'a minute longer—just a minute,' Zonella, with sorrow in her looks, seeming mutely to second the appeal. But the parting came at last, and, amid loud huzzas, and the waving of hands and scarves, and other tokens of good will, Templemore turned away and, with Ergalon, disappeared into the thicket.

Little was said by either as they made their way down the rough path, and, even when they rested in the shade of the half-way cave, neither seemed disposed for talk. Almost in silence they ate the refreshments with which the forethought of their friends had loaded them, and drank cool draughts from the rocky shallows of the stream.

Suddenly, while they sat within the cave, waiting for the sun to move so far that the path should be in shade, a heavy booming detonation like the firing of cannon burst upon their astonished ears; and they started up together and stood listening anxiously.

"What on earth can that be?" exclaimed Templemore.

Ergalon gravely shook his head.

"Falling rock, I think," he answered. "If so, it must be farther down the canyon."

"Let us hasten," cried the other, a vision rising before his eyes of the entrance-cavern blocked, and his being forced to return. "This is what I have been fearing."

Despite the sun, he started off at a rapid pace down the path, Ergalon following and striving, as well as he could, to keep up with the other's impetuous movements. During the remainder of the descent they heard two or three other similar noises; and at each of these Templemore hurried on still faster.

When they reached the bottom, they came upon the little party who had preceded them; they were standing in doubt and alarm, looking along the valley, which was already partially blocked by fallen rocks, while more continued to fall at intervals, crashing on to those already fallen and sending up clouds of dust. With the group, looking on at the scene in a sort of mild surprise, stood 'Nea' the puma.

"The stars be praised," Ergalon exclaimed, relieved, "it's all at the other end."

"What do you mean?" asked Templemore in surprise.

"Why, the rocks have not fallen near your cave," was the reply. "All is clear there," and he pointed to the hidden cave.

Then there were explanations, and, to Templemore's dismay, it now appeared that Ergalon had mistaken his instructions and placed all the things in the wrong place. He was not really to blame in the matter; for he only knew of the one cave—that to which he had accompanied Templemore when they had come down to fetch the spare weapons. He knew nothing of any other cavern, and Templemore had not remembered this.

The situation was a trying and terribly disappointing one, and Templemore found himself in a grave dilemma. If he hesitated, it was plain his way would soon be totally barred. If he went on, and risked being crushed by the falling rocks, he must go alone; leave behind him everything he had intended to take with him, save what he had on his person, and make up his mind to face the dangers of the gloomy forest by himself! Even now it was almost folly to risk death or serious injury by making for the cavern.

Templemore hesitated, the while that more boulders came crashing down. Then he thought of what it would mean for him were he to be shut up in the mountain for an indefinite period. He looked up keenly and saw enough of what was going on to grasp the fact that the whole sides of the canyon were crumbling and falling in, and it looked a sufficient quantity to make it likely that the reopening of the road would be a work of years. As that conviction dawned upon him, with a brief word of farewell he dashed away from the group, and, despite their startled endeavours to stay him and the entreaties they called after him, he ran swiftly along the valley towards the entrance-cavern. After him bounded the faithful puma; he had no time to give to the attempting to send her back, and the two went rapidly on, dodging the great masses that now crashed down faster than before. A massive boulder rolling down seemed about to crush them, but they escaped it and disappeared in a cloud of dust from the view of the spellbound witnesses of their hazardous race.

Just when they reached the cavern a great stone pitched upon one already fallen and, splitting into several pieces, sent heavy fragments flying around in all directions, like an exploding bomb-shell. One of these fragments struck Templemore in the back, smashing his rifle, and throwing him, stunned and bruised, upon the floor of the cavern.

XXXV

Just in Time!

At sunrise, one morning, a fortnight after the events recorded in the last chapter, a party of travellers, consisting of three white men and a number of Indians, set out from the Indian village of Daranato, making their way in the direction of Roraima.

The three white men were Dr. Lorien, his son Harry, and Robert Kingsford; and among the Indians was Matava. As they toiled along the rough path it was easy to see that the travellers were, for the most part, travel-worn and weary; they moved forward in a half-listless fashion, scarcely looking to right or left, and showing but little interest in the scenes that lay along their route. Only when they came to the ridge from which the first view of Roraima is to be obtained did any of the party exhibit curiosity. Here a halt was made, and they all gazed for sometime silently at the great mass that raised itself high above the surrounding landscape. This morning, clouds hung over it and it appeared sombre, dark and threatening, and gave no sign of the fairy-like lightness and beauty it sometimes assumed when seen from this same spot.

Robert Kingsford had come up from the coast, in the company of the doctor and his son, bent upon solving, if possible, the mystery that surrounded the fate of the two friends who had left Georgetown, nearly nine months before, to join with an unknown stranger in the exploration of Roraima. All that had since been heard of them was the strange, almost fantastic account that had been brought back by Matava, according to which they had actually found a way into the mountain, and thenceforth had disappeared. The very entrance by which they had made their way through the solid wall of cliff had been afterwards found fast sealed; and no trace or clue to their fate had been left behind. This had been Matava's account, and he had not hesitated to express his belief that the three adventurers had been captured by the demons of the mountain, and either eaten up then and there, or kept as prisoners and slaves in durance vile.

This story, however, did not satisfy the minds of the others, and Robert Kingsford, seeing and compassionating the deep sorrow of

Templemore's widowed mother, and the still more passionate grief of his own sister Maud, determined to investigate matters for himself. Dr. Lorien was detained longer in Rio than he had expected; but, when at last he returned to Georgetown, he readily joined the other in the proposed expedition of inquiry.

They had a very arduous and difficult journey up from the coast. It happened to be a season of exceptional drought, and cassava, and food of all kinds, were extremely scarce. The sun had been unusually fierce, and the heat abnormal; hence, by the time they reached Daranato, even the sturdy and seasoned doctor—a very veteran in tropical travel—was nearly worn out; while the other two were in still worse plight.

Add to these trials the fact that they had little, if any, hope of succeeding in their quest, and felt, in reality, that the expedition was, at best, but a sort of forlorn hope; and it will be understood why they had started from Daranato dispirited and depressed.

Thus, when they obtained their first view of the mysterious mountain, the cause of all their trouble, they were not inclined to regard it with any very friendly feelings; and its gloomy, forbidding look this morning was reflected, so to speak, in their own minds. "There is our enemy," they felt. "There is the fascinating, sinister chimera that has bewitched, and lured away from us, our dear friends, and caused us all this anxiety and useless trouble." And so, as Roraima frowned upon them, they frowned back, and returned in kind its gloomy and unfriendly greeting.

But frowns and angry looks could do them no good; so the travellers, with a very few words of comment, continued their route towards 'Monella Lodge,' where they arrived towards evening.

Here, a mile or so from the 'haunted wood,' and almost, as it seemed to them, under the very shadow of the mighty towering walls, they set about making arrangements for a stay of several days. They found everything in the cabin much as Matava had led them to expect; the place, indeed, just as Templemore had left it at his last visit. Many things had been left there that the travellers now found useful, and that seemed veritable luxuries after the discomforts of their long journey.

Kingsford's thoughts were intent upon his missing friends; and, indeed, this was also the case in only a slightly less degree with the other two. All were oppressed with vague suspicions of the Indians, even of Matava. Might these not have murdered the three travellers for the sake of the things they had with them—articles and stores which would be as priceless treasures to Indians; therefore which might quite conceivably have offered a temptation too great to be resisted?

However, amongst the tribe at the village, they had seen no signs of 'white men's' belongings to any unusual extent; and, now that they saw what a number of things had been left undisturbed in 'Monella Lodge,' their suspicions were very considerably lightened. For all that, they found it difficult to believe implicitly the fantastic tale Matava had told about the three adventurers' disappearance.

The Indians gathered wood and lighted fires, while the white men made a careful and interested inspection of the contents of the habitation and its surroundings (the two llamas had been removed to the village, where, however, they had both since died). Inside, they found a lamp and a small cask still partly full of oil, which was a discovery they appreciated when it grew dark.

After their evening meal, the three friends sat for sometime smoking their pipes and discussing the strange situation in which they found themselves. They were now within reach of their journey's end. If the tale told by Matava were correct, and the road through the forest were still fairly clear, they ought to be able to reach the mysterious cavern the next day; when they were determined, if requisite, to blow open the entrance with gunpowder. In addition to that which they had brought with them, they had found a considerable quantity at 'Monella Lodge.' This surprised them; for in this country gunpowder is more valued by Indians than almost anything else.

The three friends were sitting talking, and were thinking of retiring to rest for the night, when Matava came rushing excitedly into the place.

"Come quickly, my masters," he exclaimed. "Come! Come and see the light on the mountain!"

Somewhat languidly those addressed rose and went out. They had so often heard the usual stories of lights seen at night on unexplored mountains that they attached but little importance to them. They had treated in like manner a statement by Carenna and Matava that some Indians, camping out on the savanna a few months before, had seen strange and unusually bright lights, that they took to be signals, on Roraima's summit. The Indians had been scared and broke up their encampment at once, fearing the lights might have been placed there to lure them into the power of the demons of the mountain.

When, however, the doctor stepped outside, and looked up towards the top of the stupendous precipice, he saw a brilliant flame that had all the appearance of a signal beacon.

"It doesn't look like a forest fire," he said to Kingsford, while they were examining it carefully through their field-glasses. "And now and then I almost fancy I can make out human forms passing in front of it."

The others had the same impression, and Harry Lorien declared he could see flashes of light, as though the beings round the fire were dressed in clothes, or carried something, that reflected the firelight.

"Let us try burning a little powder," the doctor suggested, "after the fashion Matava says was arranged between him and the others, but which they never carried out."

So they sent Matava for the powder, and told him to fire it in the manner that had been settled between him and Monella. It is true none of the three messages agreed upon would be applicable to the present occasion—but that they could not help.

Presently, three tongues of flame leaped up into the air, then suddenly died out, leaving those around temporarily half-blinded by the glare. Then they stood for sometime anxiously watching through their glasses.

What seemed a long interval ensued; when, suddenly, three brilliant gleams flashed out on Roraima's height, in exact imitation, as to the intervals between the flashes, of the signals they had themselves made.

"Try another," Doctor Lorien cried, in growing excitement. "Arrange the three differently this time."

This was done, and the answering flashes came back, again in exact imitation; and this time with scarcely any delay.

Doctor Lorien seized Kingsford by the hand.

"Heaven be praised for this!" he exclaimed, his voice half-choked with emotion. "It begins to look, indeed, as though Matava's account were true; as if our dear friends may be alive after all!"

Words cannot describe the delight with which the travel-worn party hailed these signs, that so unmistakably pointed to the conclusion suggested in the doctor's words. There was one thing, certainly, they could not understand; none of the signals agreed upon between Monella and Matava had been given from the mountain; but they were inclined to attribute this to Matava's having, after the lapse of time, forgotten or mixed up what had been arranged. Only the thought that their supply of powder was not unlimited restrained them from continuing the signalling; but they were reluctantly compelled, as a matter of prudence, to discontinue it.

"Now," said the doctor, "we can attack the 'haunted wood' with a good heart. Surely, our friends will come down to meet us, now that they know we are here!"

Before daylight they were all astir, and set off at once on the journey through the forest, Matava guiding them. The road, or track, was followed with difficulty, and was almost blocked at times. Only an Indian's instinct, indeed, could have made it out. In places the rough temporary bridges that had been made over water-courses had been washed away, but, the water being very low from the long-continued drought, this caused no serious difficulty. They met with some adventures by the way, which were, however, suggestive of the dangers that lay around them rather than important in themselves. At last, towards evening, Matava told the doctor they were getting near the cavern. And now he begged him to proceed with caution. He could not get over the fear that the 'demons of the mountain' had eaten up or captured their friends, and were now awaiting more victims whom they had lured on by imitating and answering the signals of their murdered friends.

This theory did not find much favour with the doctor; for all that he so far yielded to the entreaties of the Indian as to send him on to scout in advance, while he, and the others of the party, walked in silence behind. And, since Matava now moved with especial care, they made slow progress.

As it happened, however, Matava's caution was in a measure justified; for just when they came to the part where there was an opening in the trees, and they could see ahead of them the light that came down into the clearing round the cavern, Matava stopped and raised his hand.

All stood still, except the doctor, who moved up to the Indian's side and looked whither he was pointing.

For a moment or so he could see nothing to account for the other's behaviour. To the right the stream that came out of the rock was now plainly in sight; and ahead of them was the clearing. The entrance to the cavern was as yet hidden by intervening trunks, but the light-coloured rock could be seen between the trees. Matava slowly raised his rifle and took a careful aim; then, as though dissatisfied, he lowered the weapon and stood with up-lifted hand enjoining silence upon those behind him. To make sure, he turned round and, with many gestures, impressed upon them all to keep motionless and silent; then, having satisfied himself that they understood and would obey his signs, he faced round and again raised his rifle.

And now, Doctor Lorien, following the line of the Indian's aim, became conscious of a slight movement among the trees in front of them. Presently—the Indian still waiting his opportunity to fire—he saw that a great hanging mass was swaying to and fro, passing and re-passing the space between the trunks of two trees. At first he thought it was a large mass of hanging creeper, but, remembering that there was no wind to cause the movement, he looked more closely and saw that it was the head and part of the body of a gigantic serpent that was depending from a branch above. Suddenly, Matava's rifle rang out, and a moment after an enormous mass fell to the ground and writhed and twisted about in horrible contortions.

Then a loud, hoarse roar was heard, echoing through the forest. The startled travellers looked about on every side, but could see nothing to explain the sound; then it came again and again, while the colossal folds in front of them, half hidden by the trees, continued to rise and fall, lashing against the trees and shrubs with blows that seemed almost to shake the ground.

Matava advanced and fired other shots into the struggling monster; then, watching his opportunity, made a rush and dexterously cut off the creature's head with a blow of his axe.

And now, looking towards the rock, they saw the 'window' entrance to the cavern, and the head of the big puma from which had proceeded the loud roars they had heard; and by the side of the puma was a pallid, thin, haggard face that they had some difficulty in recognising as Jack Templemore's!

"You have come only just in time," he said, in a weak voice, with a poor attempt at a smile, when the doctor had come near. "We were almost done for; at least, I know I am. I scarcely know whether I have strength enough to get the ladder out for you."

They tied two lassoes together and threw one end in; this he fastened to the ladder, and, thus assisted, it was got out. Immediately the puma sprang down it and disappeared into the forest. Then the doctor, followed by Kingsford and Harry, climbed up and entered the cavern, to find Templemore lying on the floor unconscious.

He was suffering from a sprained ankle and a badly bruised arm, and was exhausted from want of food. It was sometime before he could explain matters to his rescuers; and they, meantime, were anxiously wondering at finding him thus alone, with no sign about of his two friends. When he had briefly accounted for their absence, he told how he had been kept prisoner for more than a week by the great serpent that, all that time, had relentlessly watched and waited outside. But, apart from this, he could scarcely have got through the wood in his crippled state.

"Still," he said, "but for that serpent, 'Nea,' the puma, would have brought in some fresh meat. As it is, I have had to share with her even the small amount of tinned food we happened to have left here."

The flying pieces of rock that had injured him had broken his rifle; and he had only a few cartridges for his revolver.

"It's all been unfortunate," he said. "They put all the things in the wrong cave, and, when I came to myself after my desperate race between the falling rocks, I was in darkness and the puma was licking my hands and face. With much difficulty I found my way to the front here and pulled the stone away; then found a lantern and some oil, and got a light. The entrance to the canyon I found was all dark— buried—and I could still hear rumblings as of further falls of rock; but they sounded distant. I imagine, therefore, that the valley must be buried pretty deep. I set about making myself as comfortable as I could; and, when I put the ladder out, 'Puss,' as I call her, went out hunting while I bathed my ankle and arm. Several days she went out and brought in something pretty regularly, and I thought I should be able to nurse myself up and get well enough to struggle through the wood alone. But, one morning, she refused to go out; that day I had a visit from a pack of 'Warracaba tigers'; another time when she stayed in, looking out myself, I saw that awful serpent hanging from a bough; and there it has been day and night ever since; 'Puss' refusing to venture forth. I fired all my cartridges, except two, at it without any effect. It kept ceaselessly swaying its head about, and my arm pained me and my hand trembled; and, unless you can put a bullet through its head, it's of no use firing at a creature like that, you know. If my rifle had been all right, the thing would have been easy enough. I kept two cartridges in reserve—one for poor 'Puss' and the other for myself—and I think you came only just about in time to save us both."

And Jack's voice shook, and he felt a choking sensation in his throat. It was clear he had given up hope and had been making up his mind to face death alone.

Robert Kingsford's gratification and delight in the fact that his journey had, after all, turned out to be the means of rescuing his friend, the lover of his sister, may be imagined. Nor were the others less pleased; only the good doctor's satisfaction was clouded by his inability to get out into the wonderful valley to obtain any of the botanical treasures that lay so near at hand. But his chagrin disappeared when Templemore, as some consolation, showed him the purse of gems that had been sent to him.

"We'll give up orchid-collecting after this, lad!" he exclaimed to his son. "No need to wear out my old bones any longer in toilsome wanderings, when we've got enough to live on comfortably without."

Presently, 'Puss' came back with a wild pig, and great was the rejoicing over the meal that followed.

Then all, save Templemore—who could only look on from the window—went out to examine the reptile monster they had killed and to gaze in astonishment at its huge proportions. The Indians had already begun to skin it, but had not finished the operation when the time came for making their preparations to pass the night.

These were complete—the four white men sleeping in the cavern and the Indians bivouacking outside—when strange cries were heard echoing through the forest. Instantly there was a great stir among the Indians. With one accord they started up, exclaiming, "The tigers! The tigers are coming!" Forgetting their fear of the 'demons' cavern,' they cried out piteously for the ladder to be put out for them; and no sooner was this done than they scrambled up it with all speed into the cave, and pulled it in after them.

In reply to the amazed inquiries of the others, Matava explained that they had recognised the distant trumpetings of 'Warracaba tigers,' those fierce animals that nothing—not even fires—can stay or keep at bay. Soon, in fact, the animals could be heard on all sides around the cavern, though but little could be seen of them in the darkness. Their growls and roars and squeals were answered by hoarse roars of defiance from the puma that were deafening as they reverberated through the galleries of the cavern. Outside, the 'tigers' made frantic efforts to leap up and get in at the window, while those within had much ado to keep the puma from leaping out amongst them. They also fired a few shots at them, but in the darkness—for the fires had burned low—they were fired at random.

"Why," said the doctor, "I should think there must be a hundred of them! What an awful place this forest must be! I know that wolves hunt in packs, but I never before heard of 'tigers' doing so. Wolves can't climb trees as these can. It's awful, perfectly awful!" he added, the while he listened to the diabolical noises going on outside. It was, indeed, as a former traveller has expressed it, 'like a withering scourge sweeping through the forest.'[1]

It was hours before the din died down; and then, just when the tired travellers were falling asleep, the most appalling, human-like cries broke forth, sounding first quite close at hand, and then dying away in a long-drawn wail or shriek.

Again the new-comers started up in alarm; but Templemore, smiling feebly, bade them take no notice.

"It is only the 'lost souls'," said he.[2]

"The 'lost souls'!" exclaimed Kingsford. "What can you mean?" He began to think the other must be raving.

"I know no more than you do," was Templemore's reply. "So the Indians account for those sounds, and that is all I can tell you. Since I have been here they have serenaded me thus every night—even sometimes by day—and at times I have thought all the 'lost souls' from the Infernal Regions must have been let loose for my especial entertainment—or to frighten me to death or drive me mad—I know not which. I really think, if I had not had the company of this faithful beast—she always roars back defiance at them—I *should* have gone mad."

Towards morning the sounds ceased, and sleep became possible for two or three hours. But when, at daylight, the Indians rose and ventured out, they found the great snake had been almost completely devoured. Only some bones and a few bits of skin were left.

---

1. See Mr. Barrington Brown's 'Canoe and Camp Life Among the Indians of British Guiana,' p. 71. He says these animals hunt in packs of as many as a hundred or more.
2. See footnote, Chapter V, p. 52.

XXXVI

The End

Templemore was carried, with much difficulty, to 'Monella Lodge,' where an attack of fever supervened, and it was nearly two weeks before the doctor pronounced him out of danger.

Carenna came over from her village to nurse him, and tended him as devotedly as she had Leonard. In the height of the fever he raved constantly of the great devil-tree, of gigantic serpents, of Monella, and of 'lost souls'; and, mixed up with all, were a number of names strange to those who listened to him; for he had been too ill when found in the cavern to give more than a brief idea of the adventures he had passed through.

While he lay upon his bed of sickness, anxious friends watched from the mountain top for tidings of his fate, but received no intelligible answers to their signals; for none of those now with Templemore knew how to reply to them. Thus it was not till he was convalescent and well enough to be taken out into the open air, that any interchange of messages became possible.

Those below, looking up, day after day had seen little flashes of light, of which they could make nothing; but now Templemore explained their meaning. A search in the cabin brought to light the mirror Monella had thoughtfully packed up and hidden carefully away; and Templemore was thus able at last to open communication with his Roraima friends.

His first signalled message to them brought back the reply:—

"Heaven be praised! We are all so thankful! We have mourned you as dead! And we are in great affliction, besides, for Monella, the great, great-hearted Mellenda, is dead! He died peacefully the day after you went away."

Then, presently, when Templemore had sent back a message of sorrow and condolence, another came.

"The whole valley at the bottom of the canyon is half-filled up. It would take years to clear it. And we pictured you as lying dead beneath it all! "

Many messages passed to and fro during the remainder of the travellers' stay; and then, after a time, Templemore having thoroughly recovered, preparations were made for the journey back to the coast.

Both Carenna and Matava were grieved at the thought that Leonard had remained on the mountain for good, and that they were never likely to see him more. Carenna, alone, however, expressed no surprise. She told Templemore that the deception as to Leonard she had practised upon the good people who had received them so hospitably in their lonely mountain retreat had, all her life, been a sore trouble to her. It was some consolation to her, therefore, to know that he had, after all, been led back to his own people. She at first refused the valuable present Leonard had sent her, saying that to receive forgiveness was in itself more than she had hoped for. But, needless to say, Templemore persuaded her into accepting it. Matava's delight with what had been sent him was unbounded; especially when Templemore told him what treasures he could purchase with it: rifles, pistols, unbounded supplies of powder, and unlimited tobacco, and other things that Indians prize.

Meanwhile, Doctor Lorien and his son had been assiduous in collecting specimens of all the botanical and zoological treasures with which the neighbourhood of Roraima abounds; and, when the time for starting came, they had good reason to be satisfied with the result. They might have done still better, perhaps, if they had gone more into Roraima Forest; but this they could not make up their minds to do. Indeed, they could not venture far without an Indian guide; and this they could not get. Neither Matava nor any one of the other Indians could be prevailed upon to go into the wood again; and even the doctor was not very pressing. All had had quite enough of the 'haunted wood.' For it now came out, too, that Templemore had become a believer in the 'didi.' He declared that more than once during his imprisonment in the cavern he had seen, either at early morning or at dusk, strange human-like shapes—gigantic apes—standing watching within the shadow of the trees.

Nothing, he said, would induce him to enter that wood again. And he felt certain that only the fact that the entrance to the cavern was so high from the ground had enabled him to escape with his life.

'Nea,' the puma, alone showed no fear of the gloomy forest. She went hunting there daily, and nearly always returned with something to reward her enterprise.

When all was ready for the start, two or three last messages passed between the travellers and their friends upon the mountain.

"*Heaven keep you and all those dear to you! Your memory will always be cherished by all here,*" came from Leonard. To which Templemore replied:—

"*Long life and happiness to you and your dear wife and all your people.*"

"*God bless you, Jack!*"

"*God bless you, Leonard!*"

Thus they finally parted; and a few hours later the homeward-bound friends looked their last upon Roraima from the ridge near Daranato. The mountain was lighted with the red rays of the setting sun and towered up in glowing splendour. The greens of the wood at its base, varied and vivid in colouring, as they were, contrasted with the pinks, and purples, and reds of the precipitous walls above, that now looked again like a fairy fortress in the clouds, smiling, and fascinating in its light, aerial beauty.

"What a pity the city does not show!" said Harry. "What a glorious sight it would make!"

"At least you have conquered the secret the mysterious mountain has so long and so well concealed," Doctor Lorien observed to Templemore.

The latter gazed on the mountain gloomily. His mind went back to the morning when he saw it first and the vague forebodings that had then come into his mind.

"I don't know," he said doubtfully. "I have not brought away with me the most wonderful secret of all—the 'Plant of Life.' When I think how I was cheated out of that, by the mountain itself, as you may truly say—for its very rocks came crashing down to prevent my escape, or to kill me if I persisted; or at least, to insure my leaving nearly everything behind—when I think of this, it seems to me that Roraima has guarded most of its secrets pretty effectually, and I am almost persuaded there is something uncanny about it."

Harry laughed at this; the more so that it came from Jack.

"That's very fanciful—for you," he returned. "If it had been Leonard, now, I should not have been surprised."

"I am afraid my ideas of what is precisely practical and what is fanciful have been a good deal modified," Jack confessed. "So would yours, if you had passed through my experiences."

"Well, after all, perhaps you haven't lost much," Harry returned. "A small bundle of dried plants wouldn't have been of much use, and as to the seeds, if, as I understand you, they only thrive high up on the mountains, I don't see what you were going to do with them. Moreover, very likely they would have been eaten up by insects, or lost, or got wetted and spoiled, or something, before you got back or could have planted them in a likely spot."

Then they continued their journey, staying that night in Daranato, where the great puma at first created a scare among the dusky inhabitants, but, showing friendliness towards all, she was soon the object of unbounded wonder and interest on every side.

Some two months later there was again a little dinner party at 'Meldona,' Mr. Kingsford's residence, and the same faces were gathered round the hospitable board—all but Leonard Elwood's. Maud looked charming and happy as she glanced, now and again, first at Jack Templemore's bronzed face, and then at her brother, listening, not for the first time now, to her lover's wondrous tale.

She and Stella had shuddered before at the accounts of the great tree and its victims, and of the horrors of the 'haunted wood'; and had talked of Ulama and Zonella, and wondered, again and again, what they were like.

"Poor Leonard! I am sorry to lose him," Maud said. "Yet, I suppose, he does not need pity; for he is to be envied in many ways. Fancy his dreamings—about which we used to tease him so—coming true after all!"

"It is just a year ago today," observed Mr. Kingsford to the doctor, "that you were at dinner here and first told us about that wondrous stranger, Monella. We've had an anxious time ever since."

"I have never known a happy moment till you all came back the other day," said Maud sadly. "I am so thankful that the cruel suspense is ended at last. I have often recalled the words Dr. Lorien used about Roraima; that 'its very name had come to be surrounded by a halo of dread and indefinable fear.' I can truly declare that it has been so with me. I, too, had come to hate and dread the very name. It has seemed to me like a great, remorseless ogre that had swallowed up two of our friends, and, as I feared, was going to swallow up my brother and two more. Yet," she added, looking at Jack, "had I known how things really were, had I known of your lying lamed, and ill, and alone in the den in that horrible forest, I think I should have gone mad! What a comfort to you this dear, faithful animal must have been!"

'Nea' was by her side, and she put her tear-stained face affectionately down to the animal's head. The big puma had already established herself as a favourite with everyone in the house.

"Truly," returned Jack, "such thoughts occurred to me while I was cooped up there. I couldn't help going over things in my mind; and, when I considered how the mountain itself, and all the horrors of the forest, seemed to have combined against me to prevent my escape, I was seized with a sort of hate and detestation of the place. And, ever since, my sleep has been disturbed—and will be for years to come, I feel convinced—by nightmare dreams of the sights and sounds that haunt my memory!"

"I feel that I have a grudge against it, too," the doctor avowed. "Consider all the wonderful things you have told us that are to be found inside! Then, just when I got so near, to be shut out in that way! That 'Plant of Life,' too! I'd have given a good deal to have some specimens of that, and some seeds. *I* would have got them to grow, somehow, if the thing could be done!"

"I'm precious glad, then, that you didn't," the irreverent Harry put in. "I'm hoping to be a physician—one day—remember! And what chance would there be for me and the rest of the profession, if you taught people how to live for hundreds of years without so much as an illness?"

This very unexpected view of the matter from the vivacious 'budding doctor' had the effect of turning the thoughts of the others from the somewhat gloomy channel into which they seemed to have drifted.

After dinner, the belt, and the purses, and their glittering contents, were brought in and spread out to view.

"Whatever else may be said," Mr. Kingsford declared, with emotion, "there is not one here who will not have cause to remember the stranger Monella, and Leonard, and their friends, with grateful feelings. And you, Jack, above all; for, if I am any judge of the value of your share of these things, you are a millionaire. And that brings back to my mind the thought that is now constantly perplexing me, Who *was* this wondrous Monella after all? I really cannot bring myself to believe he was—what was his name?—Mellenda, you know."

"No," assented the doctor. "As a man, I have the greatest liking and respect for him; but, as a scientist, I am bound to disbelieve in that part."

"Since I have no claim yet to be considered a scientist," said Harry, "I suppose I am free to believe what I like. So I go the whole ticket. I believe he was what I first pronounced him to be—a magician—

FRANK AUBREY

and—I swallow the Mellenda legend—whole! So there!" This very emphatically.

"Oh dear, *yes!*" Stella exclaimed, her blue eyes opening wide at the doubting ones. "Why, of course, it *must* be true. It is so much more romantic and poetic, you know!"

Robert shook his head gravely.

"No!" he said, very decidedly. "I honour and respect the man, and his memory, from all I have heard of him, but—I cannot accept that wonderful part of it."

"Well, *I* do," Maud exclaimed, looking round with a pretty air of defiance, more particularly directed against Jack. "So that makes opinion even, so far—three for, and three against. Now," to Templemore, "of course, I know *you* will side with the others."

To everyone's surprise, however, Jack also shook his head.

"I don't know that," he answered, with a comically bewildered air. "I've really had all my old notions so mixed up and blown about, that I honestly admit I really cannot make up my mind. The whole thing is an enigma that I cannot solve as yet—probably never shall. So you may put me down as neutral—undecided—whatever you like to call it."

Maud clapped her hands; and upon that the puma gave a loud roar, evidently signifying *her* assent and approbation.

"Three for, three against, and one neutral," Maud cried "That's better than I hoped for!"

The doctor laughed, and his good-natured eyes twinkled.

"You've all but beaten us," he said good-humouredly. "But, going away from that part of the subject, I feel truly sorry to think that he should have died so soon after he had accomplished the work he had had so much at heart."

"There again I am inclined to differ," Templemore answered slowly. "I honestly believe that nothing could have happened to please him more. All his later talk clearly showed that. He said he was utterly weary of life, and anxious to be 'released,' as he called it; yet his love for his people was so great, he let no sign of this appear till he felt sure all had been finally achieved. It was the fear that that work might be upset after he had gone—and that alone—that made him so anxious to shut out all future communication with the world outside; of that I feel convinced. It was that that influenced him too, I have no doubt, in making me promise to keep my adventures there a secret from the world in general. But, just at the last, almost when I was coming away, a doubt seemed to come into his mind, and he said to me, 'I release you from that promise, if circumstances should arise in which you conscientiously believe it would be conducive to the good of my country to tell the story of your sojourn here.' What he meant I cannot conceive; I only tell you what he said. Possibly time may show. He seemed to have the 'gift of prophecy' to some extent in those days; certainly, everything went to show that he foresaw, or expected, his own approaching death."

THIS WAS ALL SOME YEARS ago.

Maud Kingsford and Templemore were married shortly after; and Stella and Harry Lorien are now married too. And, when the two sisters appear in society, they excite admiration, not only by their beauty, but also by their matchless jewels—that once glittered on the bosom of Ulama, Princess of Manoa, and that had adorned, probably, the persons of generations of descendants of former mighty kings of that once mighty empire.

But of this nothing is known to the general public. Templemore and his friends have kept the promise he gave, and preserved the secret of Roraima. It was only a short time ago that circumstances arose that seemed to him to justify a departure from the course he had hitherto observed. This was when the dispute which has been dormant for just upon a hundred years respecting the boundaries of British Guiana suddenly reached an acute stage.

"Truly," he said to his wife, then, "I think this is the contingency our friend Monella must have had in his mind when he intimated that in certain circumstances I was to be free to depart from the silence he had enjoined. It seems to me more than ever the case that he must have had 'the gift of prophecy' at that time. I cannot doubt that, if he were alive now, and saw that the future international position of Roraima was hanging in the balance, he would wish it to become permanently British territory, rather than Venezuelan. And, if he could know of the present state of indifference—or want of information—that seems to prevail in England, I feel satisfied he would wish me to do what I could to awaken the English nation to the true facts of the question that is at stake."

And that is how it has come about that, after some years of silence, this strange story of Roraima and the ancient city of El Dorado is now given to the world.

THE END

A Note About the Author

Frank Aubrey was the pseudonym of Francis Henry Atkins (1847–1927), a popular British pulp fiction writer. While not much is known about Atkins, he published widely in some of the leading Victorian pulp magazines and is seen as a pioneer in the lost world genre of science fiction. *The Devil-Tree of El Dorado* (1896), his most famous novel, is a story of fantasy and adventure set in the colony of British Guiana. Atkins' son, Frank Howard Atkins, would follow in his footsteps to become a successful pulp fiction writer in his own right, publishing stories in *Pearson's Magazine, The Grand Magazine,* and *Adventure.*

A Note from the Publisher

Spanning many genres, from non-fiction essays to literature classics to children's books and lyric poetry, Mint Edition books showcase the master works of our time in a modern new package. The text is freshly typeset, is clean and easy to read, and features a new note about the author in each volume. Many books also include exclusive new introductory material. Every book boasts a striking new cover, which makes it as appropriate for collecting as it is for gift giving. Mint Edition books are only printed when a reader orders them, so natural resources are not wasted. We're proud that our books are never manufactured in excess and exist only in the exact quantity they need to be read and enjoyed.

bookfinity™

Discover more of your favorite classics with Bookfinity™.

- Track your reading with custom book lists.
- Get great book recommendations for your personalized Reader Type.
- Add reviews for your favorite books.
- AND MUCH MORE!

Visit **bookfinity.com** and take the fun Reader Type quiz to get started.

Enjoy our classic and modern companion pairings!

Classic & Modern

Printed in the USA
CPSIA information can be obtained
at www.ICGtesting.com
JSHW022213140824
68134JS00018B/1021